THE U.S. NAVY'S ON-THE-ROOF GANG

トップシークレット VOLUME ONE トップシークレット

PRELUDE TO WAR

MATT ZULLO

A ZOOHAUS BOOK

The U.S. Navy's On-the-Roof Gang

First hardcover edition August 2020
ISBN: 978-1-7351527-0-7 (hardcover)
ISBN: 978-1-7351527-1-4 (ebook)

Book design and production by Domini Dragoone
Editorial services by White Dog Editorial Services
Maps illustrated by Ali Hval
Zoohaus logo designed by Kiri Leigh Zullo
Website design by Kecia Zullo

All photos courtesy of the Naval Cryptologic Veterans Association, except: page 28, courtesy National Archives (80-G-1024872); page 32, courtesy nsa.gov; pages 54 (NH 78374), 61 (NH 46638), 84 (NH 122695), 146 (NH 83192), 200 (NH 35834), 233 (US 51.01.51), 294 (NH 50809), and 358 (NH 64844), courtesy Naval History and Heritage Command; and pages 76 and 168, Guam Public Library System.

Published by
ZooHaus Books
www.mattzulloauthor.com
www.ontheroofgang.com

DEDICATION

This book is dedicated to all men and women, past and present, who have served in the U.S. Navy's cryptologic community. You have served your country silently, without accolade or praise. Although it was never easy to do, you kept secrets from the ones you loved most. Each of you knows the level of sacrifice and dedication required to succeed in this environment, even though it goes unspoken in the outside world. When you see each other in public, you cannot speak of the things you are most proud. You know what you've accomplished and the lives you've saved. Someday, as with the On-the-Roof Gang, perhaps your story will be lifted out of the shadows of secrecy and you'll finally be able to talk about it. Until then, all you can do is recognize each other with a subtle nod of the head or a wink to acknowledge your shared experiences. This book is for you.

CONTENTS

Foreword ix
Acknowledgments xiii
Author's Note xv
Prologue 1

Chapter 01: Harry Kidder 7
Chapter 02: Laurance Safford 21
Chapter 03: The Research Desk 27
Chapter 04: The Meeting 38
Chapter 05: The Plan 45
Chapter 06: Station ABLE 52
Chapter 07: Operational Planning 59
Chapter 08: USS *Marblehead* 62
Chapter 09: Reconstruction 68
Chapter 10: Craven's Decision 71
Chapter 11: Station BAKER 73
Chapter 12: Station HYPO 78
Chapter 13: To the Roof! 85
Chapter 14: CNO Announcement 89
Chapter 15: The Curriculum 92
Chapter 16: Class #1 96
Chapter 17: Christmas at Ma Travers's Guest House 108

Chapter 18: Class #1 Continues 113
Chapter 19: Class #2 119
Chapter 20: Station CAST 126
Chapter 21: Class #3 131
Chapter 22: Back to the Fleet 140
Chapter 23: Orange Grand Maneuvers of 1930 147
Chapter 24: Class #4 151
Chapter 25: Visit to Station CAST 155
Chapter 26: Class #5 160
Chapter 27: Visit to Station BAKER 164
Chapter 28: Class #6 172
Chapter 29: Visit to Station HYPO 175
Chapter 30: Classes #7 and #8 182
Chapter 31: Station S 186
Chapter 32: Pappy's Return 189
Chapter 33: Class #9 192
Chapter 34: President Steamship Lines 198
Chapter 35: Class #10 202
Chapter 36: Class #11 205
Chapter 37: Orange Grand Maneuvers of 1933 209
Chapter 38: Class #12 211
Chapter 39: McClaran's Appeal 216
Chapter 40: Class #13 221
Chapter 41: BAKER Moves to Libugon 223
Chapter 42: Class #14 227
Chapter 43: CAST moves to Mariveles 235
Chapter 44: Class #15 242
Chapter 45: HYPO Moves to Heeia 246
Chapter 46: ABLE Moves back to Shanghai 252

Chapter 47: Class #16 255
Chapter 48: Tragedy in DC 258
Chapter 49: CAST Moves to Cavite 262
Chapter 50: Classes #17 and #18 265
Chapter 51: Developments in HFDF 271
Chapter 52: Class #19 275
Chapter 53: Unrest in China 277
Chapter 54: Problems at Station BAKER 280
Chapter 55: Class #20 283
Chapter 56: Air Activity in China 290
Chapter 57: The Panay Incident 293
Chapter 58: Pacific HFDF Net 295
Chapter 59: Class #21 299
Chapter 60: Station V 302
Chapter 61: Class #22 305
Chapter 62: IJN Code Change 308
Chapter 63: Improvements at Station ABLE 311
Chapter 64: Station S Moves to Bainbridge Island 314
Chapter 65: Class #23 317
Chapter 66: CAST Moves to Corregidor Island 319
Chapter 67: Class #24 324
Chapter 68: Missing in Samoa 326
Chapter 69: A Schoolhouse Option 329
Chapter 70: Pappy Reinstated 331
Chapter 71: Typhoon 336
Chapter 72: Dependents Evacuated from Station CAST 338
Chapter 73: Typhoon's Aftermath 341
Chapter 74: Class #25 343
Chapter 75: Station K 346

Chapter 76: Codebreaking in DC 349
Chapter 77: Intelligence Cooperation 353
Chapter 78: Codebreaking in Hawaii 357
Chapter 79: Plans for Pappy 360
Chapter 80: Operations in Samoa 362
Chapter 81: Keeping Track of the Carriers 364
Chapter 82: Station ABLE Closes 366
Chapter 83: Station AB 368
Chapter 84: Station CAST Absorbs Station ABLE 372
Chapter 85: Dependents Evacuated across Pacific 376
Chapter 86: Station S Operations 379
Chapter 87: Winds Instructions 382
Chapter 88: Station CAST Listens for Winds Message 385
Chapter 89: Another IJN Code Change 388
Chapter 90: Station HYPO Listens for Winds Message 391
Chapter 91: Station BAKER Listens for Winds Message 394
Chapter 92: Station S Listens for Winds Message 396
Chapter 93: Station M Listens for Winds Message 398
Chapter 94: Winds Message Confusion 401
Chapter 95: Station S Intercepts 14-Part Message 404
Chapter 96: Where are the Carriers? 406
Chapter 97: The Final Part 409
Chapter 98: Kidder in Greenland 412
Chapter 99: Day of Infamy 414

Epilogue 416
Appendix A: Acronyms and Abbreviations 418
Appendix B: On-the-Roof Gang Class Rosters 420

FOREWORD

BY: WILLIAM "BILL" HICKEY
EXECUTIVE DIRECTOR,
NAVAL CRYPTOLOGIC VETERANS ASSOCIATION

It's the early part of the 20th century…imagine living without your smartphone or any of the high-tech gear we take for granted today. Life is simpler, yet just as complex for everyone living in those times. We had just been through World War I—the "war to end all wars"—and while we were celebrating that victory, we were beginning to face the reality of the coming economic downturn and depression. Guglielmo Marconi had just invented the "wireless" only a couple of decades earlier, and while it had come a long way from his primitive experiments, it was still a fledgling technology—this "radio" communication capability. What we call "amateur radio" today—a hobby occupied by enthusiasts bent on pushing technology to its limits—was still in its infancy. There were no commercial radios for amateurs available—they had to make their own equipment from scratch. And given the economic realities of the times, they had to sometimes be pretty creative to build the radios and get them working.

So, we meet Petty Officer Harry Kidder, a U.S. Navy radioman stationed in Los Baños, Philippine Islands. Harry knows Morse code, as that is the primary means of communications from ships to other ships and with shore stations. He's also a fledgling "ham"—or amateur radio operator—who has built his own station and spends his free time operating it and communicating with other similarly enthusiastic amateurs around the world. Harry even has a hard time getting to work on time because he stays up all night—when conditions are good—working other amateur stations trying to see just how far he can get with what today would be considered a QRP (low power—about five watts or less) signal with a crude long wire antenna.

One night, as he's tuning his receiver, Harry hears an unusually strong station. Initially, it sounds like Morse code, but he notices that there are some combinations of *dits* and *dahs* that just don't make any sense. He's an experienced U.S. Navy radioman, so he knows the code, but some of these combinations aren't familiar to him. Harry's curiosity gets the better of him, and when he analyzes what he's copied, he discovers that there are more character combinations than we use in typical International Morse code (in English, anyway). After a while, he's reconstructed the fact that this signal is probably not coming from an English speaking country and he spends time learning to copy the signals so he can get a better idea of where they might be coming from, and perhaps even what they are saying. This is what is probably the first inkling of a discipline called "transmission analysis" and communications intelligence, or COMINT, as it is known today.

Harry learns that the transmissions he's been copying have been Japanese katakana telegraphic code—sent mostly by Imperial Japanese Navy radio operators.

Fast-forward a number of years, Harry has made chief petty officer—the highest enlisted rank and a recognition of his professional capabilities and his leadership abilities. He's been stationed in various places and has met some pretty influential and significant names—Rochefort, Safford, and the like. Who are these influential men you might ask? They are the ones history has largely forgotten—at least the history we teach in school. They operated in a world called "cryptology" (making and breaking codes), which has traditionally been one of the most secret and protected of all military professions. As a group, these men will end up recognizing the code Harry found and its significance in preparing for what almost everyone in that closely-held circle believes is yet another war. They begin to read unencrypted messages easily, and when some turn out to be unreadable, they learn to decrypt the messages. This would become the foundation of what was then called the "Black Chamber"—people whose work was so secret that it was even kept from Secretary of War Stimson—who later declared that "gentlemen do not read other gentlemen's mail."

Together, this cadre of "code-breakers" will end up creating a school to train more radio operators in how to intercept, transcribe, analyze, and report what they hear so decision-makers can have needed information to guide the course of the country. But, their progress is slow—they can't get the funding they need, sometimes the equipment is hard to find and deploy, and not everyone they think will be a suitable candidate for the training works out.

In a nutshell, what you about to read is a fascinating story about how these people took a fledgling technology, discovered a threat on the horizon, worked against all odds proving that their "intelligence" would eventually be critical—and a difference maker in the War in the Pacific. They persevered, in spite of the heavy odds against them, out of stubborn faith and belief that the information they were providing was essential to the security of the country.

As we conclude Volume 1, we see all the signs and historic signals that are the prelude to World War II—and you will see just how important our ability to read the Japanese signals, decode them, and provide that information to war planners will be.

Stay tuned. This ride is about to get pretty wild. The "school" that Harry and the others created to do this job is literally located *on the roof* of a building because there is no other space available. They christen themselves the "On-The-Roof-Gang" and the name sticks. These men are the precursors of our Navy's cryptologic community—the Naval Security Group Command—and now the Information Warfare Community. The members of this elite group started the Naval Cryptologic Veterans Association in 1978—a group dedicated to the preservation of Naval cryptologic history. As a group we recognize the significance of the On-the-Roof-Gang, and have worked to pass on the knowledge, techniques, and discipline of cryptology to the current generation.

And, we now have Matt Zullo, a long-standing member of that "fraternity" to thank for bringing to light this story and making it much more than the typical dry and laborious history class assignment we all dreaded when we were in high school and college. For years, decades even, this history has been held in the collective memories of the NCVA members in bits and pieces. As our ranks refresh with new blood, it's important to collect this knowledge into one place for posterity. And Matt has done that with an incredible amount of research and amazing story-telling abilities. This story of the On-the-Roof Gang is a history lesson you will not soon forget!

ACKNOWLEDGMENTS

Researching and writing the story of the On-the-Roof Gang has been a labor of love for me since 2007, when I wrote my master's thesis. Back then, Dr. David Hatch was my thesis committee chairman and helped me through the process of writing the story into an acceptable academic paper. Since then, his ceaseless mentorship and guidance have proven invaluable as I continued to research and write about the On-the-Roof Gang. I can only hope to live up to his high standards of historical accuracy, while telling this story in a fashion that will keep you interested.

The National Cryptologic Veterans Association (NCVA) possesses the vast majority of the information about the On-the-Roof Gang in its holdings at the Command Display in Pensacola, on the pages of its *Cryptolog* magazine and other publications, and in the collective experience of its members. Over the years, some of the officers of the NCVA were of particular help to me. They were Bill Hickey, the NCVA Executive Director; Jay Browne, the producer of the *Cryptolog*; Public Affairs Officer J. W. Smith; and John "Gus" Gustafson. Other NCVA members provided assistance along the way, including Bob Anderson, Grady Lewis, Don McDonald, R. W. Russell, Richard Dirks, Richard Bidwell, Phil Jacobsen, Bill Lockert, Bill Moody, Bob Payne, and Peg Fiehtner.

I am humbled that I was able to meet and/or correspond with some of the On-the-Roof Gang themselves. Jim "Cappy" Capron, Warren "Al" Simmons, Duane Whitlock, and Hal Joslin encouraged me to keep pushing through the difficulties of putting a story like this together. I cannot thank them enough. Shortly after writing this book, the last surviving On-the-Roof Gang member, Hal Joslin, passed away and is now serving on the staff of the Supreme Commander. Rest easy, shipmates, we have the watch.

I also communicated with family members of some of the On-the-Roof Gang members, including Lillian Spivey, Walter Nowosad, Judy Terry, Jack Kaye, and Stephen Snyder, who provided personal detail of their loved ones. I hope these pages do justice to the memory of all the members of this elite group of Sailors and Marines.

A project like this is one that cannot be accomplished without the help of others. Along the way, I have asked numerous people for advice, help, or expertise. I would like to thank Cliff Lynn, Pat Mead, Pat McAuliffe, Edo Forsythe, David "Igor" Meadows, Matt Betley, Ali Hval, Domini Dragoone, Susan Thompson, Brad Pollard, Karen Pollard, Rob Simpson, and Rachel Kambury. You know what you did to help me, and for your contribution, I am thankful. Another note of thanks has to be given to the researchers at the National Archives, who helped me find information needed to complete this project.

I would also like to thank Jennifer Huston of White Dog Editorial Services sincerely for her expert editing of this book. She used *The Chicago Manual of Style* (CMOS) to edit these pages. However, despite her protestations, in the end, I strayed from her guidance and used the *U.S. Navy Style Guide* (2017) for some of the Navy-specific terminology. When you find a mistake in this text, please be assured that the mistake is mine, not hers. Her keen attention to detail and deep CMOS expertise was a precious help to me.

Lastly, but most importantly, I thank my wife Kecia, whose constant encouragement, help, and love has made this book possible.

AUTHOR'S NOTE

This is an account of the U.S. Navy's "On-the-Roof Gang," the group of U.S. Navy and Marine Corps radiomen who trained themselves in intercepting Imperial Japanese Navy telegraphic communications and performed other duties as part of the new radio intelligence discipline prior to and during World War II.

This story is true, told mainly through accounts from the On-the-Roof Gang members themselves. To the greatest extent possible, I endeavored to use these first-hand accounts to tell it. However, I had to fill gaps where I could not find information, and as such, this book should be considered a work of fiction. Wherever possible, I used real stories of the real men, although I had to invent some minor characters to help flesh out the story. Where there wasn't a tremendous amount of information available, I often supplemented the historical record with stories from my personal experience in the Navy or experiences of my shipmates.

In cases of controversy or disagreement, I always sided with the accounts provided by the On-the-Roof Gang. I meant no disrespect to any other points of view, but rather I sought to fully acknowledge the viewpoint of the members of the On-the-Roof Gang.

Although this is a story about intelligence operations leading up to the Japanese attack on Pearl Harbor, it does not seek to answer the question about what the United States Government knew before December 7, 1941. Instead, the book will focus on what the On-the-Roof Gang knew and what they did prior to the attack.

By all means, I meant to honor the dedication and sacrifices of the Sailors and Marines of the "On-the-Roof Gang." Between the On-the-Roof Gang and a handful of innovative U.S. Navy officers who saw the potential value of radio intelligence, they can truly be thought of as the cradle of U.S. Navy cryptology. They laid the groundwork for the U.S. Navy communications intelligence (COMINT) organizations and operations of the future.

PROLOGUE

SUNDAY, SEPTEMBER 4, 1921
GRAND CENTRAL TERMINAL, NEW YORK CITY

If New York is the city that never sleeps, this night was proof. Grand Central Terminal was teeming with people at two-thirty in the morning. It was not uncommon for people to be wandering in and out of the train station at such an hour. As usual, all sorts of people were milling around—travelers waiting for morning connections, homeless men looking for warm grates to sleep on, working girls trying to find customers, and lonely men looking to pay them.

There was another sort of person drifting through the shadows of Midtown Manhattan on this warm, late summer night. With his head held low, Russell Ford kept the collar of his trench coat up around his ears and kept his face obscured. He preferred that people looked past him rather than at him.

Ford, a lieutenant commander in the U.S. Navy, was on a three-year assignment in New York City as an agent for the Office of Naval Intelligence (ONI). After eight years of sea duty, he welcomed the assignment and the promise of a New York City apartment paid for by the U.S. Navy. Ford was a likeable guy—outgoing and the life of the party. His wife joked that he'd make friends with a burglar if one ever broke into their apartment. This sentiment made the activities on this particular night especially ironic.

Ford lingered in the shadows on Forty-Second Street outside Grand Central. He was dressed well but disheveled; anyone who passed by would've likely mistaken him for a weary traveler waiting for the trains to start running again in the morning. But it was more likely that no one would notice him at all, which suited him just fine. Unlike others at Grand Central Terminal, Ford was proceeding through the stages of a plan he and others had rehearsed in great detail. He was waiting for his three conspirators to move onto the next step.

The first to arrive was Don Edwards, Ford's buddy from the FBI, exactly as planned. Ford had met Edwards when he first arrived in New York a year earlier. Because the ONI didn't have an office in New York, Ford had been instructed to make contact with the FBI, which would provide him office space in the FBI building, if he needed it. Edwards had showed Ford around the FBI office, pointing out where he could store classified materials and which desks he could use. The two hit it off immediately, discovering from their accents that they were both Midwesterners. Ford didn't go into the FBI offices very often, unless he was there to pal around with Edwards. The two became fast friends.

The sole purpose of Ford's assignment in New York was to obtain material on the capabilities of foreign navies. High on the list of his priorities was the Imperial Japanese Navy (IJN). For over a decade, Japan had been using its navy to assert power over an ever-expanding area of the Pacific Ocean. In order to keep up with the Western world and continue its dominance over China and other areas in the Pacific, Japan required oil and rubber to fuel its industrial engine, and those resources were available in the Dutch East Indies and further south. Seeking to dominate the shipping lanes in those areas, the Imperial Japanese Navy occasionally harassed the merchant ships and navy vessels of other countries. Not surprisingly, the ONI was extremely concerned about the activities of the Imperial Japanese

Navy. Therefore, the need to obtain information about its capabilities and capacity to wage war were of the highest priority.

Edwards helped Ford on a number of occasions by supplying information on the timing of foreign navy visits to New York. Ford often posed as a tourist near the ports in Brooklyn, Staten Island, or in New Jersey. To date, the extent of Ford's espionage career consisted of taking photographs of foreign navy ships and sending the film back to Washington for processing and analysis. He never even saw the pictures or heard if he was getting the information that was expected. As far as he was concerned, no news was good news. He figured if the ONI was disappointed with the photographs he was submitting, they would have told him so.

However, this particular night was different. Edwards had clued Ford in on an especially valuable cache of information that the ONI might want. The FBI had learned about this information through a paid informant, Dorothy O'Reilly, who was known as Dot to her friends and family. Dot worked as a maid cleaning the offices of the Japanese consul general in New York. She was also an informant on the rolls of the FBI. The FBI compensated her handsomely for her work. In fact, she was paid more to keep tabs on the comings and goings of Japanese diplomats than she was to clean their offices. But it was only right; after all, she was putting her career—and perhaps her life—on the line for her country. In exchange, she diligently took note of any bit of information she could scrounge up and provided the FBI with scraps of writing that were carelessly thrown away.

Dot had recently noticed a new face in the consulate—someone who seemed to have direct access to the consul general. She passed this information on to Edwards. But Edwards, being equally diligent in his work, was already tracking the visitor from Japan who claimed to be a tourist. In reality, Edwards had already figured out that the visitor was an Imperial Japanese Navy courier, delivering important information to the consulate. As she was paid to do, Dot paid particular attention to this unknown visitor, whom she believed was bringing information regarding Japan's plans for war. As the visitor spoke with officials at the consulate, she'd heard them discussing a person known only as Yamato. Dot knew nothing of the Japanese language, but she had learned that the suffix *-san* referred to a person's name. Throughout the conversations, she'd heard the name *Yamato-san* over and over again. Edwards knew there was no one at the consulate with this name, and, given the visitor's connection to the Japanese Navy, he and Ford agreed that the name Yamato was most likely referring to the new super dreadnought battleship currently in development. They didn't quite understand why the Japanese consulate in New York would need information about a battleship that hadn't even been built yet, but if the diplomats were in possession of details about the planned battleship, Ford had to have it. Arming American politicians and diplomats with intelligence about the Yamato could be key to future negotiations.

For several years, FBI agents had been surreptitiously entering the Japanese consulate to photograph secret documents, and Edwards knew it was again time for such measures. After consulting the New York City Police Department, Edwards planned a break-in to make copies of the information that the courier had delivered. This time, Edwards invited Ford along, just in case there was some good intelligence about the Yamato battleship. For weeks, Edwards and Ford had developed and rehearsed the plan over and over down to the slightest detail.

At the exact predesignated time of 0300 hours, Edwards approached Ford along the Forty-Second Street side of Grand Central Terminal, staying as close as possible to the cool, limestone building in order to remain in the shadows. The two exchanged a glance but didn't speak a word, just as they'd rehearsed. Edwards peered across Park Avenue and saw the two policemen he was expecting. The two cops were there to ensure that other unwitting police officers did not interrupt Edwards and Ford as they slipped into the Japanese consulate. Ford and Edwards turned left onto Park Avenue, headed north, and followed about a hundred yards behind the policemen on the opposite side of the street. After the cops passed the Japanese consulate between 48th and 49th Streets, Ford and Edwards ducked into the shadows under the building's awning. Using a key—a duplicate copy of the one used for the front entrance—the pair entered without notice.

Ford and Edwards passed through the empty lobby before climbing six flights of stairs and entering the office of the consul general. Using flashlights dimmed by several layers of cellophane, the two walked directly to the safe containing the documents they were looking for. Thanks to the combination Dot had provided, Edwards had opened this safe several times before, and within seconds, he opened it again. As they had hoped, a black leather attaché case stuffed with documents appeared as they opened the drawer to the safe. The two exchanged a quick knowing smile. However, after opening the briefcase, they immediately realized that the information inside was not what they were seeking. Both men possessed a rudimentary knowledge of the Japanese katakana alphabet, so they instantly knew that this document contained neither war plans nor technical specs of the Yamato-class battleship.

At the top and bottom, each page was marked: シ ー ク レ ッ ト

Edwards and Ford both recognized the Japanese term for SECRET material; it had six characters in the Japanese katakana alphabet. What they were looking for would surely be TOP SECRET, which they knew had nine characters: ト ッ プ シ ー ク レ ッ ト

With some disappointment, they got back to work. They each took photographs of all the pages of the document, 180 in all. Highly formatted text filled the document. Each line contained a five-digit number followed by five alphabetic characters, three katakana characters, and finally Japanese words spelled out in the katakana alphabet.

After about an hour of taking photographs, Ford and Edwards exited the building just as quickly and surreptitiously as they had arrived. At the building's entrance, Russell exited first followed by Edwards a few seconds later. They parted ways without having spoken a single word to each other the entire night.

Ford was crestfallen—he was certain they would have found plans for the battleship *Yamato*. Instead, the pair found page after page of gibberish. The ONI certainly wouldn't be happy with the take from the night's clandestine activities. In his mind, he'd built up the evening as the grand culmination of his assignment with the ONI—the one big thing he could be proud of, the thing that might help him get promoted to commander with a staff job at the headquarters for the Atlantic Fleet or the Pacific Fleet. Instead, after his tour in New York, he'd likely be assigned to another ship based out of Norfolk or Pearl Harbor. Ford trudged home, dejected and humbled by an overwhelming sense of failure.

CHAPTER 01

HARRY KIDDER

SATURDAY, JUNE 7, 1924
LOS BAÑOS, PHILIPPINES

Harry Kidder was already ten minutes late for watch, but he was dead asleep. The warm sun and early morning breeze from the open window next to his bed did nothing to wake him. Outside, below his second-floor window, shopkeepers were preparing their wares for the day's customers. Muted conversations in Tagalog echoed up through Harry's window, but he was completely oblivious to them. Although the volume knob was set to zero, the radio gear on the table next to his bed buzzed with electricity.

Outside, a milk bottle crashed to the ground, finally waking Kidder from his slumber. Looking at the clock next to his radio, he cursed under his breath, hauled himself out of bed, and rushed to shave, shower, and throw on his uniform—the standard-issue long-sleeved chambray shirt and denim bell-bottom dungarees with patch pockets sewn on the front and back. Because of the tropical weather in the western Pacific, Asiatic Fleet commanders permitted Sailors to roll up their sleeves to just above the elbow. A white, Dixie cup hat topped off the uniform. It was this last piece of gear that gave U.S. Navy petty officers their nickname: *White Hats*.

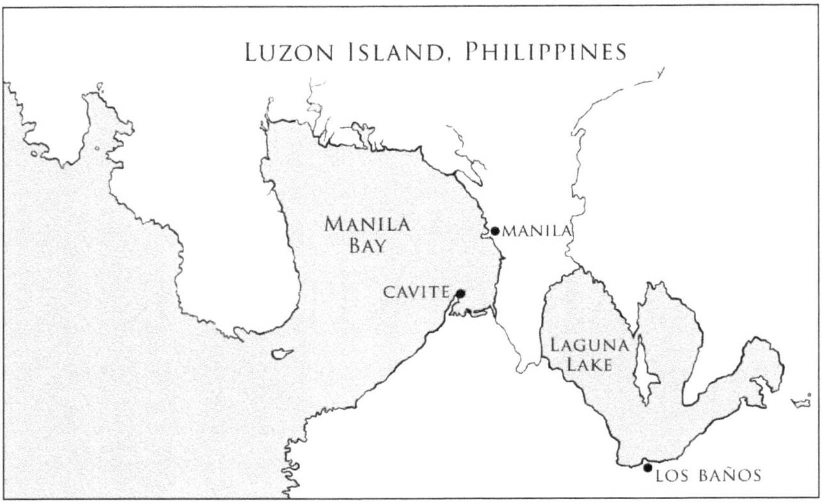

It took Petty Officer Kidder less than ten minutes to get ready and head out the door. The front gate of Camp Eldridge was only a five-minute walk from his one-bedroom apartment, but that meant he'd still be a half hour late—and his chief was going to kill him.

It was approaching 0800 hours on this particular Saturday morning as Petty Officer Harry Kidder hurried through the mostly quiet streets of Los Baños, his white hat cocked back on his head. Other than the occasional Sailor stumbling home after a night of debauchery and the fishermen preparing for a day on Laguna Lake, the Philippine Islands town was eerily quiet. Beer bottles and discarded wooden skewers from the town's famed "meat on a stick" littered the dirt roads. The meat was always pork, but the Sailors frequently joked that it was monkey or dog. In actuality, both monkey and dog meat were much more expensive than pork and were considered delicacies in the Philippines.

Harry was almost thirty minutes late for watch and picked up his pace as he neared the main gate to the naval base. When he arrived, he flashed his identification card to the guard then broke into a slow jog toward the low one-story building marked "U.S. Navy COMSTA,

U.S. Navy Communications Station, Los Baños, Philippines.

Camp Eldridge." At the door, he quickly rang the buzzer. A disinterested Sailor opened it and Harry rushed in. He hurried through two more doors as he made his way to the operations floor.

As usual, the room was dark, except for the radio dials and the occasional desk lamp dimly illuminating the watch standers' faces. Because the work that took place in the building was highly classified, the windows were painted on the inside and covered with dark curtains. Just about everyone smoked, so a dull haze hovered in the air, contributing to the subdued lighting. Harry liked it though; it made his work seem more clandestine.

With his headphones on, Radioman Second Class Phillip Johnson sat at his station. As Harry approached, Johnson looked straight at him with his eyes wide as if to warn him of immediate danger. Chief Radioman Bud Karcher stood behind Petty Officer Johnson, facing the door and waiting for Harry to arrive. Karcher looked at his watch, lit cigarette in hand, and grumbled, "Thirty-four minutes late, Kidder."

"I know, Chief. I'm sorry."

"You don't have to apologize to me; it's Johnson you've made stay on watch thirty-four . . . ," he paused, looking at his watch. "Thirty-*five* minutes extra."

"I'm sorry, Johnson."

Johnson really didn't mind that much. He actually felt sorry for Harry, knowing that the chief was about to lay into him. He shrugged at Kidder, not wanting to be a part of the tense situation any more than he already was.

"God dammit, Kidder! How many times do we have to do this?"

Recognizing this was a rhetorical question, Kidder kept his mouth shut.

"What is it this time? Late night after a bar fine?" In the Philippines, when Sailors left with bar girls before closing time, they were required to pay the bar owner a fine, allegedly to compensate him for lost income due to the girl's absence. This was in addition to any payment the girl might want based on services rendered. In all his time in the Philippines, Harry had never once paid a bar fine.

"No, Chief," Harry responded, embarrassed by the insinuation.

"Don't you like girls, Kidder?" the chief mocked.

His embarrassment growing, Kidder responded, "Uh . . . no . . . that's not it, Chief." The truth was that Kidder didn't have much experience with women, and he wasn't ever brave enough to pay a bar fine.

"Choir practice after work yesterday?" the chief chided, referring to a euphemism among Sailors in the Philippines who claimed they were going to choir practice, when they were really going drinking. "Get drunk and pass out in a gutter?"

"No, Chief," Kidder said flatly as he felt the redness in his cheeks growing.

"What, then?"

Finally, Harry sensed an opportunity to explain. "Chief, I was up late with my ham rig. I actually spoke to somebody in Maine last night!" Amateur radio, or ham radio, was Kidder's new hobby—his passion, really. Ham radio was a relatively new avocation born out of the rapidly increasing technology of radio communications. Kidder had been fascinated with radio since childhood, and he found

like-minded individuals around the globe on the airwaves. Ham radio enthusiasts communicated via international Morse code—a series of dits and dahs transmitted to represent the letters of the alphabet, numbers, and punctuation marks. In this way, it was possible to send a message in Morse code simply by turning a signal on and off in the correct manner to represent the dits and dahs. Each dit-dah combination represented a letter in international Morse code, which was the internationally accepted standard in Continuous Wave (CW) communications. Kidder was obsessed with being a ham operator and had subscribed to a relatively new magazine called QST, which was published by the American Relay League. The magazine instructed readers on how to build and operate their own ham radios and antennas. Because of his Navy job, Harry could copy up to thirty-five words per minute before he ever applied for his amateur radio license, which only required five words per minute for an entry-level license. On the day when he finally received his license, he smiled when he saw he received the call sign he requested: PI 1HK.

Despite the appearance that his frequent tardiness projected, having a job in this high-tech field was exactly what Kidder was hoping for when he joined the Navy. And his love for the job spilled over into his personal life. His self-built radio rig and rudimentary dipole antenna worked exceedingly well. Kidder considered himself lucky that his job was so similar to his hobby. At work, he and all other radiomen in the U.S. Navy used Morse code to communicate between ships and shore stations around the world. Between his job and his hobby, Kidder was undoubtedly one of the most skilled Morse code operators in the world. Other ham operators around the Pacific and across the United States were familiar with his call sign.

"That's forty-two states I've got now!" Kidder exclaimed. In his excitement, he'd forgotten the pickle he was in with the chief.

Chief Karcher took a deep breath and exhaled in Kidder's face. It took all of Harry's resolve not to react to the coffee and cigarette smell of the chief's stale breath. "Kidder, you owe me thirty-five minutes extra duty," he barked. "Relieve Johnson *now*, and see me after your watch is over."

"Aye, aye, Chief," Kidder responded immediately.

Extra duty was just another way of saying that Kidder would be swabbing the deck or shining the overhead for at least thirty-five minutes after his eight-hour shift ended. Karcher turned and walked off the watch floor. Immediately, the tension eased.

Kidder relieved Johnson and apologized in earnest this time. "I really am sorry, Jepp. I only got three hours of sleep."

Everyone called Petty Officer Johnson by his nickname: Jepp. In the Philippines, the locals had a hard time pronouncing the *f* sound, and Phil had grown weary of the locals calling him "Pill." He eventually began introducing himself to the Filipinos as Jeff, so from then on, his nickname became Jepp.

"It's all right, Harry," Jepp assured his buddy. "But you're gonna have to show me that rig of yours someday."

"You got it," Harry answered.

Kidder put on the headphones and started his watch. His job was to monitor U.S. Navy transmissions on specific radio frequencies at certain times, otherwise known as "the sked." The sked normally consisted of five to ten messages transmitted in Morse code from one naval station to another. At Camp Eldridge, most messages were destined for the headquarters of the Asiatic Fleet located in Cavite, about forty miles to the northwest. Other messages were to be retransmitted to U.S. Navy communications stations around the western Pacific Ocean.

To most Sailors, copying or sending Morse code messages was a difficult chore. To Harry, however, the dits and dahs were as clear as could be. While others struggled when the speed of the code reached twenty words per minute, Harry could easily copy thirty to forty words per minute. As he received messages addressed to ships and stations in the Philippines, he copied them and passed them to the on-duty yeoman. Other radio messages he relayed to other stations in the Asiatic Fleet before he passed them to the yeoman. On any given watch, a radioman at Camp Eldridge would likely talk to his counterparts at Pearl Harbor, Midway Island, Guam, Shanghai, and on board ships assigned to the Asiatic Fleet. For Kidder, his job was more like play than work, so his time on watch seemed to fly by.

Each shift, Kidder had seven regular frequencies to monitor—four in the high frequency (HF) band, two in the medium frequency (MF) band, and one in the low frequency (LF) band. This he did with the easy grace of a man who loves his work. In between skeds, Kidder would "spin and grin," meaning that he would turn the dial to see what else he could hear. This was not part of his assigned duties, but his curiosity always got the best of him.

Other than being late, this shift was not unlike a thousand other watches Kidder had worked. He copied all the messages destined for his station and retransmitted everything he was supposed to. But on this particular day while spinning and grinning at the low end of the HF band, Harry came across a very loud signal in a military band and on a frequency that he wasn't expecting. Knowing he'd have to leave it soon for his next sked, he jotted down the frequency—4255 kilocycles—and stuffed it in his pocket. He didn't want the chief to know that he was listening to anything off-sked. He tried to copy the loud transmission, but something didn't seem right. There seemed to be letters in the transmissions that he'd never heard before. He'd get a few letters, then miss a few. This frustrated Harry because he prided himself on a zero-mistake sked every time. This time, however, he was missing almost half the letters.

"What's going on?" he muttered to himself. He shook his head as if there were wires crossed in his brain that needed uncrossing. He concentrated harder; it was still no good. The transmission was strong, the code crystal clear, but he was still missing letters in the message, and what he was able to catch made no sense. He kept at it for several minutes, trying his best to make some sense of it.

"The sked!" he scolded himself out loud for losing track of time and forgetting about his duties while trying to figure out the riddle of the unusual code he was hearing.

Kidder quickly tuned to the frequency of his next sked and got to it just after the call signs were sent. *Thank God,* he thought. The chief would have killed him if he missed his sked—especially after showing up to work late again. He could fill in the call signs on the copy sheet later before he gave it to the yeoman.

After completing his shift, Kidder made his way to the chief's office, dreading the extra duty in store for him. He was still feeling annoyed about missing so many letters in that unusual transmission he'd heard; it just stuck in his craw.

As Kidder strode to the chief's office, he knew he was in for some trouble. He only hoped Chief Karcher wouldn't refer the issue to the commanding officer (CO). The last thing Kidder wanted was to face the old man at captain's mast. The CO was notorious for taking a stripe from any Sailor brought before him for nonjudicial punishment, and Harry did not want to lose a stripe.

When he arrived at the chief's office, he knocked loudly three times. "Petty Officer Kidder reporting as ordered, Chief," he said steadily, trying to make a good impression.

"Come in," ordered the chief.

Kidder entered the chief's office and stood in front of his desk. The chief tapped his pencil on the steel desk at stared at Kidder. "Sit down, Kidder," the chief snapped impatiently. Confused, Kidder did as he was told. Without taking his eyes off the Sailor, the chief put his pencil down, tapped a cigarette out of its cardboard box, lit it, and inhaled deeply.

On the desk, Kidder could see the chief's coffee cup, half full of steaming black coffee. As if on cue, the chief took a sip. Inside the cup, Kidder saw the coffee stains that chief petty officers seemed to take pride in. "Don't ever wash a chief's coffee cup," was well-known dogma within the U.S. Navy.

The prolonged silence was getting to Harry, so he finally blurted out, "I'm sorry, Chief. It won't happen again."

With his goal of getting Kidder to start the conversation achieved, Chief Karcher said, "Kidder, you know what happens if I'm late? Do you know what happens when a chief is late?"

"No, chief."

"Well, first his Sailors begin to think they can come in late. And then the junior officers think they can come in late. Do you understand where I'm going with this, Kidder?"

Kidder had no idea, but he replied, "Yes, Chief." He knew it was the only acceptable answer.

Chief Karcher exhaled loudly. He knew Petty Officer Kidder was the most talented communicator he had, but he didn't like him. Kidder never went to the bars with his shipmates; he never even spent any time with the other Sailors. The only other Navy man the chief ever saw Kidder talking to was a junior officer fresh out of the Naval Academy. They were both ham radio enthusiasts, and every time they spoke, it went over the chief's head. To Karcher, Kidder was more than a little odd, and that irritated him.

"Kidder, what are you gonna do when you're the chief? Are you gonna keep coming in late? Are you gonna set a bad example for your Sailors?" Karcher took another drag of his cigarette and tapped the ashes into the overflowing ashtray next to his coffee cup.

Harry had never given this any thought. Making chief was never a priority for him. And quite honestly, he didn't think it was likely to happen, anyway.

"Well, no Chief, but I don't see how that matters to—."

Chief Karcher interrupted Kidder. "Don't get smart with me, Kidder! It matters. Got it?" he barked.

Kidder was really lost now. "Yes, Chief."

More silence followed as the chief took a drag of his cigarette and drank his coffee, never taking his eyes off Kidder. After what seemed like an eternity to Kidder, the chief took another deep breath, opened his desk drawer, and produced a single sheet of paper with letterhead from the Bureau of Naval Personnel (BUPERS). "The skipper received this letter from BUPERS today. It seems you've been selected for chief petty officer," he said glumly.

"What?" Kidder said incredulously. "You're joking." Kidder knew that chief petty officers were the backbone of the Navy—senior enough to be wise, wise enough to know what's important, and separate from the officer community so as to be able to call a spade a spade, when necessary. He just never thought of himself as worthy of selection to chief.

"I wish I was," Karcher said flatly. "So, it's going to go like this. After you pin on your anchors, you're going to PCS in the fall. You're headed to NAVCOMSTA Cheltenham, in Maryland. PCS is "permanent change of station" in Navy parlance. In other words, Kidder was being transferred from his duties in the Philippines.

"That's great, chief," Harry said, half excited for his promotion and half sad to leave the Philippines.

"If you say so," Karcher grumbled as he inhaled on his cigarette again. "You've got to make it through initiation, first, though."

"Initiation, what's that?" asked Kidder.

"You'll find out, Kidder," Karcher said. For the first time, Kidder detected the faintest of smiles on the chief's face. "You'll find out, all right."

"Aye, chief."

"Now, I want you to field day these spaces. Pick up every cigarette butt you find and empty every butt-can you see. I'm leaving for the day, Kidder. When I come in tomorrow, I don't want to see a single cigarette butt anywhere in this building. I don't care how long it takes you. Got it?"

"Aye, aye, Chief," Kidder said dejectedly. He was hoping the news of him making chief would make Karcher forget about his extra duty.

"Start right here," Karcher said as he dropped his cigarette on the floor and stamped it out slowly, all the while looking directly at Kidder. "Tomorrow, you and I are headed to Cavite to meet the other chief selectees."

"But I'm off tomorrow, Chief."

"You *were* off. You wanna be a chief, or not?"

"Yes, chief."

"Then I'll see you outside the front gate tomorrow morning at 0600 hours."

"Aye, chief, 0600," Kidder said as Chief Karcher got up. Kidder picked up a pair of work gloves and a garbage bag from the gear locker and began to pick up cigarette butts. Once he knew the chief was out of earshot, he mumbled to himself, "I'm never going to be an ass like Chief Karcher. I'm going to be a damn good chief!"

After about an hour, Kidder called it quits. He'd barely made a dent in clearing the room of cigarette butts, but he realized he was never going to pick them all up unless he worked overnight. His extra duty was only supposed to last thirty-five minutes, so he threw away the butts he'd picked up so far and left for the day.

As he walked home, Kidder was on top of the world. He was going to be a chief petty officer, something he never dreamed would happen. He whistled as he strolled through town, which was much livelier in the afternoon sun than it was earlier in the day. The afternoon heat was a joy to Kidder. The meat-on-a-stick vendors were back on the street, cooking on grills stoked by wood fires. Music emanated from every bar, as scantily dressed Filipina bar girls tried to coax him inside. It was early enough in the day that Sailors on liberty for the evening had not yet claimed them. As he walked through town toward his apartment, Harry was as happy as he could ever remember. Even so, something was bothering him—something underneath the happiness—like an itch he couldn't reach.

Shaking the vague, uneasy feeling, he turned toward his apartment and saw several Filipino children playing in the street. When they saw him, they immediately ran over to him.

"Mr. Harry, Mr. Harry. Give me a penny. Give me a nickel," they cried out. Harry chuckled to himself. Every day they asked him for change, and every day he told them no.

"Mr. Harry, we want bread," they lied. He knew if he gave them money, they'd take it directly home, and bread was the last thing it would be used to buy. But this day was different. Harry had just found out he'd been selected for chief, so he was feeling generous. Without a word, he walked over to a fruit and vegetable stand on the street, the kids right on his heels. He reached down deep into his dungaree pocket for a quarter then picked out four apples. He gave one to each kid, who scampered off in all directions. He received his change from the shopkeeper and looked at it in his hand. Next to the fifteen cents was a crumpled piece of paper. *What's this*, he thought, and then he remembered . . . *the frequency*!

Harry ran the rest of the way home. Stumbling toward the small desk in his bedroom, he turned on his ham rig. As the tubes began to warm up and glow, he leaned in close. He loved the faint odor of the capacitors heating up, the low glow of the vacuum tubes, the slight hum of the electronics at work—this was his bliss. When the familiar smell of capacitors and vacuum tubes began to fill the air, he knew the rig was ready.

He tuned to the frequency he'd written down earlier—4255 kilocycles—expecting the same loud unintelligible telegraphic code. Instead, he heard only static. Disappointed, he sat for a moment, wondering who the transmitter had been earlier in the day. It was a strong signal, so it must have been someone close by. But what were those strange characters? And why were they using a military band? They should have been on an amateur frequency band. He wished he had kept the copy from earlier. He listened to the static for twenty minutes but got nothing.

Harry was just about to give up and start tuning to an amateur band when he heard the telltale tuning of a continuous wave key.

...– ...– ...–

V V V

The signal sounded louder and stronger than before. *The atmospherics must be good,* Harry thought. Although he had a pair of headphones, he liked to copy using a speaker instead. He wore headphones all day at work, and the speaker allowed him to wander around his apartment while he listened. But not wanting to draw attention to himself through the open window in his bedroom, he turned down the speaker's volume. Harry was determined to copy the code this time. Instinctively, he jotted down the time and frequency and began to copy. But it was no good. He couldn't copy it. The telegraphic code proved to be just as indecipherable as before.

Who is this? He looked at his watch; it was ten minutes to six—ten minutes before the hour, just like it had been when he'd caught the transmission earlier in the day. *They're on a sked!*

He was right. The transmissions continued throughout the night, beginning ten minutes before every hour and lasting between fifteen and twenty minutes. Each time the transmission came on the air, Harry copied all the letters he knew and recorded all the dit-dah combinations he didn't. After each transmission, Harry scrutinized his copy—but he just couldn't grasp what he was hearing.

"Dah dah dah dit dah," Harry said aloud to himself. "What the hell *is* that?"

He copied sked after sked of jumbled code deep into the night, impatiently waiting between each one. Before the night was over, Harry Kidder realized he was copying some sort of telegraphic code with at least forty-eight characters in it. It had him completely stumped.

As the sun began to rise, Harry looked at the pile of papers on his desk: one recorded times and frequencies, the rest contained his copy. He could tell that there were call signs being used, and most of the transmissions seemed to be sent in groups of three characters. On a separate sheet of paper, Harry had written all the unknown dit-dah combinations he had heard throughout the night.

As the morning light crept in through his window, Harry realized he'd been up all night—again. *At least it's Sunday, so I don't have to work today, and I can get some shut-eye*, he thought. *Sunday . . . Sunday? What's different about this Sunday?*

Harry looked at his clock, which read 0721. He scratched his head as if to draw out the feeling he had that something was different about today . . .

"Oh, no, I'm late. The chief!"

CHAPTER 02

LAURANCE SAFFORD

FRIDAY, JULY 11, 1924
YANGTZE RIVER, SHANGHAI, CHINA

Lieutenant Laurance F. Safford was the CO of the minesweeper USS *Finch*, and he was proud of his ship and his men. The *Finch*, which was assigned to patrol the Yangtze River, had certainly been pulling its weight, so Safford had every right to be proud. Commanders in the Asiatic Fleet had cited him many times for providing expert security services around the China coast and along the length of the Yangtze River.

Located at the mouth of the Yangtze, Shanghai was one of the world's largest cities in the 1920s, with well over two million residents. Only about 30,000 of those residents were of European origin, but they controlled half the city in areas called the International Settlement and French Concession. The Whangpoo River—a small tributary of the Yangtze that flows into the East China Sea—bisects the city, separating the more European western half from the traditionally Chinese eastern half.

In the early 1920's, Shanghai accounted for over half the imports and exports of China. British and American businessmen made a

great deal of money in trade and finance in Shanghai and along the full length of the winding Yangtze River. The prosperous international trade environment, in turn, attracted exploitation from river pirates all the way up to professional crime syndicates.

Tension between China and Japan had existed since the mid-nineteenth century, and in 1915, Japan issued its so-called "Twenty-one Demands" to China. This amounted to privileged trade status for Japan, which was in direct conflict with the Open Door policy initiated by the United States. The Open Door policy required countries to respect Chinese sovereignty and enjoy equal access to Chinese trade.

The bulk of American trade in China took place in Shanghai, particularly in an area known as the Bund along the Whangpoo in the western part of the city. During this time, the amount of low-level crime and the tensions between Japan and western countries adhering to the Open Door policy created the need for a protection force. For the United States, the Yangtze River Patrol was that force. It occupied several piers in the International Settlement near the Bund.

In 1924, Safford was the only commissioned officer on board the USS *Finch*—Chief Petty Officer Randy McDonald was his executive

Laurance F. Safford

officer (XO). The ship usually had another commissioned officer acting as the XO, but when Safford's second-in-command fell ill and transferred out, a replacement wasn't requested. Chief McDonald impressed Lieutenant Safford, who felt confident he could fill the role admirably. McDonald was a boatswain's mate by trade and had showed many leadership qualities. Safford often thought McDonald was the reason for the *Finch*'s success. The men saw McDonald as a mentor, someone they could aspire to be one day.

Safford appreciated McDonald's extensive experience at sea. Safford was a brilliant young man, yet relatively inexperienced compared with the chief. McDonald showed him respect while bringing him up to speed on leadership at sea and shipboard life. Eventually, Safford caught on, understanding what it took to lead Sailors at sea. Safford and McDonald made an excellent team; their crew performed well, and the results showed.

To Chief McDonald, Safford's intelligence was clearly evident, having graduated fifteenth in the U.S. Naval Academy's Class of 1916, where he demonstrated a particular proficiency in radio communications. The radio shack on board the *Finch* was among the best in the Asiatic Fleet. The *Finch*'s three radiomen were skilled at sending and understanding Morse code, and they continuously monitored U.S. fleet communications circuits in the 17-meter and 20-meter HF bands and the 160-meter MF band. But they often complained of overpowering signals drowning out their circuits and making it difficult to copy their own traffic. It sounded similar to Morse code, yet it contained characters that none of them understood. Although he didn't know Morse code, Safford was intrigued and listened to the unidentified signals a few times himself. Believing signals of that strength had to originate from a U.S. Navy transmitter somewhere nearby, Safford asked the U.S. Navy's Asiatic Fleet communications officer if they could do something about the interfering signals. Safford wanted to help his radiomen, but after asking the Asiatic Fleet communications officer several times with no response, he assumed there was nothing that could be done.

On a peaceful Friday morning in port Shanghai, the *Finch* made preparations for the 1,400-mile trip upriver to Chungking. The *Finch*'s mission was to follow a small flotilla of American commercial vessels destined for the inland markets of China—a perilous journey for unarmed commercial vessels. Pirates answered to petty warlords and bandits along the river and worked in packs. Their typical modus operandi was to swarm unsuspecting vessels and take everything they could carry off the boats. The *Finch* would protect the flotilla with its two three-inch deck guns. The mere presence of an armed U.S. Navy ship was usually enough to deter the pirates, but occasional skirmishes still broke out.

On this particular morning, Safford and McDonald were busy preparing the ship and the men for their upcoming voyage. There was much to do the day before departure. The ship was abuzz with activity as Sailors carried stores onto the ship, loaded equipment and ammunition, tested onboard equipment, and removed garbage. Everything was accomplished as expected; it was a well-rehearsed dance of procedure, which Safford and McDonald choreographed to the letter. In no time at all, the USS *Finch* was in shipshape.

The men in the *Finch*'s radio shack were also busy on this Friday morning. They were expecting a list of the commercial ships they were supposed to escort, with the *Finch*'s schedule and berthing assignments along the way. In addition to these logistical messages, the radioman on duty on board the *Finch* received one he wasn't expecting—one that Safford wouldn't want to read.

The radioman tracked down Chief McDonald on the bridge and handed him a metal clipboard containing the *Finch*'s morning messages. Standard procedure required Lieutenant Safford to read messages before anyone else, but the radioman knew he had to show one in particular to Chief McDonald first. As the chief read the messages, he initialed in the top right corner of each one indicating that he'd read it. While reading the messages, Chief McDonald paused on the message that concerned the radioman. He read this message more slowly and deliberately than the rest. While he was reading it, Lieutenant Safford arrived on the bridge. After McDonald completed his reading and initialed the last messages, he handed the clipboard back to the radioman and looked him straight in the eye. They were the only two who knew what Safford was about to read. The radioman handed the clipboard to Safford.

"The 0600 sked, sir. Six new messages," recited the radioman.

Safford began to read and initial, just as Chief McDonald had done moments earlier. When he got to the unusual message, he paused like the chief had, only he didn't continue. He read the message over and over without initialing it.

The message informed Safford that the Navy was relieving him of his duties as CO of the USS *Finch*. There was no reason given for Safford's firing, but it was never a good thing for a commander to be relieved of his command. The message merely stated that he was to report for duty in Washington, DC, as soon as possible, and Chief McDonald would assume command of the ship until proper relief arrived.

To say this disappointed Safford was an understatement. He was just gaining traction with the crew and the ship's best days were right around the corner. Besides, no one is ever relieved without reason—and the reason is almost always bad.

After several minutes, Safford looked up at McDonald. "I'm sorry, sir," McDonald said to him.

"Don't worry about it, Chief. The ship is in good hands with you. My relief should be here in just a few days. The ship will stay here in Shanghai until then."

The bridge was silent as Lieutenant Safford completed reading the morning's messages. There was no point in doing so, but Safford finished his routine, initialing each message before handing the clipboard back to the radioman. As Safford scanned the bridge, each man looked back at him as if wanting to say something, but there was nothing to be said.

Safford eventually took a deep breath and left the bridge for the final time. He went to his stateroom to pack. He was in a bit of a daze trying to figure out what he had done wrong. It only took him thirty minutes to pack his seabag and prepare himself for what came next.

The crew gathered in formation on the deck for Safford's departure. The chief made sure the crew knew what was happening so they could give him a proper send-off.

Safford turned toward McDonald, saluted, and said, "Request permission to go ashore."

The chief saluted back and responded, "Permission granted."

Chief McDonald yelled out the order, "Formation! Hand salute!" The crew saluted as Safford strode down the gangplank. As was customary, the chief rang the ship's bell twice before announcing, "Finch, departing!"

On the walk toward the pier, Safford stopped once, faced the American ensign flying on the stern of the ship, and saluted smartly. Safford choked up when he dropped his salute. His command was over, the ship no longer his. It was only a short walk over to the SS *President Fillmore*, a passenger steamship headed for the West Coast of the United States. Unlike his time aboard the USS *Finch*, Safford would be a passenger on this voyage.

CHAPTER 03

THE RESEARCH DESK

MONDAY, JULY 28, 1924

MAIN NAVY BUILDING, WASHINGTON, DC

The Main Navy Building was one of two identical buildings in Washington, DC, constructed as temporary structures toward the tail end World War I. The pair of buildings were located on Constitution Avenue between Seventeenth Street NW and Nineteenth Street NW. Along with its twin—the Munitions Building—the Main Navy Building was an eyesore to all passersby. It was only meant to house some military offices temporarily, while more permanent spaces were built. This space, which had previously been covered in a carpet of beautiful green grass, was now blighted with the two concrete and cinder block buildings. Regardless, by 1924, it was obvious that the Army and Navy would be occupying the monstrosities for years to come.

Safford's orders required him to check in at the Main Navy Building with the Code and Signal Section of the Department of Naval Communications (DNC) by August 4. This should have been his first indicator that he wasn't in any sort of trouble, but he didn't realize it at the time. If he was in any real trouble, he would've been ordered to

Main Navy Building, circa 1920. View of the building's North face seen from just west of 19th Street, looking southeasterly from across Constitution Avenue.

a headquarters element, not an obscure section of the DNC. However, this thought hadn't occurred to him, so the closer he was to reporting, the more nervous he became. He checked in a full week early, preferring to face the music had he done something wrong than agonize over it a moment longer.

A young yeoman greeted Safford in the lobby of the Main Navy Building and took him to a room on the first floor of the sixth wing. The yeoman ushered him into the office of Captain Ridley McLean, the Director of Naval Communications.

Safford marched in and said, "Lieutenant Laurance Safford reporting as ordered, sir." Although exhausted from the long journey from China, he wanted to appear as if he had all of his military bearing intact.

The yeoman closed the door behind him as he left the two officers alone. McLean's office was impressive, not unlike all the other commanders' offices on the first floor of the building. Captain McLean sat on a leather chair behind a large mahogany desk surrounded by tall wooden bookshelves. Floor-to-ceiling windows on one side of the office provided plenty of light, which was diluted only by sheer curtains. The heavy silk curtains that could be used as blackout drapes were tied to the side, flanking each window. Brass light sconces hanging from the walls matched the table lamp on McLean's desk. A thick oriental rug of elegant reds and greens covered most of the dark wood floor. Two overstuffed leather chairs sat opposite McLean's desk, and a round mahogany table and chairs in the corner offered additional seating. The office smelled of leather and wood. If McLean was a smoker, it wasn't evident—the crystal ashtrays were spotless, and there wasn't even a hint of smoke in the air. A seemingly unused pipe sat in the ashtray on his desk.

McLean, speaking in a slow southern drawl, said "Sit down, Lieutenant. Do you know why you're here?"

"No, sir," Safford replied, dreading the next few moments.

"You've been recommended to me by Admiral Washington."

Safford quickly thought about this statement and asked, "Sir, with all due respect, what interest does the Commander in Chief of the Asiatic Fleet have with me?"

"It seems you've been griping about unusual radio activity in the East China Sea. Is that true?"

"Yes, sir."

"And what did you make of it?"

"All I know is that it wasn't supposed to be on our frequencies," Safford admitted. "My radiomen complained that it overrode our nets and drowned out our communications. Some Navy chaps were obviously overzealous with the power of their transmitters. I repeatedly asked for it to be stopped."

McLean relished informing subordinate officers of facts they didn't know. "Admiral Washington believes what you were listening to, son, was the IJN," he said smugly.

"The Imperial Japanese Navy?" Safford replied. Then he paused for a moment to think before continuing, "I hadn't thought of that, but it makes sense; it was mostly gibberish to my radiomen."

"It wasn't gibberish, Lieutenant. It was Japanese. We have some reports from a chief radioman at Camp Eldridge named Kidder, who says he's figured out the code. I don't understand anything in Kidder's reports, and Admiral Washington wants it figured out immediately. He's pulled some radiomen off their ships in Shanghai and stationed them in the American consulate to try to make some sense out of the IJN comms."

"Kidder, huh? Do you have these reports?"

"They're all on your desk, Lieutenant. We've set you up with a civilian clerk and a couple of yeomen in the Code and Signal Section. We're calling your temporary effort the Research Desk. Let's keep this quiet, Lieutenant, OK?"

"Aye, aye, sir."

"The ONI is interested in this, too, Safford. They've staked you with some funds in an account that no one else knows about."

"How much, sir?"

"I don't know. Captain Welles will be your point man at the ONI, and he wouldn't tell me. I say spend until they tell you to stop," McLean suggested with a chuckle. "And I'd appreciate it if you could figure this out quick, so I can get Admiral Washington off my back and get those radiomen in Shanghai back on their ships where they belong."

"Yes, sir," answered Safford.

This was quite a turn of events. Safford had been preparing himself for the worst—some sort of disciplinary action for an unknown offense. But instead, he was being given a great puzzle to work on, and he couldn't wait to get started.

"You're dismissed, Lieutenant."

"Aye, aye, sir," Safford said as he stood up and walked toward the door.

As Safford grabbed the doorknob to let himself out, Captain McLean added, "You've got six months to figure this out, Safford. After that, it's back to sea duty."

The yeoman was waiting for Safford outside McLean's office. As they walked down the hallway and up a flight of stairs, Safford couldn't help but wonder what was happening in Shanghai. On board the *Finch*, he was less than a mile from the American consulate, but he had no idea what was going on. And who was this Chief Kidder? Were those radiomen in Shanghai able to copy the Japanese code? Why hadn't his own men on the *Finch* been able to do so?

The yeoman knocked on a door marked:

Room 2646

OP-20-G

Department of Naval Communications

Code and Signal Section

Research Desk

Lieutenant Safford had a way with numbers, so the room number immediately made sense to him. He was on the second floor of the sixth wing in front of room number forty-six. The door had a combination dial with the numbers one through ten just above the doorknob. A few seconds passed before a woman opened the door no more than two inches.

"Lieutenant Safford?" she asked. This woman, Safford would quickly learn, was Agnes Meyer, a civilian clerk assigned to the Research Desk.

Agnes Meyer Driscoll

Agnes May Meyer was a first-generation American citizen and was, quite simply, brilliant. She'd earned an undergraduate degree from the Ohio State University in 1911 and listed physics, engineering, mathematics, statistics, auditing, bookkeeping, typing, and clerical work as special skills on her résumé. She had previously worked as the music director for the Lowry Phillips Military Academy in Amarillo, Texas, and also taught math classes. Toward the end of World War I, she was one of the first women to enlist in the Navy and qualified in four foreign languages: French, German, Japanese, and Latin. She joined the Navy and worked her way up to the rank of chief yeoman, the highest rank a woman could achieve at the time. As such, she was assigned to the Code and Signal Section of the Department of Naval Communications. As the war drew to a close, she remained on the Navy's pay role as a civilian stenographer with an annual salary of $1,500. She was eventually promoted to the position of clerk and was assigned to help evaluate a new electric cipher machine being developed in the Code and Signal Section. By the beginning of 1924, Agnes was working in a new division of the Code and Signal Section known as the Research Desk. This division was responsible for understanding and breaking the code systems of foreign navies.

"Yes, ma'am," Safford answered as he was led into the room. The yeoman turned and walked away, closing the door as he left. The room was a far cry from Captain McLean's office. It was about the same size, but that's where the similarities ended. Eight gray steel desks were squeezed in, lined up in rows like good Sailors on a march. The windows were much smaller and covered with thick metal venetian blinds, which were the same dull gray as the desks. The blinds were closed, and Safford could see a layer of dust covering them. Several bare incandescent bulbs hung from the ceiling in metal shrouds, providing light for the room. Steel filing cabinets lined the three windowless walls. The uncovered floor was made of asbestos tiles in a brownish-gray color Safford had never seen before. Although the building was only five years old, Safford saw that this room was well worn. Tin ashtrays full of cigarette butts were scattered about the desks, and the stale smell of smoke hung in the air. Two yeomen sitting at their desks momentarily looked up from their work when Safford first entered the room. Their indifference was in stark contrast to the treatment he had received as the commanding officer of the *Finch*.

Meyer chuckled to herself and said, "You can stop calling me ma'am. I was a chief yeoman before this. Call me Agnes."

"Miss Aggie," one of the yeomen chimed in. The two yeomen were trying their best to look disinterested in the newly arrived officer.

"My sincere apologies, Agnes," Safford responded.

"No need to apologize. The combination for the door is 1-0-1-3, left, right, left, right."

"Nice to meet you, Agnes. I'm Laurance. 1-0-1-3? The U.S. Navy's birthday. Very clever. . . . Should be easy to remember."

Agnes was impressed; Safford obviously had a knack for numbers. "That's right," she remarked. "Well . . . ," she paused as if trying to figure out what to do next, "do you want to get started?" Without waiting for an answer, she showed Safford his desk, which was directly next to hers. "I have so much to show you; I don't know where to begin."

"Do you have Chief Kidder's reports?" asked Safford.

"Oh, yes, of course. Chief Kidder has helped us out tremendously."

"Who is this Kidder?"

"We first heard from him about six months ago," Agnes explained. "He's a chief radioman, and a good one. He was stationed at the Los Baños communication station in the Philippines and was frustrated by some code on his net that he didn't understand."

"Imperial Japanese Navy comms?"

"That's right, and the IJN is using very strong transmitters. They obviously don't know we can hear them. Or if they do, they assume their code is unbreakable. Anyway, we sent out an advisory last year for all radiomen in the Asiatic Fleet to be on the lookout for the Japanese telegraphic code."

"Why didn't my radiomen on the *Finch* get this advisory?" Safford wondered out loud.

"I don't know, but Chief Kidder certainly did. And within three months, he had the Japanese katakana telegraphic code licked. He sent us this chart."

Agnes held up a small chart that contained each of the fifty katakana symbols, each character's sound in English, and its corresponding telegraphic representation.

"Well, I'll be. How'd he figure this out?"

"Apparently, a Japanese woman he knows in the Philippines helped him figure it out."

"So, why are we here?" Safford questioned. "Sounds like Kidder has cracked it already."

"Here's why," Agnes said as she threw down a ream of paper covered with handwritten katakana in groups of three characters. "None of this is real Japanese text. It's all in code—five-digit cipher rendered in katakana characters. And this is only a week's worth of intercept. Two of those filing cabinets are full."

"Well, what can we do with this? It means nothing without a codebook."

Agnes let out a triumphant laugh. "Aha! Yes, Lieutenant Safford, you're a natural. Let me introduce you to a little friend of mine. I call it 'the Red Book.'" Agnes reached around and picked up a red binder from her desk. The binder had *RIP-2* written in large block letters across the front. She put the book down on Safford's desk and splayed the pages open for him to see.

"The Red Book is a translation of the Japanese fleet's Operations Code from 1918." On the pages of the open Red Book, Safford saw lines of text arranged in five columns. The first column was a five-digit number. Next came a five-character code followed by syllables representing letters in the Japanese katakana alphabet. The final two columns were the meaning of each of the codes in Japanese and English.

Safford quickly read a few lines of the Red Book:

59605	LYZPH	ra-chi-ra	Enshu(ni)	Practice/exercise
59606	LYZQI	ra-chi-re	Enshu ni sanyao (shi/ni)	Taking part in maneuvers
59607	LZZSK	ra-chi-ri	Enshu no tame	On account of maneuvers
59608	LZZTL	ra-chi-ro	Enshu wo okona (hi/mo)	Carry out maneuvers
59609	LYZUM	ra-chi-ru	Enshu chu (ni)	During maneuvers

Agnes explained that the Red Book contained about 100,000 phrases and had three independent code equivalents for each expression: a five-digit number, a five-letter group, and a three-character Romaji group. The Imperial Japanese Navy typically transmitted the three-character katakana group because this was the most expedient way to send messages. However, the five-character number or letter group could also be used, depending on the circumstances. Using this code, the Imperial Japanese Navy could securely communicate any message necessary while maintaining the secrecy of the message. Unless, of course, somebody else had the codebook.

"The Red Book is our bible," Agnes said reverently.

Impressed, Safford asked, "How did we get it?"

"Courtesy of the Office of Naval Intelligence. An agent named Russell Ford stole it for us several years ago, and the ONI has been providing us with updates. Of course, the original had katakana where you see the Romaji equivalent—which is the romanization of katakana—and it didn't have the English translations in it. The translations are courtesy of Dr. and Mrs. Emerson Haworth at the ONI. The ONI thought the DNC might be interested. And we were, of course, but we had no idea what to do with it. I was asked to help figure it out, but I hadn't a clue where to start. I put it in this binder and called it the Red Book because we didn't know what it really was. It wasn't until Chief Kidder began sending us some of his intercept that we realized what we had. We can now use the Red Book to decipher everything that Kidder sends us."

"Unbelievable," Safford mumbled. "So, what does RIP-2 stand for?"

"It's our serial number of the Red Book. RIP stands for Radio Intelligence Publication. I'm not sure what RIP-1 is, though," Agnes explained with a shrug.

The possibilities swirled in Safford's mind. "This is amazing! Who else knows about this? Is Kidder still sending us intercept?"

"No, he's been transferred to Cheltenham, Maryland."

"What about Shanghai?"

"Station ABLE? Who told you about that?"

Safford shrugged; he had never heard the term Station ABLE before but didn't want to sidetrack Agnes.

Agnes shook her head almost imperceptibly, but continued, "Chief Malcolm Lyon is heading up efforts there. He and his men are sending us their intercept, but only some of them seem to use the same code. All of them use five-digit cipher or three-character katakana, but only about half of them break using the Red Book. The known Imperial Japanese Navy nets break fine, but the other intercept may be diplomatic. Different frequencies, different code. Chief Lyon is also getting intercept from up the road in Peiping, where he's trained some Marines to copy the traffic. It all comes back to us here at the Research Desk.

"In addition to Kidder and Lyon, there are three other radiomen sending us intercept—," she paused as she shuffled through some papers. Finding the one she was looking for, she continued, "Chief Radioman Dorman Chauncey on the USS *Paul Jones*, Radioman First Class Orville Coonce on the USS *Huron*, and Marine Sergeant Stephen Lesko in Peiping. They all taught themselves to copy the katakana code in much the same way Kidder did," Agnes continued. "All of them have provided a significant amount of intercept back to the Research Desk. None of them are as skilled as Chief Kidder, but it's better than nothing."

"Is there anyone helping us out in the Philippines now that Kidder's been reassigned?" asked Safford.

"No, we've got no one with Kidder's expertise. These are merely radiomen spending their spare time doing this intercept work for us. The next guy doesn't necessarily have the skill or inclination to do the same. There's nothing in it for them."

"OK," Safford sighed. "We might have to do something about that."

Safford decided right away that he needed to see Chief Kidder and pick his brain. Luckily, the Naval Communications Station (COMSTA) at Cheltenham where Kidder was working was just outside Washington, DC. Safford called the commanding officer of Kidder's unit and set up a meeting.

CHAPTER 04

THE MEETING

WEDNESDAY, AUGUST 6, 1924
NAVAL COMMUNICATIONS STATION,
CHELTENHAM, MARYLAND

Harry Kidder sat in his office at his new assignment in Maryland, missing the excitement of living and working in the Philippines. Now, as the chief radioman in charge of a communication station, he rarely got a chance to listen to Morse code. Instead, he supervised more junior Sailors who did all the work. It certainly wasn't as fulfilling to him, and he frequently sat bored in his office thinking about his past assignments and his life before the Navy.

Harry Kidder was born on September 27, 1889 in Farber, Missouri, a small farming community about 100 miles northwest of St. Louis and 180 miles east of Kansas City. He excelled in the one-room schoolhouse in Farber, where science and math were his strengths. At home, he learned the farming business from his parents. Since he was an only child, they were counting on him to eventually take over the farm, which had been in the family for generations. After graduating from high school in 1907, Harry began working parcels of his family's corn farm on his own, just as his parents had planned. Despite making a good living and being on a path to take over the farm completely when his parents retired, Harry yearned for something more than the farm or his hometown could offer. Without telling his parents, he drove over an hour to visit the U.S. Army recruiter in Columbia and signed on for a three-year hitch. Devastated by his decision to abandon them, his parents disowned him; the fight they had before Harry left for basic training made it clear to him that they wanted nothing more to do with him.

Harry's father was already out working in the fields at sunup on a chilly April morning in 1911, when the Army recruiter drove up to their farmstead. His mother watched from the kitchen window as Harry climbed into the recruiter's Knox seven-passenger touring car. Feeling a mixture of shame and guilt, Harry didn't look back as the car started to roll, so he never saw his mother crying at the window as he pulled away from the house.

Because of his aptitude for the sciences and his technological curiosity, the Army assigned Harry to communications school following basic training. There, he learned all about the growing field of radio communications and how to correspond by sending and receiving Morse code messages.

After training, Private Kidder was assigned to the U.S. Army Signal Corps station in Saint Michael, Alaska. His official duties were to operate communications equipment as part of the Washington-Alaska Military Cable and Telegraph System. In reality, as the junior man in the unit, Private Kidder washed trucks and maintained the motor pool instead of performing the radio work for which he was trained. Harry loved the idea of working in the communications field, but in the army, he was a grunt first and a communicator second. Cold, disappointed, and disillusioned, Kidder completed his three-year hitch in the army and set off in search of his next adventure.

Without a family to return to, Kidder found his way to Anchorage and visited the U.S. Navy recruiter in town. Ever since Guglielmo

Marconi's wireless telegraph gained worldwide attention in 1899, the Navy had become the leader in this technology within the U.S. military. By the early twentieth century, the Navy was routinely using Morse code to communicate wirelessly across vast distances. Trained radiomen in the U.S. Navy were on the cutting edge of radio theory and practice.

Based on his time in the Army, Kidder was brought into the Navy as a radioman second class. The Navy recruiter promised him warm climates and more communications work than he could handle. He signed on the dotted line before the recruiter could ask twice.

Within weeks, Petty Officer Kidder found himself on the USS *Blackhawk*, a U.S. Navy destroyer tender assigned to the Asiatic Fleet, which was headquartered at Cavite Naval Base in Manila Bay in the Philippines. Despite being the smallest in the U.S. Navy, the Asiatic Fleet was responsible for defending the high seas between Guam, the coast of China, and the Indian Ocean. Under the command of Rear Admiral Walter C. Cowles, the fleet's primary responsibility was to maintain the United States' Open Door policy with China in the face of increasing hostility and aggression from Japan.

Kidder was in his element in the Navy. He loved the beaches of the Philippines—the warm sun and salt air were heaven to him, especially after living in Alaska for three years. His proficiency as a communicator quickly grew, and the Navy assigned him to the cruiser USS *Pittsburgh* and then the cruiser USS *Augusta* in the western Pacific. He was happy to stay in the western Pacific as long as the Navy would allow.

After he was promoted to radioman first class, Petty Officer Kidder was assigned to the U.S. Navy communications station on Camp Eldridge in the town of Los Baños on Laguna de Bay in the Philippines, about forty miles southeast of Manila, where he first ran across the katakana telegraphic code. With the help of the wife of a shipmate, he had learned the katakana syllabary and the corresponding telegraphic codes. Just when he was started to gain some traction in learning to intercept the IJN communications, he had been reassigned to Cheltenham, Maryland.

Now, Kidder waited for an officer from the Department of Naval Communications named Safford, but he didn't know why. A yeoman from Safford's office had scheduled the meeting but couldn't tell Chief Kidder the reason.

Safford arrived for his meeting with Kidder right on time. When Safford first laid eyes on Harry Kidder, he thought he epitomized what a chief petty officer should look like. His faced was deeply tanned, almost to the point that it seemed leathery—as if he'd been in the sun every day of his life. At thirty-four years old, Kidder was already a grizzled man, who spoke with a raspy voice—the effects of too much coffee and too many cigarettes. There were many things about Kidder that Safford immediately liked. He had the hard edge of a Sailor who'd seen the world. He was a fireplug of a man—he certainly couldn't have stood more than five foot six—but with his stocky build and smiling face, he was still a commanding presence. When Kidder spoke, he spoke with authority.

After some niceties and military protocol, Safford asked, "So, chief, I understand you know how to copy the katakana telegraphic code."

"That's right, sir. But how do you know that?"

"Your name is well-known at the Research Desk. We have all the intercept you sent in," Safford explained. "Can you tell me more about it?"

Kidder explained to Safford how he'd been listening to the strange telegraphic code for months while he was stationed in the Philippines. He had begun to write out the telegraphic symbols that were not part of the standard international Morse code. He had no idea what he was listening to, but as long as he could hear it, he copied it. Over time, he learned to recognize most of the telegraphic characters he was hearing and eventually became proficient at copying it. After the advisory sent out by the Department of Naval Communications in 1923, he realized he was copying the telegraphic code of the Imperial Japanese Navy, which made it that much more intriguing.

"Before the memo, how did you know what you were copying, Kidder?" asked Safford.

"I didn't. But I figured it out—there were just a few characters I had to learn," Kidder said. The problem was daunting, but he was up to the task.

"But how on earth did you ever make any sense of it?"

As luck would have it, one of Kidder's buddies in the Philippines was married to a Japanese woman named Ako, whom he asked for help. He explained to her the concept of telegraphic code and showed her the American alphabet and Morse code equivalents. Then he showed her the undefined groups of dits and dahs and asked her if she could help translate them into Japanese letters. Within two weeks, Ako had helped Kidder develop the symbol, sound, and letter chart that Agnes had showed Safford on his first day of work at the Research Desk.

Armed with his newfound katakana code skills, Kidder began to sit next to the on-watch radioman, creating a new position for himself after he became chief. He told his commanding officer it was for mentoring purposes to help get the young Sailors up to speed on copying the skeds. This was true, but he also began copying the Japanese skeds regularly. He sent all his intercept logs back to the Research Desk through his commanding officer.

Kidder eventually received orders for duty at COMSTA Cheltenham. Naturally, he was disappointed to leave the Philippines, but he knew all along it wouldn't last forever. Cheltenham was good duty—a little too close to HQ, but far enough away to remain anonymous. It wasn't long after he'd arrived in Cheltenham, though, that Lieutenant Safford came to visit.

Safford had a notepad and pencil and was ready to take notes. "Was is difficult, Kidder?" he asked.

"Sir?"

"Is this something others can do? Can we ask other radiomen to copy the Japanese code?"

"Well, yes and no. I think any radioman worth his salt can learn to copy the katakana. They'll need some training, but it can be done. There is one thing, though—" Kidder trailed off, not knowing how to proceed.

Safford looked up from his notepad, "Spit it out, chief."

Kidder knew when an officer was prepared to hear the truth, so he continued, "Radiomen are gonna resist; they're not gonna want to do it."

"Why not?" Safford was puzzled.

"Several reasons. First, there's no incentive for them to do it. You'd be asking them to squeeze in work between their skeds. Why would they want to do that? And then they're working with telegraphic code different than what they're familiar with. Promotions for radiomen depend on Morse code speed tests. The katakana code erodes the ability to copy standard Morse."

Safford nodded in understanding while writing furiously.

"Plus, we're trained to copy Morse code using typewriters, but the U.S. Navy is not equipped with typewriters with the katakana alphabet. They'd have to copy using a stick," Kidder explained.

"A stick?"

"A pencil. It's slower than copying with a mill…a typewriter. And after a while, your hand begins to ache. We'd need Japanese mills."

"Makes sense," Safford agreed. "What kind of typewriters do radiomen use now?"

"The Underwood Model 5—standard Navy issue. It's what we're trained on and what's in the fleet."

"OK, got it," Safford said, still scribbling notes.

Kidder continued to explain that after copying the code for several months, he began to recognize the Imperial Japanese Navy operators by their "fist." That is, each Japanese radio operator had his own methods and quirks when transmitting messages via telegraphic code. One man might hit the key hard and fast. Another might be more subtle and lingering. Kidder began to distinguish between operators and even anticipate what or how they would send their messages. Kidder explained that this was no different than recognizing a Morse code operator, or someone's voice.

Could come in handy, Safford thought to himself. "There is one thing you can do for me, Chief," Safford said.

"Yes, sir?"

"I'd like you to put together an information booklet that we can provide to radiomen in the Pacific," Safford said. "I want to provide them with a little more information about how to copy the katakana code than they've got now."

"No problem, sir. I can get that to you in a week."

"Thanks, Chief. That will be very helpful."

"Yes, sir."

Before he left Cheltenham, Safford asked Chief Kidder one last thing, "What got you started on this, Kidder? Why did you give it any thought at all? Why didn't you just tune past it?"

Kidder told him about his homemade ham rig in the Philippines and about how he'd stay up all night listening to the unusual telegraphic code. As Kidder described his activities over the past several months, Safford could see the excitement on his face and in the way he described it. Safford knew the answer to his own question: Chief Kidder had a passion for radio communications. That was something he had never seen before in the fleet.

This guy is something special, Safford thought. *I don't think this is the last I'll see of him.*

CHAPTER 05

THE PLAN

MONDAY, AUGUST 18, 1924
MAIN NAVY BUILDING, WASHINGTON, DC

Back at the Research Desk, Lieutenant Safford tried to imagine how much Japanese katakana traffic there was. If five self-taught operators could fill two cabinets in less than a year, imagine how much more was out there! While sitting at his desk next to Agnes, Safford wondered out loud, "How can we do this? There simply aren't enough radiomen out there to assign any to intercept duty full time.

Agnes was ready with an answer. "We have to set up some training," she said.

Agnes's words jarred Safford from his thoughts. He hadn't expected an answer, but he knew she was right—training was a necessity. But that wasn't all. The U.S. Navy needed to establish intercept sites, develop equipment, and set up a cadre of well-trained radiomen. They also needed to be able to identify these specially trained radiomen so that they weren't sent off to perform "general service" radioman duties after they were trained. Lieutenant Safford needed a plan. Despite Captain McLean's wishes, this was going to take much longer than six months.

"Training," Safford thought out loud. "We need training, and I know exactly who will be giving it."

"Chief Kidder?" replied Agnes.

"That's right. But we've got other things to get done first."

"I'm your man!" Agnes responded, pausing for comedic effect.

Safford stopped and looked up at Miss Aggie, who was looking directly back at him. They both burst out laughing. It was the first joke that had passed between them, and Safford realized how lucrative this partnership would be.

"First, I need to know how much is in this ONI 'slush fund.' Have you heard of it, Agnes?"

"I thought it was just a rumor."

"Captain McLean confirmed it. I need to know how much I have to play with." Safford turned to a yeoman and barked, "Get me the number of Captain Roger Welles at ONI."

Ten minutes later, Safford was on hold waiting for Captain Welles. A captain is never on a lieutenant's schedule, so Safford figured he might be on hold for a while. After holding for several minutes, a secretary came over the line and said, "Lieutenant Safford, stand by for Captain Welles."

A moment later, Safford heard, "Laurance! I've been eager to talk to you. Glad you finally got the nerve to call me!"

Safford asked about the ONI fund and nodded up and down while Captain Welles explained how it would work. To Agnes watching from the adjacent desk, Safford seemed completely engulfed in the conversation, as if there was no one else in the room. He nodded and occasionally swallowed hard.

"Yes, sir. Really? Anything? Yes, sir. . . . Yes, sir. . . . Yes, sir."

Agnes was dying to hear the other side of the conversation. The yeomen, equally intrigued by Safford's side of the conversation, were all smoking and staring at the lieutenant, their work at a temporary standstill.

"Yes, sir. . . . But how do I—" After many moments of silence, Safford responded, "Aye, aye, sir!"

Safford hung up and took a deep breath. As he transitioned from the telephone call to being back in the room with the others, he looked up from the phone at Agnes. He turned to the yeomen and then back to Agnes.

"Well, young lady, someone is going to get a raise!"

"Laurance, what are you talking about?" Agnes asked.

"The ONI has set aside one hundred thousand dollars for this effort—they're calling it *radio intelligence*. We can use the money how and when we want, within limits, of course. We just need to provide a justification, and the money is ours. And for that, I will need your help, Agnes."

"One hundred thousand dollars . . ." Agnes whispered. She was flabbergasted, especially if this meant a raise for her. She'd been getting paid as a clerk since she started working as a civilian for the Navy; maybe now she would get paid for what she was actually doing.

"Any ideas, Agnes?"

"Well, we need to pay the Haworths for their translation work. Who knows when we might need them again? We could also use some dictionaries, books on the Japanese language and names, Japanese atlases, information about the Japanese Navy. . . ." Agnes tried to think of more worthy uses of the slush fund.

Safford nodded and added, "We've got to get some help out to those Sailors and Marines in China too. They're our only source of intercept right now."

Over the next several months, Safford challenged himself to learn the katakana alphabet and the art of cryptanalysis. Agnes Meyer was an immense help on both fronts. She got him up to speed on everything the U.S. Navy knew about intercepting, translating, processing, decrypting, and understanding IJN communications.

In addition to this education, Safford began searching for possible

Research Desk candidates from the fleet. To do so, he posted cryptograms of varying difficulty in the monthly DNC bulletin. Individuals who successfully completed these puzzles and indicated an interest in cryptography had their names placed in a personnel file for future contact. The first pupil to come to Safford's attention was Lieutenant Joseph Numa Wenger.

Tall, thin, and exceedingly intelligent, Lieutenant Wenger graduated from the U.S. Naval Academy in 1923, after which he went directly to sea. He responded to the Research Desk cryptogram memos several times, solving the puzzles perfectly each time.

Along with five other naval officers who showed promise solving the puzzles, Wenger was brought to Washington, DC, in 1925 for a six-week initiation into cryptanalysis. Also in the group was a young lieutenant junior grade named Joseph Rochefort. The six officers spent time with Safford and Agnes learning the basics of cryptanalysis and radio intelligence before being sent back to their ships. Wenger and Rochefort were standouts in the group, and Safford filed their names away for later use, knowing he would eventually find roles for each of them.

As Safford's own understanding of cryptanalysis grew, he began thinking about Chief Kidder's explanation of having to copy the katakana code by pencil and began developing a design for a typewriter. By October 1924, he had fully developed his idea and was ready to get one built.

In an official letter to Captain McLean, Safford requested permission to solicit bids from several typewriter companies to develop a machine that radiomen could use when intercepting IJN telegraphic codes. Safford also proposed establishing sites around the Pacific where radiomen would be stationed with the sole purpose of intercepting IJN messages. His rationale was that one dedicated intercept station would furnish more valuable material than a hundred stations forwarding only such foreign traffic that they merely happened upon, as was happening in Shanghai. Safford suggested the Navy had to intercept messages by the hundreds and thousands to have enough material to solve foreign codes.

His letter also included a request for specialized training to teach radiomen how to intercept and process IJN katakana telegraphic code. Safford was stepping through all of Chief Kidder's recommendations and trying to force the slow-moving bureaucracy of the U.S. Navy into a new paradigm that utilized radio intelligence.

McLean approved the purchase of katakana typewriters but disapproved any additional intercept sites or dedicated intercept training. Safford was crushed; he thought he had made a compelling argument that radio intercept operations were a necessity against the Imperial Japanese Navy.

Still, with one victory in hand, Safford wrote to several American typewriter companies asking for bids on a machine that could type both English letters and Romaji renderings of katakana symbols. He received only one design that looked like it would work. It came from the Underwood Typewriter Company, which proposed adapting its Model 5 to type English capital letters, Romaji symbols, and numbers. Safford ordered four of these modified Model 5s, for a total cost of $640.

When the Underwood machines arrived at the Research Desk, Safford noticed that Underwood took the liberty of adding the words "Underwood Code Machine" underneath the space bar, where normally placed the words "Underwood Standard Typewriter." Safford had a U.S. Navy property plate affixed to each of them, giving them the designation Radio Intelligence Publication-5 (RIP-5). On the machines, each of the forty-six keys in lowercase typed Romaji renderings of katakana symbols, and two of the keys in uppercase typed the final two Romaji symbols. The rest of the uppercase on the RIP-5 were Japanese accent marks, English capital letters, English punctuation marks, and numbers. Two of these Underwood Code

RIP-5 Underwood Code Machine

Machines were sent to Shanghai for radiomen to use when intercepting messages. One RIP-5 was sent to the Asiatic Fleet flagship the USS *Huron*, and one remained in the Research Desk spaces for training and further development.

Safford knew his time at the Research Desk was limited, so he was eager to get as much groundwork completed before he was transferred to his next assignment. Unfortunately, this was the Navy, and progress was slow—too slow for Laurance Safford.

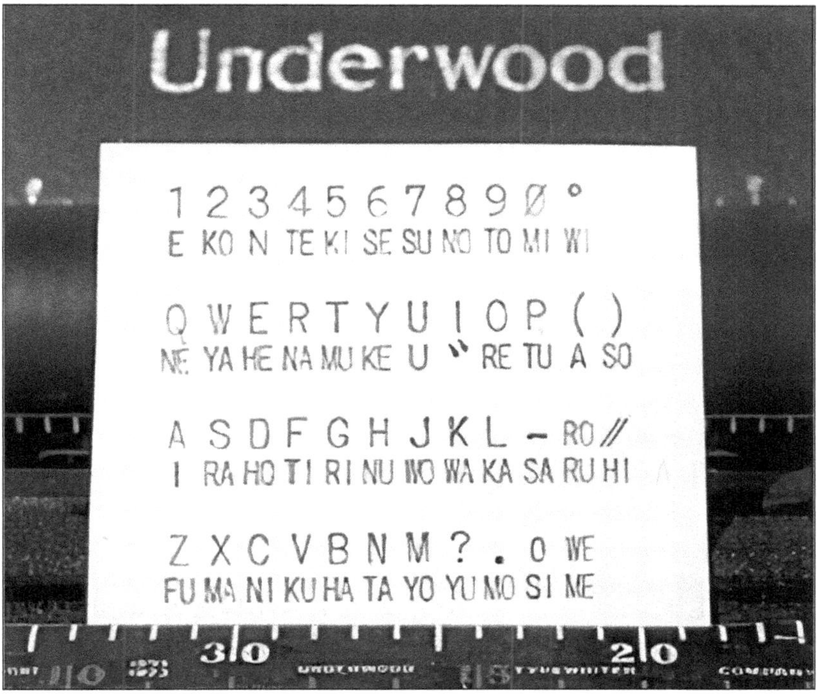

RIP-5 Underwood Code Machine typing output

CHAPTER 06

STATION ABLE

THURSDAY, JULY 14, 1927
STATION ABLE, SHANGHAI, CHINA

Almost three years had passed since Lieutenant Safford began his work at the Research Desk, and his progress on his checklist was frustratingly slow. The American consulate office in Shanghai was located in the Bund area, just north of the historic walled city center along the western bank of the Whangpoo River. The Bund housed several other foreign consulates, but the building for the American consulate was the newest and most modern. Like all the buildings in the Bund, the American consulate looked like it belonged in Paris instead of the Far East. With six stories, it was one of the tallest buildings on the western side of the city.

The U.S. flag flew high above the main entrance to the American consulate, which faced the Whangpoo River. Three half-wave dipole antennas and two loop antennas were hidden behind the flag, and thus, were not visible from the street. The three half-wave antennas were merely insulated copper wires of varying lengths that attached to another wire halfway along their lengths. This shared wire then snaked into the building. The antennas were designed to receive HF signals between 11 and 21 megacycles. The loop antennas, consisting

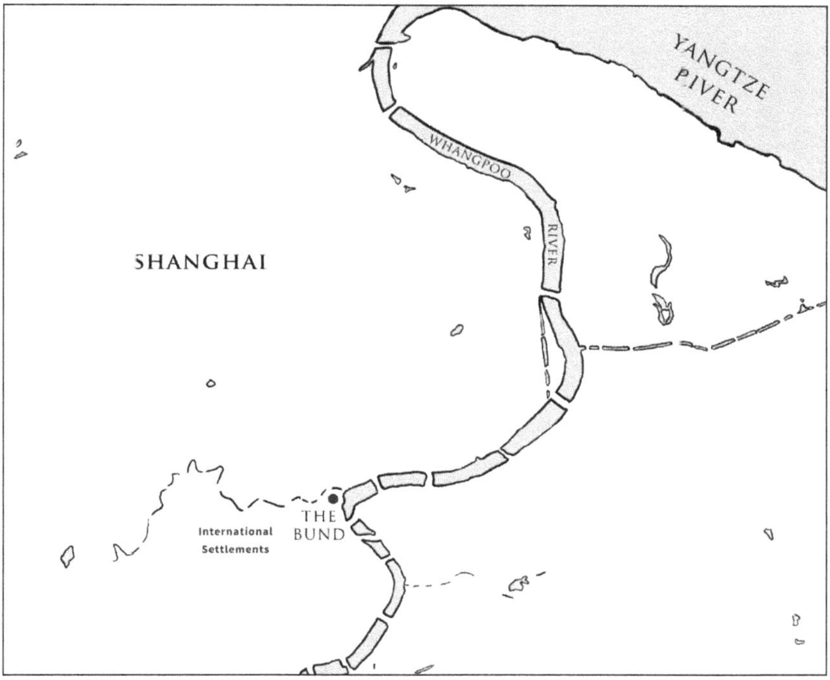

of wire wrapped around a diamond-shaped spindle, were designed to copy low frequency communications at 30 to 300 kilocycles. Even though none of the antennas were visible from anywhere on the street, they were dual-use and could easily be explained away as standard communications equipment, if anyone inquired. Their real purpose, however, was entirely different.

The U.S. Navy had been allocated a small windowless room on the fourth floor of the American consulate building. It was the Navy's only official intercept station, having been designated Station ABLE by the Research Desk. The station was equipped with several U.S. Navy LF and HF receivers, which allowed for intercept between 3 and 300 kilocycles and from 1 to 30 megacycles.

Chief Radioman Malcolm "Felix" Lyon sat in front of the brand-new RIP-5 at Station ABLE, typing the katakana symbols as he

The Bund, Shanghai, China

heard them. The Underwood Code Machine made intercepting the katakana code significantly easier. Because Lyon had developed significant skill in copying the katakana telegraphic code, he was the only radioman assigned solely to intercept duties at Station ABLE in Shanghai. Other radiomen rotated between their regular duties and intercept duties. For every intercept watch, they performed three regular watches. However, using that rotation, the radiomen's intercept skills would never improve, and dedicated intercept operators were desperately needed. Nonetheless, Lyon was responsible for training the less experienced intercept operators on the katakana telegraphic code, how to use the RIP-5, and how to analyze the traffic.

Lyon had received several copies of the information booklet that the Research Desk had provided to all Asiatic Fleet communications stations. The booklet was developed by one Harry Kidder, a chief radioman well known to most Pacific Fleet communicators. The booklet contained all the information a radioman would need to begin copying the Imperial Japanese Navy's katakana telegraphic code.

Chief Lyon saw to it that all of the radiomen in Shanghai received a copy of the information booklet. However, the radiomen he was trying to train seemed more interested in keeping their regular radioman skills up to snuff instead of experimenting with a foreign telegraphic code. Intercepting foreign communications might have been a curiosity at best, but if they couldn't perform well as fleet communicators, they'd be overlooked when it came time for a promotion.

Radioman Second Class Merle Lynch, known as "Little Beaver" to his shipmates, because of his diminutive size and industrious nature, was sitting the katakana watch with Chief Lyon, who was having a devil of a time teaching Lynch the katakana code. Little Beaver was eager to learn, but it just wasn't sticking.

Lynch was wearing headphones and listening to the same frequency as the chief, who was typing out his copy on the RIP-5. Lynch had his eyes tightly closed, desperately trying to concentrate as he used a stick to record what he was hearing. But he was simply unable to keep up with the more experienced chief.

"Dit dit dah dit dah, that's *MI*," instructed Lyon while he continued to copy and type. *MI* was the katakana character ミ and sounded like *mee*.

"Sorry," responded Lynch, opening his eyes to look at the chief.

"Keep trying," the chief consoled.

Lynch closed his eyes again and recorded a couple katakana characters on his paper.

"Dit dit dit dah, that's *KU*. You wrote V," said Lyon.

"I'm used to that being a V, Chief."

On the chief's paper, the RIP-5 rendered the single Romaji character *KU*, pronounced *koo*.

"Never mind. Just keep trying."

Lynch redoubled his efforts and recorded a few more katakana characters before setting the pencil down with an exasperated huff. He opened his eyes and watched Chief Lyon. With his eyes on the paper where his copy was being recorded, Lyon typed character after character, never missing a one. *Clack, clack, clack* went the Underwood Code Machine as Lyon copied.

"I'm sorry . . . I can't do this, Chief."

"You'll get it, Lynch. You just gotta keep trying." Despite Lynch's struggles, he actually showed more aptitude than others for intercept duty. Lyon desperately wanted Lynch to succeed.

Chief Lyon kept typing as he spoke with Lynch. The RIP-5 sounded off with each key stroke. *Clack*, *clack*, *clack*. Each Romaji character appeared on the page with every clack of the Underwood Code Machine.

"The mill makes it easier, but you have to get to a point where you think of the katakana character as soon as you hear the code. Just like you do with your Morse skeds."

"It's just not happening for me, Chief," Lynch said glumly. "I'm just not getting it."

Chief Lyon continued to type. He had to complete the sked because he knew the intercept could be important.

Lynch was not alone in his inability to grasp the art of copying the katakana telegraphic code. Chief Lyon was spending far too much time on the position, or poz, so Station ABLE could provide as much intercept copy as possible. He worked twelve to fourteen hour shifts just to maximize the station's output while trying to teach the others. Upon his return each morning, he'd find a few scant pages of poorly copied intercept from the overnight shift, which were of no use to anyone. Each morning, Lyon would start over with a new pupil, who'd invariably prove to be just as inept at copying the katakana code as the last.

Eventually, Chief Lyon found the lone exception among the group: Radioman First Class Orville Coonce. Coonce displayed an actual interest in his intercept duties and this translated into real ability. Coonce had arrived in Shanghai after completing an assignment aboard the USS *Huron*, which was scheduled to be decommissioned. As the *Huron* departed Manila for its final voyage across the Pacific, Coonce was transferred to Station ABLE. Along with Coonce's personal effects, the Navy had paid to have the lone Underwood Code Machine aboard the USS *Huron* moved to Station ABLE, bringing the total there to three. Coonce had achieved some skill at intercepting the katakana telegraphic code while on board the *Huron*, and under Chief Lyon's tutelage at Station ABLE, he became quite proficient.

This allowed Lyon to work twelve-hour shifts during the daytime, while Coonce took the night shift. The duo fell easily into this port-and-starboard schedule and continued training the other radiomen while they performed their intercept duties.

Less than 800 miles northwest of Shanghai, another fledging radio intelligence effort was taking shape. Since the dissemination of the Research Desk's information booklet, some Marine Corps radio operators in Peiping, China, were also trying to intercept the Imperial Japanese Navy's telegraphic code. Their efforts were largely ineffective, but Lyon wanted to give them a leg up.

The U.S. Marine Corps detachment in Peiping was subordinate to the Headquarters Company, Third Battalion, Fourth Regiment in Shanghai. The Fourth Regiment, under the command of Colonel Charles Hill, was deployed to Shanghai to protect American citizens and property in Shanghai's International Settlement along the Bund. The Third Battalion had detachments in several other locations where there were large concentrations of American citizens.

Colonel Hill, a ham radio enthusiast, heard about Station ABLE from his Marine communicators and was keen to meet Chief Lyon. Lyon showed the colonel the intercept spaces, and the colonel immediately wanted in on the action. He directed the Third Battalion to identify five Marine communicators for training under Chief Lyon.

Over the next several weeks, Chief Lyon trained the five operators—Private William Kiser, Corporal Paul Kugler, Private Winnett Robinson, Private First Class William Thomson, and Private Ogden Wilson—in all aspects of radio intelligence. In September 1927, the group of newly trained intercept operators boarded the USS

Cincinnati, an Omaha-class light cruiser, for the three-day journey to Peiping. They carried with them a single Underwood Code Machine, the transfer of which the Research Desk had authorized. They were all assigned to the Marine Detachment, American Legation in Peiping and immediately began radio intercept operations there.

American Legation in Peiping, China

Intercept operations in China were productive. There was a high level of Japanese katakana code communications in the area due to the tensions between Japan and China at the time. The U.S. Marine Corps intercept operators in Peiping performed well and passed along their intercept logs to Station ABLE in Shanghai. The two intercept stations stayed in touch regularly to compare notes and divide up skeds to copy. Lyon and Coonce continued to train radiomen as they rotated in and out of intercept duties.

Between the intercept sites at Shanghai and Peiping, operators began to notice an uptick in traffic being sent by the Imperial Japanese Navy. The skeds were growing from fifteen to twenty minutes in duration to as much as forty to forty-five minutes. There were more messages sent per sked, and each message tended to be longer. The intercept operators could discern that something was about to happen; they simply didn't know what.

CHAPTER 07

OPERATIONAL PLANNING

MONDAY, OCTOBER 10, 1927

MAIN NAVY BUILDING, WASHINGTON, DC

Back in the Main Navy Building in Washington, DC, they knew what was coming.

It was a balmy autumn day in the nation's capital and time for Lieutenant Safford to move on. After setting in motion the plan to establish radio intelligence as an operational activity in the U.S. Navy, Safford was transferred back to regular shipboard duties on board the USS *California*, a battleship stationed in San Pedro, California. Given the opportunity to choose his own replacement, Safford selected Joseph Rochefort, who had recently been promoted to lieutenant on board the battleship USS *Arizona* and was due for transfer orders.

On this pleasant, Indian summer afternoon, Lieutenant Rochefort—one of Safford's initial cryptanalysis students—took over as head of the Research Desk and was working alongside Agnes, who was now Agnes Meyer Driscoll, having married Michael Driscoll, a DC lawyer, in the summer of 1924.

Rochefort enlisted in the U.S. Navy in 1918, before he even graduated from Polytechnic High School in Los Angeles. He dreamed of being a Navy pilot, so he lied about his age to enlist. Just a year after he enlisted, the Navy sent him to the Stevens Institute of Technology in New Jersey, where, upon his graduation, he received a commission as an ensign. On board the USS *Arizona*, while he served as the auxiliary division officer, he was befriended by his department head, Lieutenant Commander Chester Jersey. The two played auction bridge together and compared notes about a new form of puzzle called a crossword.

When Commander Jersey received transfer orders to the Navy Department in Washington, DC, he arranged for Rochefort to come along on a temporary assignment to train in cryptanalysis under Lieutenant Laurance Safford.

In the Research Desk office spaces on this particular day in early October 1927, it was too hot to move, too hot to talk. Although the windows were open, stale cigarette smoke hung heavy in the air, unmoving. Two additional yeoman clerks were now working in the Research Desk, bringing the total to five plus Agnes and the officer in charge.

The Research Desk had recently received word from the ONI that indicators pointed to a large-scale "Orange" naval exercise in October 1927. Under U.S. doctrine, all countries were assigned a color code for planning purposes. Japan was orange, the United States was blue, Great Britain was red, France was gold, and so on. The Orange naval exercise of 1927 was predicted to be Japan's largest-ever naval exercise and a potential rehearsal of the country's plan to attack areas in the Pacific.

Along with operators in Shanghai and on board ships of the Asiatic Fleet, Lieutenant Rochefort and the Research Desk planned to monitor the Imperial Japanese Navy's communications during the exercise. Intercept operators from Station ABLE would embark the

USS Marblehead

USS *Marblehead*, a light cruiser, for the duration of the exercise. The *Marblehead* and the USS *Pittsburgh*, the new flagship of the Asiatic Fleet, would trail the exercise, remaining out of view but within range to intercept radio transmissions.

Captain Thomas Craven, who was the Director of Naval Communications at the time, approved the plan. It was unknown if the American ships would be able to intercept Japanese transmissions while underway, but the science seemed to indicate it would work.

We'll simply have to try it, thought Rochefort.

CHAPTER 08

USS MARBLEHEAD

SUNDAY, OCTOBER 16, 1927
STATION ABLE, SHANGHAI, CHINA

In the weeks leading up to the Orange Grand Maneuvers, the USS *Pittsburgh* and the USS *Marblehead* pulled into port Shanghai. They were there to pick up provisions and allow the crews to take liberty prior to their next assignment monitoring the Imperial Japanese Navy's exercise.

Lieutenant Commander Ellis Zacharias was stationed on board the USS *Marblehead* for the exercise. Zacharias, who had recently completed a brief period of cryptanalytic training at the Research Desk, now understood how radio intelligence should work. He was assigned as the Asiatic Fleet's intelligence officer in Cavite, Philippines, so he was keen to lead the first-ever attempt at shipboard radio intelligence operations.

Under the cover of darkness, Zacharias drove the short distance from the *Marblehead* to the American consulate in a nondescript box truck. The truck was purposefully unmarked so as not to draw any unnecessary attention while Zacharias picked up equipment and Chief Lyon, Petty Officer Coonce, and six other radiomen as previously arranged.

Dressed in civilian clothing, Lyon and his men waited for Zacharias on the loading dock behind the consulate. They carried full seabags and two crates of equipment with them, including radio receivers, antennas, reams of paper, and two RIP-5 Underwood Code Machines from Station ABLE.

"Who's coming to pick us up?" Coonce asked.

"Commander Zacharias, the intel boss at Cavite," Lyon replied.

"Well, I can't wait to get to sea again, but I have no idea what this is all about."

Lyon explained how they were to connect their receivers to the *Marblehead*'s antenna systems, set up their RIP-5s, and conduct intercept operations while the ship was at sea.

"Why can't we do that from here?"

The chief shrugged. It certainly was possible to intercept Imperial Japanese Navy ships from Shanghai. Indeed, they had done it before. But it was hit or miss. "Atmospherics. They may be out of range. Besides, I thought you were looking forward to getting out to sea again."

"I am," Coonce confirmed. "I'm just not so sure this is going to work."

"No one is . . . at least not until we try," the chief assured. Clearly, he was more optimistic than Coonce.

Just then, Zacharias pulled the truck around the back of the building and entered the parking lot near the loading dock. Lyon stood up and greeted Zacharias as he got out. "Evening, Commander. I'm Chief Lyon." The two men shook hands, but since everyone was in civilian clothes, no salutes were exchanged.

"Evening, Chief. Hope you and your crew are ready," Zacharias replied, excited for what lay ahead of them.

"We're ready, sir."

"Then let's get moving. And Lyon, until we get on the ship, I'm Ellis, not Commander Zacharias."

"Aye, aye, sir," Lyon replied, catching himself. "OK, Ellis. You can call me Felix."

The chief turned to his men and told them to get started. Within minutes, the truck was loaded with their gear. Lyon sat up front in the passenger seat, and the men jumped into the back.

Ten minutes after Zacharias pulled away from the loading dock, the nondescript box truck arrived at the *Marblehead*, which was berthed in a U.S. Navy leased pier on the Whangpoo River. Quietly, the men got out of the truck and began loading their gear and seabags onto the ship.

After the last of the cargo was on the ship, Zacharias turned to Lyon and said, "Let's go, Felix."

"OK, Ellis," Lyon responded, starting up the gangplank.

Petty Officer Coonce followed the chief and said to the commander with a smirk, "OK, Ellis."

Sailors being Sailors, this was an opportunity they couldn't pass up. The next Sailor after Coonce repeated, "OK, Ellis," as sarcastically as he could muster.

"Let's go, Ellis!"

"C'mon, Ellis!"

"Time to shove off, Ellis!"

"Ellis, Ellis."

After every Sailor had taken a shot at mockingly calling the superior officer by his first name, Lieutenant Commander Zacharias shook his head and chuckled to himself. *I guess I asked for that,* he thought.

As soon as all of the men were aboard, they began casting away lines so the ship could depart port. They set sail just prior to midnight. The USS *Pittsburgh* had already departed and was waiting to rendezvous with the *Marblehead* at dawn.

Simultaneously, a squadron of American destroyers sailed from Cavite Naval Base in the Philippines, ostensibly for a regular exercise but actually on a cruise to the area where the Japanese hoped they could stage their war games without being disturbed. Teams of specially chosen intelligence officers were stationed on each of the destroyers with orders to make visual observations of any Imperial Japanese Navy activity if they came within range.

Over the next three days, 170 Imperial Japanese Navy vessels deployed for the maneuvers. They were divided into a "Blue Fleet," which would simulate an attack on Tokyo from the direction of Formosa, and a "Red Fleet," which would defend the capital from the attack. The "Reds" rendezvoused east of Tokyo on October 19. The next day, the "Blues" left Tokuyama, at the southwestern end of Japan's Honshu Island in the Sea of Japan and reappeared from the east as the "enemy" fleet. A violent storm was in full force, adding considerable realism to the impending mock battle.

On its fourth day at sea, the USS *Marblehead* arrived in the general area of the Japanese maneuvers. The following day, the two opposing Imperial Japanese Navy battle fleets met 250 miles south of Yokosuka Naval Base for the mock battle.

While the USS *Marblehead* remained distant, the American destroyers sighted the Blue Fleet in the vicinity of Formosa and steamed across its path. For the first time ever, the U.S. Navy observed the Imperial Japanese Navy aircraft carrier IJN *Akagi* as it launched and recovered its planes.

The Imperial Japanese Navy's communications plan was simple and easy for the intercept operators to figure out. All ship-to-ship communications were in the HF band: the Reds communicated on three preset frequencies between 4.0 and 4.5 megacycles while the Blues used 4.5 to 5.0 megacycles. Shore-based broadcasts to the fleets were in the low frequency band at 39, 59, and 223 kilocycles. The antennas and the receivers that the *Marblehead*'s intercept team brought on board were perfect for this. The team quickly analyzed and learned the communications plan and began processing intercept. Some of the communications were encrypted using the Red Book code, while other more routine information was passed without encryption. The intercept operators were ready.

Listening to the Japanese, operators aboard the USS *Marblehead* intercepted communications indicating that the Imperial Japanese Navy's commanders were frustrated and annoyed at the sudden appearance of the American destroyers. They also intercepted directions given by the flagship ordering fast vessels to raise a smoke screen between the *Akagi* and the American destroyers. While this may have had a negative effect on visual observations, it in no way interfered with the U.S. Navy's radio intelligence efforts.

Although the goal of the Imperial Japanese Navy was to maintain secrecy while conducting the maneuvers, Lieutenant Commander Zacharias was able to reconstruct a fairly robust description of the entire exercise. And even though the USS *Marblehead* did not make visual contact with the Japanese fleet, radio intercept operators succeeded in getting Zacharias what he sought. Throughout the maneuvers, the team of American radiomen listened to Japanese radio traffic and transcribed the messages. Zacharias decrypted as much of the intercept as he could with the help of the Japanese codebooks he had on board.

On October 28, when the USS *Marblehead* arrived in Kobe, Japan, for a previously scheduled visit, Zacharias had his preliminary report ready. In the report, which was full of optimism about the results of the Orange Grand Maneuvers and the use of radio intelligence while at sea, Zacharias wrote that he was able to learn much about the Japanese exercise by reading the Japanese messages, even though they never came into contact with the Japanese fleet. He believed he had reconstructed the complete and accurate plan of the entire operation.

To Zacharias, the effort was an unmitigated success. Back in Washington, DC, Captain Craven agreed. He wrote a letter to Zacharias, which read:

Dear Ellis:
I have just read with interest a very excellent report you submitted with

regard to certain maneuvers which you had an opportunity of observing in a communication sense.

I thought I would drop you a line and tell you that I consider this report excellent, as it covers a line of Naval information which is very important for us to get hold of and the value of which we so far have failed to appreciate. With congratulations and best wishes.

Sincerely yours,
//signed//
T. T. CRAVEN
Captain, U.S. Navy
Director Naval Communications

CHAPTER 09

RECONSTRUCTION

WEDNESDAY, NOVEMBER 30, 1927

MAIN NAVY BUILDING, WASHINGTON, DC

Despite Captain Craven's high regard for the work to monitor the Orange Grand Maneuvers, the people manning the Research Desk were not as impressed with the results. In their attempt to reconstruct the exercise based on the decoded intercept, they became increasingly frustrated.

"What on earth does this mean?" Agnes asked Lieutenant Rochefort. By this time, the men of the Research Desk had begun calling Agnes "Madame X" out of utter respect for her uncanny ability to break any code put in front of her.

Rochefort shrugged. If Madame X couldn't figure it out, no one could.

Her question was a rhetorical one, of course, because at least half of the intercept she was decoding made absolutely no sense. There were enough correct code groups to indicate they were still using the same Red Book code, but most of the intercepted katakana code groups were nonsense. It was obvious that the radiomen were only partially skilled at copying the katakana telegraphic code.

"These call signs are all wrong," Rochefort groaned. "I'm glad the DNC is happy with these results, but the information is worthless. And now Admiral Bristol wants to move the entire Station ABLE operation on board the USS *General Alava* because he thinks the men would be better off at sea." Admiral Mark Bristol was the Commander in Chief of the Asiatic Fleet (CINCAF) and had the authority to do what he wanted with the men and with the *General Alava*.

The USS *General Alava* was a converted yacht being used by Asiatic Fleet commanders to carry senior naval officers between the Philippines and several ports in China. The CINCAF believed the ship would make a better intercept location than the stationary American consulate in Shanghai.

"What can we do?" Agnes asked Rochefort.

"Those operators just weren't up to snuff. We need to get them better trained, just like Lieutenant Safford said. And we need more of them," Rochefort answered.

"How are we going to do that?" Agnes asked. "This isn't something those operators want to do. We're borrowing them from their real jobs. This will never work."

"We need full-time operators, don't we?"

"Yeah. That's what Laurance said time and time again," Agnes agreed.

"What else did he say?"

Agnes turned and headed directly for one of the filing cabinets. "He kept the plans in here." She pulled out a manila folder stuffed with Safford's notes. Agnes unfolded a map of the Pacific Ocean. On it, Safford had detailed his ideas for listening stations. "Guam, Midway, Hawaii, Alaska, Australia, Subic Bay in the Philippines—these are the sites where he wanted to set up intercept stations."

"Why didn't he?"

"Red tape. Lieutenant Safford wasn't very good with bureaucracy, and he thought everyone who didn't see things his way was a fool. He told Captain McLean as much, which did nothing toward getting his way."

"Did he have a plan for training?"

"You bet," Agnes replied as she pulled out another sheet of paper from the folder. "He and Chief Kidder figured it would take a year to get good radiomen up to snuff on the katakana code."

"DNC will never go for a year. We need to get Kidder back here to see if we can do it quicker." Rochefort turned and barked, "Yeoman!"

A young third class petty officer hustled over, as if he was just waiting for the officer to beckon.

Rochefort said, "I want three things, yeoman. First, I want Chief Kidder here tomorrow morning. Second, I want memos drafted to the DNC requesting listening posts in Hawaii, Guam, and the Philippines. Last, I want a message drafted to commanders worldwide requesting the best radiomen they've got. Can you handle that, yeoman?"

"Aye, sir," the yeoman responded confidently.

"Tomorrow morning."

"Aye, aye, sir!"

CHAPTER 10

CRAVEN'S DECISION

MONDAY, DECEMBER 19, 1927

MAIN NAVY BUILDING, WASHINGTON, DC

Over the next several weeks, Captain Craven, the Director of Naval Communications, had several in-depth telephone conversations on the subject of radio intelligence with Captain Alfred Johnson, the Director of Naval Intelligence. They also had one uncomfortable face-to-face meeting where Johnson threatened to absorb all of the radio intelligence operations into the Office of Naval Intelligence, insisting that all forms of intelligence should be controlled out of the ONI. Craven was certainly supportive of the new intelligence discipline, but he wasn't so keen on removing radiomen from their primary duties as communicators. For starters, there were only a finite number of them. If he assigned some of the radiomen to the ONI, he'd lose them permanently, thus shorting at-sea commanders of their ability to communicate. However, if he held on to all radio intelligence operations, he could at least control how many radiomen were doing it and where.

Craven's hand was being forced, and he was ready to be bold.

Back in his office in the Main Navy Building, Craven bellowed, "Yeoman! Memo!"

A yeoman scurried to the side of Craven's desk, and said, "Yes, sir."

"Number one, for CINCAF, Top Secret."

"Yes, sir."

"For Action: Establish radio intelligence sites at Guam, Hawaii, and the Philippines immediately. Assign appropriate and sufficient radiomen so as to stand up intercept operations in those three locations ASAP," Craven dictated to the yeoman.

The yeoman waited for more.

"Next, for the Chief of Naval Operations: Request memo to all commanders at sea and ashore. We're looking for the best radiomen in the fleet for 'special radio service.' All applications to be sent to this office for immediate consideration for training."

"Aye, aye, sir."

"That's all, yeoman. You're dismissed."

"Yes, sir."

Captain Craven couldn't decide whether he was pleased with his decision to hold onto the radio intelligence operations or not. Captain Johnson had a good point that all intelligence should belong to him, but Craven argued that he would not give up any of his radiomen to the ONI. For the time being, at least, radio intelligence still belonged to the Department of Naval Communications.

CHAPTER 11

STATION BAKER

MONDAY, FEBRUARY 6, 1928
AGAÑA, GUAM

Dorman Chauncey was the only chief radioman aboard the USS *Paul Jones*, a Clemson-class destroyer assigned to the Asiatic Fleet. As such, Chauncey had the luxury of not having to work a rotating shift. Instead, he managed the radio shack while working a regular day schedule. Since the arrival of the Research Desk's information booklet, he'd been dedicating several hours each day to learning the katakana telegraphic code. As instructed in the booklet, he turned in his intercept logs to the ship's communications officer, who, in turn, sent them to the Asiatic Fleet's intelligence officer. As far as Chauncey knew, that's as far as it went.

After only six months on board the *Paul Jones*, Chauncey unexpectedly received transfer orders to Piti Naval Base, Guam. His division officer told him that the Department of Naval Communications had ordered him to Guam to establish a listening post there.

The United States had gained control of Guam in 1898 following the Spanish-American War. A year later, the U.S. Navy established a base located about halfway up the west coast of the island along Agaña

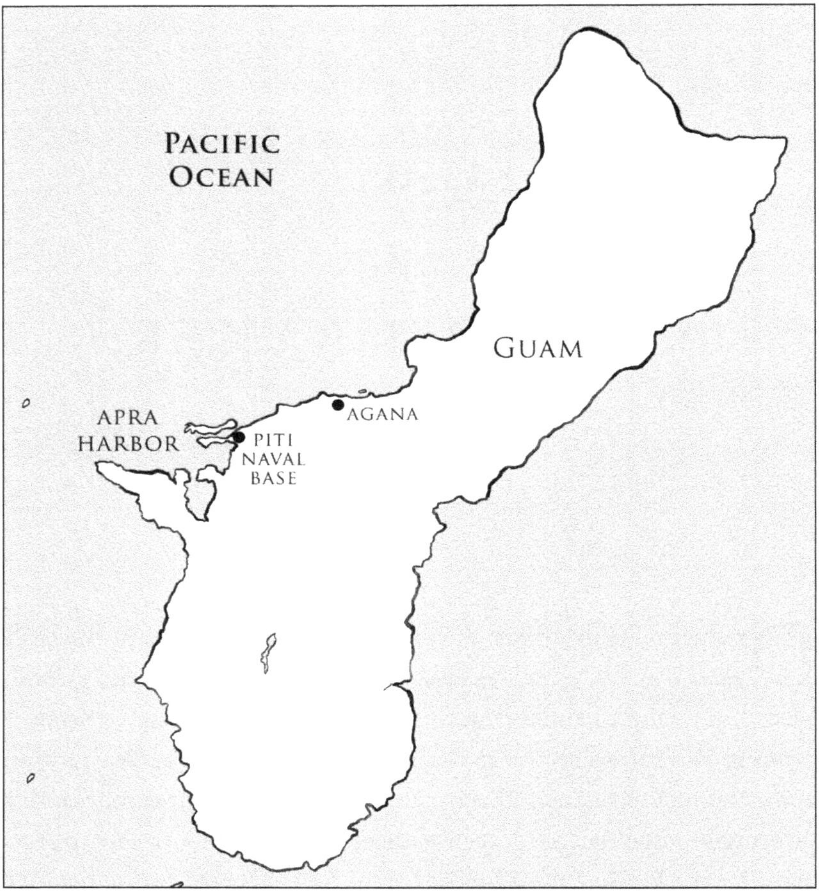

Bay. Just inland, the U.S. Navy built the Government House for the Naval Governor of Guam, as well as a small hospital and barracks in the oldest part of town called the Plaza de España. Dulce Nombre de Maria Cathedral—the first Roman Catholic church in the Mariana Islands—stood on the opposite side of the plaza. Over time, the town of Agaña sprang up around these buildings and became the largest village on the island. Mountains covered with dense jungle surrounded the town on three sides. Foot paths, some wide enough to accommodate small motor vehicles, crisscrossed the jungle between villages.

The indigenous people of Guam—known as the Chamorro—were ancestrally connected to other Pacific Islanders. Even so, the Chamorro were unique to Guam and the Northern Mariana Islands. On Guam, the Chamorro culture had been heavily influenced by centuries of Spanish occupation, which began when Ferdinand Magellan first set foot on the island in 1521.

Due to Guam's strategic location about a quarter of the way from the Philippines to Hawaii, the U.S. Navy has had a long-standing interest in the island. Guam had initially served as a coaling station for the Navy prior to the advent of oil-burning ships. In the early twentieth century, it was an important communication relay station before advancements in long-distance HF technology.

Upon Chauncey's arrival to Guam, the naval communications officer informed him that the new intercept station would be housed in the Old Spanish Guardhouse, where the guards who protected the colonial governor's palace during the Spanish occupation stood watch. The naval governor of Guam selected the site for the intercept station because it was the only unoccupied building that the U.S. Navy was already leasing. It was an old, decrepit building located in the Governor's Garden just off the Plaza de España. He was the only radioman selected for this duty; others would have to come from the Navy COMSTA at Libugon Hill, about a mile inland and uphill from Agaña.

Chauncey stepped into the abandoned space inside the Old Spanish Guardhouse and wondered if he was the victim of a practical joke. The place simply didn't seem appropriate for radio intercept. Spanish soldiers had constructed it out of coral mortar blocks, but at this point, it featured loose wooden floorboards over hard earth, and the main room was damp and humid.

"I cannot imagine this place in the middle of the summer," he said aloud to himself.

Recalling his training during his chief petty officer initiation, Chauncey decided to look past the negatives and focus on the

Naval Governor's Palace with flagpole. The Old Spanish Guardhouse is to the right of the Palace.

potential of the site. And over the next few weeks, he was able to piece together a functional intercept site—the first one outside of China. The Research Desk dubbed it Station BAKER. Chauncey procured receivers and antennas from the local U.S. Navy supply system at Piti Navy Base, which provided parts and supplies to meet the local Navy community's needs. He also received a large wooden crate labeled:

SECRET—FOR CRM CHAUNCEY ONLY

In the crate were four RIP-5 Underwood Code Machines. The Underwood Typewriter Company had been continuing to build the code machines for the Research Desk, which then distributed them to the intercept sites as fast as possible.

"What on earth is this?" Chauncey said as he inspected the modified Underwood mills. Once he saw the Japanese Romaji on the keys, he quickly understood their purpose. *Ingenious*, he thought. He quickly taught himself how to use the RIP-5 machine and was thrilled with its performance.

A handful of general service radiomen from Radio Libugon, the large Navy COMSTA on Guam, took rotating shifts at Station BAKER attempting to perform intercept operations with instruction and assistance from Chief Chauncey. Just as they had been at Station ABLE, the results from the general service radiomen at Station BAKER were not good. Some radiomen showed some promise, but others showed none at all. Regardless of aptitude, none of the part-time operators dove in headfirst. The radiomen were not interested in performing intercept duties; they preferred to hone their primary skills as fleet communicators using international Morse code so they could compete for promotions more successfully.

In addition to the lack of dedicated intercept operators, Station BAKER had other problems. Inside the dilapidated building, paper and equipment mildewed rapidly. Dengue fever was not uncommon in Guam and was particularly rough on the radiomen who stood watches in the Old Spanish Guardhouse. Even worse, proximity to powerful Radio Libugon frequently overwhelmed the site with interference, rendering intercept operations even more challenging. All things considered, Chauncey recognized the need for a better work environment if the Research Desk wanted any real results in Guam.

Still, Chief Chauncey did his best to train other operators to perform katakana intercept and sent the logs back via courier to the Research Desk. Chauncey had the place up and running, even if it had gotten off to a slow start.

CHAPTER 12

STATION HYPO

MONDAY, FEBRUARY 6, 1928
PEARL HARBOR, TERRITORY OF HAWAII

The USS *Henderson*, slowly pulling into Pearl Harbor, passed several port facilities under construction before arriving at a pier in Quarry Loch, east of Ford Island. Radioman First Class Orville Coonce strolled off the gangplank of the *Henderson*, having just arrived for duty in Hawaii. After a stint on board USS *Huron* in the Far East and additional time at Station ABLE, Coonce had become quite proficient at copying the katakana telegraphic code.

Hawaii had officially been a U.S. territory since 1898 when President McKinley signed the Newlands Resolution, which had already passed Congress. This followed the overthrow of the King of Hawaii by mostly foreign instigators five years earlier. To protect the large number of American civilians living on the island at the time, a contingent of Marines from the USS *Boston* went ashore. The Marines never entered the palace grounds nor fired a single shot, but their presence served to effectively intimidate royalist defenders, thus sealing the fate of the Hawaiian monarchy. For the next five years, American businessmen set up a provisional government in Hawaii with lawyer Sanford B. Dole as president. On August 12, 1898, a ceremony was

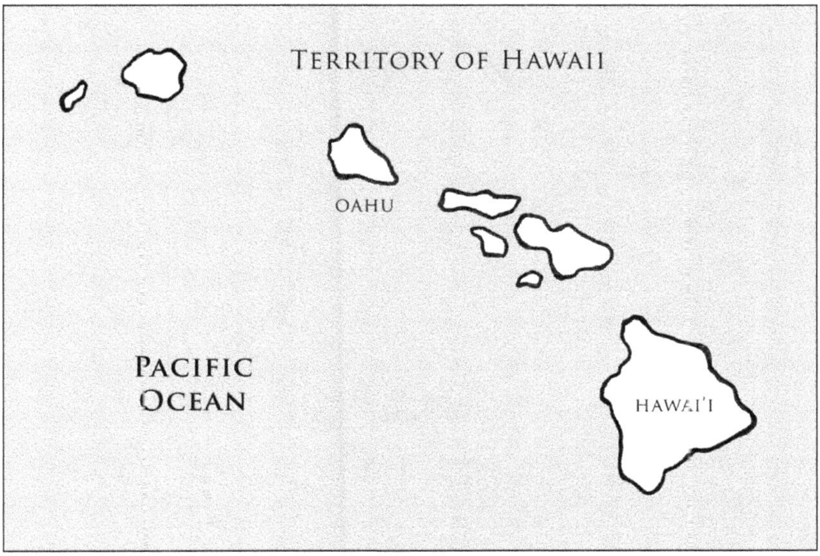

held on the steps of Iolani Palace in Honolulu where the Hawaiian flag was lowered, and the American flag was raised.

Ten years later, the United States began looking for new commercial markets in the Pacific. Access to these new markets required three main things: a merchant fleet to transport commercial goods, an armed navy to protect the merchant navy, and a network of naval bases capable of providing fuel and supplies for both the merchant and navy fleets. Hawaii was the ideal location for setting up a naval base where ships could refuel and resupply, and Pearl Harbor, being one of the largest natural harbors in the Pacific, seemed like a perfect fit. Following the American annexation of Hawaii, the U.S. Navy began developing Pearl Harbor into a key stronghold in the Pacific. By the 1920s, Pearl Harbor and Cavite Naval Base in the Philippines were the two major American naval bases in the Pacific.

The winter weather here is so much different than in Shanghai, Petty Officer Coonce thought to himself as he felt the warmth of the sun on his face and the heavy humidity in the air. Closing his eyes for a

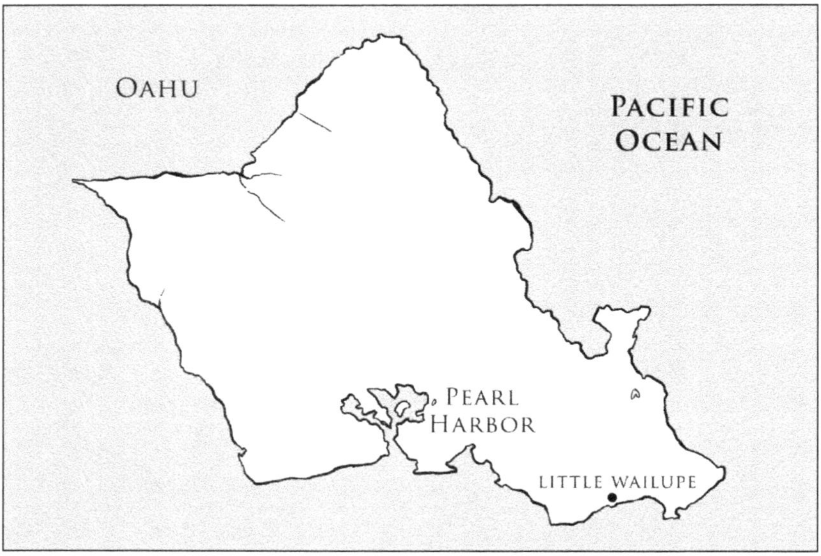

moment as he walked along the pier, he relished the tropical feel of his new home. He wouldn't miss the chilly winters or the hustle and bustle of the Chinese metropolis.

He walked into the Fourteenth Naval District administration offices and handed a large brown envelope containing his service record to the clerk standing behind the counter. "Checking in to Radio Wailupe," Coonce said.

Radio Wailupe—call sign NPM—was the primary Navy COMSTA for all Navy forces in Hawaii, responsible for communications with Navy headquarters and for radio relay to Pearl Harbor, Cavite, and ships at sea in the Pacific Ocean. Coonce was looking forward to the duty, although he would miss the interesting nature of the intercept work he had been doing in Shanghai.

Without saying a word to Coonce, the clerk read the orders stapled to the front of the envelope, tore off the papers, and then disappeared behind a door. Moments later, he reappeared with a small stack of paperwork for Coonce.

"You're owed a paycheck," the clerk said. "Fill these out, and I'll give you a chit for the pay you're owed, and they'll cut you a check over there," he said with a nod toward another counter.

"Great!" Coonce exclaimed, excited at the news of this unexpected windfall.

"Oh, and one more thing, Petty Officer Coonce," the clerk added. "You're not going to Radio Wailupe."

"What do you mean?" Coonce asked.

"Your orders were changed to an office called OP-20-G at Wailupe. I don't know what that means; I've never seen it before."

Coonce knew what it meant, but it didn't make any sense to him, either. OP-20-G was the Research Desk in Washington, DC, not Hawaii.

"After you get your paycheck, you're supposed to report to the DCO, up on the second deck," the clerk told Coonce. "Once you're done with him, there's a bus every hour from the front of this building to Wailupe. Take that to the barracks there, and they'll assign you a room."

Coonce completed the paperwork, returned it to the personnel clerk, and retrieved his paycheck before heading upstairs.

Lieutenant Dan Wilson was the Fourteenth Naval District Communication Officer (DCO). As Petty Officer Coonce walked into his office, he said, "How can I help you, Sailor?"

"I'm Petty Officer Coonce, sir. I was told to come see you about my orders."

"Oh, yes, Coonce . . . of course. We've been expecting you." Wilson's demeanor changed as soon as Coonce announced his name. The lieutenant seemed robotic and short with the Sailor, although just moments before, he'd been cheery and helpful.

"I think there's some confusion, sir. I was originally told I'd be going to Radio Wailupe. Has that changed?"

"Yes, it has, Coonce. You're still going to Wailupe, but you're not going to be attached to the radio station. You're going to work directly for OP-20-G," Wilson replied as he fumbled through his top desk drawer. He pulled out a sealed envelope, on which was stenciled:

CONFIDENTIAL—FOR RM1c O. COONCE

"I've got strict instructions to destroy that letter as soon as you've read it," Wilson barked. "So, go ahead . . . read."

Coonce read the letter as instructed. After doing so, he finally understood the situation. The letter said he'd be setting up a new intercept station at Wailupe, which would be called Station HYPO, and he needed to get it operational ASAP. Coonce knew that if he was going to be successful, he'd have to rely heavily on his experience with Chief Lyon at Station ABLE. He handed the letter back to Lieutenant Wilson, who set it aflame with his Ronson Wonderlite cigarette lighter and dropped it into the empty ash tray on his desk.

"I don't know what you're going to be doing, Petty Officer Coonce, but you're not working for me." Wilson again reached into the top drawer of his desk. This time he pulled out a set of keys and tossed them to Coonce. "Building number ten at Wailupe is yours. Good luck, Coonce."

"Sir, how do I—"

Before Coonce could finish his question, the lieutenant interrupted him, "I told you, you're not working for me, Coonce. I've already spent too much time with you. You're dismissed."

Resigned to the fact that he would get nothing more from the lieutenant, Coonce headed back down the stairs and waited out front to catch the bus to Wailupe.

Located about fifteen miles southeast of Pearl Harbor, Wailupe was a small peninsula and the site of Radio Wailupe the receiving and relay station for the Fourteenth Naval District at Pearl Harbor.

After Coonce's bus passed through Honolulu, he saw what was undoubtedly the radio station. With its 100-foot tall antenna tower,

Radio Wailupe was built just west of the peninsula. Residing on a large dock supported by pilings driven deep into the sand, the station jutted out over the lagoon leading to Maunalua Bay. At the front of the dock, Coonce read a large white sign:

U.S. NAVAL
RADIO STATION
WAILUPE
ABSOLUTELY
NO—ADMITTANCE
KAPU

The word *kapu* refers to an ancient Hawaiian code of laws, which can be translated as "keep out."

Coonce stayed on the bus one additional stop before arriving at the barracks. After checking in and being assigned a room, he walked across the highway and headed back toward Radio Wailupe.

As he walked toward the peninsula opposite Radio Wailupe, he noticed a garage, shops, storage space, and the new spaces designated for Station HYPO. Building number ten was basically an abandoned storeroom about twelve feet by fifteen feet. Inside, the small space was crammed with six wooden tables.

Over the next few weeks, Petty Officer Coonce got to work setting up the intercept site. Since radio equipment was easy to find in the Navy supply system at Pearl Harbor, he procured multiple LF, MF, and HF receivers, frequency scopes, and ancillary radio equipment, connecting it all to the antennas from Radio Wailupe. He also received a shipment of four RIP-5 typewriters, courtesy of the Research Desk, and set them up.

As Coonce began operations at Station HYPO, he realized that the intercept station's proximity to Radio Wailupe interfered with his work during the daylight hours, when the radio station was

Radio Wailupe on pier with intercept facilities for Station HYPO on right.

operating almost continuously. As a result, he found that the best time to intercept Japanese communications was between the hours of mid-afternoon to late evening, so he began working from 1400 hours to midnight.

Despite his success at getting Station HYPO up and running, Coonce failed to find others to man the intercept positions. As a first class petty officer, he didn't have the pull of a chief, especially in a large naval community like Hawaii. As such, he was unable to convince the commander of Radio Wailupe to give up any radiomen for intercept duty, even on a part-time basis, so he was a one-man show at Station HYPO. Nevertheless, he did the best he could to copy Imperial Japanese Navy communications and forward them to the Research Desk. He could only hope Washington, DC would be sending reinforcements soon.

CHAPTER 13

TO THE ROOF!

FRIDAY, MARCH 9, 1928
MAIN NAVY BUILDING, WASHINGTON, DC

Chief Kidder sat at the desk directly in front of Lieutenant Joseph Rochefort, the officer in charge at OP-20-G. Since Kidder had been reassigned from his general service radioman duties at the communications station in Cheltenham two months earlier, all eight desks in the Research Desk had been occupied.

On this blustery Friday morning, Kidder was diligently working on the training plan Rochefort had tasked him with creating. He was developing a curriculum for the inaugural course in radio intelligence, which he assumed would take up to twelve months to teach. Despite Kidder's recommendation, Rochefort decided that the class should last only three months. Kidder knew this wasn't long enough, but he did the best he could to squeeze the pertinent information into such a short period of time. He believed that after teaching the first class, he could persuade Rochefort that the radiomen needed more training.

As Kidder worked at his desk, Rochefort was on the phone behind him. Suddenly, Rochefort slammed the phone's receiver down and yelled, "Damn it!" Everyone in the office stopped what they were doing and looked at Rochefort. Normally, the lieutenant was an easy-going officer—very difficult to anger. To hear him not only slam the phone but also curse was a shock.

"What is it, Lieutenant Rochefort?" Agnes asked.

"Idiots! That's what. We've got a chief here figuring out the curriculum for training the radiomen who will be here before the end of the year. But we've got nowhere to train them. Admiral Taylor just turned down our request for a classroom." Rear Admiral David W. Taylor was chief of the Bureau of Construction and Repair, and his office was in charge of all office allocations within the Main Navy Building.

"Why would they turn it down? What are we supposed to do?" Agnes asked.

"I don't know. I need time to think," Rochefort grumbled as he pinched the area between his eyes in an attempt to stave off an imminent headache.

Chief Kidder chimed in, "Sir, I've got some friends in the Chiefs Mess that might be able to help. They work for Admiral Taylor in Construction. Let me see if I can get the real scoop."

"OK, check with your friends, Chief. Agnes, any other ideas?"

"None," she replied.

Kidder immediately got on the phone and started talking to another chief petty officer. Moments later, he got up and strode toward the door, tossing a wink in Lieutenant Rochefort's direction. Seconds later, he was gone.

"I think we'll have an answer soon, Agnes. Once Chief Kidder sets his mind to something, it gets done," Rochefort said.

"I believe you're right!" Agnes agreed, as she returned to her stack of intercept.

An hour later, Kidder came back in the room wearing a smug grin. "Done!" he said. Everyone in the office looked at him with surprise.

"What's done, Chief?" Rochefort inquired.

"The engineers said we're overflowing this building. There's simply no space left to give. It's not just our request that was denied—everyone is getting told no," Kidder explained.

"That doesn't sound like a good answer, Chief," Rochefort said impatiently. He was anxious to hear what Kidder had come up with.

"The chiefs in Constructions are pressing the admiral to approve the construction of a few spaces on the roof. It'll only be one small structure on top of each wing because they don't want to stress the roof with too much weight. There are already several requests from offices in each of the wings; I added our request for a classroom."

"Again, that doesn't sound very promising, Kidder."

"Sir, don't you trust me? It's a done deal. They prioritized the list right in front on me; our request is at the top of the list for the sixth wing."

Everyone in the room smiled. This was surely the power of the Chiefs Mess, and Kidder was a great chief.

"That's great, Kidder! Let's get this moving quickly."

"Aye, aye, sir."

Since it was important to maintain the secrecy of the content of the training, Rochefort thought a rooftop classroom would be a perfect location.

Over the next several weeks, Chief Kidder was extremely busy. Not only did he have a curriculum to develop, he was acting as the general contractor for the new rooftop classroom project. With the help of his chief friends in Construction, he had consulted with Turner Construction Company—the firm that had built the Main Navy Building—on the design of the new classroom.

The structure was to be very similar in design to several sheds that Kidder helped his father with back on the farm. It would be built completely out of reinforced concrete block like the rest of the building and would be twenty-five feet long, fifteen feet wide, and ten feet tall with two windows and a door along one wall. This would provide sufficient room for eight students plus the instructor. The only way to access the rooftop classroom would be by taking a steep, steel staircase from the third floor.

With money from the ONI slush fund, Turner Construction Company was contracted to build the rooftop classroom. Turner would supply all the material and equipment as well as the technical specifications and connection to the building's power grid. However, in order to keep costs low, the Navy would need to supply some manual labor to complete the job. In this case, the manual labor was Chief Kidder.

With his experience building similar structures as a teenager in Missouri and his desire to make sure the classroom was perfect, Kidder was the natural choice to help Turner build the structure. He was so enthusiastic about the job that he routinely put in ten- to twelve-hour days: eight hours helping to build the classroom and then additional time in the office developing the curriculum. For Kidder, the classes themselves couldn't start soon enough.

CHAPTER 14

CNO ANNOUNCEMENT

July 16, 1928

From: Chief of Naval Operations
To: Commander in Chief, Battle Fleet
Commander Scouting Fleet
Commander Control Force
Subject: Training of radiomen for special radio service

1. The Navy Department will establish at the Department a school for training radiomen in special radio work commencing about 1 October 1928. The class will consist of ten men, divided approximately as follows:

2 Chief radiomen
4 Radiomen first class
4 Radiomen second class

2. The present plan contemplates a three-month course at the Department, followed by detail to the Asiatic Station. The selection of proper personnel is essentially important.

3. Submit to the Chief of Naval Operations (Director of Naval Communications) at as early a date as practicable, a list of radiomen, by name and rate, recommended for this duty. In preparing recommendations, the following points must be carefully covered:

   (a) The men must have excellent records and be qualified in every respect for important and responsible duty of this nature. They must be known to be of high moral character and trustworthy.

   (b) They must have at least two and one-half years of service on their current enlistment or be willing to provide for this period of service.

   (c) They should desire this service.

4. This matter is to be considered as highly SECRET and all possible publicity avoided. The Chief of Naval Operations desires that this subject be given prompt and careful attention.

C. F. HUGHES
ADM USN

Copy to:
CinC, U.S. Fleet
Comdr, Fleet Base Force

CHAPTER 15

THE CURRICULUM

WEDNESDAY, SEPTEMBER 19, 1928
MAIN NAVY BUILDING, WASHINGTON, DC

Chief Kidder finished the curriculum with just weeks to spare before the first radio intelligence class was scheduled to convene on October 1, 1928. Just a month earlier, Turner Construction Company had completed the rooftop classroom, and it was almost ready for occupation. Kidder busied himself painting the steel-reinforced concrete blockhouse, both inside and out. He used white for interior and exterior walls and dark brown for the door, door frame, and window frames. He would have picked a different color scheme, but this is what the Navy had available.

Chief Kidder's curriculum was complex. While the Japanese used international Morse code to communicate with the rest of the world, at home they avoided the use of that code for both domestic and military purposes. Instead, they'd developed their own system of dits and dahs that was somewhat more responsive to their needs and certainly more efficient than the one Samuel Morse had developed. In Morse code, for example, it took a total of eight dit-dah combinations to transmit the letters in the word *Yokosuka*, whereas in the Japanese katakana system, it took only four:

In Morse code: Y o k o s u k a:

— · — —   — — —   — · —   — — —   · · ·   · · —   — · —   · —

In katakana code: Yo ko su ka:

— —   — — — —   — — — · —   · — · ·

The reason for this was quite simple: the katakana alphabet consists of symbols represented in Romaji by a consonant and vowel combination. In katakana, the word Yokosuka is spelled with four symbols: ヨ コ ス カ

Using the katakana code, the Japanese used roughly half the telegraphic code symbols of Morse code, making communication quicker and more efficient.

The first and primary focus of Kidder's curriculum was the Japanese katakana alphabet and the corresponding telegraphic code equivalent. Kidder developed a katakana code reference card for the students:

A	ア	— — · — —	**HA**	ハ	— · · ·	**KA**	カ	· — · ·
E	エ	— · — — —	**HE**	ヘ	·	**KE**	ケ	— · — —
I	イ	· —	**HI**	ヒ	— — · · —	**KI**	キ	— · — · ·
O	オ	· — · · ·	**HO**	ホ	— · ·	**KO**	コ	— — — —
U	ウ	· · —	**FU**	フ	— — · ·	**KU**	ク	· · · —
(n)	ン	· — · — ·						
MA	マ	— · · —	**NA**	ナ	· — ·	**RA**	ラ	· · ·
ME	メ	— · · · —	**NE**	ネ	— — · —	**RE**	レ	— — —
MI	ミ	· · — · —	**NI**	ニ	— · — ·	**RI**	リ	— — ·
MO	モ	— · · — ·	**NO**	ノ	· · — —	**RO**	ロ	· — · —
MU	ム	—	**NU**	ヌ	· · · ·	**RU**	ル	— · — — ·
SA	サ	— · — · —	**TA**	タ	— ·	**WA**	ワ	— · —
SE	セ	· — — — ·	**TE**	テ	· — · — —	**WE**	ヱ	· — — · ·
SI	シ	— — · — ·	**TI**	チ	· · — ·	**WI**	ヰ	· — · · —
SO	ソ	— — — ·	**TO**	ト	· · — · ·	**WO**	ヲ	· — — —
SU	ス	— — — · —	**TU**	ツ	· — — ·			
						YA	ヤ	· — —
						YO	ヨ	— —
						YU	ユ	— · · — —

The radiomen would have to learn the basic katakana alphabet, followed by numbers, punctuation, and some characters unique to the Japanese language. Many of the telegraphic codes were the same as in Morse code, but they represented completely different characters. For instance, • ▬ • epresented the letter *r* in Morse code, but in katakana, • ▬ • represented ナ or the *nah* sound.

Perhaps the most difficult thing to grasp was hearing a katakana telegraphic code and then writing or typing the corresponding katakana character. Students would learn this skill on live radio traffic using the same receivers they'd encounter at the intercept stations. Operators would first have to learn to copy the katakana telegraphic code by hand before they could start using the RIP-5 Underwood Code Machines. The RIP-5s made things easier for the radiomen, but they weren't meant to be a shortcut or crutch. Copying the katakana by stick ensured the radiomen were completely skilled in the practice even if they went to a station without a RIP-5. The RIP-5 allowed operators to hit the same key they were used to in cases where the Morse and katakana codes intersected. If the operator copied • ▬ •, he would hit the *r* key on the mill, but the Romaji characters *NA* would appear on the paper.

The curriculum also included traffic analysis, which enabled operators to glean some value from encrypted messages without the benefit of being able to decrypt them. The technique involved studying the message headings to determine who originated any given message, where it was being sent, and to whom it was being addressed. For example, operators might see a message heading such as the following:

```
TI SUTINI1 TUHO EEI // HASITO2 HA HAFU6
```

The message is addressed for action (TI) to the Japanese minesweeper #136 (call sign SUTINI1), for information (TUHO) to Sasebo Naval Base (call sign EEI), and to the Japanese cruise ship

Torishima Maru (call sign HASITO2). The message originated (HA) at naval headquarters in Tokyo (call sign HAFU6) and has already been delivered to the *Torishima Maru* as indicated by the double slash that precedes that ship's call sign. From this message heading, a traffic analyst could deduce that the *Torishima Maru*, known to be employed as a naval transport, was departing Tokyo Bay en route to Sasebo Naval Base. Not only did information such as this aid in deciphering encrypted messages, but in wartime situations, that alone could provide valuable intelligence to U.S. commanders.

The radiomen would also be taught how to develop an intercept plan based on the skeds of the target network. Every network operated differently, and a proper intercept plan was key to being able to fully exploit its communications.

Lastly, Chief Kidder's curriculum introduced the radiomen to cryptanalysis, the art and science of breaking enemy ciphers. This was a skill Kidder had only recently been exposed to at the Research Desk. It wasn't intended to be a primary skill of the radio intercept operators, but it was a chance for the Research Desk to screen for Sailors who might have a special aptitude for the work.

It was an awful lot to learn in three months. Harry Kidder thought back to when he was learning to copy the katakana code—how strenuous and intellectually challenging it was. He knew it would take some very special operators to be able to do what was being asked of them. And that's exactly what he got.

CHAPTER 16

CLASS #1

MONDAY, OCTOBER 1, 1928
MAIN NAVY BUILDING, WASHINGTON, DC

On the first day of class, Chief Kidder waited in civilian clothes in the lobby of the Main Navy Building for the eight radiomen who had been selected for training. After the memo that Chief of Naval Operations Hughes sent out to the fleets, the Research Desk had received over thirty nominations. Despite the memo asking for lower rates, every nomination was for a radioman first class or chief petty officer. Apparently, CNO Hughes's memo set extremely high standards for the initial offering of radio intelligence training—standards that few junior radiomen could attain.

Chief Kidder and Lieutenant Rochefort had pored over all the nominations and organized them into three piles. The first was for the eight radiomen that would be selected for the inaugural class on the roof. The second was for those who might be considered for a future class, and the third pile was for those radiomen deemed not qualified for the training, the duty, or the responsibility.

The eight radiomen selected for the first class were clearly the best of the lot. The roster included one chief radioman, Joseph Goldstein.

The remaining students were all radiomen first class: Guy Billehus, Burton Cloyd, Keith Goodwin, Robert Hoffman, Truett Lusk, Michael Roberts, and Martin Vandenberg.

Each of the students had arrived in Washington, DC, the week prior, except for Petty Officer Roberts, who hadn't been heard from since his departure from the USS *Pillsbury*. Chief Kidder reported Roberts's status to the Personnel Support Detachment as "U/A," meaning Unauthorized Absence. After twenty-four hours, Roberts would be marked as "AWOL," Absent Without Leave. Chief Kidder made sure the rest had checked in to the administrative offices. More importantly, he ensured the students would be paid properly for their current assignment in Washington. The students were each given a daily stipend for food and lodging. They were also given a one-time allowance of fifteen dollars for civilian clothing, as uniforms were not permitted for anyone associated with the Research Desk.

All of the students were billeted in Ma Travers's Guest House, less than a mile north of the Main Navy Building. Ma Travers was actually Gertrude Hampton, the widowed aunt of Yeoman First Class Sam Hampton in the Navy's administrative office. Aunt Gertrude was doing her nephew a favor by reserving rooms at her bed-and-breakfast for all eight men.

When Chief Kidder heard about these arrangements, he paid Ma Travers a visit to make sure everything was up to snuff for the Sailors before they arrived. The place was a bit run-down, but it was certainly good enough for Sailors recently off sea duty. The guesthouse was located at 611 Twenty-Second Street NW, between F and G Streets NW—not far from the campus of George Washington University in the Foggy Bottom neighborhood—and within walking distance of the Main Navy Building. The guesthouse had eight rooms and served breakfast daily. As Kidder was checking out the accommodations, he happened upon a maid as she made up one of the rooms. Her back was turned, unaware of Kidder's presence.

"Nice place," he said.

The young woman was startled by his words. She turned, and, wary of the stranger in the house, took a step back. Kidder was immediately taken by the maid's pretty features—short blond hair, green eyes, and tall, at least three inches taller than Kidder.

"I'm sorry to have startled you," Harry said. "I should introduce myself. I'm Chief Kidder. I'm just checking on the accommodations for our Sailors that are coming to stay."

The young woman smiled slightly and answered, "I'm Susan."

Susan Williams, or Susie to her friends, was a twentysomething girl trying to do more than just make ends meet. She grew up with six brothers and sisters in a two-bedroom wood-framed row house on Willow Tree Alley, just blocks away from the Capitol. Her family was dirt-poor, quite literally—the main floor of their home was hard-packed dirt. Her parents raised their children the best they could under the circumstances, even though neither had permanent employment. Instead they each worked odd jobs during Susie's childhood. Roger Williams, Susie's father, worked as a laborer across the city. More often than not, his jobs consisted of hauling bricks, stone, or cement to construction sites as new office buildings were being built in the nation's capital. Susie's mother, Agatha, cleaned houses in wealthy neighborhoods whenever she could find the work, which was becoming increasingly difficult.

To help make ends meet in the Williams household, Susie's brothers and sisters resorted to petty crime from an early age, but Susie resisted the urge to behave that way. Instead, she went along on jobs with her mother when there was enough work for two. She loved to help clean houses that had real furniture and decorations. She imagined herself living in those houses and decided at an early age that she would escape her miserable existence by saving every penny she got her hands on. Her life's goal was to live in a house like the ones she'd been cleaning.

As a child, Susie hid her savings behind a loose board in the wall of her bedroom. Occasionally, she thought some of the money went missing, and she suspected her brother Phillip of stealing from her. As the youngest, though, she never dared accuse him.

Years later, working as a maid at Ma Travers's Guest House was only a temporary situation for Susie. Her ambition to escape poverty had never faded.

"You can call me Harry. How long have you been working here?" Harry asked.

Her guard still up, Susie hesitated before answering. Despite her best attempt to remain aloof, she blushed and answered, "Just a couple weeks. Ma hired me because of all your Sailors coming to stay." Because she viewed Harry as an authority figure, Susie felt compelled to continue. "Ma is good to me, so I don't mind. She has a bed for me, feeds me two meals a day, and pays me OK. I'm trying to earn enough money to start my own business."

Harry was glad for the opening to continue the conversation, "Business? What kind of business are you going to start?"

"I have friends who need work, and there are plenty of hotels in Washington. I'd like to start my own company that supplies good workers to the hotels."

"That's a great idea." Harry was genuinely impressed with the idea, but even more so, he felt a spark of attraction toward this young woman. He hoped, somehow, the feeling was mutual.

Kidder liked the arrangements at Ma Travers's place, so he figured it would make for good lodging for this and future classes. As an added bonus, Harry thought it would be nice to come around the place every now and then to see Susie.

⚓ ⚓ ⚓

After the arrival of all the students, Kidder met with Chief Goldstein at Ma Travers's place, as he was the senior man in the class and would be in charge of the group of students. While at the guesthouse, Harry made sure to say hello to Susie.

Kidder invited Goldstein to the next Chiefs Mess meeting. All the chief petty officers stationed in the Main Navy Building gathered on the first Friday of every month at a pub just a block away. The Chiefs Mess meetings were where things really got done—chief petty officers knew how to network, especially when they had a cold mug of suds in hand.

On the first day of class, Chief Kidder waited for his students to arrive by the quarterdeck in the lobby of the Main Navy Building. The quarterdeck was the official entry point onto any U.S. Navy facility—ships and buildings alike—and it was usually manned with a junior Sailor (the messenger of the watch), a more senior Sailor (the petty officer of the watch), and an officer of the deck.

Kidder was tense with anticipation. Like a kid on Christmas morning, he had been awaiting the start of this first class for months, and the day had finally arrived. He chatted idly with the petty officer of the watch. The chief loved talking to Sailors and getting to know them.

Chief Goldstein was the first of Kidder's students to arrive at the quarterdeck. As the only chief petty officer in the class, Goldstein wanted to set a good example by showing up a little early. Chief Kidder greeted Goldstein as he walked in through the front doors.

"Joe! Great to see you again!"

"Nice to see you, too, Harry!" Goldstein responded as the two shook hands.

"Did Roberts ever show?"

"No sign of him."

"Lost his spot, then. Even if he shows up now, an AWOL won't look good on his record. They'll never give him clearance to come in the spaces now. Where's the rest of the crew?" Kidder asked.

"They're a couple minutes behind me. I wanted them to see me walking out the door to be early for class. They were just finishing up their breakfast. Ma Travers does it up right."

"That's good to hear." Every mention of Ma Travers brought up Susie's face in Harry's mind, almost to the point of distraction. Just then, the six other Sailors in the class came rumbling into the building together. Young and confident, they were some of the best radiomen in the fleet. They all wore civilian clothes as instructed—brand-new white shirts courtesy of their special clothing allowance for the class. Civilian clothes and all-expenses paid in the nation's capital—these Sailors were living high on the hog.

Kidder greeted each of them and introduced himself. They all gathered around and showed their identification cards to the petty officer of the watch, who checked their names on a list of authorized personnel. After each received permission to enter the building, Kidder began walking them to their classroom. He walked down the front passageway to the sixth wing and then up a flight of stairs so he could walk the students past the combination-locked Research Desk office that required special clearance to enter.

Kidder pointed toward the door and said, "This is where decryption happens. Don't worry if you don't know what that means right now; I'll be explaining everything to you soon." Just then, a Sailor walked toward them from the other end of the building. Kidder paused and waited for the man to pass. Sensing the awkward silence due to his presence, the Sailor put his head down and quickened his pace to pass. Kidder continued, "Lieutenant Rochefort and Mrs. Driscoll run the show in here. You'll each get to spend some time in the office, but not until you're ready."

"I'm ready now!" Petty Officer Goodwin quipped, and the rest of the group chuckled. Keith E. Goodwin, nicknamed "Keg" by his shipmates aboard the USS *Pennsylvania*, was certainly the class clown in this group.

"I'll tell you when you're ready," Kidder quickly responded with a wry smile, appreciating Keg's sense of humor. "Let's get to the classroom."

Kidder walked the group back to a stairwell and up to the third floor. Walking down the passageway along the third floor, they passed room after room. The Sailors wondered which of the rooms was their classroom. Finally, Kidder passed the final room and approached a narrow, black, steel staircase that reached toward the ceiling.

As he started up the stairs, Goodwin asked, "Where are we going, Chief?"

With a flourish, Chief Kidder pointed straight up and responded, "To the roof!"

A sign on the door said, "Emergency Exit Only," but Kidder told them not to worry. He opened the door to sunlight and fresh air. The chief walked through the door and held it open until the entire group was gathered on a catwalk outside the door. Harry closed the door behind them to reveal a ladder with hooks at the top. He hooked the ladder to the edge of the roof and began to climb up. The group followed one by one.

Once everyone got up, Chief Kidder said, "Gang, you're going to learn to love it up here on the roof. Just look at the view!"

They all looked around, squinting as the sun rose over the Washington Monument just to the east. Further in the same direction, they could see the Capitol. Turning counterclockwise, they saw the White House to the north, the Lincoln Memorial with the winding Potomac River behind it to the west, and the Tidal Basin to the south.

After spending several minutes admiring the views, the group walked across the roof to a reinforced concrete structure with windows on either side of a single door, which was elevated from the roof of the building by about a foot. A small, wooden staircase led the team to the door. Kidder opened it wide and announced, "Welcome to your home for the next three months, gentlemen!"

Inside, the radiomen saw a large, wooden rectangular table. Along the sides of the room were eight positions that looked extremely familiar to them: each position had an LF receiver, an HF receiver, and an Underwood typewriter. The only two differences between these positions and those they were accustomed to were the lettering on the typewriter keys of the typewriter and the lack of a telegraphic key. After all, they wouldn't be sending any messages during this course. A small desk and podium were located in the front of the classroom; another smaller desk was at the rear. Through the windows, the Sailors could see a long-wire dipole antenna strung along the edge of the roof.

"Grab a seat at the center table, gentlemen, we have some things to go over," Kidder instructed. As they all sat around the table, one empty seat marked the spot that would've been for Petty Officer Roberts.

Kidder began, "What you are about to learn is considered top secret. Only a handful of people in the entire U.S. Navy know what's going on in this classroom, and we'd like to keep it that way. You were all selected for this training not only for your skill as fleet communicators, but because you were deemed to have a trustworthy nature. Let me repeat, gentlemen, the information you will learn in this classroom is never to be discussed outside these walls. Is everyone clear on that?"

Silence filled the classroom as none of the Sailors wanted to be the first to respond.

Chief Goldstein broke the ice. "Got it, Chief," he said.

One by one, the men all agreed to Chief Kidder's terms.

Chief Kidder handed them each a sheet of paper with an oath of secrecy that repeated his orders. "Write your name and service number at the top, then sign the bottom. This will go into your service records." The U.S. Navy kept records of everyone who had access to this classified information.

They all signed, and Chief Goldstein collected the papers.

Kidder continued, "OK, then . . . How many of you have already seen the information booklet?" He held up a copy of the instructional pamphlet that he'd created months earlier. All but one student raised their hands.

"Good!" Kidder said. Since the booklets were classified, the students had to leave them back on their ships. Kidder handed a stack of the pamphlets to Chief Goldstein, who handed one to each of the students.

"Did anyone give it a go?" A few hands went down, leaving only Petty Officers Billehus, Goodwin, and Vandenberg with their hands raised.

"Good. Any of you able to copy the code?" All three shook their heads. Chief Kidder wasn't surprised.

"OK, then, this is what we're about to learn." Kidder had their attention now. "Japan is preparing for war with the United States," he said point-blank. "This is my opinion and there is no proof. But I believe it."

Chief Kidder's matter-of-fact announcement drew raised eyebrows from all the students. The Great War was long since over and sentiment in the United States was that it was the war to end all wars. Kidder continued, "You're here to stop that from happening. The Imperial Japanese Navy has been exercising their Combined Fleet against a mock Pacific Fleet. As they do, they're communicating via CW."

"Morse!" Petty Officer Cloyd chimed in.

"CW, yes. Morse, no," Kidder responded. "They're using their own telegraphic code. It's just like Morse, but it has more letters—katakana letters." The students were already lost.

"Katakana is the Japanese alphabet," Kidder continued, "only, it's an alphabet like you've never seen before." Kidder made his way to the chalkboard at the front of the room and started to write the katakana alphabet:

ン ア エ イ オ ウ マ メ ミ モ ム

As he wrote, Kidder recited the accompanying sound, "*Ah*, *eh*, *ee*, *oh*, *oo*, *mah*, *meh*, *moh*, *moo*, *mee* . . ."

Although they were following along in their pamphlets, the students were still not fully grasping what was going on. When Kidder finished writing all the katakana symbols on the chalkboard, he turned around to look at his students, who stared back at him dumbfounded.

"Looks like hen tracks!" Keg exclaimed. The rest of the class laughed, as did Kidder.

"Yes, this is tough stuff. But you're all here because your chain of command thought you had the smarts to do this job. And I believe them. We'll get there, don't worry," he said.

⚓ ⚓ ⚓

As the weeks passed, the weather turned cooler in DC. But the rooftop classroom was cozy and warm with two hot water-fed radiators and the combined body heat of eight men.

Kidder practiced the katakana syllabary every day with his students. He began each class by standing at the front of the classroom and reciting katakana sounds in groups of three.

"*Hah*, *mee*, *noh*. *Seh*, *ruh*, *kee*."

As Kidder spoke the words, the students wrote each of the katakana symbols, or hen tracks, as Keg so eloquently put it. Kidder started the students at about five groups of three katakana characters per minute. The pace was nice and slow and gave them time to think about what they were hearing before writing the corresponding katakana symbol.

Kidder recited the katakana symbols rhythmically—symbol, symbol, symbol, pause. Symbol, symbol, symbol, pause. The students were permitted to have their copy of the information booklet in front of them while they copied Kidder's recitation, and after a couple weeks of this, the students began to catch on. After each session of writing the katakana characters, the students transliterated them into Romaji symbols.

"Why can't we just write the Romaji while we're copying, Chief?" Petty Officer Lusk asked.

"You need to be able to write the katakana, Tru," Kidder answered. "There are times when the actual katakana is important. And you need to practice the transliteration for the codebreakers."

Chief Kidder's last word caught all the students' attention. Codebreakers! They were intrigued, but no one asked the obvious question: What codes were they breaking? As time went on, Kidder began to increase his recitation speed. As the speed increased, he maintained his rhythm: symbol, symbol, symbol, pause; symbol, symbol, symbol, pause; symbol, symbol, symbol, pause. . . . Regardless of the speed, the rhythm cadence remained the same, which helped the students keep up even if they missed a character here or there.

Next, Kidder introduced the students to the corresponding telegraphic code for each katakana character. Each day, he added five new katakana telegraphic codes. Every morning Chief Kidder began by reciting the same katakana sounds, but every day, he went faster and faster. After Kidder had introduced the students to the telegraphic code for each of the katakana symbols, he had the men practice copying the codes in addition to his recitations. Kidder used a telegraph key on his podium attached to a speaker in order to "send" the katakana code for the students to copy.

By week six, Kidder had the students writing up to twenty groups per minute as he recited katakana in groups of three. Even though the speed increased, the rhythm remained the same: symbol, symbol, symbol, pause; symbol, symbol, symbol, pause; symbol, symbol, symbol, pause. They continued to practice this every morning. After lunch, they switched to practicing the telegraphic code—starting at five groups per minute—with the students following along writing the hen tracks. The students heard:

· — · · ·   — · — — ·   · —   — · — ·   — · —
— · · · —   — — — · —   — ·   ·

They wrote:

オ ル イ ニ ワ メ ス タ ヘ

Which in Romaji transliterated as:

O RU I NI WA ME SU TA HE

Despite the fact that the students were now copying the telegraphic code instead of the chief's voice, the rhythm remained the same: symbol, symbol, symbol, pause; symbol, symbol, symbol, pause; symbol, symbol, symbol, pause.

Each day, Kidder slowly increased his speed as he practiced with his students, reciting both the verbalized sound and the telegraphic code. And each day, the students improved their speed and accuracy.

Symbol, symbol, symbol, pause; symbol, symbol, symbol, pause; symbol, symbol, symbol, pause. Kidder knew that repetition was the key to improvement. The students started to dream in katakana telegraphic code. Each day, the students got better and better at copying the code with fewer and fewer mistakes.

By Christmas, the students were copying both the telegraphic code and writing the hen tracks at twenty katakana groups per minute.

Finally, it was time for a break over the holidays. Because Christmas Day fell on a Tuesday, all nonessential personnel in the Main Navy Building were given the Friday and Monday before the holiday off, as well as the day after Christmas. The students were considered nonessential, so they had six consecutive days off. In Kidder's view, they'd certainly earned the break.

CHAPTER 17

CHRISTMAS AT MA TRAVERS'S GUEST HOUSE

TUESDAY, DECEMBER 25, 1928

MA TRAVERS'S GUEST HOUSE, WASHINGTON, DC

In 1928, Christmastime at Ma Travers's Guest House was a festive one. Gertrude—or "Ma" as everyone called her—decided to cook a fabulous Christmas dinner for all her boarders. Gertrude's nephew, Sam Hampton, and Harry Kidder were also in attendance at the feast. Susie Williams and Stephanie Nelson, the two maids who lived and worked in the guesthouse, helped prepare the meal.

Gertrude was in an especially cheerful mood. She had never had seven of her rooms occupied for such an extended period of time, and the income she was receiving for it meant she could provide a veritable feast for her guests. The U.S. Navy continued to pay for all eight rooms, even though Petty Officer Roberts had never showed. She wanted to express her gratitude by cooking a traditional holiday meal for everyone. Before dinner began, Kidder let her know that the Navy wanted to reserve the entire house again for the next group of students, who would be arriving in May. Gertrude was over the moon with this news. This Christmas, Ma Travers gave her two maids a modest raise as their gifts.

As Gertrude, Susie, and Stephanie prepared the dinner, the men mingled in the large front room enjoying some eggnog spiked with whiskey. Classical Christmas music played on a Victrola in the corner while a fire blazed in the fireplace, adding to the convivial mood. All of the invited guests were in the front room—except for Harry Kidder.

Harry was drinking his eggnog in the kitchen. He stayed out of the way but lingered to steal flirtatious glimpses at Susie as she and the other women busily prepared the meal. As if performing a highly choreographed dance routine, the ladies moved swiftly and efficiently between the sink, icebox, and oven. The aroma was perfect. *Just like Christmas on the farm*, Harry thought. It was a bittersweet memory for Harry, who hadn't spoken to his parents in over ten years. He hoped they were well, but he honestly didn't know if they'd welcome contact from him.

Any melancholy thoughts quickly dissolved when Harry realized Susie was paying as much attention to him as he was to her, glancing at him at every opportunity. Ma could tell what was going on, so she pitched in to do some of the work Susie was supposed to be doing. Ma thought the situation was adorable and allowed it to continue, despite it causing her extra work.

"You two need to join the others in the front room," she said to Harry and Susie. "You're not doing me any good in here."

They didn't have to be told twice. Susie looked directly into Harry's eyes as they smiled at each other and scurried off. As Susie led Harry down the corridor from the kitchen to the front room, Harry touched her elbow from behind. She stopped and turned back toward him. He wasn't sure what he was going to say, but he wanted a little time alone with her in the hallway.

As she turned, she backed up until she leaned on the wall,

smiling at Harry. He took a step closer to her, and still couldn't find any words to say. Instead, he leaned in and kissed her. To his great delight, she kissed him back.

"Merry Christmas, Susie," Harry murmured, slowly opening his eyes.

"Merry Christmas, Harry." They stood in the hallway together for a moment, enjoying the fact that they were alone in a house full of people. They kissed again. After a few moments, the pair continued into the front room. As they approached, they heard the men sharing stories from their time at sea, as Sailors typically do—especially when they've had a drink or two. When Susie and Harry walked in, the conversation stopped—all eyes were on them. It was immediately apparent to everyone in the room what had just happened, Susie's Christmas-red lipstick was smeared all over Harry's mouth.

Before sitting down, the pair walked over to a small table and Harry filled two cups with eggnog. Harry sat in an empty armchair, and Susie perched herself on its arm. Joe Goldstein handed Harry a handkerchief and motioned toward his face. As Harry wiped the evidence from his face, Susie blushed.

"Why, Pappy, you old dog!" Keg exclaimed. This was the first time any of the students had called him "Pappy" to his face, but they had been doing it in private for some time.

"Pappy?" Harry was surprised by the nickname, but not offended. At thirty-nine years old, he was clearly the elder statesman among the Sailors.

"It's because they like you, Harry," Joe said as he leaned in.

"Great . . . well, Pappy it is, then," Harry said with a smile. Nothing could have upset him on this day.

A little tipsy on the eggnog, Tru Lusk finally scrounged up the courage to ask Kidder a question. "So is it true, Pappy, that the Japs know who you are?"

Kidder opened his eyes wide, surprised by the question—particularly since they shouldn't have been talking about anything work-related outside the classroom. Regardless, Harry replied, "What on earth are you talking about, Tru?"

"Everybody says they sign on to their weather broadcasts every day with G-M-H-K."

Harry was stumped. "So, . . .? What is that supposed to mean?"

"G-M-H-K. Good morning, Harry Kidder!"

Everyone in the room laughed, but they had all heard the story. No matter what Kidder answered, they were still going to believe it. Chief Kidder was already a legend in the small radio intelligence community.

Embarrassed by the attention, Harry wanted to deflect it elsewhere. "Get outta here! That ain't true! Keg, I heard you were copying forty groups per minute on the *Pennsylvania*."

Everyone groaned. Martin Vandenberg chimed in, "There's no way. Keg can't copy in the forties!"

"Can too, Van!" Keg defended himself.

"You'll have to prove that one to me, Keg."

"You're quite the gang . . . ," Kidder shook his head and laughed, "a gang from the roof. You're the On-the-Roof Gang. How do you like that?"

"Is that who we are, Chief?" asked Keg. "We're the On-the-Roof Gang?"

"Yeah, that's a good one," Kidder acknowledged. He liked the name a lot. "It's settled, then," he said proudly. "Here's to the On-the-Roof Gang!"

Everyone raised their glasses and toasted the new name of their group.

Ma eventually called Susie back into the kitchen. Not long after, the women summoned the men to the large dining room opposite the front room. The feast placed on the table in front of them was immensely beautiful, both in sight and smell. Roasted duck, the main dish, was accompanied by every Christmas trimming imaginable—mashed potatoes, green beans, yams, corn, pickles, olives, cheese, bread, and more. Four candles lined the center of the table. The music from the front room flowed into the dining room. Ma Travers had created a Christmas to remember.

Ma motioned for Harry to sit at the head of the table. Everyone else filled in around him, including Susie and Stephanie. Anticipation for the meal ahead caused a hush to fall on the room. Harry took this opportunity to say a Navy prayer. He folded his hands, closed his eyes, and prayed:

> *O eternal Lord God, who alone spreadest out the heavens, and rulest the raging of the sea; Vouchsafe to take into thy almighty and most gracious protection our country's Navy, and all who serve therein. Preserve them from the dangers of the sea, and from the violence of the enemy; that they may be a safeguard unto the United States of America, and a security for such as pass on the seas upon their lawful occasions; that the inhabitants of our land may in peace and quietness serve thee our God, to the glory of thy Name; through Jesus Christ our Lord. Amen.*

The prayer took everyone by surprise, but they all joined in saying, "Amen." Kidder was a religious man, but until this point, no one knew it. If at all possible, the prayer made everyone respect the chief that much more. No one more so than Susie.

CHAPTER 18

CLASS #1 CONTINUES

THURSDAY, DECEMBER 27, 1929
MAIN NAVY BUILDING, WASHINGTON, DC

Upon their return to class after the Christmas break, the students had to brace themselves against the wintery weather walking toward the Main Navy Building. When they pushed open the door leading to the roof, the wind caught the door and exposed them all to the harsh, biting cold. Although they surely felt it walking from Ma Travers's place to the Main Navy Building, the wind on the roof made it seem twenty degrees colder. There would be no lollygagging on the roof this morning.

When they entered the classroom, Kidder began his routine: an hour of recitation followed by an hour of copying the katakana code by hand. At 1000 hours on this particular day, Kidder told the students to pick an intercept position instead of sitting at the center table. The students were excited to try something new.

"Time to learn how to use the mill in front of you. We call it the Underwood Code Machine, or RIP-5," Kidder explained. "For the katakana symbols that have an equivalent in Morse, the keystroke will be the same. For instance, the *C* in Morse is dah dit dah dit. If you hit the *C* on your typewriter, *NI* will be printed out, which is dah dit dah dit in the katakana code. For those codes that don't have a Morse equivalent, you'll have to learn what key to hit. You can see each key has both the American alphabet and the Romaji syllable. You just have to get used to where each key is."

Even though the keyboard was clearly labeled, Kidder handed each of the students a cheat sheet showing the keyboard layout.

1	2	3	4	5	6	7	8	9	0	°	
E	**KO**	**N**	**TE**	**KI**	**SE**	**SU**	**NO**	**TO**	**MI**	**WI**	
Q	W	E	R	T	Y	U	I	O	P	(	)
NE	**YA**	**HE**	**NA**	**MU**	**KE**	**U**	**Đ**	**RE**	**TU**	**A**	**SO**
A	S	D	F	G	H	J	K	L	—	RO	//
I	**RA**	**HO**	**TI**	**RI**	**NU**	**WO**	**WA**	**KA**	**SA**	**RU**	**HI**
Z	X	C	V	B	N	M	?	.	0	WE	
FU	**MA**	**NI**	**KU**	**HA**	**TA**	**YO**	**YU**	**MO**	**SI**	**ME**	

"We'll start slowly," Kidder continued, "one character at a time. I'll say the character and you type what you hear.

"Tee," he said. *Clack, clack, clack, clack*. Some were still looking for the right key to hit. It was where the *F* was on a standard American typewriter. *Clack, clack, clack*. Finally, everyone found it.

"Nee," Kidder said next. Same result. Some were quick to find the *nee* sound on the *C* key; others needed more time.

"Tah."

"Kee."

"Soh."

"Rah."

"Koh."

Kidder recited katakana sounds for hours, until the students finally started to remember where the keys were. They practiced this recitation with the RIP-5 for the rest of the week.

On the following Monday at noon, Chief Kidder declared, "Ropeyarn," which needed no explanation to the Sailors. Traditionally in the U.S. Navy, on the day the tailor boarded a ship in port, the crew knocked off early and mended clothes with the yarn that was used to make rope. But the term *ropeyarn* had simply come to mean "to knock off work early." As soon as Chief Kidder said the word, the Sailors all jumped out of their seats, as if by instinct.

On the morning of Wednesday, January 2—the first workday of 1929—snow flurries were falling on the roof of the Main Navy Building as the men shuffled through an inch or so of powder to the classroom. Kidder stood at the front of the classroom as always. "Man your poz, time to copy some katakana," he ordered.

After the men settled into their positions, Kidder began to send katakana code with his telegraphic key at about five groups per minute. As always, the rhythm was the same. The keys of all the typewriters sounded like several horses' hooves hitting a cobblestone street—no two clacks happened simultaneously. Still, Kidder persisted. Hour after hour, day after day—symbol, symbol, symbol, pause; symbol, symbol, symbol, pause.

By mid-January, after two weeks of continuous practice, Chief Kidder had choreographed a perfect dance. Finally, symbol, symbol, symbol, pause; symbol, symbol, symbol, pause; symbol, symbol, symbol, pause was followed immediately on the RIP-5 with *clack, clack, clack, pause*; *clack, clack, clack, pause*; *clack, clack, clack, pause*—all in unison. Kidder smiled.

However, there was still more work to be done and little time to do it. All seven of the operators would soon be assigned to Station BAKER in Guam, but Kidder felt they weren't ready. He had adjusted the pace of the curriculum to meet the performance of the students, and it wasn't until recently that copying the code had become routine for them. Kidder hadn't even turned on the receivers in the classroom to expose the group to live Japanese traffic. Nor had he gone over developing intercept schedules or traffic analysis. He had so much left to teach them.

In order to prepare them for the real world of intercepting coded Japanese messages, Kidder turned on the receiver closest to the front of the room, connected his speaker, tuned it to 39 kilocycles—a known broadcast frequency for Tokyo Radio, call sign JJC—and waited for it to warm up.

The men waited as the tubes began to glow inside the radio. They all recognized the low humming of the receiver as it slowly came to life. The sound of static could faintly be heard through the speaker as the tubes continued to warm. The static grew in volume, until eventually it was audible throughout the classroom.

"It's just a couple minutes from the sked," Kidder said.

"They run skeds too, Chief?" Petty Officer Lusk asked.

"Yes, they do, Tru. Their procedures are only a little different than our own. You'll get used to it."

Just then, a Japanese radio operator began to tune his transmitter.

· · · —   · · · —   · · · —

"He's sending *V*s!" Hoffman exclaimed.

"That's *KU*, Rob," Kidder reminded him.

"Oh, yeah . . . , that's right," Hoffman shamefully agreed.

· · · —   · · · —   · · · —

When the katakana paused, Kidder said to his students, "Get ready." As the broadcast began, Chief Kidder took out his stick and began to copy symbol, symbol, symbol, pause; symbol, symbol, symbol, pause; symbol, symbol, symbol, pause. The Japanese radio operator sent his code at about twenty groups per minute, which was no problem for Kidder.

The students tried their best but couldn't keep up. While the katakana telegraphic code was recognizable, it was choppy and faded in and out with a haze of continuous static in the background.

Kidder tried to encourage them. "You'll have to practice this when you get to Guam. We'll send you frequencies and sked times. The Old Spanish Guardhouse is kitted up and waiting for you. For the first month or so, I want you to listen for transmissions on the frequencies we send you. Try to figure out the skeds. Figure out what the right intercept routine is. And above all, practice copying actual transmissions. Practice, practice, practice." Kidder felt like a mother bird pushing her babies out of the nest before they were ready to fly.

⚓ ⚓ ⚓

There was no graduation ceremony for the group. Friday, January 18, was their final day of instruction, and Kidder told them to check out of Ma Travers's place before they came to class the following Monday morning.

When they reported to the rooftop classroom on Monday, January 21, Kidder said, "We've got three things to accomplish today. First: orders."

Kidder handed out large brown paper envelopes to everyone. Inside each envelope was the Sailor's medical file and his personnel record, which had been fully updated the previous week. A copy of the Sailor's typed orders to Guam were stapled to the front of each envelope.

"Next: travel documents." Kidder handed out another smaller envelope to each student. "This is important. These envelopes contain your train tickets from Union Station to San Francisco. Your orders will get you on board USS *Chaumont* to Hawaii, then on to Guam. Do not lose them."

"Woo-hoo!" Keg exclaimed. "We're goin' to Guam!"

Van chirped excitedly, "Paradise!"

"Has anyone ever been?" Kidder asked. Van, Billehus, and Hoffman raised their hands. "Ah, yes. Asiatic Fleet Sailors," Kidder said knowingly. "Good liberty in Guam, for sure."

Lusk chimed in, "You said there were three things, Chief. What's the third thing?"

"Right, yes. Well, now it's time for choir practice." As he said this, he reached behind the back of the podium. Everyone looked puzzled, except Chief Goldstein, who knew exactly what was about to happen.

Petty Officer Cloyd asked, a bit confused, "Chief, do we have to sing? I don't sing."

"Who said anything about singing?" Kidder said playfully. "I said it's time for choir practice." He pulled out a bottle of whiskey then retrieved several glasses and began to pour.

The men finally understood.

"Choir practice, huh?" a bemused Hoffman said.

The men laughed, raised their glasses, and toasted the successful culmination of the inaugural class of the On-the-Roof Gang training.

CHAPTER 19

CLASS #2

MONDAY, MAY 6, 1929

MAIN NAVY BUILDING, WASHINGTON, DC

On this lovely spring day, Chief Kidder had just returned from visiting Ma Travers's Guest House to make sure everything was ready for his second group of radio intercept students. He also made sure to find Susie so he could spend some time with her. After his first class graduated, Kidder frequently found reasons to visit the guesthouse—rent payments, reservations for upcoming students, coordination of the shipment of personal effects, and so on. In reality, he was there to see Susie and found convenient excuses to visit.

Harry was smitten with Susie, and he would do anything to spend time with her. He couldn't believe a woman as young, pretty, and smart as Susie would have anything to do with a crusty, old Navy chief like him, but Susie seemed to return his feelings. This was his first real girlfriend, and he was going to do everything in his power not to blow it.

Aside from visiting the guesthouse as often as possible, Kidder had also been strategizing how to get additional time for training the next rooftop class. Three months just wasn't enough. He'd drafted a request to Lieutenant Rochefort asking for two additional months, even though he only wanted one. Rochefort agreed and forwarded the request to the Director of Naval Communications, who approved an extension, but of just one month. Chief Kidder knew how to play the game to get exactly what he was hoping for.

Harry whistled as he walked to work on this sunny spring morning. The sun peeked intermittently through the leaves on the trees, flashing warmth on and off his face as he made his way down Virginia Avenue. Being in love awakened his appreciation of how beautiful spring was in Washington, DC.

As he stepped into the Research Desk office, he immediately noticed something different. Whereas normally there was a buzz of activity in the office, there was an unmistakable shroud of silence and sadness. Agnes had a frown on her face as she looked at Lieutenant Rochefort, who was on the phone and speaking in hushed tones. The yeomen looked up at Kidder as he entered the office. No one smiled.

Kidder walked up to the desk closest to the door and asked the yeoman, "What's up?"

The Sailor shrugged and answered, "Not sure, chief, but it ain't good." He nodded toward Rochefort.

Kidder strode toward his desk in front of Rochefort, switching his gaze between Agnes and the lieutenant. Agnes returned his glance. Something was up, for sure, but no one was going to say anything while Rochefort was on the phone. Finally, he hung up the receiver gently.

"Well, it's done," Rochefort declared.

Kidder was a little afraid to ask, but he did so anyway, "What is, sir?"

"Yardley's Black Chamber. Stimson closed it."

Secretary of State Henry Stimson had only been in his post since March, when the newly inaugurated President Herbert Hoover appointed him. He was a New York lawyer who was still learning all the ins and outs of the State Department.

The Black Chamber—the popular nickname for the Cipher Bureau, the nation's top codebreaking organization, which was under the direction of Herbert Yardley—was jointly funded and operated by the U.S. Army and the State Department. Upon being briefed of the Black Chamber's operations, Stimson firmly believed the work was highly unethical.

Stating that "Gentlemen do not read each other's mail," Stimson immediately ceased State Department funding to the Black Chamber, essentially closing it down for good. This was bad news for the Code and Signal Section within the U.S. Navy. Although the Secretary of State had no authority over any part of the Navy, there was a very real fear that this was the first domino to fall in Hoover's new postwar administration.

Rochefort and Miss Aggie sat at their desks, dispirited. Chief Kidder, ever the optimist, said, "They don't even know where my classroom is. How would they even find us to close it down? We're the On-the-Roof Gang, they can't shut us down!"

This lifted the duo out of their malaise. Kidder was right—the State Department had no idea about this small Navy outfit. They might have to take some steps to remain under the radar, but for now at least, the Research Desk and the rooftop training were safe. Rochefort would have to keep an ear to the ground for any possible grumblings about shutting them down.

⚓ ⚓ ⚓

Two weeks before the second On-the-Roof Gang class was scheduled to begin, Sailors began checking in with the personnel department and moving into Ma Travers's Guest House. The roster for the class included Chief Radioman Max Gunn; five radiomen first class: Donovan Broughton, Charles Daniels, Oliver Grew, Clarence Reynolds, and Murrel Wood; and one radiomen second class, Earnest Edwin Dailey.

On the first day of class, the students reported to the Main Navy Building in civilian clothing at 0800 hours. Kidder gave the students the same tour of the building that he'd given to his inaugural class before finally taking them up to the rooftop classroom. Again, he made a point of establishing a more personal connection with the only chief assigned to the class, Chief Radioman Max Gunn. Once in the classroom, Kidder administered the oath of secrecy to the group, after which he got right to work.

Just as he'd done the first time around, Chief Kidder used the crawl-walk-run method. He started with the alphabet and the information booklet before moving into recitation of the katakana sounds and then the telegraphic code. The class responded just as well as the first—catching on quickly to the katakana telegraphic code. By midsummer, the class was copying twenty groups per minute as Chief Kidder sent the code with the telegraphic key on his podium.

Having learned from mistakes he made during the first class, Kidder started to sprinkle in the concepts of traffic analysis and developing intercept plans. He also started turning on the receivers for a few minutes at the end of each day. This, at the very least, gave the students an idea of what they'd be up against out in the fleet.

One student who showed particular promise as an intercept operator was Radioman Second Class Earnest E. Dailey, whom his classmates called E. E. Despite the fact that he was the most junior man in the class, he quickly demonstrated why he was selected for the training. He copied the katakana code almost effortlessly, while others labored with the task. Chief Kidder took a mental note to make sure to get to know Dailey a little better.

One morning in early August, Chief Kidder walked into the Research Desk office and received a surprise. Sitting at Rochefort's desk was none other than Laurance Safford, who'd recently been promoted to lieutenant commander.

"Chief Kidder, great to see you again."

"This is a surprise, sir. Great to see you too. So, I hear you're a lieutenant commander now, huh? Congratulations. What are you doing in DC?"

"This may or may not be pleasant news for you, but I'm here to relieve Lieutenant Rochefort," he told the chief. "He's heading to Tokyo to study Japanese for three years."

For years, ONI had been sending several junior officers to Japan to study the language, and Rochefort was an excellent candidate for the training. Once he was selected, a replacement was needed at the Research Desk, and Safford was due for transfer orders. It was an easy choice.

"That's swell, sir. Lieutenant Rochefort has been great, but it'll be good to have you back in the fold," Kidder said sincerely.

"I hear the training has been going well, Chief. Your graduates are doing great things in Guam."

"Yes, sir. We're getting some good intercept from the On-the-Roof Gang."

"The On-the-Roof Gang? That's good, I like it."

"We can really see the difference between their work and everyone else's," Kidder boasted.

"Excellent work, Chief! The operators are a credit to you," Safford said. Kidder accepted the compliment with an uncomfortable nod, but didn't respond, so Safford continued, "We're going to have to increase the staff here if we're going to keep up with the volume of intercept they're producing. What else is left to do from the original plans?"

Kidder thought back to the original plans he and Safford had worked on and realized they had made some amazing progress. Still, there was more to do. "We still need to open a site in the Philippines and get some trained operators to Stations ABLE and HYPO. We could also use an intercept site in the Aleutians and maybe Australia. And we haven't done anything about creating DF sites."

DF, or direction finding, was the measurement of the direction from which a received radio signal was transmitted. DF equipment used rotating antennas that compared signal strengths on each line of bearing. The stronger the signal was on any line of bearing, the more likely the transmitted signal was coming from that direction. By slowly rotating the antenna in extremely small increments, it was possible to point directly at a transmitted signal. By combining the direction information from two or more suitably spaced receivers, the source of a transmission could be located through triangulation. This was revolutionary science in the early days of wireless radio communications, so it would be difficult to gain approval to have radiomen stationed at remote sites around the Pacific, especially at sites that didn't have traditional communications or intercept missions. Still, it was part of the overall plan to establish these sites to be able to track Imperial Japanese Navy ships in addition to intercept activities. This was something Safford felt needed to get done, and he planned to work on that while he was back at the Research Desk.

"There is something else I need to bring you up to speed on, sir. It's about one of the students," Kidder said.

"Which student, Chief? What's the problem?"

"Well, Petty Officer Dailey swears his division officer on the USS *Concord* promised him a promotion to first class if he accepted orders to this training. Now that his class is almost done, he's expecting to be promoted."

Safford furrowed his brow.

Kidder continued, "He's good, sir. He's got everything we need—skill, integrity, smarts. I'd like to try to keep him in the outfit."

"Chief, you know how this goes. We can't get anyone promoted without competing against everyone else. Dailey's going to have to make a choice."

Chief Kidder nodded, a little disappointed. He had heard the same through the chiefs' network but was hoping a newly minted lieutenant commander would want to take up the mantle for a fight like this. Kidder would have to break the news to Dailey that he wasn't going to be promoted. He hoped that Dailey, having completed nearly all of the rooftop training, would decide to stick it out anyway.

But that wasn't going to happen. When Chief Kidder told him the news, Dailey became agitated and angry. If there was no automatic promotion, what was in it for him? He certainly wasn't going to be able to pass a Morse code test if he continued with intercept duties, and he was ready to get back to the fleet.

Chief Kidder obliged. He sent Dailey directly to the administrative office, and he was out of training the very same day; the class was down to six students.

The rest of the training continued without incident. The extra month allowed the chief time to train the students on those topics that the first class had glossed over—traffic analysis, intercept plan, codebreaking. Even before they finished, Kidder felt this class was much more ready for the real world.

After completion of training in September, five of the six On-the-Roof Gang class members were sent to the Philippines to establish Station CAST, the fourth dedicated intercept site in the Pacific Ocean. Chief Max Gunn was this class's sole graduate to receive orders to American Legation in Peiping, China, to help the Marine Corps with intercept operations there.

Again, there was no graduation ceremony, but as he'd done before, Chief Kidder held "choir practice" with his students. Then the students traveled together via train to San Francisco where they boarded the USS *Chaumont*, this time destined for Subic Bay in the Philippines.

With a lot of diligence and determination, along with the dedication and hard work of Chief Kidder, Lieutenant Commander Safford's plans were gaining momentum.

CHAPTER 20

STATION CAST

THURSDAY, OCTOBER 10, 1929
OLONGAPO, PHILIPPINES

Admiral Frank Upham, the Commander in Chief of the Asiatic Fleet (CINCAF), was so impressed by the results of the radio intelligence work at Stations ABLE, BAKER, and HYPO that he wanted his own intercept site. Specifically, he had requested that an intercept unit—complete with a decryption center—be located at or near Manila Bay with the intention of preventing a surprise attack on the Asiatic Fleet. He believed Subic Bay in the Philippines was a suitable location for such a site.

During the more than 300 years that Spain controlled the Philippines, Subic Bay—an inlet on the west coast of the island of Luzon about fifty miles northwest of Manila—had served as the site of a naval base and stronghold. Beginning in the early twentieth century, the U.S. Navy used Subic Bay as a naval facility, but access was a problem. The main U.S. Navy facilities in the Philippines were in Manila Bay, and the only efficient way to get to and from Subic was by sea—there was no direct vehicular route from Manila or Cavite Naval Base.

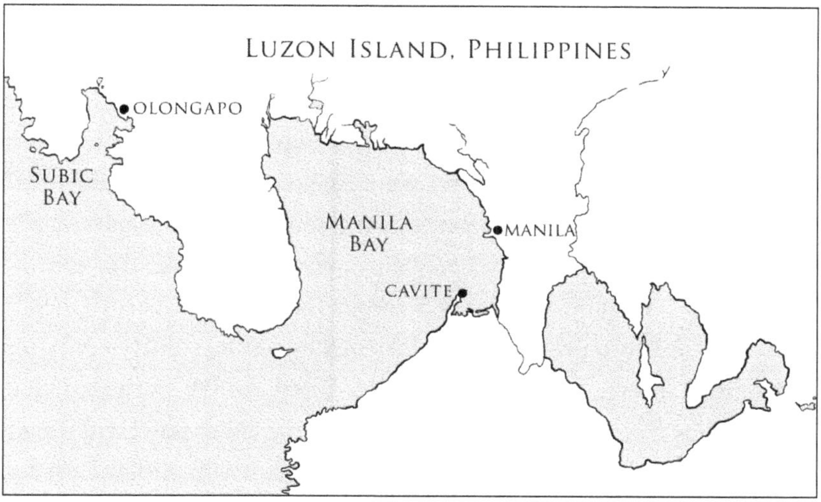

In 1925, after some negotiation with U.S. Navy commanders in the Philippines, the provincial government in Zambales authorized the construction of a paved road cutting across the mountains along the north side of Manila Bay, which made travel to Subic Bay much easier. Soon after, a small village known as Olongapo began to develop along Subic Bay just outside the naval base on the mouth of the Santa Rita River.

According to popular legend, the town received its name from the severed head of an ancient, local tribesman named Apo, who wanted to unite two warring tribes in the area. There were, however, some who bitterly opposed his idea, and one day, Apo disappeared without a trace. After a search, his body was found without its head, and tribesmen continued to look for Apo's severed head. A young boy eventually found it perched on top of a bamboo pole. While holding the decapitated head of Apo on the bamboo pole, the boy ran back to his people yelling, "ulo ng Apo," which means "head of Apo" in Tagalog. The phrase stuck, and eventually gave Olongapo its name.

After construction of Manila Road, more and more shops, restaurants, and bars sprang up in the area to meet the demands of the growing local population. Admiral Upham requested that the Director of Naval Communications send an investigatory party to assess the feasibility of an intercept site in Olongapo. Chief Joe Goldstein and Petty Officer Tru Lusk—graduates of the initial On-the-Roof Gang class—who were assigned to Station BAKER in Guam at the time, were selected for the duty. They embarked the Asiatic Fleet flagship USS *Isabel* and arrived in Subic Bay within two weeks. As they approached Subic Bay on October 10, 1929, they used the ship's radios to perform an initial feasibility study for a potential intercept site in Olongapo. Their results indicated that interference from Radio P. I.—the largest and most powerful broadcasting site in the Asiatic Fleet—made it a less-than-optimal site for intercept operations.

After the USS *Isabel* pulled into port in Olongapo, Goldstein and Lusk walked the short distance to the radio station where Admiral Upham's aide, Lieutenant Commander Peter Lovejoy, greeted them. "Welcome to your new home, boys!"

Chief Goldstein spoke for the pair, "Thank you, sir. Not sure this will be the right location for us, though." He remembered the severe difficulties at Station BAKER in Guam, where Radio Libugon repeatedly interfered with the ability to perform intercept operations.

"It's the right location, Chief. Admiral Upham says it's the right location," Lovejoy said sternly. Just then, Lieutenant Donald Rogers, the commander of Radio P. I., joined the group.

"With all due respect, Commander," Goldstein said somewhat more forcefully, "we're here to assess the feasibility of this place for intercept duties. And it's plain to see that it's not an ideal location for such duties."

"Now, Chief, you haven't even seen the place yet. Radio P. I. is quite a facility," Rogers assured the visitors from Guam. "We've set aside a room specifically for your intercept operation. I think you'll be impressed."

Lieutenant Commander Lovejoy was less forgiving, "Chief, there is only one possible outcome in this situation. I'm sure you're not planning to tell Admiral Upham that he can't have an intercept site here. I won't *let you* tell him that."

"Aye, aye, sir," Goldstein replied dejectedly. He was caught between a rock and a hard place. He had been given instructions to conduct a real assessment of the location, but he could tell that being so close to Radio P. I. would be problematic. Yet he also knew that the Research Desk had a strong desire to build a site in the Philippines. He didn't want to get into a pissing match with the admiral's aide, nor with the admiral himself. That was never good for one's career.

"Follow me, gentlemen," Lieutenant Rogers said as he began to walk down the passageway. Petty Officer Lusk was the first to follow, then Chief Goldstein, and finally Lieutenant Commander Lovejoy. When the group arrived at a combination-locked door, Lieutenant Rogers quickly dialed the code, and they went inside the room.

The room was large, clean, and ready to be occupied. Despite the fact that the Philippine Islands were susceptible to the same monsoons as in Guam, the facility felt new, bright, clean, and airy. Ten tables lined three of the four walls. Antenna cables streamed from an opening overhead and snaked onto each of the tables. A smaller, rectangular table was centered in the space with six chairs surrounding it. Although there were no windows, air seemed to be flowing through the room. Goldstein and Lusk gave each other a look that said, "Someone did their homework." The space alone made Radio P. I. a significantly better location than the Old Spanish Guardhouse, where Goldstein and Lusk had been working in Agaña, Guam. Even if the site wasn't effective in conducting intercept operations, the men would be comfortable.

"You just have to let us know what equipment you need, Chief, and we'll get it for you ASAP," Rogers said. Goldstein felt like he was being sold a used car, but he obviously had little choice.

Lieutenant Commander Lovejoy confirmed this, "Chief, I suppose you haven't heard. All of the radiomen from the second class of your gumshoe outfit are on their way here for duty." Choosing his words carefully, Lovejoy was clearly taking a swipe at the location of the radio intelligence classroom on the roof of the Main Navy Building. Walking on the roof, Sailors likely got tar on their shoes—something that was obviously very distasteful to the fine sensibilities of the lieutenant commander.

"No, I hadn't heard, sir," Goldstein replied, feeling the cards being stacked against him.

Lovejoy continued, "Well now you have, and they'll be here by November. The CINCAF wants you to have your intercept site up and running by the end of the year. You'll both stay here until then to get the place ready. More recent grads will come from the next class. Admiral Upham will have his intercept site . . . and it will be here in Olongapo. Understood?"

"Aye, aye, sir." Chief Goldstein knew when he was beaten. A new intercept site—known as Station CAST—would soon open in Olongapo.

CHAPTER 21

CLASS #3

MONDAY, NOVEMBER 4, 1929
MAIN NAVY BUILDING, WASHINGTON, DC

The self-trained Marine Corps operators at the American Legation in Peiping were in need of help from formally trained intercept operators, particularly after the Sailors from Station ABLE moved from Shanghai to the USS *General Alava* in 1927. When that happened, the Marine Corps site in Peiping was the only intercept operation remaining on mainland China.

In order to reinvigorate intercept operations there, Lieutenant Safford decided he would work to bolster the Marine Corps site in Peiping. In the fall of 1929, Safford solicited names of Marine Corps radiomen for intercept duty in much the same way he had done for Navy operators. The Marine Corps Communications Department finally nominated four radiomen from the Fourth Marine Regiment in Shanghai just two weeks before Harry Kidder's third On-the-Roof Gang class was scheduled to begin. The Marines were soon on board the USS *Chaumont* en route to Washington, DC, for Kidder's class, even though the Research Desk hadn't properly vetted them yet.

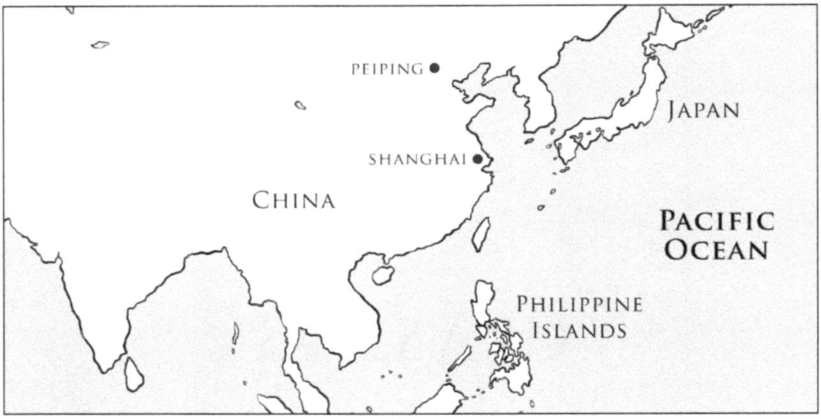

After having received the nominees' names late, the Research Desk quickly reviewed the backgrounds and records of the Marines. Safford rejected three of the four immediately for repeated alcohol-related incidents in China. Only one Marine, Private First Class Charles Cameron, was placed on the training roster. Together with Cameron, the rest of Harry Kidder's third class of recruits included four U.S. Navy radiomen first class: Ludolph Guillet, George Hopkins, Laurence Myers, and Daryl Wigle.

Meanwhile, the Research Desk was expanding. Lieutenant Commander Safford had reported to Captain Stanley C. Hooper—the new Director of Naval Communications—that the Research Desk had accumulated five years' worth of intercepted and untranslated Japanese diplomatic messages and two years' worth of intercepted Japanese naval messages. Every safe was stuffed with reams of intercept logs. They even began storing intercepted communications in their desks, which was against security protocol. But there was no way around it; the Research Desk simply needed more people, more equipment, and more space.

Captain Hooper—another staunch supporter of the new radio intelligence discipline—agreed and gave the Research Desk additional office space in the sixth wing of the Main Navy Building, this time on the third floor. Ten additional yeomen were assigned to duty in the Research Desk along with several more commissioned officers, who were trained in either Japanese, cryptanalysis, or both.

Harry Kidder was scheduled to teach his third and final group of On-the-Roof Gang students beginning in November. When the class was over, he would transfer to the Asiatic Fleet for assignment. The news of his transfer loomed over him like a dark, ominous cloud. While he missed the tropical climate of the Pacific Ocean, he couldn't bear the thought of leaving Susie behind.

Safford tried to console Kidder. "We'll get you back here as soon as we can, Chief. You'll do two or three years in the fleet and then come right back here to teach. It'll go quicker than you think."

"I appreciate that, sir. Three years to a forty-year-old lug like me is nothing. But to Susie, it'll seem like a lifetime."

"You two will work it out. Why don't you take some time off and go see her," Safford suggested.

With a week to go before class was scheduled to begin, Harry visited Susie at Ma Travers's place. Sitting in the front room, Harry broke the news to her.

"Nooooo, Harry!" she cried. "Why do you have to go?"

"It's just time, Susie. I've been stateside for almost five years; it's time to go out to sea again. That's just how it works," he explained. "But if we got married, you could come with me!" He knew the answer to this before he blurted it out.

"Harry, you know I can't leave," she reminded him. "I'm saving money for my business. I'm almost there. I can't give up on my dream now."

"I know, Susie. I understand. I was just looking for a way to keep us together."

"Then stay," she pleaded.

"I can't, Susie." He wanted desperately to tell her what he was working on in the Navy so she would understand how important he was to the effort. But the oath of secrecy he'd signed prevented him from doing so.

"But I think I'll be able to come back in a couple years."

"Really? Two years is a long time, but by the time you get back, I might be able to quit this job and start my own business."

"I'll save, too, Susie. I'll save so we can get married." Harry saw the glimmer in her eyes and knew this was the only real solution to their problem.

The two made a pact to stay true to each other for the duration of Harry's assignment in the Far East. And they had four months before he had to leave, so they agreed to spend every possible moment together.

As the two were comforting each other in the front room, Daryl Wigle, the senior radioman in Kidder's upcoming class, walked in the front door and raised his eyebrows at the site of Harry and Susie arm-in-arm. "I think I'm going to like this place!" he said jokingly.

Harry laughed and stood up. "I'm Chief Kidder. . . . And who are you?"

"Petty Officer Wigle. Not wiggle, Wigle." He made sure to stress the long *i* sound in his name.

"Your first name's Daryl, right? How 'bout we just call you DW?"

"That'll be just fine, Chief. Can I call you Pappy?" Kidder's reputation had preceded him.

"Out here that's fine. In class, it's Chief Kidder."

"No problem. Is anyone else here yet?"

Susie answered, "You're the first. Go see Ma in the office behind the kitchen. She'll check you in, and I'll show you to your room."

"Thanks," Wigle said with a gracious nod before heading toward the kitchen.

⚓ ⚓ ⚓

When the third class of the On-the-Roof Gang convened on Monday, November 11, Chief Kidder ran through his typical orientation with his five new students. It was soon obvious that Private First Class Cameron wasn't just the sole Marine in the class, he was by far the most junior. The four Navy students were first class petty officers, so they had years of experience on the Marine. Some good-natured ribbing was the norm in Kidder's class. Even though it was always lighthearted, Cameron stood six foot six and had the build of a linebacker, so the Sailors didn't really want to mess with him too much.

The smaller class size allowed Chief Kidder to give each of the students more personalized attention, and it clearly paid off. The students caught on more quickly and retained information better than the first two classes had. By the Christmas break, they were already copying katakana communications at twenty-five groups per minute as the chief used the telegraphic key on his desk.

Despite the downturn in the economy following the stock market crash less than two months prior, Christmas 1929 was again a festive occasion at Ma Travers's Guest House. After receiving rent from the U.S. Navy for another full house, Gertrude was as solvent as she'd ever been. This year, she'd even hired a cook to come in and prepare Christmas dinner. She also gave Susie and Stephanie raises and bonuses as Christmas presents. Susie was particularly thrilled.

Everyone was in good spirits relaxing in the front room—even Harry and Susie, who were celebrating as if time was no issue. The students all called each other by their nicknames. Ludolph Guillet was "LG"; George Hopkins was "Red"; Laurence Myers was "Frankie"; Daryl Wigle was "DW"; and of course, Harry Kidder was "Pappy." Charles Cameron made the rest of them laugh when he told them his nickname was "Private."

"The Marine Corps gave me my nickname," he explained. "But I guess they'll have to change it when I make corporal."

There was one unfamiliar face in the group. Chief Radioman Dorman Chauncey was going to be the instructor for the next three classes after Kidder shipped out to sea, so he'd arrived in time to celebrate Christmas with everyone. Even though Chauncey was an experienced operator, having stood up Station BAKER, he hadn't attended the On-the-Roof Gang training, so he needed to learn Kidder's techniques as an instructor. He sat quietly, not wanting to interrupt the obvious chemistry within the group.

In the five years prior to his arrival in Washington, DC, Chauncey had gained intercept experience at Station BAKER in Guam and while on board the USS *Trenton* in the Asiatic Fleet. More importantly, he had helped train general service radiomen from Radio Libugon in the art of copying the katakana telegraphic code. It was this experience that convinced Safford to select Chauncey as Kidder's replacement as instructor of the On-the-Roof Gang.

In the front room, the students were drinking eggnog and exchanging sea stories. Wigle captivated the group with a story he'd heard about a young Chief Kidder. "Did you know he once built his own ham rig in the P. I.?" he said, regaling his classmates. "And he was talking to someone in Maine in just an hour and a half!" The group was amazed.

Uncomfortable as the center of attention, Harry said, "Chief Chauncey is the real magician." He motioned toward Chauncey and continued, "He turned a ramshackle stone house on Guam into an intercept station in a month."

Wigle asked, "Is that true, Chief?"

"Yeah, it's true, DW," Chauncey responded. "But it wasn't magic. They gave me the space and the equipment; I just put it all together."

Pleased that the attention had been diverted to someone else, Harry returned his own attention to Susie, who was sitting on the chair's armrest, her hand resting on Harry's shoulder.

Before dinner, Harry again recited the special Navy prayer. Just as it had been the year before, the feast was spectacular. After the meal, the guests bonded over port wine, pie, and Christmas cookies. By the end of the evening, everyone had made Chauncey feel at ease within the group.

Before everyone retired to their rooms, Chief Kidder stood and said, "I have some toasts to make." A hush fell over the group after he got everyone's attention. "To the On-the-Roof Gang. We know you're out there, and we're listening."

Everyone raised their glasses and cheered, "To the On-the-Roof Gang!"

Still standing, Harry continued, "To Chief Chauncey. You're one of us now; you're part of the On-the-Roof Gang." Harry raised his glass and nodded toward Chauncey.

Everyone repeated, "To Chief Chauncey!"

"And to the U.S. Navy. Long may she rule the waves!"

"Hear! Hear! To the Navy!" the men hollered as they took another drink.

By midnight, Chief Chauncey had left for his apartment a few blocks away, and everyone else had retired to their rooms, leaving Harry and Susie alone in the front room. The Victrola had ceased playing music, but the record continued to spin on the turntable. The loving couple didn't notice any of it—they were too lost in each other's company.

Harry promised several things to Susie that Christmas night. He promised he would come back to her. He promised he would be true to her. He promised to save money so that when he returned, they could get married. And most sincerely, Harry promised to never stop loving her. To Harry's delight, Susie nestled her head against his neck. He was hoping to hear her make some promises in return, but his disappointment faded when she fell asleep as the fire crackled in the fireplace.

Chief Kidder and his students returned to class after the Christmas break, reinvigorated after a wonderful, relaxing holiday. Kidder was a little subdued knowing that he was in the final stretch before he'd have to leave his love. Chief Chauncey was sitting at the small desk at the back of the room observing the class. By this time, all of the students were extremely proficient, and they continued to get better with each passing day. After class ended each day, Kidder and Chauncey remained behind in the classroom to discuss Harry's techniques for teaching the katakana alphabet and how to copy it.

In early January 1930, Lieutenant Commander Safford produced a report for the Director of Naval Communications on the status of radio intelligence operations in the fleet. Spread across Stations ABLE, BAKER, CAST, and HYPO, seventeen qualified operators were performing intercept duties, and the five students in Harry's class would soon be heading out as reinforcements. Safford was pleased with the progress that had been made, yet one issue or another still hampered each of the sites. Station HYPO was undermanned. The damp weather in Guam plagued the men at Station BAKER and routinely made them ill. And Kidder's specially trained intercept operators at Station CAST were being used to augment the general service communications watch. All three sites also had to deal with interference from the large U.S. Navy radio transmitters drowning out their intercept operations. But Safford's biggest problem was in China, where Station ABLE had been moved aboard USS *General Alava*, which was eventually decommissioned. Safford designated the U.S. Marine Corps intercept site at the American Legation in Peiping, which was the only intercept happening in China, the title Station ABLE. Because of the intensifying unrest between China and Japan, the safety and security of the intercept operations at the new Station ABLE were at risk. Safford resolved to improve the situation at each of the intercept sites.

By early March 1930, all the students in the rooftop class were ready to transfer to the fleet. On the final day of class, Chief Kidder handed out orders. Guillet, Hopkins, and Myers were going to Station CAST in the Philippines. Daryl Wigle was to transfer to Station BAKER in Guam. Perhaps in retaliation for dropping three of the four Marines from the class, the Marine Corps had ordered Cameron back to general service radio duty instead of sending him to Peiping for intercept duty. Cameron was good at copying the katakana code, but to the Marine Corps, it didn't matter. Kidder was frustrated with the wasted opportunity.

Chief Kidder received orders to report to the USS *Isabel*, in the Asiatic Fleet. Upon learning of Kidder's orders, Lieutenant Commander Safford remarked, "Chief Kidder, you're going to be working with a good man, Lieutenant Wenger. He's good at this game, he's smart, and you and he will get along famously." Wenger had previously spent some time learning cryptanalysis from Safford at the Research Desk.

"I look forward to meeting him, sir," Kidder said slowly as he tried to process the reality of receiving his orders. He was still having difficulty with the thought of leaving Susie, regardless of who he would be working with. Safford could see it in Kidder's body language.

"Chief . . . Harry . . . we'll get you back here, I promise. Go to sea, do good things with Wenger. The time will go by more quickly than you think."

Harry prayed Safford was right.

CHAPTER 22

BACK TO THE FLEET

TUESDAY, APRIL 15, 1930

USS *HENDERSON*, PACIFIC OCEAN

Chief Kidder and four of his recent On-the-Roof Gang graduates sailed from Long Beach, California, aboard the USS *Henderson*, an armed troop transport ship named for Brigadier General Archibald Henderson, who served as the commander of the U.S. Marine Corps in the 1800s. Kidder enjoyed the company of his former students, but they were berthed in different locations. Kidder was staying in chief's berthing, which was one deck below the main deck and had sufficient racks for the forty chief petty officers on board. There was also a separate living space, known as the Goat Locker, where the chiefs could eat and relax in comfort away from the rest of the ship's passengers. The Goat Locker was looked after by two stewards, whose responsibility it was to keep the space clean, serve the chiefs their meals, and do the chiefs' laundry. In contrast, Kidder's former students on board, who were first class petty officers, were put up in troop berthing on the fourth deck below the main deck. Troop berthing had hundreds of racks stacked four high in a very large open space. Because the ship operated twenty-four hours a day, there was rarely quiet or complete darkness.

Although Chief Kidder had full access to the Goat Locker, he spent much of his time with his former students. Typically, when a chief chose to eat with the men in the crew's mess instead of the Goat Locker, he would have head-of-the-line privileges. But Kidder instead decided to wait in line with his fellow On-the-Roof Gang members.

The USS *Henderson* had spent the past six years transiting between the West Coast of the United States, Hawaii, and the Far East. During that time, Sailors on the *Henderson* began the tradition of initiating others into "the Realm of the Golden Dragon." Each time the ship would cross the international date line in a westerly direction, those already initiated would put on a ritual that required the inexperienced to participate. Exactly what happened during the Golden Dragon ceremony was a closely kept secret. Although Kidder and his men had all been across the international date line before, the ritual was still unique to the *Henderson* at the time, so the entire group had to participate. Each man took his turn crawling through garbage, being swatted with paddles, eating unidentifiable food scraps, pleading for mercy in front of a kangaroo court, and finally receiving a certificate proving he had been inducted into the Realm. The tradition was a bonding experience for the ship's crew and was a way for the men to prove that they could handle the rigors of shipboard life, regardless of the conditions. Despite the discomfort of the ritual, Kidder and his men were all glad they had completed it.

The USS *Henderson* arrived in Manila Bay after a seventeen-day journey from Long Beach. Chief Kidder stood on the weather deck and recalled his previous time spent there. Despite missing Susie, the Philippines felt like home. As the warm sea breeze buffeted the rim of his khaki combination cover, he closed his eyes, took a deep breath of the salt air, and enjoyed the warmth of the sun on his face.

Kidder stood on the port side of the ship to admire the rocky shoreline of Corregidor Island, the largest of the rocky islands at the entrance of Manila Bay. Behind the steep rocky cliffs of the shoreline,

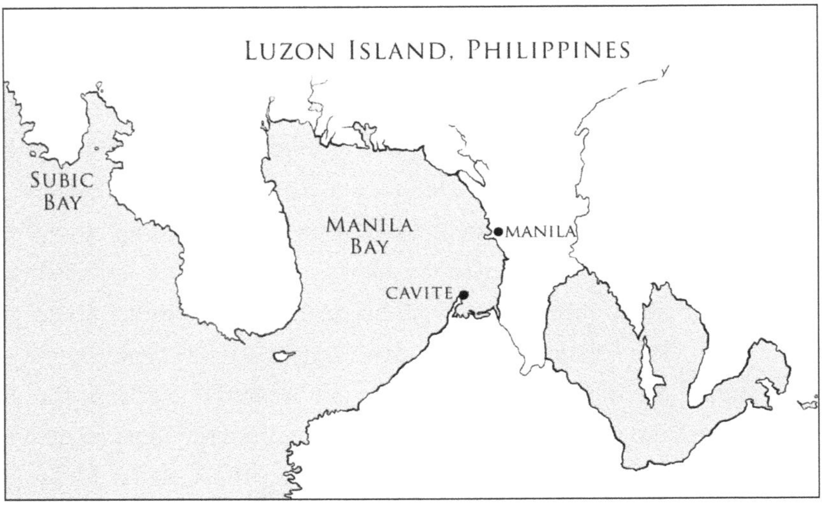

he saw nothing but dense jungle peppered with palm trees. He knew from his previous time in the Philippines that the U.S. Army had some facilities on Corregidor Island, but he wasn't sure what they were. One thing he did know, Corregidor wasn't the "Gibraltar of the Pacific," which the Army claimed it was. It might have been the "Gibraltar of Manila Bay," but that was the extent of it.

After passing Corregidor Island, Kidder strolled to the starboard bow to watch the activity along Cavite Peninsula. U.S. Navy planes were conducting flight operations at Sangley Point at the very tip of the peninsula. *Henderson* rounded Sangley Point, and Cavite Naval Base came into view on the far side of a small inlet called Canacao Bay.

As the *Henderson* continued to turn starboard, passing another peninsula that divided Canacao Bay and Bacoor Bay, Kidder saw Cavite Naval Base and, for the first time, his home for the next few years—the USS *Isabel.* He was looking forward to his new job on board the *Isabel.*

He was also looking forward to meeting his new division officer, Lieutenant Wenger, who, like Kidder himself, had a reputation for excellence in the fledgling field of radio intelligence. Before Kidder had arrived at the Research Desk, Wenger had spent some time at the Research Desk under the tutelage of Agnes Meyer Driscoll and Laurance Safford, from whom he'd learned the basics of radio intelligence and cryptanalysis. He'd showed real promise at decrypting enemy codes. By the spring of 1930, he was the Asiatic Fleet intelligence officer on the flagship, USS *Isabel.* Remembering how Safford had praised Wenger, Chief Kidder figured he must be a good man.

As Chief Kidder prepared to depart the *Henderson*, he wished his men success and luck in their new assignments. Three of them would be boarding the USS *Dapdap*, a ferryboat that would take them out of Manila Bay and north to Olongapo and Station CAST. Petty Officer Wigle would continue on board the USS *Henderson* for an additional week to Station BAKER in Guam. The rest checked off the ship together just after breakfast, taking turns requesting permission to go ashore and saluting the U.S. flag at the stern of the *Henderson.*

As the group gathered on the pier one last time, Chief Kidder once again wished them well.

Petty Officers Hopkins, Myers, and Guillet had all spent some time at Cavite, so they knew where to go. They walked along the waterfront to the westernmost and smallest pier at Cavite. The USS *Dapdap* was docked outboard of two other ferryboats: the USS *San Felipe* and the USS *Camia*. In order to get to the *Dapdap*, the trio had to request permission to cross the two other ferries first.

The seventy-two-foot-long USS *Dapdap*'s keel and hull were identical to those of a tugboat: wide and strong. Above deck, however, the ferryboat was designed to carry passengers around Manila Bay. It had a wooden housing with sliding doors and windows to allow passengers to see out. The entry to the bridge was inside the housing along with several long wooden benches where passengers could rest. Outside, ladders were placed on either side of the housing so passengers could also sit on benches topside on the weather decks.

While underway, a Sailor stood watch as a lookout. As the trio of On-the-Roof Gang graduates checked on board the *Dapdap*, Sailors were preparing the ferryboat to get underway for the eight-hour trip to Subic Bay.

⚓ ⚓ ⚓

Meanwhile, Chief Kidder lingered a while on the pier below the *Isabel*'s gangplank. He took in the sights, sounds, and smells of being on a real U.S. Navy base again—he hadn't realized how much he'd missed it. Eventually, he picked up his seabag and headed toward the waterfront and then to the adjacent pier. He walked up the gangplank, saluted the American flag, and, at the quarterdeck, requested permission to come aboard for duty. The petty officer of the watch welcomed the chief aboard then called down to the ship's Goat Locker on the ship's telephone. Shortly, a chief boatswain's mate approached and greeted him.

"I'm Harry," Kidder said.

"Call me Boats. Nice to meet you." Harry chuckled to himself, thinking about the fact that on every ship he'd ever been on, the chief boatswain's mate was nicknamed "Boats." And every hospital corpsman was nicknamed "Doc."

Boats showed Harry the Goat Locker and assigned him a rack.

"I'd like to get to the radio shack right away," Kidder told Boats.

"OK, let's go."

The USS *Isabel*, originally designed as a personal yacht, was smaller than any ship on which Kidder had ever been stationed. There was less headroom in the passageways and the ship's fire suppression system was obviously added well after construction. All in all, to Chief Kidder, the Isabel seemed to be piecemealed together.

When Kidder arrived at the radio shack, he knocked on the door. After a few seconds, a radioman third class opened the door and let him in. As the door closed behind him, Chief Kidder noticed how cramped and cluttered the room was, not unlike many radio rooms he'd been in before. The smell of capacitors and hot vacuum tubes filled Harry's nostrils, and he had a flashback to the last time he'd been at sea. He took a deep breath to enhance the experience.

The door opened behind him; it was Lieutenant Wenger.

"Chief Kidder. I was wondering when you'd show up. I saw the *Henderson* alongside and figured you'd be here soon." Wenger stuck out his hand to greet the chief. "Great to finally meet you, Chief Kidder. I've heard a lot about you."

"None of it's true, sir," Kidder responded, and they both chuckled. "But I'm glad to meet you, too."

"I know you want to check out the radio room, but if you don't mind, let's go to my stateroom," Wenger said. "We've got a lot to discuss."

Lieutenant Wenger led Chief Kidder through a small passageway toward the front of the ship and then through an unlocked door. In his stateroom, Wenger explained to Chief Kidder his vision for the immediate future. The pair would travel aboard the USS *Isabel* while sailing the western Pacific, visiting intercept sites whenever they arrived at a port that had one. In other locations, they would conduct studies to assess the feasibility of adding a direction finding site there. Wenger told Kidder that the USS *Houston*, when construction was complete, would relieve USS *Isabel* to become the new Asiatic Fleet flagship and their new home.

Kidder was impressed with Wenger's plan and his energy. They were both excited about the opportunity they had before them and the possibility of doing a lot of good together. Kidder was also looking forward to seeing how some of his earlier students were faring at the intercept sites they would visit.

"Where to first?" Kidder asked.

"We'll start locally, Chief," said Wenger. "Station CAST is up at Subic Bay. Have you been there?"

USS Isabel

"No, sir. Subic is a little sleepy for my taste."

"It's changed, Chief. Olongapo is a great town now."

"I'll take your word for it, sir. Looking forward to it," Kidder said.

"Me, too."

In addition to Lieutenant Wenger's plan, Chief Kidder intended to conduct some intercept from the USS *Isabel*'s radio shack and teach the ship's radiomen how to do the same.

Wouldn't want to waste this opportunity, Kidder thought.

CHAPTER 23

ORANGE GRAND MANEUVERS OF 1930

SUNDAY, MAY 4, 1930
STATION BAKER, OLD SPANISH GUARDHOUSE, AGAÑA, GUAM

The last time the Imperial Japanese Navy held one of its larger Grand Maneuvers was in 1927, which was when the U.S. Navy first attempted to intercept radio communications during such an event. The Research Desk and the U.S. Navy's radio intelligence operations were significantly more prepared for the Grand Maneuvers scheduled for 1930. This time, intercept operations would be centered around Station BAKER in Guam, where Malcolm "Felix" Lyon, the chief radioman in charge, had implemented an around-the-clock intercept plan.

As the date of the Orange Grand Maneuvers of 1930 approached, the On-the-Roof Gang graduates at Station BAKER, who were under the guidance of Chief Lyon, noticed a gradual yet steady increase in radio traffic and a higher percentage of encrypted messages contained in the intercept. The intercept logs of Guy Billehus, Keg Goodwin, Tru Lusk, and Martin Vandenberg all showed an increase in radio activity from the Japanese radio stations at Saipan (call sign JRV), Chichijima (call sign JJG), Tokyo (call sign JJC), and Palao (call sign JRW) as they communicated with the ships participating in the exercise.

Lyon complained to the Research Desk about the continued interference coming from Radio Libugon and was pleased to hear that Lieutenant Commander Safford had convinced the Director of Naval Communications to suspend broadcast operations there for the duration of the exercise. During the spring of 1930, the volume of radio traffic continued to grow. On-the-Roof Gang alums Billehus, Cloyd, Goodwin, Hoffman, Lusk, Vandenberg, and Wigle—all radiomen first class—stood ten-hour watches in the weeks leading up to the Orange Grand Maneuvers of 1930. Eight of those hours were devoted to intercept and two were spent on traffic analysis and reconstruction. Lyon and Goldstein—the two chief radiomen—worked twelve-hour days, seven days a week to conduct traffic analysis, perform reconstruction, and write summaries.

As the days progressed, the signal strength of the Combined Fleet transmissions continued to grow, as the Japanese fleet was moving closer toward the Mariana Islands. The daily increase in signal strength of the IJN *Ashigara*'s 157-kilocycle transmissions revealed to the intercept operators that the ship was gradually nearing Guam. During the exercise, Imperial Japanese Navy ships approached so close to Guam that their radio transmissions boomed though the operators' headsets; the operators could actually hear clicking of telegraphic keys as the Japanese sent their katakana code.

Communication levels reached their peak on June 13. The On-the-Roof Gang operators performed well, copying both plaintext and encrypted messages. For them, the encrypted messages were easier to copy. Chief Kidder had done an incredible job beating the rhythm into their heads: symbol, symbol, symbol, pause; symbol, symbol, symbol, pause. Plaintext messages contained words of varying lengths and had no repeating rhythm, making them more difficult to copy.

Although messages were intercepted at Station BAKER, decryption could only be completed at the Research Desk because the men at Station BAKER didn't have a copy of the Red Book. After the Orange Grand Maneuvers of 1930 concluded, the On-the-Roof Gang prepared a complete report, which included intercept logs, clear and encoded message texts, traffic analysis, and summaries, and forwarded it via officer courier to the Research Desk for decryption and final reconstruction.

To Lieutenant Commander Safford back at the Research Desk, it was plain to see that the Imperial Japanese Navy was conducting a full rehearsal of its plan to invade Manchuria and that the investment in training the On-the-Roof Gang operators was paying off. After the reconstruction of the exercise was complete, Safford prepared a secret memorandum to Secretary of the Navy Charles Adams, dated September 21, 1930, which read, in part:

> The U.S. Navy has at the present moment as complete an ascendancy over the Japanese Navy in the matter of radio intelligence as the British Navy had over the German Navy during the Great War.

Safford's assessment further stated that the Grand Maneuvers of 1930 were of particular importance for several reasons, which included:

1. The Grand Maneuvers were a dress rehearsal for war, proving that Japan was prepared;

2. The mobilization of the Imperial Japanese Navy was conducted in secret, and no other intelligence indicators outside of the radio intelligence group recognized this mobilization;

3. The information obtained by the radio intelligence group was a direct contributor to the formulation of the U.S. Navy's own war plans;

4. The difficulty in tracking Japanese naval ships demonstrated the need to establish direction finding sites throughout the Pacific Ocean; and

5. The successes of the radio intelligence group gave everyone involved confidence in the ability of the On-the-Roof Gang to keep track of the Imperial Japanese Navy during war-time conditions.

All in all, the Grand Maneuvers of 1930 demonstrated to fleet and national leadership that the On-the-Roof Gang could provide a tactical advantage if war ever came. The On-the-Roof Gang had gained its first intelligence victory, and commanders took notice.

CHAPTER 24

CLASS #4

MONDAY, MAY 19, 1930
MAIN NAVY BUILDING, WASHINGTON, DC

After the third class of the On-the-Roof Gang graduated and Chief Kidder departed, Chief Chauncey had the opportunity to get to know Lieutenant Commander Safford and the rest of the Research Desk team. He knew it would be difficult to replace Kidder, but he was confident in his ability to provide excellent radio intelligence training to the selected radiomen.

Originally from Oregon, Dorman Chauncey was a big man. At six foot two, he weighed in at over 200 pounds. He was slightly balding and had a round face, which the round wire-rimmed glasses he wore only accentuated. To a casual observer, Chauncey didn't fit the standard image of a military man. Nonetheless, he was an outstanding radioman, and with the help of Kidder's instruction booklet, he'd picked up the katakana code independently with ease.

For the six weeks between classes, Chauncey familiarized himself with Kidder's curriculum and the work happening at the Research Desk. He and Safford got along well, although their relationship didn't come close to the deep mutual respect Safford and Kidder shared. Chauncey was also less relaxed and confident around the Sailors working at the Research Desk than Kidder had been, so Miss Aggie did her best to make him feel at home.

In early 1930, Safford had solicited nominations from the fleet for the next On-the-Roof Gang class. Since the first three classes had been composed mainly of chiefs and first class petty officers, this time around, Safford had requested radiomen second and third class. After reviewing all the nominations, Safford and Chauncey selected six Sailors for the class, including Chief Petty Officer Leroy "LD" Lankford and First Class Petty Officer Antone "Tony" Novak. The other four were third class petty officers: John Cooke, Albert Geiken, Edward Keesey, and James Pearson.

The students all arrived and checked into Ma Travers's Guest House. On May 19, 1930, Chief Chauncey ran them through the orientation that Kidder had established and then began the class.

Thinking back on the Orange Grand Maneuvers of 1930, Lieutenant Commander Safford had one major concern: the U.S. Navy's largest and most capable intercept site was located on an undefended island that could be captured if war broke out. Indeed, the latest Grand Maneuvers indicated that attacking Guam was part of Japan's war plan, which would put Station BAKER at significant risk.

In an effort to identify locations for intercept operations that were more secure than Station BAKER, Safford sent an exploratory team to Seattle to the Thirteenth Naval District headquarters, which encompassed all of the northwestern states.

Another location of interest to Safford was Bar Harbor, Maine, which seemed to be a good location for intercepting messages when Japan was communicating with European partners. Safford believed a short survey would help determine if the site was suitable for long-term intercept operations. Radioman First Class Clifton Shumaker was sent to Bar Harbor to establish and lead the intercept effort there. Although not formally trained on the roof, Shumaker had demonstrated some ability while working part-time at Station HYPO when he was assigned to Radio Wailupe in Hawaii.

As spring turned into summer, the radiomen of the fourth On-the-Roof Gang class proved themselves capable of learning the katakana code and how to copy it. Chauncey supplemented Kidder's curriculum with stories of his own experience in copying the katakana code. He was amazed at how quickly the students mastered the skill. One student in particular stood out as extremely gifted: Jimmy Pearson challenged himself to have zero errors in anything he copied, whether in English or Japanese, and he was usually up to the task.

During the summer of 1930, as the fourth On-the-Roof Gang class neared its graduation, Chief Chauncey added a wrinkle to the curriculum. He had recorded several cuts of katakana code at different speeds, and he wanted to test the students at their speed and accuracy using both the stick and the Underwood Code Machine. Using three katakana characters per group, he started at fifteen groups per minute (gpm), then increased to twenty gpm, then twenty-five gpm, and finally thirty gpm. All the students scored 100 percent at fifteen gpm. At twenty gpm, all but one scored 100 percent. At twenty-five gpm, three scored 100 percent, but at thirty gpm, only Jimmy Pearson had a perfect score. When McClaran learned of Pearson's performance on the test, he wrote a letter to the Secretary of the Navy regarding the state of radio intelligence operations in the fleet. He included Pearson's tests to prove the efficacy of the rooftop training.

In August, on the final day of class, Chief Chauncey walked into the rooftop classroom with a familiar pile of service records and orders attached.

"Who wants to go to Guam?" he asked the class. Each man raised his hand.

"Anyone for the Philippines?" he teased. "I've got five sets of orders to Station BAKER and one to CAST."

They all wanted to go to Guam. Its reputation as a tropical paradise was alluring, and there was no major naval command on the island. In other words, there weren't as many officers stationed there, and fewer officers meant fewer rules.

Tony Novak tried to get an answer out of Chief Chauncey, "Who's going to the P. I., Chief? Is it me?"

"It ain't you, Novak," Chauncey responded. Petty Officer Novak was relieved to hear it.

"Me?" asked Johnny Cooke.

"Nope."

"Me?" Al Geiken tried.

"No." There were only three operators left, and they all exchanged glances. "It ain't you either, Keesey."

This left Jimmy Pearson and LD Lankford, who both wished they were going to Guam.

"It's me," Pearson chimed in.

Chauncey imperceptibly shook his head up and down. Pearson was going to Station CAST in the Philippines. Chief Lankford breathed a sigh of relief at the knowledge that he'd be joining the rest of his classmates at Station BAKER in Guam.

Wanting to relieve the tension of orders day, Chauncey continued the tradition started by Chief Kidder. He reached behind the podium and said, "And with that, it's now time for choir practice."

CHAPTER 25

VISIT TO STATION CAST

WEDNESDAY, SEPTEMBER 10, 1930

STATION CAST, OLONGAPO, PHILIPPINES

In early September 1930, having finally coordinated a date to visit Station CAST, Lieutenant Wenger and Chief Kidder set out on the USS *Dapdap* for the daylong journey. As they arrived in Subic Bay, Lieutenant Don Rogers, the commander of Radio P. I., greeted Wenger and Kidder on the quarterdeck in the lobby of the broadcasting station. Wenger quickly explained that their purpose for visiting the site was to observe intercept operations and determine if any improvements could be made.

"Chief Kidder and I are here on behalf of the CINCAF," Wenger said.

"Good. Let me show you the operations floor," Rogers replied with a smile. Then he led the pair into the passageway toward the broadcasting room.

As they walked, Kidder purposefully fell behind. Engrossed in their conversation, Wenger and Rogers continued ahead while Kidder took his time checking out the signs posted on doors. Various signs indicated the command duty officer's bunk room, a couple of broom closets, and the head. A large wooden plaque marked the commander's office. Across from the commander's office was a room with a much smaller sign that said: OP-20-G—the designator for the Research Desk in Washington, DC. Radio P. I. obviously used the same designator for the intercept activities in Olongapo. *Bingo!* Kidder thought. *This is what I'm looking for.*

Kidder wondered why Wenger and Rogers were still walking; after all, this was what they'd come to see. He watched them enter another door at the end of the passageway a good fifty feet away. The door to OP-20-G had a cipher lock; Kidder tried it with no luck, so he headed back to the quarterdeck to see if he could talk the petty officer of the watch into letting him into the room. As he made his way through the lobby, a familiar face walked in the front door.

"Hey, Petty Officer Grew!" Kidder exclaimed as his old student approached. Oliver Grew had been assigned to Station CAST following his graduation from the On-the-Roof Gang class the year before.

"Chief Kidder? What are you doing here?" Grew asked with a big smile on his face.

"Just checking the place out. How are things here?"

Petty Officer Grew's face suddenly changed from a big smile to an awkward grin. "Uh . . . just fine, Chief."

"What's wrong?"

"Well, if you're here to check things out, you'll see."

"That bad?"

Grew shrugged.

"OK, well, let's go check out your spaces." The two began to walk down the hall. As they approached the room labeled OP-20-G, Kidder slowed, but Grew kept going. Confused, Kidder stopped. Grew walked a couple extra steps, then turned back to the chief.

"Aren't we going in, Ollie?" Kidder asked.

"Not in there. We haven't been working in there for months."

"Isn't this the intercept room?"

"Sure is, Chief. We work in the broadcast station. We haven't been doing any intercept at all."

"Can we go in, anyway?" Kidder asked.

"Sure." Grew unlocked the door, and they walked in. As Grew flicked on the overhead lights, Kidder was happy to see a first-rate intercept room. It was lined with positions equipped with Underwood Code Machines and several brand-new HF and MF receivers, but they were all powered down. Headphones hung from a hook on the front of each desk.

As he slowly approached the closest position, he noticed a fine layer of dust covering everything. The equipment hadn't been touched in quite a while. Stale cigarette butts remained in some of the tin ashtrays, so they had obviously worked in there at some point. Kidder pursed his lips and shook his head in disbelief.

"Ollie, you have to tell me what's going on."

Grew exhaled nervously, then quietly closed the door.

⚓ ⚓ ⚓

Meanwhile, down in the broadcast operations room, the environment was much livelier. Radiomen sat at positions around the large operations floor. Some typed out messages as they were copied. Others were busily sending out Morse code on telegraphic keys. Two chief yeomen walked back and forth behind the operators, grabbing sheets of paper as the operators held them up. Wenger could see that the station was obviously extremely busy.

Don Broughton and Murrel Wood, two more graduates of Kidder's rooftop training, were working on the operations floor. Along with all the other On-the-Roof Gang operators at Station CAST, Broughton and Wood had been assigned to perform general service radio duties due to staffing shortages across the Asiatic Fleet.

Wenger turned to Rogers, "This is a nice operation you have going here, Don, but where's the intercept happening?"

"Two of your operators are over there," Rogers responded, pointing to Broughton and Wood. "They're two of my best radiomen."

"Then why aren't they performing intercept duties?"

"The CINCAF says the intercept operations are supposed to be happening on a 'not-to-interfere basis.' We've got a manning shortage here, so I need these radiomen on my ops floor." Rogers explained.

"That's ridiculous! CINCAF also said he wanted an intercept site here!"

"It's not ridiculous. It's a matter of priorities."

"These men were trained for four months specifically for intercept duty. They should be doing what they've trained for," Wenger argued.

"They're radiomen. They're doing the work they were trained for. You're not going to convince me to put them back on intercept duty until I get all my billets filled."

Wenger knew he couldn't do anything about Rogers's misuse of the On-the-Roof Gang operators. As the commander of Radio P.I., Rogers could use his people however he saw fit. Wenger recognized there was only one real solution to this problem: he needed to move the On-the-Roof Gang operators to a different location. This would be his immediate recommendation to the Research Desk.

⚓ ⚓ ⚓

Back in the intercept room, Petty Officer Grew told Chief Kidder about the difficulties the graduates of the On-the-Roof Gang were having with Lieutenant Rogers. They were eager to start their intercept work but were not allowed. Instead, they were redirected to perform general service radio duties.

Kidder could sense the frustration in Grew's description of the situation. In an effort to calm Petty Officer Grew, Kidder explained that he would try to fix the issue, but in the meantime, Grew and the other On-the-Roof Gang graduates would have to follow Lieutenant Rogers's orders until something changed.

Kidder and Grew stepped out of the intercept room into the main passageway. As they made their way down the hall, they encountered Rogers and Wenger, who were silently returning from the operations floor. Rogers had the same fake smile on his face as always. Wenger's jaw was clenched, and his cheeks were flushed a vivid red.

Wenger looked at Kidder and growled, "Let's go."

Kidder nodded toward Petty Officer Grew and then turned to match Wenger's stride. They quickly separated themselves from Lieutenant Rogers and continued toward the lobby.

When they were out of earshot, Wenger said to Kidder, "The man's an idiot. It's like talking to a Labrador retriever. When I talk, he smiles and wags his tail, but he has nothing intelligent to say in return."

As they approached the exit, Kidder held back his laughter as best he could. He pushed the door open and looked at Lieutenant Wenger, whose eyebrows were raised. As they exited the building, their laughter echoed throughout the quarterdeck.

CHAPTER 26

CLASS #5

MONDAY, DECEMBER 8, 1930
MAIN NAVY BUILDING, WASHINGTON, DC

The Imperial Japanese Navy had been using the same Operations Code since 1918, so it was only a matter of time before the IJN changed their code in order to protect their communications. Intercept being forwarded to the Research Desk at the beginning of December 1930 indicated that it had finally happened. Agnes could no longer break any of the intercepted code groups using the Red Book. All of the recently intercepted messages contained katakana groups of four characters rather than the previous three-character groups. Unfortunately, this time, the employees of the Research Desk didn't have the luxury of a stolen copy of the codebook, so they would have to manually break the new code. The training and practice they'd had in cryptanalysis were about to be put to the test.

Lieutenant Commander John McClaran had arrived to take over as the officer in charge of the Research Desk. In addition to Agnes, three naval officers, including Lieutenant Junior Grade Thomas Dyer, and several additional yeoman clerks were now working at the Research Desk. Their primary task was to work on breaking the new code, which they referred to as "Code A."

The change of the Imperial Japanese Navy's Operations Code wasn't the only challenge facing the Research Desk in late 1930. McClaran had recently received the report from Lieutenant Wenger and Chief Kidder regarding the situation at Station CAST. It was obvious that McClaran had to move the intercept operations in the Philippines, but the Asiatic Fleet Commander, Admiral Charles McVay, had full authority over the matter. Unfortunately, McVay's own men were telling him that everything was fine, so if McClaran wanted to move Station CAST, he'd be in for a fight.

In his first move to bolster the skills and capacity in China, McClaran decided that the incoming Class #5 of rooftop students to begin in December 1930 would consist solely of radiomen from the U.S. Marine Corps, and the graduates would all be sent to the new Station ABLE at the American Legation in Peiping, China. McClaran made sure to solicit sufficient nominations to have a full class of Marine Corps operators in the class. He didn't want to have to turn away three-quarters of the Marine nominees like Safford had to from the third training class. In addition, McClaran and Chauncey only considered Marines who had already served in China. They assumed it would be less risky to only select men who knew what they were getting into. After careful screening, they settled on six Marines: Sergeant Hubert Thomas, Corporal William Wilder, Private First Class Walter Robertson, and privates Phillip Miller, Maurice Overstreet, and Charles Smith.

As usual, the students stayed at Ma Travers's Guest House. Ma was happy to have the continued rent, and Susie and Stephanie were happy to continue working there. Susie was still saving money for her housecleaning business, but, at the time, because she was a woman, it was illegal for her to open a bank account. When her brother Phillip offered to open a joint account with Susie, she hesitated. Since childhood, she hadn't trusted Phillip, thinking he'd stolen from her all those years ago. But she was in a difficult situation: if she wanted to start a business, she needed a bank account, and her brother offered the only solution. Susie felt she had no choice, so she accepted Phillip's offer, and together, they opened a bank account for her growing savings.

⚓ ⚓ ⚓

In the Main Navy Building, Chief Chauncey modified the instruction for this latest class based on the new katakana groups with four characters. To be safe, he taught the Marines to copy both three- *and* four-character codes. This slowed the instruction a little, and by the end of the term, their speed wasn't as fast as previous classes. However, they were more prepared for any traffic they might encounter in Peiping.

On the day the students received their orders in March 1931, it was no surprise that everyone was assigned to Station ABLE. The only unknown was how they were going to get there. Chief Chauncey broke the news, "First, you're on a train to San Francisco. Then, you'll board the USS *Chaumont* for the trip to Peiping, via Pearl and—"

A collective groan from all the students drowned out the end of Chauncey's sentence.

"What's wrong with the *Chaumont*?" Chauncey asked.

"You really want to know, Chief?" Sergeant Thomas asked.

When Chauncey replied in the affirmative, Thomas looked at his fellow Marines and nodded. In unison, they all recited the Marine Corps mnemonic for *Chaumont*, "Christ, Help All Us Marines On Navy Transports!"

Laughter filled the classroom as Chief Chauncey reached behind the podium. It was time for choir practice.

On-the-Roof Gang Class #5, circa 1931. L-to-R: CPL William Wilder, PVT Charles Smith, CRM Dorman Chauncey (instructor), SGT Hubert Thomas, PVT Phillip Miller, PVT Maurice Overstreet. PFC Walter Robertson missing from photo.

CHAPTER 27

VISIT TO STATION BAKER

MONDAY, FEBRUARY 2, 1931

USS *ISABEL*, CAVITE NAVAL BASE, PHILIPPINES

The USS *Houston*, the brand-new heavy cruiser of the Northampton class, built in Newport News, Virginia specifically to serve as the flagship of the Asiatic Fleet, had just arrived in the Philippines. As the USS *Isabel* motored past the *Houston*, Kidder was amazed by the sight of the two large eight-inch guns on the bow and two Curtiss SOC Seagull scout-observation floatplanes sitting on amidships catapults. He understood the ship could make a speed of almost thirty knots.

Chief Kidder stood on the deck and was filled with awe as the *Isabel* pulled alongside the *Houston*. *What a beauty*, he thought. Although he had not yet set foot on board the *Houston*, he was suddenly filled with a sense of pride to be a member of its crew.

Eager to get on board his new ship as soon as possible, Chief Kidder had his seabag packed, and he waited on the *Isabel*'s deck until the gangplank was lowered. He immediately crossed the pier and rushed over to the USS *Houston*. He hurriedly checked onto the quarterdeck and asked the petty officer of the watch where the radio room was.

"Go forward from here, Chief. It's in Section A, Level 1. You can't miss it."

Despite having never been on board the ship before, Kidder instinctively knew what that meant and how to get there. All ships since the turn of the century had the same compartment marking scheme. All compartments forward of the forward fireroom bulkhead were in Section A. Compartments from the forward fireroom to the after fireroom bulkhead were in Section B. Those from the after fireroom to the engine room bulkhead were in Section C. And all compartments abaft the engine room were in Section D. Levels above the unprotected weather deck were labeled with three-digit numbers, and those below the weather decks were labeled with one-digit numbers. Kidder would find the radio room near the bow of the ship, one level below the weather deck. Wanting to get acquainted with his new home, he meandered around the ship first, marveling at its size and cleanliness, for almost an hour before finding his way to the radio shack.

He rang a buzzer and a Sailor opened the door. The Sailor had bright red hair and freckles, and to the Kidder, he looked like he was about ten years old. Kidder noticed the Sailor's name tag; his last name was Ritchie.

"Chief Kidder?" Ritchie asked.

"That's right, Petty Officer Ritchie," Kidder answered.

"We've been expecting you, Chief."

"Happy to be here, Ritchie. Did you make the trip from Virginia?" he asked the Sailor.

"Yeah."

"How do you like it here, Ritchie?"

"It's just fine, Chief," Ritchie replied excitedly.

Harry noticed that the radio room was the best he'd ever seen on a ship: clean, well-equipped, and spacious. It was no wonder that Petty Officer Ritchie was happy on board USS *Houston*. Kidder thought he would like it as well.

⚓ ⚓ ⚓

Two weeks later, the USS *Houston* slowly slipped into port at Apra Harbor in the village of Piti, about six miles southwest of Agaña on Guam's western shore. There were port facilities in Agaña, but the *Houston* needed deeper water facilities that were only available in Piti. The *Houston* berthed next to the USS *Penguin*, a Lapwing-class minesweeper that was assigned to patrol the waters near Guam and protect the U.S. Navy resources there. Lieutenant Wenger and Chief Kidder disembarked the *Houston* in their khaki uniforms and crossed the *Penguin* in order to go ashore. Once on the pier, they were met by Chief Lyon, who was driving a car that he'd borrowed from Radio Libugon. The car—a haze gray 1928 Dodge Victory Six sedan—had been converted for use by the U.S. Navy. The front doors on both sides of the car had the words U.S. NAVY SHORE PATROL painted in dark blue block letters with a six-digit U.S. Navy registration number below.

Chief Lyon greeted the lieutenant first, then stuck his hand out toward Kidder. "I'm really glad to meet you, Chief Kidder. Everyone here who has been through your rooftop class has nothing but great things to say about you."

Chief Kidder, who'd always been uncomfortable with compliments, replied, "Chief Lyon, you know half their stories aren't true. And you can call me Harry."

"Call me Felix. And if only half are true, I'm still impressed. Let's go see the site."

Chief Lyon got in the driver's seat, while Lieutenant Wenger climbed into the front seat and Kidder got in back. The back had two bench seats that faced each other and could fit six to eight passengers. Kidder wondered how many drunken Sailors the car had transported to the brig. Lyon started the car and drove out of the port facility, turning left toward Agaña.

Wenger and Kidder enjoyed the short drive from Piti to Agaña. Warm, moist air flowed in through the car's open windows. The breeze was sweet with the scent of saltwater spray, tropical flowers, and palm trees. As the *Houston* slowly disappeared in the rearview mirror, the men were treated to some beautiful scenery. On their left, white sandy beaches with the deep blue waters of Agaña Bay and the Pacific Ocean painted a spectacular backdrop. On their right, dense, green jungles reached up into the hills surrounding Piti and Agaña. The jungle seemed to stretch on for miles along Guam's curving spine. In the distance, Kidder noticed the antenna tower of Radio Libugon perched on a hill on Libugon Vista Point.

As Chief Lyon cruised eastward, Agaña appeared before them. About halfway into town, Lyon turned right toward the Plaza de España. He drove along the west side of the square to the far corner where he parked the car. Spanish-style arches and walls made of white stucco and black cast-iron gates ringed the grassy rectangle of the Plaza de España. Dirt paths crisscrossed the grass between several small structures, a baseball field, and a badminton court. The two most impressive buildings on the square faced each other. In the traditional Spanish style, both were made of white stucco with terracotta tile roofs. The historic Governor's Palace stood on one side of the plaza while Dulce Nombre de Maria Cathedral blanketed the other. On the far side of the square, adjacent to the Governor's Palace, was the much less impressive Old Spanish Guardhouse, the site of Station BAKER.

As the men made their way toward the front of the guardhouse, Kidder looked for antennas on the roof, but none were visible. Lyon pulled out a large, silver-colored skeleton key, unlocked the door, and walked in. Wenger and Kidder followed.

As they walked inside, Kidder immediately noticed the absence of a lobby or quarterdeck. The front door led directly to the operations floor, where intercept was underway. At three of the eight positions, Sailors sat with headphones on, intently listening and typing on the

Plaza de España, Agaña, Guam.

Underwood Code Machines before them. Kidder instantly recognized his former student Martin Vandenberg sitting next to another operator that he didn't know. *Clack, clack, clack, clack, pause. Clack, clack, clack, clack, pause.*

It was immediately apparent to both Kidder and Wenger that the conditions at the site were less than ideal. The floor was comprised of simple wooden planks that loosely sat directly on the hard, uneven dirt. Kidder even noticed a puddle in one corner of the room that he assumed got worse during monsoon season. The ceiling was high—maybe twelve feet tall—but sunlight peeked through the space where the ceiling and the tops of the walls intersected. Large areas that clearly used to be windows were bricked up and painted white to match the walls. Although light bulbs hung from the ceiling, the room still seemed dark and dank. In one corner of the room, several derelict receivers were stacked onto a table. The humid air hung heavy in the room, and it had a strange odor to it: a pungent combination of mold, sweat, stale water, and cigarette smoke that reminded Lieutenant Wenger of his high school's locker room.

After allowing his visitors to observe the intercept operation for several minutes, Chief Lyon led them to a passageway on the far side of the room. Several offices lined the passageway, which ended in a door that led to the back of the building. The three entered one of the offices.

"Chief Lyon, the conditions here are deplorable!" Wenger commented. "How can your men stand it?"

"Well, there's more to life than work, sir. Guam is a pretty nice place to live. Besides, we may be working in a dump, but the intercept is pretty good here," Lyon replied. "Except when the big transmitter is singing. When that happens, we just take a break."

"That reminds me, Chief. I'd like to see Radio Libugon while we're here. How can I do that?" Wenger asked.

Chief Lyon reached into his pocket, pulled out the car keys, and tossed them to Lieutenant Wenger. "Take the car. We need to return it to Libugon, anyway. They've got an officer's mess up there. Go see the station, have lunch, and Chief Kidder and I will meet you up there in a couple hours."

"Which way is it?" Wenger asked. "I'm still a little lost on this island."

"It's easy. Stay straight on the road where the car is parked now. The road winds up the hill. You'll run right into the place. You can't miss it."

"Got it. See you soon," Wenger said as he turned and headed out. As he left the room, Chief Joe Goldstein walked in.

Kidder greeted him with a hearty handshake. "Joe! Great to see you again!"

"Hiya, Pappy! What do you think of our little station here?"

"It's a bit run-down, don't you think?"

"Yeah, but the copy . . . you gotta put the cans on and see. The atmospherics are incredible here. We can hear when someone farts in Yokohama Bay!"

They all laughed. "I bet you're right, Joe. But first, I need you to tell me everything you want to see changed." Kidder was glad Wenger was gone. Between the three chief petty officers, they could really get down to business.

Felix and Joe explained the hardships they faced because of the location of the intercept station. Many of the problems concerned the building itself, which was old and dilapidated. Not only were the conditions at the intercept site in Agaña poor, but the men were housed outside of town in rented rooms. And because there was no public transportation available, they had to walk for miles to and from work each day.

But there were positives. Guam was a tropical paradise, and the intercept conditions were excellent. If they only had a newer, more modern facility for their operations, it could be the jewel in the crown of the Research Desk.

After their discussion, the three chiefs made their way onto the ops floor to do some intercept. They sat next to each other in three consecutive positions. When they turned on their receivers, Chief Lyon suggested they tune into 157 kilocycles. Almost immediately, the three simultaneously began to type on their Underwood Code Machines:

```
NU RI SO KO   TE HE WE FU   MI MU WO HI
TU SO MO YU   NI HO RA KU   KE HA TO WI
NA TE MA SA   SE NE TI RO   TA HO WE YU
NA TO SI MA   MA TU KI WE   RA NO MU U
```

The RIP-5s sounded of in unison. *Clack, clack, clack, clack, pause. Clack, clack, clack, clack, pause.*

The code was coming fast—nearly twenty-five groups per minute. Chiefs Goldstein and Lyon were barely keeping up, occasionally missing a character here or there. Kidder, on the other hand, was dominating. He tapped his foot in time with the four-character traffic. Goldstein stopped copying and simply watched Kidder in awe. Lyon stopped next, overwhelmed by the speed of the telegraphic code. To the others, Kidder's ability to copy at top speed seemed effortless. His eyes were closed as he concentrated on the code in his headphones. His fingers moved instinctively with each katakana syllable. He was a maestro on the keyboard; it was truly a sight to behold.

After the sked, Harry seemed to snap out of a trance. They all looked at each other and exhaled. "That was fun!" Harry remarked.

"Pappy, that was amazing! You're unbelievable!" Joe exclaimed. Harry just chuckled to himself.

⚓ ⚓ ⚓

Later that evening, back on board the USS *Houston*, Lieutenant Wenger invited Chief Kidder to his stateroom. He had some news that he wanted to deliver to the chief in private. Kidder was worried that something was wrong with Susie because he hadn't heard from her in over a year since his transfer to the *Houston*.

"Chief, while I was up at Radio Libugon, I read the *Houston*'s messages. I have some bad news for you," Wenger began. "Sit down, Harry."

Kidder sat and braced himself for the worst. "Yes, sir?"

"Your parents have both passed away." Kidder felt immediate relief that Susie was all right, but then guilt immediately followed. He hadn't talked to his parents in over twenty years. Certainly, he should have tried to reach out at some point. But the timing was never right, and they'd made it clear that they didn't want to hear from him. For Kidder, it had been easier for him to simply put them out of his mind.

"Are you OK, Harry?"

"I'm OK, sir." He didn't know what else to say. He was shocked and saddened, but he didn't feel any real loss. The reality was, he'd lost them years ago. "Don't worry about me, sir."

"All right, Chief. Just tell me if you need anything."

"Yes, sir." Kidder headed back to the Goat Locker.

CHAPTER 28

CLASS #6

MONDAY, AUGUST 10, 1931
MAIN NAVY BUILDING, WASHINGTON, DC

By early August, Wenger and Kidder's report on the conditions at Station BAKER reached John McClaran, now a full commander, who was becoming distressed with all the problems at the intercept sites in the Asiatic Fleet's jurisdiction. Commanders in the Asiatic Fleet were assigning the worst available spaces to intercept operations; they basically paid no attention to the requirements of such sites. Commander McClaran was surprised at the hypocrisy of it all and couldn't square it away in his mind. On the one hand, Asiatic Fleet commanders were clamoring for the intelligence the On-the-Roof Gang graduates were producing. But on the other hand, they weren't willing to invest in dedicated personnel or space for them to work.

Needless to say, McClaran was not the least bit surprised when he heard that Japan had invaded Manchuria. On September 18, 1931, in a covert operation near Mukden, Manchuria, Japanese Army officers detonated dynamite near the Japanese-owned South Manchurian Railway. The Japanese then blamed Chinese dissidents for the act, using it as a pretense for an invasion of Manchuria, which quickly led to a full-scale occupation. While the Japanese invasion was not good news, it did at least validate one of the primary results of the analysis of the 1930 Grand Maneuvers: for the first time in history, radio intelligence had predicted real-world events over a year in advance.

The Japanese invasion of Manchuria solidified McClaran's resolve that he needed to enhance intercept operations in China. By adding to the ranks of the Marine intercept operations in Peiping, the sixth installment of On-the-Roof Gang students would prepare to do just that. Six Marines were identified for the training, but by the time it was scheduled to start in August 1931, only three were still available. Joel Easter, Carl Gustaveson, and John Hibbard were all corporals at the time.

Just before class began, McClaran selected Radioman First Class Clifton Shumaker—a general service radioman who'd been experimenting with high frequency direction finding (HFDF) in Bar Harbor, Maine—to fill one of the vacant slots and attend the training.

The class performed well, learning how to copy both three- and four-character katakana traffic. After graduation in December 1931, the three Marines were ordered to Station ABLE in Peiping, while Petty Officer Shumaker was sent to Station HYPO in Hawaii.

Over at the Research Desk, the entire team was consumed with trying to break the new "Code A" being used by the Imperial Japanese Navy. Agnes Meyer Driscoll devoted herself to the task full time, and Lieutenant Commander Safford helped when he wasn't otherwise occupied. Lieutenant Junior Grade Thomas Dyer was adept at pouring through large amounts of intercept and finding patterns, repeats, and mistakes that the Japanese made as they encrypted their messages. He was able to identify character groups that appeared in traffic most often, frequent group combinations, and other statistical data. The Japanese radio operators often fumbled the code and even occasionally passed something in the clear after attempting to send it in code. Eventually, this led to a break in the code, which Agnes had started referring to as the Blue Book, again named for the color of the binder in which it was stored.

It was Agnes, of course, who got the initial break. She worked out that the Blue Book code used a transposition cipher in which the katakana characters were shuffled into a different order known only to the users of the code. For instance, if the code encrypted a message by reversing the letters of each word, but not the order in which the words are written "a simple example" would become "a elpmis elpmaxe." She also figured out that a two-character differential was used to encipher the four-character katakana groups. Once this was established, it was only a matter of receiving enough intercepted four-character traffic to recover all the code groups.

They got to work.

CHAPTER 29

VISIT TO STATION HYPO

THURSDAY, JANUARY 28, 1932
USS *HOUSTON*, AT SEA IN THE PACIFIC OCEAN

Station HYPO was next on the inspection list for Lieutenant Wenger and Chief Kidder. USS *Houston* steamed toward Hawaii, scheduled to observe an exercise aimed at testing the U.S. Pacific Fleet's defense of the Hawaiian Islands—an exercise dubbed Fleet Problem XIII—before pulling into Pearl Harbor.

Rear Admiral Harry Yarnell—who, in 1927, had taken command of the aircraft carrier USS *Saratoga*—commanded the attacking force for the exercise. Yarnell had made quite a name for himself developing tactics for a new class of ships known as aircraft carriers. At the time, aircraft carriers were classified as "fleet scouting elements," and the onboard aircraft were used primarily for observation purposes only. Before Yarnell changed the way the U.S. Navy employed them, aircraft carriers were not valued as legitimate war-fighting ships and were considered expendable.

Throughout his career, Yarnell consistently maintained that Japan had repeatedly engaged in wartime operations by attacking China prior to a declaration of war. Accordingly, he designed an exercise for Fleet Problem XIII during which aircraft and their carriers would be used to simulate a surprise invasion of Pearl Harbor.

Prior to the exercise, defenders in Pearl Harbor had anticipated that Yarnell would attack with his battleships. Instead, he left his battleships in San Diego and steamed the aircraft carriers USS *Saratoga* and USS *Lexington* to a point roughly 200 miles north-northeast of Hawaii.

As the USS *Houston* lingered at a safe distance from the exercise participants, Wenger and Kidder had a bird's-eye view of the exercise. At dawn on Sunday, February 7, Yarnell launched his attack with a force of 152 fighters, bombers, and torpedo bombers from the two carriers. Approaching from the south, Yarnell's attack force flew directly for Oahu and banked east to follow the coastline around the island toward Pearl Harbor, first hitting the airfields and then the ships docked along Battleship Row. Kidder, who was in the *Houston*'s radio shack monitoring the Pacific Fleet nets, listened for communications coordinating the defense of Pearl Harbor. Those communications never came.

The attacking force achieved total surprise. The aircraft scored multiple hits on airfields and battleships, dropping sacks of white flour to simulate bombs. The airfields were put completely out of commission, having been hit by multiple bags of flour. Not a single plane on the ground at Pearl Harbor got airborne during the mock attack. The battleships all received similar treatment from the attacking force. It was clear that at least half of them would have been sunk, and the remainder would've received major damage.

On board the USS *Houston*, Chief Kidder continued to monitor for any signs of defensive activity from the U.S. Pacific Fleet. Eventually, he gave up. The attacking force had obviously won the exercise.

The local Hawaiian newspapers and news radio programs gave the exercise in-depth coverage, all of which was mirrored in the *New*

York Times. Japanese diplomats at the consulate in Honolulu took note and reported back to their national leadership.

Controversy ensued when, under pressure from Pacific Fleet commanders, the referees of the exercise changed their initial ruling and declared the defensive side the victors of the mock battle. In their updated ruling, the referees stated that no nation with the power to strike so far from home would attack the United States without a declaration of war. Even if a nation did, no decent enemy would attack so early on a Sunday morning. Admiral Yarnell was incredulous. However, he had no choice but to accept the ruling of the exercise's referees. Lieutenant Wenger and Chief Kidder were equally as baffled—not necessarily by the official result, but that the defenses on Hawaii were so unable to mount any kind of resistance.

After the exercise, the USS *Saratoga* and USS *Lexington* turned around and headed back to San Diego. The USS *Houston* pulled into Pearl Harbor early the next morning for its scheduled visit. As the *Houston* passed by the occupied piers on her way to her berthing assignment, Wenger and Kidder stood on the deck and saw Sailors using fire hoses to wash the flour off their ships.

Petty Officer Clifton Shumaker greeted Wenger and Kidder as they disembarked the *Houston*. Shumaker had recently been assigned to Station HYPO following his graduation from the On-the-Roof Gang training. He was the only rooftop-trained intercept operator permanently assigned to Station HYPO, but leaders at Radio Wailupe had gotten better at providing Station HYPO with part-time general service radiomen to help with intercept duties.

"Hi, Lieutenant Wenger . . . Chief Kidder. I'm Petty Officer Shumaker. We'll need to walk off the pier. After the training exercise yesterday, they're not letting anyone drive on. They've really tightened things up. I'm parked just at the end of the pier, though. It's not far."

As they began to walk, Kidder asked, "Did you know about the exercise beforehand?"

"We knew there would be an exercise, but no one realized it would happen yesterday morning. I was in the barracks at Wailupe when it went down. I thought it was strange to hear so many planes that early on a Sunday morning," he said.

Kidder had been to Hawaii before, but he'd never ventured beyond Pearl Harbor. Radio Wailupe was famous in the fleet for its scenic location, and since Station HYPO was co-located, Kidder was legitimately excited to visit.

The three climbed into the car Shumaker had borrowed from Radio Wailupe. Similar to the car they'd been transported in back in Guam, this was a haze gray 1930 Willys-Knight converted for use by the Navy. Shumaker put the car in gear, and they were on their way.

Pearl Harbor was a large naval base, so it took a few minutes before they were past the industrial and populated areas and traveling along the coastal road. Once they did, Shumaker steered the car east toward Honolulu. Just as they had been in Guam, the windows of the car were down, so the men all enjoyed the fresh breeze as they drove along the coastline.

"It's breathtaking here, Shumaker," Kidder remarked.

"Yeah, we'll take the scenic road along the coast. I want you to see Diamond Head up close."

About midway through the roughly fifteen-mile drive, they reached Honolulu. After they passed the white sand beaches of Waikiki, the car approached Diamond Head, an imposing yet extinct volcanic cone that had once exploded, leaving a ring-shaped ridge with a deep crater within.

Shumaker explained, "Fort Ruger is there. I hear the Army has tunnels deep inside the mountain, but I've never been up there to check it out," he said with a shrug. Fort Ruger was the first U.S. military installation on the island of Oahu, and big Army guns could be seen sticking up and out from the rim of the crater. "Who knows?"

As they passed south of Diamond Head on the coastal road, the cliffs of the extinct volcano towered over them on the left side of the car. Waves crashed along the beaches on the right.

"Just wait 'til you see this view," Shumaker teased. As Diamond Head disappeared in the distance behind them and the road curved northeast toward Wailupe, a jungle-covered mountain range that stretched all the way to the beaches appeared before them. It truly was a breathtaking sight.

As Shumaker continued driving northeast, an antenna tower came into view right along the shoreline. As they approached, they could see that the tower was actually built out over the water on a man-made pier. It was adjacent to a building that stood on the small Wailupe Peninsula.

Kidder couldn't take his eyes off the immense pier with the tower at the end. "Looks like a great place to work," he gushed.

"That's not it, Chief," Shumaker corrected, as he steered the car onto the peninsula just beyond the pier.

Confused, Kidder asked, "Where are you going?"

"That's HYPO, right there," Shumaker said, pointing toward a row of small shacks in front of them. It was then that Kidder remembered Station HYPO wasn't located in the same building as Radio Wailupe; it was only close by.

Station HYPO was one of six small buildings on the peninsula across from Radio Wailupe. Kidder couldn't tell what the other buildings were used for, but it was obvious that Station HYPO had some affiliation with radio work. Several small antennas protruded from the roof of building ten. Long dipole antennas that reached across several of the small buildings were also connected to the roof of Station HYPO.

"Good thing we're in Hawaii and not China," Kidder said, only half joking as he pointed toward the roof. "You're not fooling anybody with that setup."

Shumaker agreed and led them toward the door. Just like at Station BAKER, the entrance led directly to the operations floor, which was crammed with equipment. However, no one was working at any of the positions, which were all powered down.

"Where is everyone?" Kidder asked.

"Oh, we don't work day shifts here, Chief," Shumaker said. "We never get any copy at all during the day. Things start to pick up at around 1900 hours."

Lieutenant Wenger excused himself, saying he wanted to visit Radio Wailupe. As he left, Kidder suggested that he and Shumaker listen to some traffic. "What do you say we chase some ditty-bops?" Kidder asked, using radioman slang for Morse code.

Kidder and Shumaker sat side by side, powered up the receivers, and waited for the vacuum tubes to heat up. Kidder could hear the familiar hum, but it was his sense of smell that gave him the strongest sensation. He closed his eyes and leaned toward the receivers, smelling the heat coming off the tubes as they began to glow inside the metal case of the radios.

Kidder put on headphones, but Shumaker did not. Kidder tuned to frequencies he knew would have traffic. At 157 kilocycles, he heard nothing but static. At 39 kilocycles, nothing. Tuning up to the HF band, he tried 5160 kilocycles. Nothing. Surely 11980 kilocycles would be active. He tuned there, but he still heard nothing but static.

"I told you, Chief. We won't hear anything until the swing shift. It's no use."

"You're right, Shumaker, I guess I was just hoping to get some copy time while we were here."

"Stick around, Chief. It'll heat up tonight. I promise." After all, Shumaker wanted to see the incomparable Harry Kidder in action.

"I wish I could, but the *Houston* pulls out at 1700 hours tonight. Gotta be back on the ship by 1600."

"That's too bad, Chief," Shumaker said, legitimately disappointed.

"It's OK, Shumaker, I'll tune in on board the *Houston*. We've got a pretty good setup there too."

The two walked over to Radio Wailupe and collected Lieutenant Wenger before they headed back toward Pearl Harbor. On the drive back, Shumaker took the quicker route north of Diamond Head, which gave Wenger and Kidder a different view of the tremendous volcanic crater.

From the front passenger seat, Wenger turned to Kidder and said, "I have some news for you, Chief."

"Not that again, sir."

"Good news this time.... At least, I think you'll think it's good news."

"Fire away, sir."

"Seems you've got orders," Wenger said with a smile.

Kidder's ears perked up. "Really?"

"Really," Wenger confirmed. "I saw them on the read board at Radio Wailupe. You're going back to DC to teach again!"

Kidder grinned from ear to ear. "When do I leave, sir?"

"Settle down, Chief. I know you're anxious to return to that lady of yours, but you have to finish your two years on the *Houston*. You'll head back this summer."

All Harry could think about was Susie. He would finally be able to see her again. Overwhelmed with joy, he couldn't wait to write to her to let her know.

The car bypassed Waikiki Beach as it sped through Honolulu, and before long the men arrived back at Pearl Harbor. The site of so many battleships lined up in a row impressed Kidder. It was an imposing display of power, but the weekend's exercise certainly exposed the danger of having them all docked in the same place. After seeing flour splattered all over the battleships, Kidder was sure the Pacific Fleet would shore up its defenses around Pearl Harbor.

CHAPTER 30

CLASSES #7 AND #8

MONDAY, FEBRUARY 1, 1932
MAIN NAVY BUILDING, WASHINGTON, DC

By the beginning of February, the results from the exploratory teams that Laurance Safford had sent to the northwestern United States finally filtered back to the Research Desk. After surveys from multiple locations and discussions with planning officers, the Thirteenth Naval District reported that there were several acceptable locations for an intercept site in the northwest. McClaran needed an experienced chief radioman to select from the two sites and lead the establishment of the new intercept station there. He asked Chief Chauncey if he'd be willing to do it. Chauncey jumped at the opportunity; after all, Chauncey was a native of the Pacific Northwest, and Oregon was his home state.

⚓ ⚓ ⚓

As part of his earlier report to the Research Desk on Station BAKER, Chief Kidder included a personal account of the morale and abilities of each of the enlisted men. He tried to be as objective possible, setting aside the respect and admiration he felt for each of the operators he had trained on the roof. His assessment was that all of the operators were performing adequately, but there were a few standouts. Petty Officers Vandenberg and Novak were extremely skilled and could be trusted with independent duties, if needed. Based on their skills and personable dispositions, he also recommended Chief Malcolm Lyon and Petty Officer Guy Billehus as good candidates to someday teach the rooftop training.

Aware of the promise Laurance Safford had made to Chief Kidder, Commander McClaran ordered him back to DC to teach. However, Kidder wouldn't be arriving until August. Since Chauncey was leaving for his new assignment in the Pacific Northwest in February, McClaran needed someone to teach at least one class in the interim. His solution was to order Chief Lyon, who had gained experience and skills at Stations ABLE and BAKER, to DC for a temporary six-month assignment. Because Chief Lyon had only recently been at Station BAKER for a year, he wasn't eligible for Permanent Change of Station (PCS) orders for another two years. However, McClaran could send him to Washington, DC for a temporary assignment for six months. After that, Lyon would return to Station BAKER.

McClaran, after reading the report on intercept operations at Station HYPO, decided Hawaii needed more full-time operators. As such, he immediately ordered several experienced On-the-Roof Gang operators, including chiefs Billehus and Vandenberg and Petty Officer Coonce, to Station HYPO.

Chief Lyon arrived in Washington, DC in early February and familiarized himself with the On-the-Roof Gang curriculum and the classroom. He was fully prepared to teach a full classroom, but CINCAF was nominating fewer and fewer radiomen for the training. Of those nominated, even fewer met the performance and integrity standards required. They were Jesse Bryan Byrd and Walter "Sandy" McGregor, both chief radiomen, and Radioman First Class Fred Freeman.

Chief Byrd, whose friends and family called him by his middle name, was the first married Sailor selected for the rooftop training. When he transferred to DC for training, his wife and their four children remained in Charleston, South Carolina. To outsiders, Bryan seemed quiet and aloof. The truth was that his favorite pastime was reading letters from his family and writing back to them. This took most of his free time, which left little opportunity to pal around with his shipmates.

As usual, the students stayed at Ma Travers's Guest House, but to the women working there, things had changed. Since Harry had left, reservations for rooms and the payment of rent were formalities that the Navy carried out via U.S. mail. They all missed Harry's personal involvement. Susie was accumulating letters from Harry, although had yet to respond to a single one. She just couldn't seem to put pen to paper. She didn't know what to say.

After completing their formal intercept training on Friday, April 28, Chief Byrd and Petty Officer Freeman were ordered to Station CAST in the Philippines, and Chief McGregor went to Station BAKER in Guam as a replacement for Chief Billehus.

Since the breaking of the Blue Book code the year before, the Research Desk was busily decrypting months of intercepted messages that had been sent in from the fleet. It wasn't lost on anyone in the Research Desk that this underscored a big problem: between the time the Imperial Japanese Navy ceased using the Red Book code and the Research Desk broke the new one, the U.S. Navy's radio intelligence effort was clueless to enemy activity. If this happened again during wartime, it could be disastrous. Luckily, at least this time nothing major happened directly after the Red Book code was changed.

The Research Desk only had Chief Lyon for six months, so his next class began immediately after the previous one ended. On Monday, May 2, eight radiomen reported to the Main Navy Building for the eighth offering of On-the-Roof Gang training.

McClaran decided he needed to augment each of the intercept sites. Upon graduation, Sidney Burnett, Carl Congdon, and Victor Long went to Station HYPO. Petty Officers Prescott Currier, John Roop, and Richard Willis were sent to Station CAST. Radioman Third Class Joseph "Mac" McConnel went to Station BAKER, and Petty Officer R. P. Clifford went to the Thirteenth Naval District to help establish a new intercept site after a location was selected based on Chief Chauncey's recommendation.

Chief Kidder arrived just as the men shipped off to their new locales, and Commander McClaran was excited to finally meet the famous Pappy.

He hoped Kidder lived up to his reputation

CHAPTER 31

STATION S

WEDNESDAY, JULY 6, 1932
FORT STEVENS, ASTORIA, OREGON

Chief Dorman Chauncey had spent the past several months in the Thirteenth Naval District in Seattle, Washington, and had narrowed his search to two possible locations for a new intercept station in the northwestern United States—Bainbridge Island, Washington and Astoria, Oregon. In the end, the choice would be an easy one.

Bainbridge Island, despite superior intercept conditions, was an unacceptable location because the U.S. Army still used it as an active coastal defense site. Its mission was to guard military facilities in Puget Sound with its three-, five-, and eight-inch guns standing at the ready. Gunnery activity, regardless of the caliber, would be detrimental to any attempt at radio intercept.

Like Bainbridge Island, Fort Stevens—which was located on the southern shore of the mouth of the Columbia River just west of Astoria, Oregon—was also an old coastal defense site. But unlike Bainbridge Island, the U.S. Army had officially closed Fort Stevens and turned it over to the U.S. Navy in 1917. When the Army moved out, the Thirteenth Naval District had decided to establish a radio

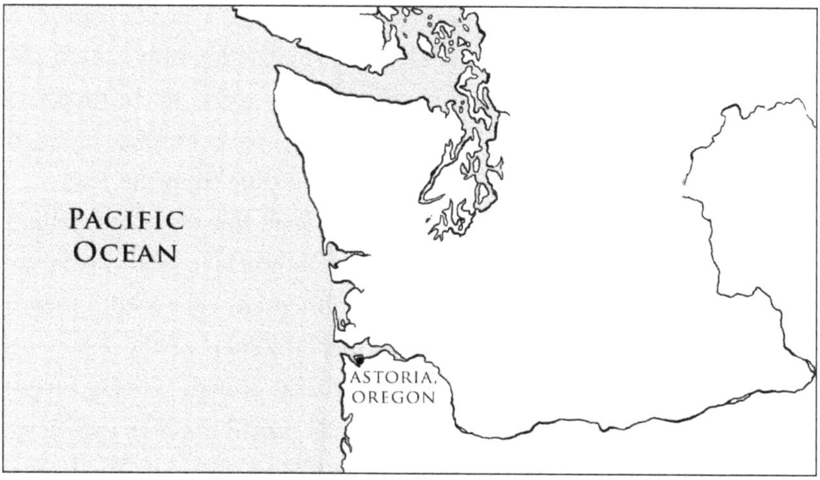

station there with the call sign NUZ. Although Chauncey's investigation revealed that intercept from this location wouldn't be optimal, there was plenty of room to build a new intercept site to co-locate with the Navy radio station, and there was no chance of gunnery operations interfering.

Toward the end of the Civil War, the U.S. Army built Fort Stevens, which was named for General Isaac Stevens, a former governor of the Washington Territory. The fort's purpose was to protect against an invasion from Canada should the British join the Civil War on the side of the Confederacy. By the time Chauncey visited, it was mostly abandoned with several brick buildings standing vacant. The only active tenant of the site was the U.S. Naval Radio Station.

Fort Stevens was well known in U.S. military lore for a shipwreck that occurred there—still visible at low tide. Built in 1890 for the British shipping firm Iredale & Porter, the *Peter Iredale* was a four-masted ship made of iron and steel. The *Iredale* left Salina Cruz, in southern Mexico, on September 26, 1906. The ship was en route to Portland, Oregon, where it was scheduled to pick up a cargo of wheat for transport to the United Kingdom. At the mouth of the Columbia

River in the early morning hours of October 25, a heavy southeast gale blew the ship aground at Clatsop Beach. The ship struck the shore so hard that on impact, three of its masts broke off. In the years since, the elements had slowly been breaking apart the ship. Even so, the wreck of the *Peter Iredale* was still quite visible from the fort.

Aside from the absence of heavy artillery, the most compelling argument for choosing Fort Stevens over Bainbridge Island was the presence of an existing Navy radio station there. The radio station would provide a cover story for why the radiomen of the Research Desk were on the base. The station would also provide a ready supply of electronic equipment, which would help curtail maintenance costs for the new intercept site. In July, Chief Chauncey made his recommendation for Astoria via official letter to the Research Desk, and the district communications officer concurred.

When choosing a designator for the new intercept site, the Research Desk had to decide which naming convention to follow. The first three intercept sites were named for the first three letters of the alphabet—ABLE, BAKER, and CAST. For Station HYPO, the intercept site at Wailupe, the first letter of the word *Hawaii* was used. They couldn't use the first letter of Astoria because Station ABLE already started with the letter *A*. Commander McClaran decided to designate the site Station S for Stevens.

Chief Chauncey, having completed the task of finding the location of the new intercept site, decided to retire from the Navy. As his replacement, the Research Desk ordered Truett Lusk—who'd recently been promoted to chief radioman—to PCS from Guam to Astoria. Petty Officer Clifford, a recent On-the-Roof Gang graduate and waiting for official word while assigned to the 13th Naval District in Seattle, was also assigned to Station S.

Commander McClaran felt relieved that the Navy now had another intercept site on U.S. soil. After all, if the United States ever went to war with Japan, Station S would be less susceptible to attack.

CHAPTER 32

PAPPY'S RETURN

SATURDAY, AUGUST 13, 1932
UNION STATION, WASHINGTON, DC

Harry Kidder stepped off the USS *Houston* when it pulled into port at San Diego for supplies and some minor upkeep. A little over two weeks later, his cross-country journey was nearing its end as his train pulled into Union Station in Washington, DC, on August 13.

As soon as the train stopped, he hefted his seabag over his shoulder and immediately set out for Ma Travers's Guest House. He'd slept poorly on the train, so he was exhausted, and the three-mile walk seemed daunting to him. Still, he couldn't wait another minute. Susie hadn't written once in the entire time he was gone, and his imagination was running wild.

As he walked, the adrenaline from arriving in DC started to wear off, and his legs became heavy with exhaustion. Each step was an effort, but the image of Susie's face kept him trudging forward, hoping for the best while fearing the worst. After what seemed like an hour, he walked in the front door of the guesthouse and dropped his seabag on the floor.

He first saw Ma, who was dusting knickknacks in the front room. She ran to Harry and hugged him. "Well, aren't you a sight for sore eyes!" she exclaimed. "Welcome home, Harry!"

"It's really nice to see you, Ma. I missed this place," he said.

"Susie's gonna be really happy to see you."

"I hope so, Ma. Where is she?" he asked.

"She's around here somewhere. I asked her to clean the floors, so she might be anywhere. Go find her."

Harry checked the kitchen and the dining room, but Susie wasn't there. He bounded up the stairs, loud enough that Susie heard his footsteps and entered the hallway to see what the ruckus was.

"Harry!" She moved in his direction, perhaps to hug him, but he caught her arms at the elbows to stop her.

"Hi, Susie," he said flatly.

She dropped her arms to her sides. "You're back, Harry. I missed you." she said, but her words rang hollow in Harry's ears.

"You did? Then why didn't you write?"

"I tried, Harry. I really did."

"I kept waiting for a letter from you."

"I was just . . . staying busy, Harry . . . trying to save money."

"I was busy, too, but I found the time to write to you—a lot."

"I'm sorry, Harry. I'm just no good at writing."

"I wrote over and over again. I asked you to write me back . . . I begged you to!"

"I know. I'm really sorry, Harry . . ." her words trailed off.

He saw by the tears welling in her eyes that he was being too harsh, and he didn't want to push her away. He only wished Susie had a better reason for not writing. And he wished she seemed more excited to see him. But his exhaustion was taking over, and he didn't have the energy for a longer conversation. "OK," he said. "It doesn't matter. It's over now. I'm back, and I've missed you."

They finally greeted each other warmly, hugging for several

moments. To Harry, it still felt forced, as if Susie would've rather been somewhere else.

Harry pulled her closer. "And I've got some news."

"More news? Isn't this enough?" she asked.

Harry was again disappointed in her reaction but was too tired to debate. Their embrace relaxed him from head to toe, and he began to notice his extreme fatigue. The walk from Union Station had taken every last ounce of his energy. He decided that he wanted to be more alert when he had the next discussion with her. "You're right. It can wait. I'm dead on my feet. Do you think Ma will let me have a room for the night?"

"Why not? The Navy's paying for them anyway." She led him to the closest room, and he sat on the bed. "Get some sleep. I'll see you in the morning." She kissed him on the forehead.

Harry took off his shoes and shirt and lay down on the bed. He was asleep before his head hit the pillow. Susie watched him for a few moments before she tiptoed out of the room and turned out the light.

CHAPTER 33

CLASS #9

SUNDAY, AUGUST 14, 1932
MA TRAVERS'S GUEST HOUSE, WASHINGTON, DC

After twelve solid hours of sleep, Harry awoke at Ma Travers's Guest House a happy man. He could smell bacon cooking downstairs, and he noticed the sun shining and the birds chirping. He sprang out of bed for what he hoped would be an even happier day than the previous one. He went downstairs and saw Susie in the kitchen.

"Good morning, Harry. I hope I didn't wake you," she said, smiling. He leaned in to kiss her, but she turned her head. He kissed her on the cheek.

Again, Harry wished for a more loving response from Susie. It seemed to him that she was still miles away, not in the same room. He desperately wanted to be closer to her. "It smells great down here," he said as he took a seat at the table.

For Harry, the time and distance of their separation only made his love for Susie grow stronger. But he was starting to fear it had worked in the opposite direction for Susie. It seemed as if Susie was just going through the motions instead of being overjoyed at his return. Because of his inexperience with women, he didn't have anything to compare her reaction to, so he prayed they simply needed to get to know each other again.

She poured him a cup of coffee and said, "Ma gave me the day off so we can spend some time together." She brought two dishes of scrambled eggs and bacon to the table and sat across from Harry.

Before he touched his food, Harry set aside his concerns and said, "I need to tell you something, Susie."

"Is this what you were going to tell me last night?"

"Yeah."

"OK, go ahead."

"I don't know how to say this properly," he said, searching for the right words. "My parents passed way." He heard himself say the words out loud, and it was jarring even to himself.

"Oh, I'm so sorry, Harry!"

He shook his head. "It's OK," he said as he closed his eyes to hide the shame he was feeling. "We weren't close. Besides, that's not really what I wanted to tell you."

"What then?" she asked.

Harry took a sip of coffee to settle his nerves. "I inherited everything from them," he explained. "As soon as it clears probate, I'm going to sell their house and the farm. I should get several thousand dollars."

"That's nice, Harry. I'm happy for you." Again, Harry was surprised at her nonchalance; he would have to connect the dots for her.

"Susie, that money is for *us*. I want you to marry me. You can start your business."

As if waking from a deep sleep herself, Susie's face lit up—the message was received.

"What?! Really?" She got up and hugged and kissed Harry. She whispered to him, "Yes, I'll marry you, Harry! You've made me so happy!"

Harry was relieved, having finally gotten the emotional response he'd been expecting from Susie, hugging for several minutes before

Susie sat back down. He couldn't remember ever being so happy, but he couldn't shake the idea that Susie was just going through the motions.

They spent the rest of the day together walking around town before going back to Ma's guesthouse, where Harry would stay until he found an apartment.

"Why do you need an apartment?" Susie asked. "The Navy is paying for all Ma's rooms, so why don't you just stay here? We could spend more time together."

"I don't know if the personnel department will go for it."

"Will you check? I'd love for you to be around more."

"Of course, I'll check. It's a great idea," he said.

⚓ ⚓ ⚓

On Monday morning, Harry checked in at the quarterdeck in the Main Navy Building and immediately went to the administrative office. The pay clerks approved his request to live at Ma Travers's place because it would save the Navy from having to pay Kidder a housing allowance. Kidder knew this would make Susie happy.

After settling into his new room at Ma Travers's place, Harry was ready to get back to work. The Marine Corps had nominated a dozen radiomen for the next On-the-Roof Gang class, but the Research Desk only approved two of them: Sergeant Richard Hardisty and Private First Class Virgil Morgan. The Marines were still nominating radiomen based solely on their transfer dates instead of conducting appropriate screening for the best candidates for intercept training. At the last minute, McClaran added U.S. Navy Radioman Second Class William Knefley, from the First Naval District in Bar Harbor, Maine, to the class as well.

In late August, Chief Kidder returned to the classroom and fell right back into his routine. But after four years of use, the rooftop classroom was showing some signs of wear. Stains from rainwater leaking into the classroom discolored the paint in each of the four corners. The wooden windowsills were starting to warp from the rain, heat, and cold of the DC weather. Floorboards were beginning to separate from each other. The place needed an overhaul, and Harry resolved to see to it in between classes.

This group was the smallest number of students Kidder had ever taught on the roof, which made for excellent learning conditions. He was able to give each of them personal attention, which reflected in their performance. The students excelled and were listening to live traffic by December.

For the first time in three years, Ma put on a Christmas feast for her guests. Although it was a smaller event than in years past, Harry reveled in the Christmas spirit and Susie's company. Harry's students felt as if they were at a family meal and Harry was the patriarch.

After the holidays, class resumed with Harry accelerating the pace of his instruction because of the smaller class size. When the students graduated in early February 1933, the Marines were sent to Station ABLE in Peiping, and Petty Officer Knefley was ordered to Station HYPO in Hawaii.

⚓ ⚓ ⚓

Harry continued to wait for his parents' estate to clear probate, and Susie asked him about it often. He was frustrated, partly because probate was taking so long and partly because of Susie's continual questions about it.

"It will happen when it happens, Susie," he'd tell her each time she asked.

Meanwhile, in the Research Desk, Commander John McClaran had a problem. He had contracted with the Naval Research Laboratory located in the Bellevue area of Washington, DC, to develop radio technology that could be used for intercept operations at sea.

The Naval Research Laboratory was ready to deliver, but McClaran had no way to test the new technology. Because of the Great Depression, budget concerns in the Navy meant that ships were spending less time at sea.

Times were tough across the nation, and the U.S. Navy was not immune. As a result of the economic downturn, fuel was more expensive, which kept Navy ships stationary longer. Ships in port were less expensive than ships burning fuel at sea.

McClaran needed to find a way to test radio intercept technology at sea, and he found the answer to his predicament in the President Steamship Lines. The U.S. Weather Bureau, seeking to better understand the weather over the Pacific Ocean to improve forecasting, had struck a deal with President Steamship Lines, which lumberman Robert Dollar had founded at the turn of the century. Dollar had established a fleet of schooners to carry lumber from his mills in Northern California and Oregon to cities and railheads in Southern and Central California. Dollar's fleet grew and expanded its services, and by 1930 was carrying passengers, cargo, and mail across the Pacific Ocean between the United States, China, and Japan. The deal with Dollar's company allowed the Weather Bureau to place civilian observers on ships traveling to the Far East.

The cruise company was happy to help the Weather Bureau, but only if the Navy would provide radiomen that would warn if their ships were sailing into danger in the Far East, where Japan and China had repeated skirmishes. Commander McClaran immediately agreed and planned to send On-the-Roof Gang operators to the passenger ships so they could continue experimenting with intercept while at sea, even when U.S. Navy ships were staying in port. The radiomen were to be treated as first-class passengers on board the ships, which would cost the ONI's slush fund thirty dollars per month per man for transportation and subsistence. Four On-the-Roof Gang alumni were selected for the assignment: Martin "Van" Vandenberg from the inaugural class and Johnny Cooke, Tony Novak, and Jimmy Pearson from the fourth class.

Electronics engineers from the Naval Research Laboratory in Bellevue briefed the four operators on a new receiver developed specifically for this assignment. The receivers, which were small enough to fit inside a suitcase, were designed for frequencies between 40 kilocycles and 480 kilocycles. The operators also received training on how to conceal their receivers and antennas to maintain security in foreign ports such as Shanghai, Hong Kong, Manila, and Kobe, Japan.

One by one, the men were sent to the West Coast to board ships as they arrived from the Far East. The men were instructed to pose as Weather Bureau civilians. They were each given an additional fifteen dollars a month in spending money—also paid from the ONI slush fund—which was a pretty sweet gig considering the economic difficulties across the country.

Each of the men would complete a yearlong stint on his assigned cruise ship: Martin Vandenberg on the SS *President Taft*, Johnny Cooke aboard the SS *President Jefferson*, Jimmy Pearson on board the SS *President Cleveland*, and Tony Novak on the SS *President Madison*. Over the course of twelve months, each of the ships would conduct six round-trip voyages from the West Coast of the United States to the Far East—a trip that would normally take about forty-five days.

At-sea intercept and On-the-Roof Gang training would be put to the test.

CHAPTER 34

PRESIDENT STEAMSHIP LINES

MONDAY, FEBRUARY 20, 1933
SS *PRESIDENT CLEVELAND*, SEATTLE, WASHINGTON

Engineers from the U.S. Weather Bureau had built a shelter on the weather deck of the SS *President Cleveland* to house their equipment: a survey theodolite (an instrument for measuring angles), a tripod, hydrogen gas canisters, and uninflated weather balloons. Jimmy Pearson also received permission from the ship's captain to string a dipole antenna along the wooden outboard rail of the weather deck, as long as it did not interfere with the ship's gear. From the center of the antenna, a wire dangled over the side of the ship and entered the porthole of Pearson's cabin one deck below. While in favorable position to conduct intercept, he would lock his door, connect the suitcase receiver to the antenna, and put on headphones to silently perform his intercept duties. He did not have the benefit of an Underwood Code Machine on the ship, which might have given away his real mission, so he would have to copy the katakana code by stick. When the ship was not in a favorable intercept position, the antenna could also be connected to a broadcast receiver to listen to music and news.

After each round trip, the President Steamships stopped in Seattle for supplies and any necessary repairs. During this time, the On-the-Roof Gang operators took the opportunity to report to Thirteenth Naval District Headquarters, let the Research Desk know they were alive and well, and receive their pay and any mail that had accumulated for them. The men were permitted to remain on board their ships while they were docked in Seattle, however, they typically rented rooms at the local YMCA to relax after the long journey.

Although only posing as Weather Bureau employees, the need for better forecasting in the Pacific Ocean became very real for Jimmy Pearson on board the SS *President Cleveland*. In October, as the *Cleveland* was en route to Nagasaki, it encountered heavy seas and gale force winds in the East China Sea. The ship bucked and rolled in the swell, and it soon became clear that a typhoon was building. The *Cleveland* was not the only ship caught in the maelstrom; the Japanese steamship *Yashima Maru* was directly ahead of the *Cleveland*. Both ships were scheduled to arrive at Nagasaki the following day.

Jimmy Pearson manned his intercept position in his cabin throughout the storm. However, instead of conducting intercept, he was listening for possible mayday calls coming from ships in peril. Around midnight, Pearson suddenly heard the telltale international Morse code transmission:

··· ——— ··· ··· ——— ··· ··· ——— ···

SOS SOS SOS

The *Yashima Maru* was in distress. The tempest had caused the ship's steam plant to fail. Without power, the ship was being turned parallel to the swell—the worst possible scenario for a ship in rough seas. Pearson called the bridge of the *Cleveland* to inform the captain of the *Yashima Maru*'s predicament, but the *Cleveland* was in some trouble as well. Heavy swells had hit it broadside and ripped three

SS President Cleveland

lifeboats—half the ship's complement—from their davits. As one of the lifeboats fell, the ship pitched to one side, exposing its propeller. A lifeboat hit the propeller directly, causing some damage before the lifeboats were swept out to sea.

Limping but still making progress, the *Cleveland* moved closer to the reported position of the *Yashima Maru* and saw her listing badly to port in the swell. Any Sailor looking at the awkward position of the ship could tell immediately that it was going down. And because the vessel was on its side, the crew couldn't orderly abandon ship—none of the abandon ship stations were accessible, and all the lifeboats were unusable.

Somehow, although flat on its side, the *Yashima Maru* remained on the surface through the night. As the seas calmed and dawn broke, the *Cleveland* pulled close to the *Yashima Maru* and sent its remaining lifeboats to the ailing ship. Stunned by the events overnight, passengers of the *Yashima Maru* stood on the side of the ship awaiting rescue. Boat by boat, at total of sixty passengers were shuttled from the *Yashima Maru* to the SS *President Cleveland* by midday on October 20. Unfortunately, sixty-four passengers were lost in the storm. As the *Cleveland* steamed away from the foundering hulk of the *Yashima Maru*, the Japanese ship slowly sank, its bow pointing downward. Passengers on board the *President Cleveland* could only watch.

When the *Cleveland* finally pulled into port at Nagasaki, Pearson learned through a news broadcast that over a thousand fishermen from the Japanese prefectures of Saga and Kumamoto were missing after the storm. He prayed and thanked his maker for his own safety.

⚓ ⚓ ⚓

On board the SS *President Jefferson*, Johnny Cooke had a slightly different experience on his first voyage to the Far East. To his great delight, the passenger list for the journey included eighty college girls and only six men. Johnny made it a point to spend a lot of time outside of his cabin on that trip.

On one particular day, he met Isyl Florence Johnson, a young woman from Tacoma, who attended the University of Washington and was on the *Jefferson* as part of a sorority field trip to visit Japan and China. Cooke was immediately smitten and spent as much time as possible with her during the trip. By the time the ship returned to Seattle, the two were engaged to be married.

Although the collaboration with the U.S. Weather Bureau was cut after the first year, the On-the-Roof Gang operators had proven the value of performing intercept while at sea. Commander McClaran learned that intercept operators could provide the same type of direct support to U.S. Navy ships as they sailed in the Far East as they did while stationed on land.

CHAPTER 35

CLASS #10

MONDAY, MARCH 6, 1933
MAIN NAVY BUILDING, WASHINGTON, DC

Harry Kidder walked to Ma Travers's place to make the reservations for the tenth On-the-Roof Gang class, which was scheduled to begin later that month with the maximum eight students. There would be four second class radiomen: Benjamin Groundwater, Orville Jones, Homer "Charlie" Kisner, and Walter Rathsack, and four third class radiomen: Donald Barnum, John Gelineau, Thomas "Ted" Hoover, and E. H. Marks.

Because Harry was staying in one of the rooms, he decided to make the third class petty officers pair up and share rooms. This was no different than the lodging they'd have in the fleet, so he didn't anticipate any problems from the men. He told Ma of these plans, and she agreed. Two of the rooms would be modified to accommodate two men each.

Harry also had some good news for Susie. He'd finally gotten word that his parents' estate had cleared probate and was his to sell. The executor of the estate, a family friend from Farber, offered Harry $10,000 on the spot for the farm, the house, and all of his parents' belongings. Harry thought that everything was probably worth more

On-the-Roof Gang Class #10, circa 1933. L-to-R (front): RM2c Orville Jones, RM2c Homer Kisner, RM3c E. H. Marks, RM3c Thomas Hoover. L-to-R (rear): RM2c Walter Rathsack, RM3c Donald Barnum, RM2c Benjamin Groundwater, RM3c John Gelineau.

than that, but at the end of the day, he just wanted to be done with the farm and receive his inheritance so he could begin his life with Susie.

Susie was thrilled with the news. "Harry, you can finally retire from the Navy, and we can start our business!" she said gleefully.

This caught Harry off guard. "I'm not ready to retire yet, Susie," he said. "We still have a lot of work to do. I want to see a few things through before I hang it up."

"Oh, Harry, can't you?" Susie pouted.

"You don't understand, Susie. It's important that I stay in a few more years." He wished again that he could tell her about his job and how important it was.

"I guess," she lamented. "I'm not very happy about it, though."

"We'll be fine. I promise."

"OK. When will you get the money?"

"The check is on its way. I'll just have to go open a bank account when it gets here." Harry had never had the need for a bank account before; he had no savings and simply lived paycheck to paycheck off his Navy earnings.

"Harry, we're engaged. We're going to be married. We should start combining our lives. We can just put your name onto my bank account so that we have a joint account."

"Are you sure about that? You must have a thousand dollars saved already. Are you sure you trust me on your account?" He was actually quite relieved—opening a bank account seemed like a daunting task to him.

"Don't be silly, Harry. Of course, I trust you."

It was settled. When Harry received his inheritance in the mail, they would go to the bank together to put his name on Susie's account and deposit the check.

CHAPTER 36

CLASS #11

SATURDAY, JULY 1, 1933
MA TRAVERS'S GUEST HOUSE, WASHINGTON, DC

Aside from the time they were working, Harry and Susie spent all their waking hours together. Harry felt as close to Susie as ever, and when his inheritance arrived, they walked arm in arm to the bank at the corner of Twentieth and H Streets to deposit it.

On the way there, Harry steered them into a jewelry store on I Street. They stood over the counter looking through the glass at engagement rings.

"Harry these rings are beautiful, but they're too expensive."

"They're not too expensive, Susie. I want you to have one."

She paused, torn between being drawn to the sparkling diamonds and the inability to spend this kind of money. Her eyes locked on a solitaire diamond set in a simple gold band.

Harry, noticing her gaze on the ring, asked the salesman, "How much is that one?"

"Five hundred dollars," the salesman answered flatly.

"Can you take it out for us?"

"Sure," he answered, opening the back of the counter with a key from his pocket. He handed the ring to Harry.

"Do you like it, Susie?"

"Of course, I do, Harry, but—"

"Don't worry about the money, Susie. You deserve this," he said, turning toward the salesman. "We'll take it. We just have to go to the bank first; we'll be right back."

The couple walked to the bank, and, after filling out a few papers, Harry was added to Susie's bank account, to which he promptly deposited $9,500. He was only slightly curious when he learned that Susie's brother was also on the account. When she explained that she couldn't open the account independently because she was a woman, he understood and put any concerns out of his head. Susie and Harry were well on their way to owning a business, married bliss, and their own "happily ever after."

Back at the jewelry store, Harry put the engagement ring on Susie's finger. The two were beaming as they left the store—a quarter carat diamond on Susie's finger.

On Independence Day, Harry took Susie to the Main Navy Building so they could watch fireworks from the roof. Harry brought out two chairs and a small table from the classroom, and they picnicked while enjoying the show. It was a beautifully warm summer evening, perfect for watching the fireworks. They held hands as the fireworks lit up their faces every few seconds. Harry's happiness was immeasurable.

The following morning, the four Sailors and three Marines who were enrolled in the eleventh rooftop class arrived for their first day of training. The class included Marines Clarence Gentilcore, Alvin Rainey, and Charles Southerland, all privates first class who'd recently arrived from duty with the Fourth Marines in China. Petty Officer Donald "Red" Ritchie, whom Chief Kidder had met on board the USS *Houston* was also on the roster. When Kidder first saw Ritchie's name on the list of nominees, he immediately put him on the acceptance list. Ritchie was exactly the right sort of fellow for this assignment. The other Sailors in the class were Petty Officers William "Joe" Edens, Ralph "Happy" Horne, and William "Willie" Muse.

Harry was already halfway through his two-year assignment, and time was moving too quickly for him. He considered trying to convince Susie to marry him immediately so she could join him when he received his orders, but he knew she'd never agree to that. She was dedicated to planning her business and had mentioned several times that she would start it when Harry was ready to retire from the navy. In Susie's plan, they would marry *after* Harry's retirement. Harry knew she wouldn't change her mind, so he just tried to enjoy every single moment with her.

In the Research Desk spaces, Lieutenant Commander Howard Kingman had relieved Commander McClaran, who moved up to become the commander of the Code and Signal Section, in May 1933. McClaran was struggling with the reduced budgets of the U.S. Navy. The ONI had rescinded the remaining money in the slush fund, which was keeping the Research Desk afloat. McClaran requested that Station CAST be moved to *Los Baños* to escape the misuse of his intercept operators at Radio P. I. in Olongapo. However, the request was turned down due to the lack of available funds. McClaran repeatedly protested as high as the Chief of Naval Operations (CNO) but was rebuffed each time.

The CNO's official response stated that reduced appropriations would necessitate the closing of about forty U.S. Navy radio stations, drastic reductions in the operating and maintenance costs of those remaining open, and the elimination of alterations or improvements of any sort. Intercept sites would have similar reductions.

This was not good news for the Research Desk, as many of the established intercept stations were in dire need of new equipment, repair, restoration, or relocation. Station ABLE in Peiping was a revolving door of operators, as the Marine Corps continuously rotated operators specially trained in intercept to general service duty. Station BAKER was isolated and working out of a decrepit facility. Station CAST was nonoperational because of the misuse of intercept operators. Station HYPO was undermanned and constrained by a lack of space, and Station S had only just opened. Without the ability to tap into the slush fund for improvements, maintaining the momentum was going to be extremely challenging. Something needed to change.

CHAPTER 37

ORANGE GRAND MANEUVERS OF 1933

MONDAY, JULY 31, 1933
USS *HOUSTON*, IN PORT AT TSINGTAO, CHINA

Despite the dire financial circumstances, Commander McClaran felt the On-the-Roof Gang and the Research Desk were more prepared than ever for the impending Orange Grand Maneuvers of 1933, which were scheduled to take place in August. Earlier in the year, Lieutenant Wenger, who was still on board the USS *Houston*, had started planning for coverage of the large-scale Japanese naval exercise. By the end of July, the *Houston* was in port at Tsingtao, China—roughly halfway between Shanghai and Peiping—for a regularly scheduled visit.

Like a seasoned maestro, Wenger orchestrated the intercept operation during the 1933 Orange Grand Maneuvers from on board the *Houston*. Thirty-plus On-the-Roof Gang alumni were standing at the ready at Stations ABLE, BAKER, CAST, HYPO, and S as well as in Peiping. They were augmented by additional intercept operators on board the USS *Gold Star*. Wenger ordered all the intercept stations to implement round-the-clock coverage of the exercise. This would mark the first full-scale test of radio intelligence in the U.S. Navy.

As in 1930, Wenger's plan included a three-step process to most effectively exploit the Imperial Japanese Navy's communications. This three-step process included: 1) intercept operations and follow-up analysis to be conducted to the greatest extent possible at each site; 2) Lieutenant Wenger's daily and post-exercise traffic analysis from on board the USS *Houston*; and 3) following the exercise, the Research desk would decrypt and translate all intercepted messages. The first two steps happened fairly quickly; local analysis was complete within twenty-four hours of receiving the intercept. Full decryption at the Research Desk, however, could take months.

The results of the intercept and traffic analysis were so compelling that the Director of Naval Communications wrote a memorandum to the Chief of Naval Operations, stating that radio intelligence results included a complete list of the Japanese ships and units taking part in the maneuvers, the organization of the Imperial Japanese Navy forces, the disposition and movement of forces and the strategic plan of defense of the Japanese homeland. Perhaps the most troubling revelation, however, was an indication that any attack by Imperial Japanese Navy forces could be made without previous declaration of war or other intentional warning.

Although there were other indicators, intercept and traffic analysis conducted during the Orange Grand Maneuvers of 1933 proved to be the primary contributor to the overall level of knowledge of Japanese operations. This further cemented the credibility of the radio intelligence program as a reliable source of information for U.S. Navy decision-makers. Back in Washington, Commander McClaran already knew that. He saw the Navy's investment in radio intelligence as imperative, and now he had proof.

CHAPTER 38

CLASS #12

WEDNESDAY, NOVEMBER 29, 1933
MAIN NAVY BUILDING, WASHINGTON, DC

Following the last day of instruction for the On-the-Roof Gang class eleven at the end of November, the students were transferred to the fleet. The three Marines—Gentilcore, Rainey, and Southerland—were headed for Station ABLE in Peiping. Petty Officers Edens and Horne were transferring to Station BAKER in Guam, while Muse and Ritchie were going to Station CAST in the Philippines.

In the Research Desk, decryption of the intercept from the 1933 Imperial Japanese Navy's Grand Maneuvers was winding down. Led by Lieutenant Junior Grade Thomas Dyer, the decryption confirmed and reinforced the earlier traffic analysis and reconstruction that Lieutenant Wenger and the On-the-Roof Gang operators had performed during and immediately following the exercise.

The On-the-Roof Gang's success during Japan's 1933 Grand Maneuvers could not have come at a better time. Commander McClaran was preparing a logical, incontrovertible defense of the U.S. Navy's radio intelligence activities along with a request for continued funding. He planned to send a letter to the Chief of Naval Operations as soon as he had it drafted.

Hearing the results from the Orange Grand Maneuvers, Chief Kidder was very proud of his students. Across the Pacific Ocean, On-the-Roof Gang operators had put into real practice the lessons he'd taught them. After the final day of class, the day before Thanksgiving, he wandered down to the Research Desk to get more details from Lieutenant Dyer.

"Lieutenant, I hear your decryption confirmed our traffic analysis. Is that right?" Chief Kidder said as he greeted Dyer.

"Sure is, Chief," Dyer confirmed. "Your guys beat us to the punch across the board."

"Great! We can learn an awful lot through good traffic analysis."

"Well, there is one area where it falls short, Chief, and that's enemy intentions. Reconstruction certainly tells us what has *already* happened, but if you want to know what their plans are in the future, you need to read their messages in real time. When we do it after the fact, we're just confirming things that have already happened," Dyer explained.

"Well, I'm just pleased it's all coming together," Kidder said with some pride in his voice.

"Your On-the-Roof Gang did a marvelous job, Chief. You should be proud."

"Thank you, sir."

Just then, a nervous yeoman stepped through the door and into the office. "Chief Kidder, Lieutenant Commander Kingman is asking to see you."

"Thanks, Sailor. Tell him I'm on my way," Kidder responded. When the yeoman left, Kidder continued. "I have one question for you, sir."

"Go ahead, Chief."

"The kind of decryption you and your team are doing . . . don't you think we'd be better off doing it at the intercept sites . . . you know, eliminate the time it takes for couriers to bring you the intercept?"

"No doubt about it, Chief. I think we'd do well to set something up in Hawaii, at least."

"Right, my thoughts exactly. Thanks for your time. I'd better see what Kingman wants."

Kidder excused himself and headed downstairs. When he arrived, he could see by the look on the commander's face that he had some unpleasant news.

"I've got orders for you," Kingman announced point-blank, as he held up a sheet of paper. "You're going to Hawaii to relieve Chief Billehus as chief radioman in charge at Station HYPO."

The news deflated Chief Kidder's good mood, and the smile disappeared from his face. He knew this day was coming but was hoping it was still at least a few months away.

"Aye, sir," Kidder responded morosely.

"Chief Billehus is on his way to relieve you," Kingman explained. "You'll teach the next class. When Billehus gets here, you'll start class number thirteen with him—get him up to speed, so he can teach the next few classes. At some point, we'll ship you out to Hawaii.

"Aye aye, sir." Kidder was gutted, but he didn't want to show any emotion in front of his superior officer. "May I go now?"

"There's more, Chief. We want to move Station HYPO to Heeia."

Heeia was a small town on Kaneohe Bay on the eastern coast of Oahu. The U.S. Navy was planning to decommission a 100-kilowatt transmitting station there, which would allow the Research Desk to lay claim.

"If we can get the funds, you'll lead the move. There's no one else out there who can handle this, especially with all the big brass in Hawaii. We need you out there."

Feeling the need to be alone with his thoughts, Chief Kidder was only half listening to the commander at this point. Kingman could see the impatience on his face.

"You're dismissed, Kidder." Kingman didn't mean for the encounter to be so impersonal; he'd meant to break the news gently to the chief. To Kingman's regret, it just didn't play out that way.

Within the next few days, four Marine operators—all privates—had arrived for class twelve. Harry Butler, Harold "Poochie" Jones, Joseph Petrosky, and Norman Robertson had all recently been general service radiomen in China.

Having broken the news to Susie, Harry wanted to spend more time with her, so he met the new students at Union Station and walked them to Ma Travers's place. Once there, Gertrude showed the newcomers to their rooms. When Harry saw Susie in the front room, he walked toward her, but she turned away.

"Susie, why are you acting like this?"

"Harry, you know why. I want to marry you. Please retire," she pleaded. "Retire now, and we can get married."

"You know I can't do that, Susie. I have to go to Hawaii. Come with me. You'll love it—you can start your business there."

"If you won't retire for me, I won't move to Hawaii for you," she protested. Then she stormed up the stairs without looking back.

Harry wasn't equipped for this kind of reaction. As he watched her disappear up the stairs, he just stood there dumbstruck. Susie bumped into Gertrude, who had witnessed the final moments of the encounter as she made her way back down the stairs.

"She'll be all right, Harry. Give her a little time. When do you leave for Hawaii?"

"Not for a few months."

"Good. I'll talk to her after you leave. When you get back from work tonight, she'll be ready to talk."

"Thanks, Ma. You're the best." Harry had gotten used to calling Gertrude "Ma." Even though it was only a nickname, he hadn't had a mother figure in his life since he'd left for the Army, so it was nice to have someone looking out for him. Still, he worried about Susie's reaction to the news, especially since they both knew his transfer orders would eventually come.

As Ma had predicted, that evening when Harry returned from

work, Susie was waiting for him. She hugged him as soon as he walked through the door. Her eyes welled up with tears as she said, "I'm sorry, Harry."

"I'm sorry too."

"I wish we didn't have to go through this again."

"Me too," Harry agreed.

They held each other tightly until Susie said, "We'll make it through this again."

"Of course, we will. I'll come back again, and we'll get married, I promise."

"That's all I want, Harry."

Ma watched from the dining room as the pair sat on the sofa, happy again.

⚓ ⚓ ⚓

At Christmas, Ma Travers put on another fabulous meal for Harry and the students preparing for class number twelve. Before dinner, Harry recited his now traditional prayer at the dinner table. Determined not to dwell on his impending separation from Susie, Harry put it out of his mind and concentrated on enjoying Christmas break.

For Harry, as the calendar turned to 1934 and winter blossomed into spring, time seemed to accelerate. Although Harry was still distracted with where things stood with Susie, he gave his students the kind of exceptional instruction that he had a reputation for. His expertise and teaching style, now honed to perfection, forged the students into excellent intercept operators in no time. In March, as the end of Class #12 approached, Chief Guy Billehus arrived from Hawaii and sat at the small table in back of the classroom to observe.

By the first week of April, the class of newly-minted U.S. Marine Corps intercept operators was ready to face radio intercept in the real world.

CHAPTER 39

MCCLARAN'S APPEAL

OP-20-G
March 5, 1934

From: Director of Naval Communications,
Code and Signal Section
To: Chief of Naval Operations
Thru: Director of Naval Communications

Subject: Training of radiomen for special radio service

1. Radio intercept stations are maintained at the following places: Astoria, Hawaii (Wailupe), Guam, Philippines (Olongapo), and China (Peiping). These stations come under three classifications as follows:

(a) Stations established for the sole purpose to have them available in war.

The stations comprising this category are Astoria and Hawaii (Wailupe). Although their peacetime functions are not of the greatest importance, their development for wartime is considered vital.

(b) Stations established in peacetime to obtain the maximum amount of material for research activities. These stations are Guam and China (Peiping). They are the most valuable stations we have today. It is assumed that they would be lost in war, but, even so, we are fully justified in maintaining them in peace not only for the material collected by them but also for the probable and vital advance warning that they might give.

(c) Stations established for peacetime operation with the hope that the station will continue operating at least through the early stages of a war. This station is Olongapo. There is no doubt that in its present location the station could not hold out, and, therefore, it is essential that it be moved to a more suitable location where it could be defended. However, scarcity of funds prevents any such shift for the present.

2. At stations where there are other radio activities, the actual cost for maintenance of the intercept sites is insignificant. However, if those other radio activities are curtailed, the maintenance cost will have to be borne by the intercept activity. Take for example Astoria. The annual cost of maintenance of Astoria is $3,500. Bainbridge Island, in Puget Sound, apparently is a much superior receiving location, but would cost significantly more to maintain as an independent station.

   The other stations—Wailupe, Guam, Olongapo, and Peiping—are located with radio activities that cannot be closed down regardless of how drastic a cut is made. Since the cost of maintenance is such a small percentage of the total cost of upkeep of the buildings and grounds, there is no benefit to closing the intercept activities at these locations.

3. The stations at Guam and Olongapo were established and are utilized for obtaining enemy naval traffic. As was shown above, it is most probable that those stations will be lost in the early stages of a war. That would mean a complete cessation of navy traffic.

Therefore, we must exert every effort to provide a means of continuing this activity, and the Hawaiian station is the one we are attempting to develop for that purpose.

4. The station at Peiping is the one we most rely on for obtaining diplomatic traffic. In the event of war with Japan, this, like Guam, will either be wiped out or closed down, but even if not closed down it will be almost impossible to get the intercepted traffic back to the United States. Therefore, to keep in touch with the political situation, we will rely on both Astoria and a new station at Bar Harbor, Maine. Both of these stations are doing excellent work under the circumstances and lack only modern equipment to make them really efficient. Astoria is now getting a considerable amount of traffic that passes between Tokyo and Manchuria—it could be diverted to intercepting traffic between Tokyo and America, but in view of the fact that such traffic would cease in war, it is considered prudent to continue current operations.

5. Although I am anxious to curtail expenditures in every possible and

reasonable manner to make it easier for others, I conscientiously feel that there is hardly a single activity of this section that is not being conducted for the primary if not sole purpose of preparation for war rather than for peacetime operating purposes. Therefore, it is recommended that none of the radio intercept activities be in any way curtailed.

JOHN MCCLARAN
CDR USN

CHAPTER 40

CLASS #13

MONDAY, APRIL 23, 1934

MAIN NAVY BUILDING, WASHINGTON, DC

Chief Guy Billehus was an excellent intercept operator, there was no denying it. However, he'd been selected to teach the On-the-Roof Gang class solely on the fact that his rotation date matched up with the start of class number thirteen. The timing for the swap was perfect.

Students for Billehus's first On-the-Roof Gang class arrived in Washington, DC in early April. The eight students consisted of three radiomen second class: Albert Burton, Hilary Cyr, and Garwin Diehl; and five third class petty officers: Frank Estes, Eugene Givler, Charles Johns, Wilson Mason, and Markle Smith. Chief Kidder would supervise and evaluate Billehus as he began to teach.

Chief Billehus dutifully ran through Kidder's training curriculum, but the students didn't seem to grasp the material as previous classes had. Billehus was struggling in his new role as instructor.

After three months of instruction, the students were behind in the curriculum, and it appeared as if four months of class would not prepare them to be sufficiently ready to perform intercept operations in the fleet. As a result, Lieutenant Commander Kingman extended the class for an additional month and asked Kidder to complete the training with the students. They would graduate in September instead of August, and Kidder would remain in DC for the duration of the class. Kidder welcomed the extension; he desperately wanted to remain in Washington, DC with Susie.

The additional month of training with Chief Kidder had the desired result, and in September, the students were ready for orders. The entire class was headed to Station HYPO in Wailupe, Hawaii.

Kidder asked for some lenience in his departure date, wanting to extend his time in DC with Susie even more than it already had been. Believing Billehus wasn't quite ready to teach on his own, Kingman approved the request. Class #14 would begin in October 1934 with both Kidder and Billehus as instructors.

CHAPTER 41

BAKER MOVES TO LIBUGON

MONDAY, SEPTEMBER 3, 1934
STATION BAKER, OLD SPANISH GUARDHOUSE, AGAÑA, GUAM

The men at Station BAKER had been working in less than ideal conditions in the Old Spanish Guardhouse since it opened, and they assumed it would continue that way. Despite the obvious need for a new location, a lack of funds had continued to prevent any movement or refurbishment of the intercept site.

Suddenly, as if something miraculously had changed the minds of the bureaucrats, the On-the-Roof Gang graduates in Guam received word that money had been made available to move Station BAKER to the site of the recently abandoned Navy radio station on Libugon Hill. Located in much more modern buildings at an altitude of almost 600 feet above the Plaza de España, it was clearly a better place for an intercept site than the Old Spanish Guardhouse.

McClaran's impassioned plea to the CNO seemed to have the desired effect, as the U.S. Navy made a strategic decision to invest in radio intelligence as a primary means of preventing surprise attacks.

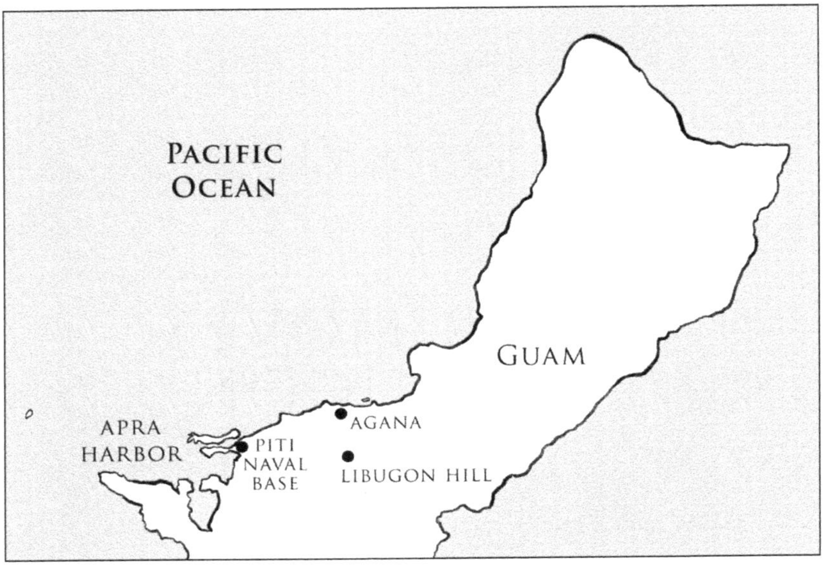

As a result, the Chief of Naval Operations directed the U.S. Navy Bureau of Engineering to establish a formal material allowance and modernization program for radio intelligence sites, specifically Station S at Fort Stevens in Astoria, Oregon; Station HYPO in Hawaii, which would move from Wailupe to a more suitable location; Station CAST in the Philippines, which would move from Olongapo to a more suitable location; Station ABLE in Peiping; and Station BAKER in Guam, which would move from Agaña to Libugon Hill.

The modernization program specified that each intercept site would be equipped with the most up-to-date radio equipment available in the U.S. Navy's supply system, including LF, MF, and HF receivers, as well as Boehme automatic wire recorders and the best frequency meters available.

At Station BAKER in Guam—the first location to reap the benefits of the Navy's investment in radio intelligence—Malcolm "Felix" Lyon served as the chief radioman in charge. He and Chief Radioman Murrel Wood—a graduate of the second On-the-Roof Gang class—were put in charge of planning and executing the move from the Old Spanish Guardhouse to Libugon Hill. They immediately realized the spaces that had previously housed Radio Libugon represented a major improvement from the old location.

However, there was work to be done. Physically moving all the equipment from Agaña up the steep hill to Libugon would require trucks and would take days. In addition, the antenna towers at Libugon weren't necessary for intercept operations. Instead, they would need to string long-wire antennas to ensure coverage of all the Imperial Japanese Navy's communication nets they wanted to copy. And something had to be done about the mosquitoes and flies that had infested the building since the departure of Radio Libugon. But the biggest problem facing Lyon and Wood was the task of transferring the operation without incurring any gaps in coverage. There were no spare receivers available to double up during the move, so they'd have to execute the move in a phased approach.

The Navy sent in the engineers, technicians, and construction workers to refurbish the barracks, the mess hall, and the operations building at Libugon, after which the work of moving the intercept station began. The chiefs had eight other On-the-Roof Gang operators available to help with the move: Sidney Burnett, Carl Congdon, Joe Edens, John Gelineau, Ted Hoover, Happy Horne, E. H. Marks, and Mac McConnel.

The plan itself was relatively simple. Installing antennas was the first order of business. Petty Officers Burnett and McConnel would do the honors since they had attended the Radio Materiel School (RMS) in Bellevue for this very purpose. Even with the pair working twelve-hour days, the task took almost a week to accomplish. After antennas were strung and ready to be used, it was time for the move. Chief Wood took charge at the Old Spanish Guardhouse until it shut down. He was responsible for running operations and orchestrating the transfer of equipment from Agaña. Sid Burnett and Ted Hoover

Station BAKER, Libugon Hill, Guam circa 1934.

would remain behind to conduct intercept there until the new location was up and running. Gelineau, Edens, and Horne shuttled equipment up the hill from Agaña to Libugon. Chief Lyon was in charge of the new site as equipment arrived and was installed for use. With the help of the transport team, Carl Congdon and E. H. Marks installed gear; they began operations as soon as the first receivers were installed. Once intercept began on Libugon Hill, operations at Agaña ceased and the rest of the gear was brought up the hill.

All told, the move took less than two weeks before the new site was operating at full capacity. Even though they were still using the older generation receivers, the relocation of the intercept station to Libugon Hill immediately increased the intercept volume by 60 percent. Perhaps the biggest improvement was in the men's living arrangements—they now had a barracks within a two minute walk to the operations building. Things were much better for the men of Station BAKER at Libugon Hill.

CHAPTER 42

CLASS #14

MONDAY, SEPTEMBER 24, 1934
MAIN NAVY BUILDING, WASHINGTON, DC

Chief Guy Billehus so dreaded the thought of teaching another class that he formally requested a transfer; he simply wasn't comfortable as an instructor. Lieutenant Commander Howard Kingman, officer in charge of the Research Desk, was keen to approve the transfer. Feedback from the students in the class Billehus had taught wasn't good. However, the main impediment to transferring him from instructor duty was that Billehus had just recently arrived in Washington and technically couldn't receive orders for at least another two years. There would be no further extensions for Chief Kidder—he had to get out to Station HYPO by the first of the year to lead the move to Heeia. Therefore, Kingman needed to come up with a clever solution. Until he did, Billehus would have to keep teaching.

The eight students in Class #14 arrived in Washington in September and were assigned rooms at Ma Travers's Guest House. The class was comprised of three radiomen second class: Norman Lewis, Leo Potvin, and Meddie Royer; and five radiomen third class: Ivan "Benny" Benjamin, Carl "Swede" Jensen, Edward Schroeder, Howard Troup, and James Willmarth.

On-the-Roof Gang Class #14, circa 1934. L-to-R (front): RM3c Ivan Benjamin, RM3c Edward Schroeder, CRM Guy Billehus (Instructor), RM3c Carl Jensen, RM3c Howard Troup. L-to-R (rear): RM2c Meddie Royer, RM3c James Willmarth, CRM Harry Kidder (Instructor), RM2c Leo Potvin, RM2c Norman Lewis.

Under the watchful eye of Chief Kidder, Chief Billehus ran through the training but he struggled again with getting the students to perform. Once again, Kingman decided to extend the class by a month in order to allow the students time to become proficient enough to transfer to intercept duties in the fleet.

As the end of 1934 approached, it was finally time for Chief Kidder to transfer to Station HYPO. He was scheduled to board a train bound for San Francisco on Saturday, December 29 and spent as much time as possible with Susie. As the inevitable approached, their hearts ached; there was nothing they could do to slow time.

On the Friday evening before the men shipped out, the mood in Ma Travers's Guest House was somber. Harry and the students ate together in the dining room as Susie served the meal. An awkward silence dominated the room.

After dinner, Harry went to his room to pack his seabag. Susie had done all his laundry and left it folded on his bed. Joining Harry in his room, Susie sat in the chair in the corner with her arms folded.

"This isn't right, Harry. You shouldn't be leaving."

"I'm sorry, sweetheart," he tried to console her. "You know I have to do this."

"I do. I just don't want you to leave."

"The time will go by quickly, Susie. I just need you to write to me from time to time." He stopped packing and sat down on the edge of the bed, hoping she would sit next to him. She didn't move. "Come here," he said, patting the edge of the bed.

As she looked up at Harry, he saw something in her eyes that he'd never seen before. He wasn't sure what it was—perhaps some level of detachment—but it made him very uncomfortable. She finally relented and walked over to him. She sat on the bed and rested her head on his shoulder; her tears dampened his shirtsleeve. He put his arm around her shoulder, and she wrapped her arms around his waist. They just held each other; eyes closed.

After several minutes, Harry got up to finish packing. When his seabag was full, he tossed it into the corner and lay down on the bed. Susie crawled up next to him and fell asleep. Harry lay awake for a few minutes, wishing he could make time stand still.

Harry's train departed at nine o'clock on Saturday morning. Despite having made this cross-country trip several times, he knew this would be the longest and loneliest.

⚓ ⚓ ⚓

Around this same time, Kingman received word from Station CAST about a security concern involving Radioman Second Class Prescott

On-the-Roof Gang operators at Station CAST in Olongapo, circa 1933. L-to-R: RM3c John Roop, CRM Walter McGregor, RM3c Prescott Currier, RM2c Richard Willis.

Currier, who had graduated from On-the-Roof Gang training in 1932. After arriving in the Philippines for duty, Currier reportedly taught himself Japanese. It was not unusual for intercept operators to gain some proficiency at recognizing simple Japanese words in plain-text messages, but Currier's proficiency greatly exceeded mere word recognition. In fact, his skill was equal to or better than any of the language officers assigned to the Research Desk, most of whom had spent three or more years in Japan studying the language.

Additionally, Currier single-handedly broke an Imperial Japanese Navy double-transposition code system that changed ciphers at random intervals. The Material Code system, also known around the Research Desk as the "HE" code, was used to transmit technical details of ship construction, including speed, tonnage, height and beam length, weaponry, and other specifications. Cryptanalysts at the Research Desk and at Cavite Naval Base were unable to break the code. Currier succeeded where others had failed, using his ability to recognize and translate the decrypted technical details. His superiors, who were fully trained language officers, were suspicious of his abilities not only to break the code but also to translate the Japanese language with such ease. As a result, they reported him to the Research Desk as a potential security risk.

In a written report to the Research Desk regarding Petty Officer Currier's accomplishments, the language officers at Station CAST reported:

> The general opinion here is that the cryptanalytical part of it might be within his capacity were it performed in a known language. Our opinion is that the text, as submitted, is too accurately translated and smacks very strongly of outside assistance. The accuracy of the translation indicates probable assistance from a Japanese national.

In other words, Currier was better at the Japanese language than the officially trained officers, and they assumed he was getting outside help.

Commander Kingman agreed with the concern that Currier might be receiving assistance in breaking the code, stating in his official response:

> If Currier carried this out alone, it is an excellent piece of work, and he deserves considerable praise. On

```
the other hand, if he obtained any
unauthorized assistance, we need to
hold him accountable for the unauthorized
disclosure of secret operations.
```

Kingman drafted orders to have Petty Officer Currier transferred immediately to Washington, DC for investigation.

⚓ ⚓ ⚓

In February 1935, as Class #14 of On-the-Roof Gang students continued training under Chief Billehus, the Research Desk received word of the crash of the USS *Macon* and that Radioman First Class E. E. Dailey had been on board. Dailey had been a member of the second On-the-Roof Gang training class before he dropped out when he learned that he would not be receiving a promotion.

The USS *Macon* was one of the largest helium-filled airships ever built. On the afternoon of February 12, 1935, as the *Macon* flew about ten miles west of Big Sur, California, it encountered a gale that critically damaged a stabilzing fin that had been damaged earlier and hastily reparied with wooden planks and nails. Dailey, having achieved the rank of first class petty officer that he desired, radioed for help in Morse code. Shortwave radio operators in San Luis Obispo were the first to hear his distress call.

Dailey transmitted, "We have a casualty." A few moments later, he sent, "SOS SOS SOS falling AS." *AS* was the Morse code procedural sign for "wait a minute."

The USS *Macon*'s commanding Officer, Lieutenant Commander Herbert Wiley, opened the door to the radio room and addressed Dailey directly. Dailey, nervously chomping on a wad of gum, stopped transmitting, took off his headphones, and waited for Wiley to give him instructions.

USS Macon in flight over San Francisco Bay.

"Dailey, transmit our position," Wiley said, handing him a slip of paper with the ship's latitude and longitude. "We're going to abandon ship as soon as we land on the water."

Dailey put his headphones back on and transmitted the USS *Macon*'s final plea for help.

"SOS SOS We will abandon ship as soon as it lands on water. We are twenty miles northwest of Point Sur, probably ten miles at sea." He then transmitted the ship's latitude and longitude several times.

With a crew of eighty-three men on board, the USS *Macon* was slowly and uncontrollably losing altitude over the ocean as the sun set. U.S. Navy and Coast Guard patrol craft sortied from San Francisco and converged on the location given in Dailey's distress calls.

Around the ship, the alarms were sounding, and announcements instructed all Sailors to their abandon ship stations. Dailey remained at his station, continuing to transmit the ship's location. He planned to leave the radio room using the emergency escape hatch right outside the radio room at the last possible moment—just in time to abandon ship when it landed. He repeatedly took off his headphones to check on the status of the announcements and their altitude. He heard the sound of waves getting louder each time he checked.

As Dailey manned his communications position, the *Macon* shook violently and rolled side to side on its uncontrolled descent toward the ocean. Dailey, believing the ship had hit the water, threw off his headphones and ran out of the radio room toward the exit. He forced the exit door open and jumped, but instead of hitting the water, he fell from the airship from an altitude of over 100 feet.

Petty Officer Dailey was one of only two men who died as a result of the *Macon*'s crash—a number that could have been considerably higher if not for Dailey's courageous efforts to report the ship's location. Even though Dailey was never assigned to intercept duties after dropping out of On-the-Roof Gang training, for all intents and purposes, he was a member of the brotherhood. His heroics on board the USS *Macon* cemented his standing among the group.

The news of Dailey's passing cast a sadness over the Research Desk.

A few weeks later, in March 1935, when the On-the-Roof Gang class completed its training, three of the men—Benjamin, Jensen, and Royer—received orders for Station BAKER in Guam. The other five graduates were heading to Station CAST in the Philippines.

Kingman was ready to make a change after Billehus completed his second attempt at instruction. Billehus would be transferred to the Research Desk to work on the decryption team, something to which he was well-suited. Billehus would essentially switch places with Chief Radioman Jesse "Bryan" Byrd, who was currently assigned to the decryption team. To Billehus's relief, he was finally relived of his duties as an instructor.

CHAPTER 43

CAST MOVES TO MARIVELES

SUNDAY, APRIL 21, 1935

USS *HENDERSON*, CAVITE NAVAL BASE, PHILIPPINES

All eight graduates of the fourteenth On-the-Roof Gang class disembarked the USS *Henderson* at Cavite Naval Base in Manila Bay, after the two week transit from San Francisco via Hawaii.

The five Sailors remaining in the Philippines for duty—Lewis, Schroeder, Troup, Potvin, and Willmarth—had their seabags over their shoulders as they walked down the gangplank. Chief Radioman Keg Goodwin, a graduate of the very first On-the-Roof Gang class who was now in charge of Station CAST, was waiting for them on the pier. "Welcome to the Philippines, Sailors!" he greeted the group. After introducing himself, he nodded in the direction of the three Sailors without seabags and said, "You three . . . don't get used to this place."

"Yeah, we get to enjoy the *Henderson* for another week!" Swede Jensen said sarcastically.

"Everything OK on board?" Goodwin asked.

"Oh, yeah. Fine, Chief," Swede replied. "There's just not much to do. If I play another game of spades, I'll throw myself overboard!"

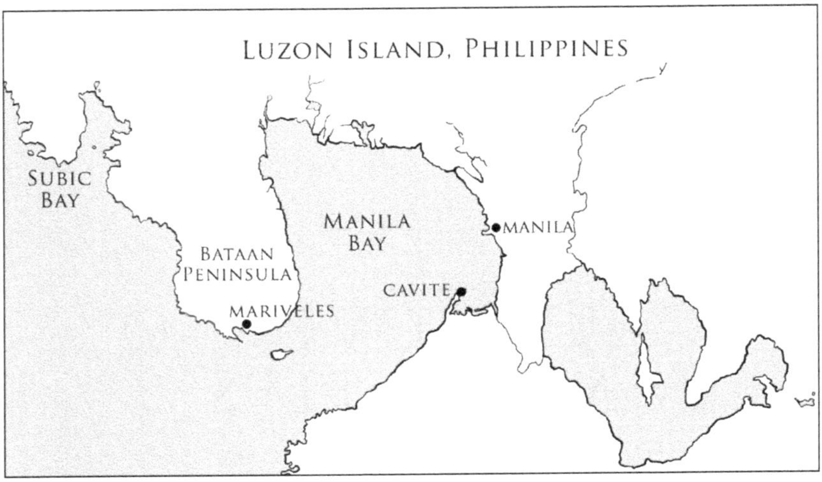

"It's all right, Chief," Petty Officer Meddie Royer added. "We're just getting off the ship to stretch our legs for a little while."

Happy to hear the men were in good spirits, Goodwin continued, "Well, our trip is much shorter. We're getting on the *Jennie* over there to cross the bay to Mariveles." The *Jennie* was actually the USS *Genesee*, a fleet tugboat that was being used to ferry men and equipment around Manila Bay.

"We've just got a short walk to pier three," Goodwin added, pointing west. Then he said to the three heading back onto the *Henderson*, "You guys will love Guam—it's an island paradise. And Chief Lyon is a good man; I'm sure you'll like working for him. Plus, you've got new digs there. I hear the reception from Libugon Hill is amazing."

"Looking forward to it, Chief," Petty Officer Benny Benjamin said.

Goodwin turned and headed off the pier with his new operators, while Benjamin, Royer, and Jensen all headed back toward the *Henderson*.

While walking along the waterfront, Chief Goodwin explained that Station CAST had recently moved from Olongapo to Mariveles, so the new spaces would allow them to do their intercept work without any interruption from Radio P. I. "This is our own place. No one bothers us here. Every now and then, Lieutenant Goodwin visits us from Cavite, but that's about it."

"*Lieutenant* Goodwin? Any relation, Chief?" Potvin asked curiously.

"None at all. Just a coincidence."

Lieutenant Junior Grade Ernest Sidney L. Goodwin had relieved Lieutenant Wenger as the Asiatic Fleet intelligence officer and had established an office for decryption in Building G of the U.S. Naval Prison at Cavite Naval Base. The decryption office was known as the Combat Intelligence Unit, and Lieutenant Goodwin spent most of his time there; he only visited Mariveles occasionally to become more familiar with the intercept operation.

The group boarded the USS *Genesee* for the brief trip across the bay to Mariveles. After departing Bacoor Bay, the *Genesee* headed slightly southwest across Manila Bay toward the Bataan Peninsula. While the crew kept the *Genesee* a safe distance from the shoreline, the recent On-the-Roof Gang grads could see some beautiful beaches dotting the southern coast of the peninsula. As they continued west, they first saw Alas-Asin Beach, then Dinginen Beach, and eventually Sisiman Beach. In between the long patches of white sand, the shore was made up of densely forested jungle. They occasionally heard what might have been the call of a large bird—or perhaps a monkey—echoing in the jungle. In any case, this was a largely uninhabited area of the Philippines. They all assumed they had a long distance yet to travel when the boat suddenly turned into Mariveles Bay.

The USS *Genesee* pulled up to a small dock at Caracol Point inside the bay. From there, the On-the-Roof Gang didn't see much other than a pier jutting out from a steep jungle-covered hill. The crew of the *Genesee* hopped off the boat, tied it up, and immediately began off-loading supplies destined for Station CAST.

"Don't just stand there—turn to, Sailors! Get your seabags off the boat, then help with the supplies!" Chief Goodwin barked

On-the-Roof Gang operators in Hawaii, en route first assignment after rooftop training, circa 1935. L-to-R: RM3c Carl Jensen, RM3c Leo Potvin, RM3c Ivan Benjamin.

at the newcomers. Each Sailor grabbed his seabag and tossed it onto the pier before lending a hand to the crew off-loading supplies.

After everything destined for Mariveles was off the boat, the newly arrived Sailors looked at each other, confused. The end of the pier seemed to disappear into the dense jungle covering the hillside. The only structure they saw was a small building housing an electrical generator at the front of the pier. The structure was about half the size of the rooftop classroom in Washington, DC, so it was obviously far too small to be the intercept site. Electrical lines and ropes were strung into the thick jungle and up the hill. A small walking path led away from the pier. There was no way a vehicle could travel on that path.

"What next, Chief?" asked Petty Officer Willmarth. "Where are we taking this stuff?"

"Ah!" The chief walked toward the shore. "I've been looking forward to this."

At the front of the pier, next to the powerhouse, he opened a small electrical box on a post. Inside the box were two large buttons: a red button on top of a black one. When the chief pressed the black button, the men heard an engine engage at the top of the hill, and a rope turned on a large pulley over the powerhouse.

"Petty Officer Ritchie rigged this up for us after we moved here from Olongapo," the chief explained as a large basket moved along a steel cable out of the jungle down toward the men—much as a ski lift worked. The basket eventually came to rest at the chief's feet. "Get your seabags in there; they'll be waiting for you when you get topside."

The men followed the chief's orders and dropped their seabags into the basket. When Goodwin pressed the red button, the basket took off up the hill. A few minutes later, the basket returned, and the men loaded the rest of the supplies. Chief Goodwin again pressed the red button to send the supplies uphill.

"OK," Goodwin said. "Now, we walk."

As they set off on the jungle path, Chief Goodwin explained to the men that they had taken over some buildings on the Mariveles Navy Camp after they'd been abandoned a few months earlier. The buildings were less than ten years old and still in good shape. He also told the men that their work in Mariveles was top secret. If anyone asked, they were to say the site was not intercept Station CAST but rather "Los Bañitos Security Station."

The path made several hairpin turns as it wound its way uphill toward the intercept site. Finally, the men emerged from the jungle and entered a clearing. They saw the top of the makeshift lift Red Ritchie had fashioned leading from the jungle toward a large, square, concrete building that was surrounded by a wraparound porch. Three Sailors sat on the porch, grinning at the newly arrived intercept operators. Their five seabags were piled in a pyramid on the porch next to the basket, which was still full of supplies for Station CAST. The three Sailors stood as the five new operators approached.

"Fresh meat!" Willie Muse smirked. "I'm Wille. Glad to meet you," he said, sticking out his hand to greet the new men. Don Barnum and Happy Horne, the other two experienced operators, followed suit.

"Red has the watch. I'll go get him," Willie said to the group as he stepped in through a wooden door. Moments later, Red and Willie came back out.

Chief Goodwin felt like a proud father. With the arrival of the five recently minted On-the-Roof Gang graduates, the size of his team had just doubled from five to ten operators. "Well, this is it, fellas," he said to the new operators. "This is the team."

The group made small talk for a while as the old hands gave the newbies the lowdown on the place.

"We're pretty isolated here," Goodwin told them. "But the chow is good. We've got a galley and our own cook. He'll rustle up anything we ask for—within reason, of course."

"Balut for dinner tonight!" Willie Muse said excitedly. "New guys always eat balut on their first night!"

None of the new guys had been to the Philippines before, but they had certainly heard of balut, which was a nearly ready to hatch duck egg boiled until ready to eat. It was typically eaten as street food by drunken Sailors. None of the newcomers were looking forward to this dubious delicacy, but they knew they had to follow the tradition.

"We'll meet for dinner in a couple hours. The balut is optional," Chief Goodwin informed the new operators. "Until then, you've got some time to get moved into your berthing."

Petty Officer Barnum reached into his pocket and pulled out five keys, each of which was attached to a small, numbered keychain. He handed the keys to the chief, who held them out to the men. They all picked one from his hand.

"Your rooms are on the other side of the building," he said. "Guys, show them their quarters. See you at 1800 hours for chow."

Barnum, Muse, and Horne walked the men around the building toward their rooms. Chief Goodwin looked at Petty Officer Ritchie and said, "C'mon, Ritchie, let's get back to the sked." The two walked into the building where the operations floor immediately opened up inside the door to a very large room, which was approximately forty feet by forty feet with windows on all sides. Along the opposite wall, another door led outside to the men's quarters. To the left, a door led to a rec room with a Ping-Pong table and chairs for relaxing and reading. The galley and mess decks were also on that side of the room. Across from the rec room, a very long workbench was set up for repairing equipment. Goodwin stood at the workbench watching Don Barnum show the new men around the operations floor. From there, a door led to the quarters for the radioman in charge, which was where Chief Goodwin lived. Windows on three sides of the room had sea views.

In the center of the main room, ten desks were arranged in a square, surrounding a hollow pylon with antenna leads reaching up to and out of the ceiling. The desks were equipped with multiple LF, MF, and HF receivers, frequency meters, and RIP-5 Underwood Code Machines.

From his intercept position, Red Ritchie also watched Barnum and the new arrivals. As katakana telegraphic code began to sound off in his headset, he turned to his typewriter and began to copy. *Clack, clack, clack, clack, pause. Clack, clack, clack, clack, pause.*

Barnum turned to the nearest newbie, Ed Schroeder, and said, "Let's copy." Barnum sat at the intercept station next to Ritchie and motioned for Schroeder to do the same. The three sat side by side in front of their Underwood Code Machines, typing out in unison what they heard. *Clack, clack, clack, clack, pause. Clack, clack, clack, clack, pause.*

The intercept from Mariveles was superb, and the operators were able to copy Imperial Japanese Navy and diplomatic nets equally well. However, outside of the intercept shack, there was nothing at Mariveles for the Sailors to do. For a night out, they had to board a ferry and take a trip across Manila Bay to Cavite or Manila. All in all, Mariveles was an excellent location for intercept operations, but it was extremely isolated for a group of young Sailors. Chief Goodwin worried that eventually the men would go stir-crazy without anything to do.

CHAPTER 44

CLASS #15

MONDAY, MARCH 4, 1935
MAIN NAVY BUILDING, WASHINGTON, DC

Immediately upon Prescott Currier's arrival in Washington, DC, the Navy interviewed and investigated him for possible unauthorized disclosure of classified material in contradiction to the security oath he swore to uphold during his On-the-Roof Gang training. After painstaking inquiries, the investigation fully exonerated Currier, stating officially that his skills were due to nothing other than being an extremely intelligent and industrious man—the type which the Research Desk had been searching for over the years. Instead of being reprimanded or discharged for security issues, the U.S. Navy immediately offered Currier a commission as an ensign in the U.S. Navy Reserve, sent him to George Washington University for advanced training, and gave him a job at the Research Desk. Commander Kingman assigned him to work with Agnes Meyer Driscoll—Madame X herself—for mentorship.

Searching for stability across all the intercept sites, Kingman needed to send some new operators to the site in Station ABLE. Stations BAKER, CAST, and HYPO had recently been augmented with new On-the-Roof Gang graduates, and Peiping was in need of new operators. However, Peiping was a particular problem for the Research Desk because Kingman had little control over the Marine Corps operators. Not only was it difficult to find Marines qualified for the rooftop training, it was hard to keep them on intercept duties. The Marine Corps treated intercept duty as a temporary assignment. The Marine radiomen would receive training, do a single tour as intercept operators, and then return to general service duties. With the fifteenth On-the-Roof Gang class, Kingman aimed to bolster the number of operators stationed in Peiping, at least temporarily, by training a full class of Marines. But when the class began in March 1935, only six privates had been selected: Cecil Carraway, Curtis Crowe, Lombard Hingle, Jesse Randle, Carl Suber, and James Winborn.

In Foggy Bottom, Ma Travers was busy preparing to accommodate the six Marines with new staff. Susie Williams, her first and last remaining employee, had quit just weeks earlier, telling Ma she was finally ready to start her own business. Ma hoped she could be Susie's first client as she was in need of new staff to work at the guesthouse. But Ma never heard from Susie again. Desperate for help, she advertised in local newspapers for two new maids. She eventually hired sisters Evelyn and Ethel Stewart, just in time for the arrival of the next round of rooftop students.

Coincidently, the new On-the-Roof Gang instructor, Chief Bryan Byrd, lived a mere two blocks from Ma Travers's place in a studio apartment in an old mansion on the corner of G Street and Eighteenth Street NW. Byrd's wife and four children were still in South Carolina, so he regularly sent the majority of his pay and housing allowance home to support them. He minimized his own housing costs by settling on a single room at the very low rent of three dollars per week. It was a small, stark room furnished with only a bed, an armchair, a small desk, and a kitchenette. Three aging gas lamps provided light in the room. All Byrd needed was a place to cook an easy meal and sleep. He shared a bathroom with the tenants of two similar rooms.

When he moved into his room, the landlady had given him explicit instructions on how to operate the lamps, since improper use of coal gas lamps could be dangerous. The key to these older gas lamps, as the landlady explained, was to make sure the gas flowed freely so that there was no chance of the flame extinguishing.

Across Washington, DC, electric lights were slowly replacing indoor gas lamps in most residences. Still, the gas lighting was deemed safe if used properly, so it was only replaced if and when a homeowner decided to spend the money to upgrade to electric lighting. Since he had to pay for the gas on top of his rent, Byrd never burned more than a single light at a time, and he always kept the flame as low as possible.

As instructor of the rooftop class, Chief Byrd was very determined to have all his students succeed. He was in better shape than most chief petty officers, so he decided to use his fitness to connect with the Marines he was teaching. During breaks from class, he challenged the Marines to push-up contests outside the rooftop classroom. The students routinely pumped out more push-ups than he could and kidded him about it. Undeterred, he continued to have the contests of strength, knowing it would keep him ingratiated with his students.

Chief Byrd used Kidder's curriculum to bring the Marine Corps radiomen up to speed on the katakana telegraphic code. He first taught them the symbols and the code equivalents before transitioning to reciting the code verbally and then finally sending the code with the key. The students began copying with the stick, and only after reaching proficiency, did they move to the RIP-5 Underwood Code Machines. They picked up the skills quickly—and Chief Byrd continued to do push-ups with the Marines.

As he often did after class, Chief Byrd wandered down to the Research Desk office to see if there was any decryption he could help with. As he entered the space, a yeoman approached and said, "I hope you don't mind, Chief. I signed for this for you." The yeoman handed him a small, buff-colored envelope with a return address that read:

```
After 10 days return to
The Western Union Telegraph, Co.
Incorporated
```

As Chief Byrd took the envelope from the yeoman's hand, his heart immediately began to race. *Telegrams are never good news*, he thought.

With his hands shaking and fearing the worst about his family in South Carolina, Byrd opened the envelope as quickly as he could. Inside was a single sheet of paper of the same light yellow color. He took a deep breath, unfolded the paper, and read to himself:

```
BRYAN—
APPRECIATE HELP OF PERSONAL NATURE.
COUNTING ON FELLOW CHIEF FOR DISCRETION.
HAVEN'T HEARD FROM SUSIE IN WEEKS AND
GETTING WORRIED. PLEASE CHECK ON HER AND
LET ME KNOW ASAP.
  PAPPY
```

Byrd was relieved that it didn't have anything to do with his family. He closed his eyes and let his heartbeat settle down for a minute. Taking one last deep breath, he read the telegram again. Harry Kidder needed his help. *Of course, I'll help the famous Harry Kidder*, he thought.

The only problem was that he'd heard the students talking about the maids at Ma Travers's Guest House, so he knew Susie had been gone for quite some time. Still, he'd check with Gertrude to see if she knew where Susie might be.

CHAPTER 45

HYPO MOVES TO HEEIA

FRIDAY, JUNE 14, 1935

STATION HYPO, HEEIA, TERRITORY OF HAWAII

As the chief radioman in charge of Station HYPO, Harry Kidder developed a plan to move intercept operations from Wailupe to Heeia, on the eastern, windward coast of Oahu. The VLF (very low frequency) transmitting station, which was previously at Heeia, had been relocated to Lualualei, on the leeward coast. This presented the Research Desk an excellent opportunity to move into a newer facility without the constant interference from the 100-kilowatt transmitter at Radio Wailupe.

Chief Kidder had the assistance of two other chief radiomen: Truett Lusk and Charles "Dan" Daniels. Kidder had trained them both, and the three worked very well together. Over the course of two months, the trio obtained brand-new receivers from the Navy supply system at Pearl Harbor and installed them at Heeia. With the help of some of the other On-the-Roof Gang operators, they strung long-wire antennas for use at the new site. Kidder had ordered six new RIP-5 Underwood Code Machines, which were ready for installation at Heeia.

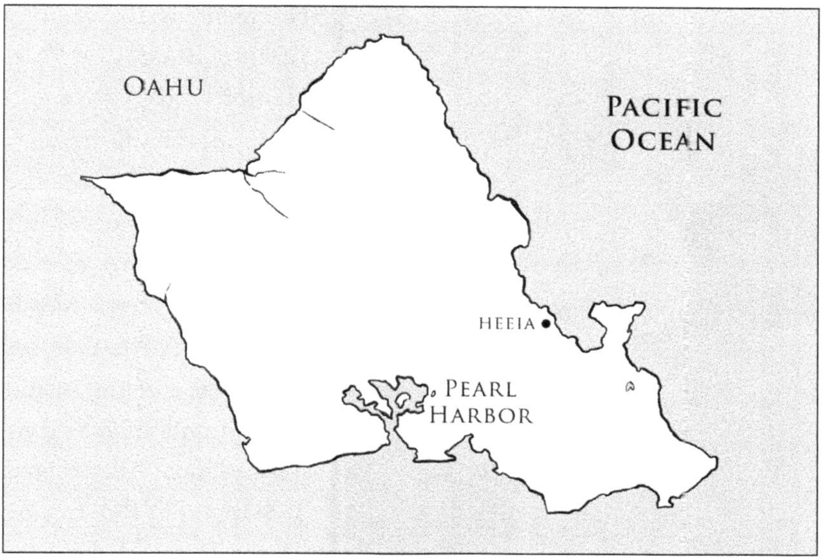

By the time the three chiefs completed outfitting the new operations floor in Heeia, Station HYPO was the best-equipped intercept station in the U.S. Navy. Intercept was excellent at the site; little to no interference and good propagation from the western Pacific Ocean ensured almost complete coverage of the Imperial Japanese Navy's communication nets. The only real limiting factor was the number of men that could work simultaneously, since only eight intercept positions could fit on Heeia's ops floor.

In addition to the excellent intercept conditions, the small nearby town of Kailua offered family housing and arguably the best swimming beach on Oahu. As the chief radioman in charge, Kidder lived in the only stand-alone house at the Heeia facility. Lusk, Daniels, and their wives lived in a duplex unit near Kidder's house. The site also had tennis courts, garages, electronic workshops, a paint locker, and a mess facility.

While Chief Kidder set up the new site at Heeia, the Fourteenth Naval District established a decryption and cryptanalytic cell in the

Chief Radioman Harry Kidder, Heeia, Hawaii, circa 1935.

basement of the Administration Building at Pearl Harbor. Like its equivalent in the Philippines, it was referred to as the Combat Intelligence Unit. Instead of having to wait for analysis from Washington, DC, the Combat Intelligence Unit could decrypt and analyze communications intercepted at Station HYPO, freeing up the Research Desk to concentrate on breaking new codes. Some of the officers and men assigned to the Combat Intelligence Unit mistakenly called themselves Station HYPO, believing *H* for Hawaii included the Combat Intelligence Unit. However, Kidder and the rest of the intercept operators knew this was wrong: HYPO was the designator for the intercept station, not the Combat Intelligence Unit at Pearl Harbor.

Despite the successful move to Heeia, Tru and Dan noticed that Chief Kidder seemed increasingly distracted. They knew he was pining for a girl back in DC, so they gave him the space he needed. But one day, when Kidder received a telegram, they noticed that he became very upset.

Their concern grew over Kidder's flagging demeanor, so they asked him to get a beer after work. The three sat at Castle Bar overlooking the Pacific Ocean. On any other day, this would have been a very pleasant after-work outing. However, on this particular day, they were too worried about their shipmate to enjoy the sea breeze. Sitting in between them, Harry stared down into his beer glass.

"Harry, are you OK?" Tru asked, genuinely concerned.

"Hmm? What? Oh, yeah, I'm fine," Harry muttered.

Tru could tell this was a lie. He had never seen his mentor look so down. "C'mon, Harry. Tell us what's gotcha down. You can tell us."

"I just got some bad news, that's all," Harry said before asking the bartender for a shot of whiskey, which he drank in one quick gulp.

"What happened?" Dan asked.

Harry shook his head. "It's nothing," he said. He wasn't comfortable sharing his problems with others. He caught the attention of the bartender and pointed at his empty whiskey glass. The bartender filled his glass, and Harry shot it again.

Tru and Dan stayed with Harry as he sat there, stewing quietly and drowning his sorrows in alcohol. Tru finally broke the ice, "Well, Harry, if there's anything you need, you just let us know."

"Of course. Thanks, fellas." Harry's response seemed robotic and forced. The three sat in silence as they finished their beers.

"C'mon, let us take you home, Harry," Tru suggested.

But Harry wasn't ready to stop drinking. "No, I'm gonna stick around a while longer. I'll catch a taxi home in a little while."

Dan and Tru were not convinced Harry was all right, but their wives were waiting for them at home, so they had to leave. Despite their concern, they left Kidder alone at the bar.

Not long after, Harry didn't notice when a couple of chatty local girls sat down next to him. They ordered cocktails and had a sip or two before they went to the dance floor. Kidder's gaze didn't stray from his beer glass, as he sat alone. The girls had left their purses and drinks on the bar next to Harry, but he barely noticed. He was still trying to process the news he had received in a telegram from Bryan Byrd earlier in the day.

Susie was gone. Gertrude had told Bryan she'd left the guesthouse weeks earlier to start her business, but since then, no one had heard from her, and nobody knew where she'd gone.

After Harry read the bad news from Bryan, he placed an expensive long-distance phone call to his bank in Washington to check on his account. The balance of his account, they told him, was zero—his bank account was completely empty. In one fell swoop, he'd lost Susie and his inheritance. At a loss for how to react, Harry decided to get drunk.

Unfortunately, drinking only made him feel worse. After he finished his last beer, he just wanted to get home to sober up. Despite the loss of Susie and a small fortune, Harry had come to the realization that as long as he concentrated on work, he'd be all right. He resolved to go home, get a good night's sleep, and apologize to Tru and Dan in the morning. He pushed his beer glass away and asked the bartender to call him a taxi.

As he sat at the bar waiting for his taxi, the two local girls returned from the dance floor. After they picked up their purses, one of them immediately began yelling at Harry.

"You stole my money! You're a thief! Call the Shore Patrol!" she yelled. This attracted the attention of the bartenders, one of whom tried to calm down the girls. The other bartender dialed the number for the Shore Patrol.

"Hold on, girls. He's been here all night. He ain't hurtin' no one. Leave him be."

"No! He has my money. Give me back my money!" she demanded.

"I don't have your money, sweetheart," Harry said dismissively.

But she persisted, "Call the SP! Call the police! He stole my money!"

Harry just shook his throbbing head, hoping this would all end soon. He didn't steal anyone's money, and he was ready to go to bed.

When the Shore Patrol—two very large petty officers in dress whites with wooden batons in hand—entered the bar, the accusing woman made straight for them and pointed a finger at Kidder. "Check his pockets!" she ordered. "He's got my money."

One of the SP officers asked, "How much are you missing, ma'am?"

"A dollar fifty."

"Sir, empty your pockets," the Shore Patrol instructed Harry.

"What? No! I didn't steal anything," Harry insisted.

"Sir, it's not a request. Empty your pockets on the bar, please."

Resigned, Harry reached into his pockets, pulled out some bills, coins, and his house key, and placed them on the bar. Among the other small bills and coins were two quarters and a dollar bill.

She yelled, "There! That's my money!"

"Don't be ridiculous," Harry said as he turned toward the SP officer. "Sailor, you have to believe me! That's not her money, it's mine!"

"Sir, you're going to have to come with us," the larger of the two SP officers instructed. Harry felt the officer grab his wrist and turn him around. Before he could resist, he was bent over the bar with handcuffs clasping his wrists together behind his back.

CHAPTER 46

ABLE MOVES BACK TO SHANGHAI

MONDAY, JUNE 24, 1935
AMERICAN LEGATION, PEIPING, CHINA

Since the closure of intercept operations in Shanghai in 1929, the Marine Corps' American Legation in Peiping, now called Station ABLE, was the only U.S. intercept station in China. The Marines primarily copied diplomatic nets, but they also covered some Imperial Japanese Navy communications nets as well. Even so, the Research Desk was looking for a way to reestablish intercept operations in Shanghai. The increasingly aggressive Japanese military activity in northern China provided the Research Desk with an opportunity to do just that.

Due to the proximity of Peiping to the Japanese-controlled city of Jehol, the security of the Marines carrying out intercept operations at the American Legation was becoming precarious, forcing the hands of decision-makers. The Research Desk, Asiatic Fleet, and the Commander of the Fourth Marine Regiment agreed to relocate Station ABLE from Peiping to Shanghai.

By this time, Chief Daryl "DW" Wigle, On-the-Roof Gang graduate of Class #3 in 1930, was the radioman in charge at Station

On-the-Roof Gang operators, mostly from Classes #12 and #15, probably on the roof of Fourth Marine Headquarters in Shanghai, circa 1935. L-to-R (front): SGT Jesse Randle, PFC Cecil Carraway, PFC Carl Suber, CRM Daryl Wigle (Radioman-in-Charge), SGT Stephen Lesko. L-to-R (rear): PVT Joseph Petrosky, PVT Harold Jones, PVT Harry Butler, PFC James Winborn, PVT Curtis Crowe, Captain Richard Zern (Officer-in-Charge).

ABLE. Wigle and Sergeant Stephen Lesko—who despite never having trained on the roof was the most experienced Marine Corps intercept operator, developed the plan for the move.

Chief Wigle left Peiping first and traveled to Shanghai to the headquarters of the Fourth Marine Regiment to discuss the new location for Station ABLE. While secrecy was of primary importance during the move, continuity of operations was also essential. The new station in Shanghai would have to be fully up and running before operations in Peiping were shut down.

Integral to the success of the plan to reestablish Station ABLE in Shanghai was to divert the Marine Corps graduates of the latest On-the-Roof Gang Class—who were already en route to Peiping—to Shanghai instead. However, the Marine operators currently at Peiping would not be told about the move. In fact, three of them—Walter Robertson, Harry Butler, and Norman Robertson—were rotated back into general service duty. Three others—Charles Southerland, Harold "Poochie" Jones, and Joseph Petrosky—all boarded the USS *Augusta* for what they believed to be a monthlong temporary assignment. In reality, they were being transferred to Shanghai. The trio arrived just days after the newly trained On-the-Roof Gang operators.

Despite agreement at the commander level, finding free space at the headquarters of the Fourth Marine Regiment Compound was a challenge. Chief Wigle was unable to secure any office space in Shanghai. Instead, the operation would be given only a small wooden shack on the roof of a two-story building at the rear of the compound. The shack, which measured about sixteen feet by six feet, was alone on the roof. A wooden desk extending along one side of the room held the receivers and housed four operating stations. Another side of the room, which contained a second desk, had a door leading onto the roof. Station personnel would be housed on the second floor of the same building. Although not ideal, the rooftop intercept site would allow the station to be operational while better spaces could be negotiated.

For the operators at the new Station ABLE, they felt right at home on the roof!

CHAPTER 47

CLASS #16

MONDAY, JULY 8, 1935
MAIN NAVY BUILDING, WASHINGTON, DC

Commander Kingman sat in his office at the Research Desk, reading the message in his hands over and over. A yeoman had delivered it moments earlier, and Kingman was having a hard time believing what he was reading.

The official U.S. Navy memo was from Lieutenant Commander Carl Holden, the DCO at the Fourteenth Naval District in Pearl Harbor. In the letter, Holden explained that Chief Harry Kidder had been arrested for drunk and disorderly conduct and petty theft. Kingman was baffled. Chief Kidder was the unimpeachable patriarch of the On-the-Roof Gang, and by all accounts, an upstanding Sailor and chief. In his long career, he was never known to drink excessively, and his integrity had never previously been in question. What was stated in the report was so far out of character for Chief Kidder that Commander Kingman felt compelled to do something about it.

But it was too late. The local courts in Hawaii moved quickly on complaints made by locals against *haole*—the local term for outsiders—especially when they were Sailors. In Chief Kidder's case, the courts ruled that he would be imprisoned for three years unless the U.S. Navy discharged him and transferred him away from the Hawaiian Islands. The Fourteenth Naval District complied. Taking into consideration his excellent record, Chief Kidder was permitted to retire in lieu of incarceration. In his absence, Tru Lusk took over Kidder's duties as radioman in charge of Station HYPO.

Not surprisingly, Harry was devastated. In addition to losing his love and his inheritance, he'd lost his one true passion—the U.S. Navy. Unceremoniously and forcibly retired from active duty, he moved to Florida. If the U.S. Navy was to going complete the job of setting up a fully functioning radio intelligence operation around the fleet, they would have to do so without the expert leadership of Chief Radioman Harry Kidder.

Among the Sailors and officers at the Research Desk, news spread of Kidder's misfortune. Agnes Meyer Driscoll took the news particularly hard. Agnes was a private person who didn't socialize with anyone at work, but if there had been anyone she felt close to in the office, it was Chief Kidder. She and Harry had forged a close professional relationship that Miss Aggie would miss. No matter when or where Harry left for sea duty, she always assumed he would return again to teach more radiomen the art and science of intercepting the katakana telegraphic code. Agnes's expectations would not come to pass now that Harry was officially out of the Navy, and she mourned the loss of her coworker.

Not only was Chief Byrd upset by the news, he also felt culpable since he'd delivered the bad news that had led to Harry getting drunk that night. He'd only met Kidder briefly, but he knew the legend of Pappy. The On-the-Roof Gang wouldn't be as strong without him.

Despite the blow to the Navy's radio intelligence efforts, Chief Byrd knew he had to get back to business. He had another class to teach. All eight students in his next class were radiomen third class:

Isaac Bemis, Elmer Dickey, Alfred DuRoss, Joseph Granger, Robert Maxwell, Kenneth Selch, Rodney Whitten, and Clifford Wilder.

One of the students, Joseph Granger, was dropped before the class even began. Despite excellent endorsements from his chain of command, a quick background check by the staff security officer at the Main Navy Building revealed two separate alcohol-related incidents that had occurred while Granger was on liberty in the Philippines. After the trouble with Chief Kidder in Hawaii, the Research Desk was especially careful about alcohol-related incidents. Granger was immediately made available for orders and departed before the first day of class.

Chief Byrd got right back to work teaching on the roof. His Navy students weren't as interested in push-up contests, and that suited him just fine. He'd recently experienced a flare-up of gastroenteritis, suffering repeated bouts of nausea from the condition he'd battled since he was young. It wasn't exactly how his chronic condition had presented itself in the past, but his gut had always given him one problem or another. Strangely though, he'd also been having headaches, something he hadn't experienced before. He dismissed these as stemming from the stress of living in a big city. He missed the slower pace of country life with his wife and children.

Despite his ailments, when Byrd was teaching, he felt great. Perhaps it was the distraction of having a real passion for the work he was doing. He missed his family terribly, but teaching provided a welcome change from the loneliness he experienced in his studio apartment. While at home, the nausea and headaches always seemed to be worse.

CHAPTER 48

TRAGEDY IN DC

SUNDAY, SEPTEMBER 22, 1935
G STREET AND 18TH STREET, WASHINGTON DC

Bryan Byrd returned home from the Main Navy Building where he had just eaten his Sunday dinner. Although he was given an allowance for meals, he regularly ate at the mess hall, even on weekends, where he could eat for free by simply showing his ID card. His family needed the money more than he did.

Byrd returned to his apartment and prepared for his favorite pastime—writing to his wife, Laura. The room was dark, so he needed to light one of the gas lamps. He stood at his desk and reached for the closest lamp, which was mounted directly to the wall. Following his landlady's instructions, he turned the knob on the lamp and waited for the gas to start flowing. At the right time, he struck a match and held it close to the nozzle.

With a soft whoosh, the lamp began to emit a bright white light. Bryan turned the knob again to lower the flame so that it was barely on. He only needed a little light to see what he was doing, and he didn't want to burn too much gas. Every penny counts! He sat down to write. Opening a desk drawer, he pulled out a pen and paper and placed them on top of the desk.

Bryan closed his eyes and imagined what he was going to write. He couldn't say anything about his work, so it would be more about life in DC and how he was feeling. His gastroenteritis was bothering him, but he would tell Laura he was feeling fine although he was missing her and the kids something fierce. He longed to play with his children and read them bedtime stories.

Stretching out, he reached his hands in the air toward the ceiling. His eyes were still closed, and he took a deep breath as he stretched. When his hands came down, he opened his eyes and looked at the blank paper. He took a couple more deep cleansing breaths as he contemplated his opening words to Laura.

Bryan glanced out the window at the warm September sunshine. Birds were singing and the traffic was light. He thought it had been too long since he'd last visited his family; he'd have to change that soon. He choked up a little, fondly remembering the good times when he and his family were all together. He breathed deeply again to let the tearfulness pass.

Suddenly, he felt a sharp pain in his forehead, painful enough to make him wince. He had been suffering from headaches lately, but this was the worst of them. He put his elbows on the desk and cradled his head in his hands. He took more deep breaths to try to help the pain pass. He gently shook his head to try and clear it, but the pain continued.

Bryan stood, again trying to clear his head. He took another deep breath to help with the pain, but it only intensified. He started to feel a little dizzy, and then the nausea crept in. Feeling the need to lie down, he backed up two steps and sat on the edge of the bed. By this time, he was having trouble catching his breath, so he breathed even more deeply several times. He lay back on the bed as another wave of dizzying nausea came over him.

Using his elbows, he crept back on the bed, so that his head was on the pillow. He was suddenly very tired and felt like he needed to close his eyes. Fighting the urge, he opened them wide and took another deep breath. He noticed the light above the desk sputtering as if the gas was turned down too low. Remembering his landlady's warnings, he knew it was important for him to get up and fix it. But his legs felt like they weighed a thousand pounds each and wouldn't move. No matter how hard he tried, he couldn't move. He tried to yell for help but had no breath in his lungs to make a sound.

Panic started to set in as he saw the flame flickering but couldn't do anything about it. He was completely paralyzed. His eyelids began to weigh heavily, and he was having a hard time keeping them open. He blinked slowly and noticed that the flame had gone out. Gas was seeping into the room, but still, he could do nothing about it.

The panic slowly faded as a peaceful calm washed over him. Just before he closed his eyes, he turned to look out the window once again. Sunlight streamed into his apartment. The warm glow grew brighter in the room as he closed his eyes for the last time and drifted off to sleep.

⚓ ⚓ ⚓

A week after the untimely death of Chief Jesse Bryan Byrd, the police report concluded that Byrd had committed suicide by turning on a gas spigot in his room. The coroner agreed.

Chief Walter "Sandy" McGregor, an On-the-Roof Gang classmate of Bryan Byrd's, knew that his friend would not have committed suicide. Bryan was a deeply religious man, and suicide was simply against his principles. Besides, Bryan had a beautiful family at home in South Carolina; he simply wouldn't have left his children without a father.

McGregor had recently arrived in Washington to work in the decryption section at the Research Desk. When he heard of Bryan's death, he immediately volunteered to take over as instructor.

Commander Kingman, thankful for a volunteer, reassigned McGregor to teach on the roof.

With only a few weeks left before the end of the sixteenth class, Chief McGregor completed the curriculum and helped the Sailors graduate, despite the loss of Chief Byrd. Following their training, each of the students was assigned to Station CAST with the exception of Petty Officers Dickey and Whitten, who were sent to Station S in Astoria for a four-month temporary assignment before heading to Station HYPO in Heeia, Hawaii.

CHAPTER 49

CAST MOVES TO CAVITE

SATURDAY, JANUARY 4, 1936

CAVITE NAVAL BASE, PHILIPPINES

After Station CAST moved to Mariveles, the isolation of the site became immediately problematic. The lack of any recreational facilities, the primitive and inadequate facilities for living, and the difficulty in getting anywhere else in Manila Bay began to create doubt about the wisdom of remaining there. To Chief Radioman Max Gunn, who recently replaced Keg Goodwin as radioman in charge of Station CAST, the need to relocate the intercept site was plainly obvious. The morale of his eight intercept operators demanded it.

Recognizing the need to once again relocate Station CAST, the Research Desk and the Department of Naval Communications proposed a plan to develop a new intercept site on Corregidor Island in the mouth of Manila Bay. Despite the U.S. Army's initial resistance to the Navy occupying any land on Corregidor, the powers that be eventually relented and agreed to a plan that would allow the Navy to occupy a location on the extreme eastern side of the island. The intercept site would be housed in a tunnel dug into the island's bedrock, much like the Army's Malinta Tunnel, the location of the Army's headquarters in the Philippines. And like the Malinta Tunnel, the Navy's facility would take years to dig and fully develop.

With the Corregidor project approved, the Research Desk then had to decide what to do with the intercept site in the interim. One option was to leave it at Mariveles until the Corregidor Tunnel was ready for occupation. However, recognizing the desperate need to get out of Mariveles, the Research Desk decided to temporarily move Station CAST closer to the Combat Intelligence Unit at Cavite Naval Base.

Cavite was a beehive of Navy activity. The area between Sangley Point and Cavite Naval Base had high-tech equipment along with a radio station, powerhouses, a commissary, a brass foundry and ice plant, numerous wharves, storage facilities, bowling alleys, recreation halls, and schools. Across Sangley Point and along the shore of Canacao Bay was Dreamland, the largest cabaret in Asia where a live orchestra played dance music all night long until the church bells signaled the first Catholic Mass of the day.

While the Combat Intelligence Unit remained in Building G of the Naval Prison, the intercept operation moved onto the second floor of a building right next door to the Radio Laboratory. In addition, an experimental HFDF site was established at Sangley Point. Several On-the-Roof Gang alumni were assigned to take turns trying to operate the experimental equipment.

Although Cavite represented an improvement over Mariveles for the morale of the operators, conditions for intercept were much more difficult. The vast amount of electrical machinery in the naval yard caused tremendous interference across all frequency bands. The problem was so severe that it made intercept operations impossible during the day.

Lieutenant Jack Holtwick, the Asiatic Fleet's newly assigned intelligence officer, directed Red Ritchie to organize a study of electrical equipment and motors to try to figure out a way to mitigate the terrible interference. Ritchie conducted a very thorough survey and found that there were over 470 electrical motors, including 200 fans, that contributed a significant portion of the interference. To alleviate some of the interference, Ritchie designed and installed filters and shielding, finally making intercept operations from Cavite possible.

The city of Cavite was well known for its nightlife. While most Sailors gravitated to Dreamland, members of the On-the-Roof Gang frequented a strip of bars and restaurants known as "The Alley," which was home to bars such as the Dixie, Santa Ana, and Miranda. However, the group's favorite haunt was Manila Tom's.

By Cavite standards, Manila Tom's was a relatively sedate bar. Instead of employing dancing girls, Manila Tom's catered to the men who simply wanted to unwind after work or on the weekends in a quiet, friendly atmosphere. The On-the-Roof Gang became regulars at Manila Tom's, where they started a tradition of buying, personalizing, and reusing their own beer mugs. Each man purchased his own mug and had it hand-painted by a local artist with his name or a unique design. In between visits to Manila Tom's, the mugs would be stored in built-in cubbyholes behind the bar. Chief Gunn's mug had an anchor painted on it. Others had their first names painted on their glasses. Some had their nicknames, like "Red" Ritchie, and "Snuffy" Schroeder. And for some reason that he wouldn't explain, Norman Lewis had "Sugar Lou" painted on his mug. His shipmates could only wonder.

CHAPTER 50

CLASSES #17 AND #18

MONDAY, JANUARY 13, 1936
MAIN NAVY BUILDING, WASHINGTON, DC

Since he'd only taught the final weeks of the sixteenth On-the-Roof Gang class, the next one—which began in January 1936—was Chief Sandy McGregor's first full class as an instructor. In the weeks prior, he worked tirelessly to prepare. In early January, seven students arrived in Washington for training. Paul Hively Jr. and Harold Layman were both radiomen second class; Kenneth Carmichael, Robert Ledford, Merle Lynch, Clarence Taylor, and Robert Williams were all radiomen third class.

Each man had his own room at Ma Travers's place. Gertrude was thankful for her new staff, but the girls working for her seemed merely like employees. She missed having Susie and Stephanie around, who felt more like family to her. Neither of the two new employees stayed at Ma's place; they were both married and lived at home with their own families.

In May 1936, Laurance Safford, having been promoted to commander, returned to Washington, DC to take over the helm of the Department of Naval Communications Code and Signal Section,

On-the-Roof Gang Class #17, circa 1936. L-to-R (front): RM2c Paul Hively, RM3c Clarence Taylor, RM3c Merle Lynch. L-to-R (rear): RM2c Harold Layman, RM3c Robert Ledford, RM3c Kenneth Carmichael, CRM Walter McGregor (Instructor), RM3c Robert Williams. Photo was taken next to the rooftop classroom.

which included the Research Desk. After settling in and checking on the status of radio intelligence operations around the fleet, he realized there were several issues requiring his attention.

After hearing what had happened to Chief Kidder, Safford didn't believe a single word of the story surrounding Harry's unceremonious dismissal. He believed that Kidder was railroaded out of the U.S. Navy merely to appease the local Hawaiian press. Safford's first priority was to try to get Kidder reinstated to active duty. He'd learned that Kidder was living in Port Saint Lucie covering the Florida State Baseball League for *The Evening Independent* newspaper. Since the courts in Hawaii no longer had any jurisdiction, Safford immediately offered Kidder an annulment of his retirement and full reinstatement into the U.S. Navy with an assignment to the communications station in Cheltenham, Maryland.

Kidder humbly declined the offer, telling Safford he was happy in his post-Navy life. In a compromise, Kidder agreed to be brought back into the active Navy Reserve with his drill site at Cheltenham. It was a small victory for Safford, who would at least have Chief Kidder available one weekend a month and for two weeks every summer to help train some of the more junior intercept operators.

Meanwhile, Safford received a letter from Charles "Dan" Daniels, who at this point was the radioman in charge of Station BAKER, regarding some problems he was having in Guam. Despite the fact that the U.S. Navy radio station had closed, Guam still had a senior communications officer assigned there: Lieutenant Junior Grade John Chester, who, with no radio station to run, interfered with the daily operations of the intercept site. Safford recognized something had to be done.

Safford also communicated with Chief Daryl Wigle, the radioman in charge of Station ABLE in Shanghai, regarding the manning and readiness of the Marine Corps operators there. Wigle provided Safford with an honest assessment of the intercept site, stating that he believed the site was fighting a losing battle trying to keep trained Marine Corps operators.

At the time, Station ABLE had two sergeants, one corporal, five privates first class, and one private in addition to Chief Wigle. All of them had been trained on the roof except Sergeant Lesko, who had been engaged in intercept work for over a decade. Other than Lesko, all the Marine Corps operators left intercept work after a single assignment, permanently returning to general service radio duty.

Safford drafted a letter for the Chief of Naval Operations to send to the Commandant of the Marine Corps. The letter made several specific recommendations toward the improvement of personnel conditions at Station ABLE and the quality of Marine Corps intercept personnel in general. Safford made it clear that unless the Marine Corps could reach the same manning standards as the Navy had established, then the Navy was prepared to discontinue training Marine Corps intercept personnel and replace them with Navy personnel.

The commandant of the Marine Corps responded via official letter, saying that he appreciated the need for sufficient operators for intercept duties. However, he declined to establish a permanent cadre of intercept operators for a couple of reasons. First, the Marine Corps was already short staffed. In addition, Marine Corps radiomen were trained to provide communications for the Fleet Marine Force. Therefore, it was not possible to divert trained radiomen to duties other than those for which they had been initially intended. The commandant offered that the Marine Corps would take steps to reduce personnel turnover, improve promotional opportunities, and assign trained personnel to intercept duties as much as possible.

This response was completely unsatisfactory to Safford, who believed it threatened the continued existence of Station ABLE. The CNO agreed and announced that the Research Desk would no longer train Marine radiomen for intercept work. Furthermore, Navy intercept operators would replace the Marines at Station ABLE. As such, the Navy assumed all Marine operators would be reassigned to general service duties at their rotation dates. Safford drafted a letter to Chief Wigle in Shanghai to inform him of the developments.

Disappointed in the outcome of two of his top priorities, Safford needed a win, and the Imperial Japanese Navy presented him with the opportunity in the form of the super-dreadnought battleship *Nagato*.

The *Nagato* was built in 1920 and had recently been updated and upgraded at Yokosuka Naval Base. Now, it was undergoing sea trials and the On-the-Roof Gang was monitoring its activities. The reconstruction, decryption (using the Blue Book code), and translation of intercepted communications of the *Nagato*'s sea trials in January 1936 indicated that its top speed was 26 knots—a fact that contradicted the information reported by the Office of Naval Intelligence, which stated the *Nagato* could only make 23.5 knots. But several times during the *Nagato*'s sea trials, the ship's self-reported top speed was 26 knots. This would be a tremendous disadvantage to U.S. Navy commanders since the Navy's new battleships were designed with a maximum speed of only 24 knots. As a result, the information on the *Nagato* was conveyed to the U.S. Navy's shipbuilding community, which ultimately raised the top speed for the first two battleships of the North Carolina-class, the USS *North Carolina* and the USS *Washington*, to 27 knots. For subsequent battleships, the maximum speed requirement would be raised to 28 knots. Based solely upon information gained through radio intelligence, twelve new U.S. Navy battleships under construction would have superior speed over their Japanese counterparts. Safford had his win.

⚓ ⚓ ⚓

When the On-the-Roof Gang class finished up in May, Petty Officers Carmichael, Hively, Lynch, and Williams transferred to Station CAST in Cavite, while Layman, Ledford, and Taylor were sent to Station HYPO in Heeia.

By the spring of 1936, nearly three years had passed since the Imperial Japanese Navy's last Grand Maneuvers exercise, and Commander Safford had already begun developing extensive plans for the exploitation of communications during the 1936 maneuvers. He made sure that Stations BAKER, CAST, and HYPO were prepared and planned to deploy several On-the-Roof Gang operators aboard the USS *Gold Star* to cover the exercise, which was scheduled to take place from May to June and was to be the largest Imperial Japanese Navy exercise ever.

On-the-Roof Gang Class #18, circa 1936. L-to-R (front): RM3c Chester Bissell, RM2c Walter Johnson, RM2c Samuel McCurdy, RM3c Frank Weiland. L-to-R (rear): RM2c Rex Jule, RM2c Albert Pelletier, CRM Walter McGregor (Instructor), RM3c Fred Thomson, RM3c Roy Sholes. Photo was taken next to the rooftop classroom.

However, in late April, decrypted and translated intercept indicated that the Japanese had indefinitely postponed the maneuvers for an unspecified reason. This was the first departure from the exercise schedule in over a decade, so Safford and the On-the-Roof Gang members were stumped as to why.

When the next On-the-Roof Gang class convened in July, a full roster of second and third class radiomen were ready for Chief McGregor to train them, including Chester Bissell, Walter Johnson, Rex Jule, Sam McCurdy, Albert Pelletier Jr., Roy Sholes, Fred Thomson, and Frank Weiland. Upon graduation, Bissell, McCurdy, and Pelletier each transferred to Station CAST. Johnson, Jule, Sholes, Thomson, and Weiland went to Station HYPO.

CHAPTER 51

DEVELOPMENTS IN HFDF

SATURDAY, JANUARY 25, 1936
STATION CAST, CAVITE NAVAL BASE, PHILIPPINES

Although the U.S. Navy had been conducting direction finding in the medium frequency band since the Great War, the DF capabilities were primarily used for station-keeping and navigational purposes, not for locating enemy ships. But over time, new techniques and equipment were required to be able to perform HFDF on Japanese communications. As such, the Naval Research Lab had secretly been developing these HFDF capabilities since 1930 and had deployed two experimental units: one to Mare Island, California, and the other to Station CAST at Cavite Naval Base, which the Naval Research Laboratory dubbed CXK-1.

The CXK-1 was a radio shack mounted on a wooden platform on wheels that—with the aid of motors—rotated around a center point on a circular cement base. A small motor mounted on the right side of the operator's chair controlled a larger motor located under the building in the cement foundation. To obtain a bearing, the operator had to learn to rotate the shack in either direction with a handle on

CXK-1 HFDF set, similar to CXK-1 installed at Sangley Point, Cavite Naval Base, Philippines. Note tracks at bottom right corner for tires to follow as entire building rotated.

the small motor. A forward spin on the handle caused the shack to rotate clockwise and a reverse spin did just the opposite. The oscilloscope display flattened down to a horizontal line, known as the null, when the operator pointed directly toward the transmitter in question. At that point, the operator had to shift his gaze from the scope to the tabletop in front of him, where the bearing could be read. Although awkward and clunky, the CXK-1 provided accurate readings of enemy communications.

In the Philippines, Lieutenant Junior Grade Raymond S. Lamb, the Asiatic Fleet intelligence officer, removed Radioman First Class Meddie Royer, who recently arrived from Station BAKER and had been promoted, from intercept duties and assigned him to operate the experimental CXK-1 HFDF equipment. In order to test the effectiveness of the new HFDF equipment, the CINCAF directed the USS *Paul Jones* to perform pre-choreographed maneuvers west of

Manila Bay. For test and calibration purposes, the *Paul Jones* would also transmit every three minutes on 8000, 12000, and 16000 kilocycles. The test took five days, but the results were only partially successful. Over the next several weeks, Royer tested various configurations of the equipment, including tilting the arms from vertical, trying different feed wire placements, placing wire coils in series with the arms, and increasing the airflow in the DF shack to reduce overheating, in order to try to improve the consistency and accuracy of the bearings.

When Royer finally believed he'd found a configuration that was most successful, he tested it in early February 1936, just as ships of the Japanese fleet departed Yokosuka Naval Base. With Royer measuring the bearings of the Japanese navy's positions and comparing them to results deduced through traffic analysis, the results proved extremely accurate. Lamb reported these results to the Research Desk via official letter.

Safford responded to this report with a letter to Lamb in which he stated:

> You and your operators did a splendid job, and you have my heartiest congratulations. You have made history, as this is the first occasion when an HFDF station has tracked a foreign ship. As a result of your good work another HFDF suite will be sent to Cavite for reconditioning and then to Guam for use.

At the Naval Research Laboratory, engineers continued to develop new-and-improved equipment for HFDF. Soon they had designed a system that utilized a rotating array of four vertical elements called a rotating Adcock. The Model DT, as it was known, was an efficient directional antenna, that, when mounted on a platform, could be rotated to measure signal strength coming from different bearings. Given some success at the Naval Research Lab, Commander Safford wanted to procure several of these new rotating HFDF systems to deploy around the Pacific Ocean. However, this would require a significant financial expenditure that Safford couldn't imagine the Department of Naval Communications approving. Still, he decided to try since this was likely the best and only way to keep track of Imperial Japanese Navy vessels if war were to come.

Model DT HFDF set.

CHAPTER 52

CLASS #19

MONDAY, JANUARY 11, 1937
MAIN NAVY BUILDING, WASHINGTON, DC

The nineteenth class of On-the-Roof Gang students was scheduled to begin in early 1937 under the tutelage of Chief Sandy McGregor. The students assigned were all radiomen second class: Clarence Detterich, Robert Dormer, Harvey Howard, Edward Kelly, Raymond Parrott, Alva Squires, Theodore Wildman, and William Young.

Because the results of the HFDF experiments at Station CAST were encouraging, all the students in this On-the-Roof Gang class were sent across town to the Naval Research Laboratory in Bellevue for a month of training on the Model DT HFDF equipment. After completing their additional training, the newly minted intercept operators were sent to the fleet. Detterich, Dormer, and Kelly were sent to Station BAKER; Howard, Parrott, and Squires transferred to Station CAST; and Wildman and Young went to Station HYPO.

On-the-Roof Gang Class #19, circa 1937. L-to-R (front): RM2c Edward Kelly, RM2c Robert Dormer, RM2c Harvey Howard, RM2c Raymond Parrott. L-to-R (rear): RM2c Alva Squires, RM2c William Young, CRM Walter McGregor (Instructor), RM2c Theodore Wildman, RM2c Clarence Detterich. Photo was taken next to the rooftop classroom.

CHAPTER 53

UNREST IN CHINA

THURSDAY, JULY 8, 1937
STATION ABLE, PEIPING, CHINA

Shortly after the nineteenth On-the-Roof Gang class graduated in July 1937, the reasoning behind the Imperial Japanese Navy's the cancellation of the 1936 Grand Maneuvers became clear. Since the invasion of Manchuria in 1931, Japanese forces had been pushing further north into China seeking to obtain raw materials to boost their industrial capacity. Occasional skirmishes broke out between Japanese forces and Chinese resistance, but these typically lasted only a few days before dying down. By July 1937, Japan had roughly 15,000 soldiers located throughout China, which stoked progressively worse feelings among its citizens.

In the early morning hours of July 8, another small skirmish occurred near Marco Polo Bridge, a crucial access point to Peiping over the Yongding River. By sunrise, Chinese and Japanese forces had gathered on either side of the bridge and gunfire rang out. Despite an official cease-fire agreement between the combatants, the gunfire never stopped; in fact, it escalated into a full-scale battle for the bridge and eventually for the city of Peiping.

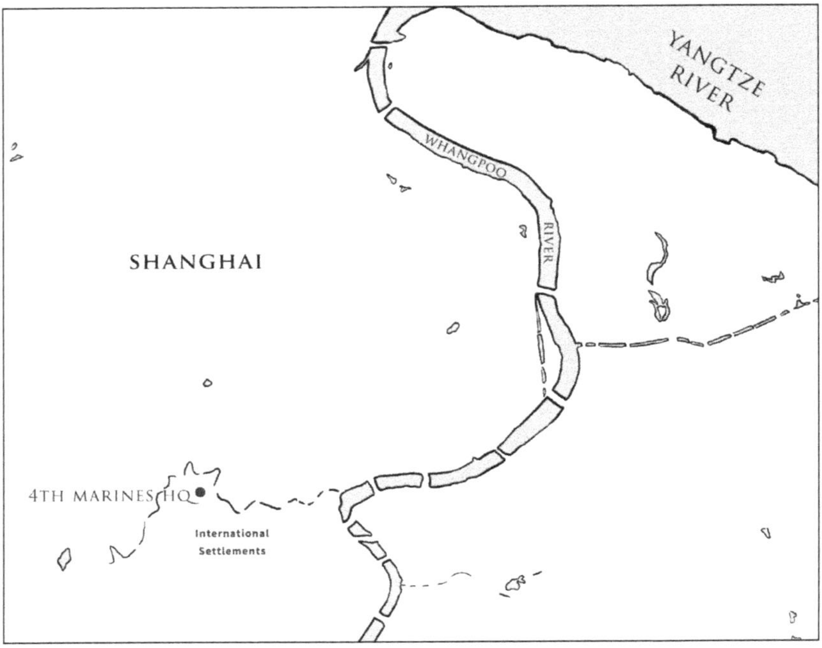

Additional soldiers were ferried from Japan on Imperial Japanese Navy ships, which remained to form a blockade around China. What began as a series of confused, sporadic skirmishes around China spiraled into a sweeping Japanese invasion of the country—an event that the U.S. Navy had predicted based on the analysis of intercept obtained during the 1933 Grand Maneuvers.

In defense of their homeland, Chinese forces laid siege to the Japanese area of the International Settlement in Shanghai. Occasional gunfire and explosions erupted mere blocks from the headquarters of the Fourth Marine Regiment. Station ABLE's intercept shack on the roof of the building was exposed and in danger of being hit by a stray bomb or even a direct attack.

In the same letter in which Safford informed Wigle that Marines would no longer be trained for radio intelligence duties, he also requested that Station ABLE be relocated inside the headquarters

Fourth Marines Headquarters, International Settlement, Shanghai, China.

of the Fourth Marine Regiment at Shanghai, as soon as possible, for safety reasons.

The powers that be at the Fourth Marine Regiment agreed to relocate seventy-five Marines housed on the top floor of the Headquarters Building so that Station ABLE could be moved into the vacated space. The new location inside the building was larger than the wooden shack previously occupied and was less conspicuous since it shared existing antennas with the general service radio room.

Once approved, Wigle immediately delegated the task to his two Marines—Sergeant Stephen Lesko and Private Jesse Randle—to execute the move. Less than a week later, the task was complete and Station ABLE operations in Shanghai were restored inside the Fourth Marines headquarters building.

CHAPTER 54

PROBLEMS AT STATION BAKER

TUESDAY, JULY 20, 1937
USS *AUGUSTA*, UNDERWAY IN THE WESTERN PACIFIC OCEAN

In response to Commander Safford's letter regarding interference from Lieutenant Junior Grade John Chester, Admiral Harry Yarnell—the Commander in Chief of the Asiatic Fleet—dispatched his intelligence officer, Lieutenant Junior Grade Raymond Lamb, from Cavite to Guam on board the USS *Augusta*. Lamb and several On-the-Roof Gang operators, including chief radiomen Max Gunn and Martin Vandenberg, were also on board the Asiatic Fleet's flagship, and the timing had been arranged so that it took place during the Japanese Fleet Maneuvers of 1937, a smaller IJN exercise than the triannual Grand Maneuvers. If, by chance, the maneuvers were to take place in waters in or near the Mandated Islands, Lamb hoped to be close enough to obtain some unique intercept from the Imperial Japanese Navy.

Lamb was also scheduled to inspect Station BAKER at Libugon to investigate the cause of friction between Chief Daniels and Lieutenant Chester, who was apparently creating many obstacles hindering effective intercept operations at the site.

During his investigation in Guam, Lamb discovered that Chester regularly ordered the men of Station BAKER to perform trivial duties for his own benefit. Using the authority Admiral Yarnell had granted him, Lamb replaced Chester on the spot with Lieutenant Bertrum Allen, who had also traveled from Cavite on board the *Augusta* for this very purpose. Chester was sent back to San Francisco for further assignment away from any intercept sites.

⚓ ⚓ ⚓

Around this same time, Johnny Cooke, a graduate of the fourth On-the-Roof Gang class, had returned to Guam after a yearlong stint on the SS *President Jefferson*. This time, however, he was there as an employee of Pan American Airways, having been honorably discharged from the U.S. Navy earlier in the year. Pan Am operated a flight service they called the China Clipper, which traveled from Alameda, California, to Hong Kong, making stops in Honolulu, Midway Island, Wake Island, Guam, and Manila. The airline used Morse code operators familiar with communications in the Pacific region to copy Japanese plaintext weather messages. Pan Am depended on those messages for safe air navigation and operations across the vast Pacific Ocean, and Cooke was one of its operators.

The Imperial Japanese Navy used an hourly sked to send current and forecasted weather reports to all Japanese navy and merchant ships operating in the Pacific and Indian Oceans. But suddenly in mid-July 1937, without warning, Japanese radio stations discontinued sending weather broadcasts for their island bases in plaintext international Morse code, instead switching to an encrypted system using the katakana telegraphic code. Without these reports, the Pan Am weather centers in Alameda, Honolulu, and Manila could not prepare forecasts or safe navigational routes for the China Clipper flights.

On-the-Roof Gang operators at Station BAKER, Guam, circa 1937. L-to-R (standing): CRM Charles Daniels (Radioman in Charge), RM2c Orville Jones, RM3c Fred Thomson, RM2c Robert Dormer, RM2c Ivan Benjamin, and RM2c Clarence Detterich. L-to-R (front): RM1c Hilary Cyr, RM2c Chester Bissell, RM2c Carl Jensen, RM2c Edward Kelly.

Luckily, the encryption system had to be simple enough for the Japanese merchant fleet to use, and Cooke was able to break the code—it was a simple transposition code wherein all the Japanese words were spelled backward yet transmitted in the correct sentence order. Cooke began to copy the weather broadcasts, decrypt the codes into plaintext, translate the weather reports, and then forward the reports twice daily to Pan Am.

Cooke shared his new solution for the weather code with his old friends at Station BAKER, who, in turn, shared it with the Research Desk. Within a week, all intercept stations in the Pacific were using Cooke's solution to copy the new Japanese weather broadcasts, which provided the only reliable weather forecasts for the entire Pacific Ocean.

CHAPTER 55

CLASS #20

MONDAY, NOVEMBER 1, 1937
MAIN NAVY BUILDING, WASHINGTON, DC

The twentieth group of On-the-Roof Gang students was about to arrive, and Chief Sandy McGregor was prepared. After checking in at the quarterdeck in late October 1937, the students checked in at Ma Travers's Guest House for lodging.

Due to a mix-up at the Bureau of Naval Personnel (BUPERS), nine radiomen were ordered to Washington for the katakana rooftop training, even though the classroom could only accommodate eight. Five of the students—Henry Ethier, Glenn Evans, James Johnson, Charles Walters, and Duane Whitlock—were all radiomen second class. The rest—Ralph Briggs, Elliott Okins, Pearly Phillips, and Samuel Winchester—were radiomen third class.

Commander Safford reviewed the records of all nine of the recently arrived radiomen, looking for one to hold back until the next class began. All had impeccable records and could copy up to forty words per minute in international Morse code. They each came highly recommended by their commanding officers. And not a single one of them had a negative mark on his personnel file. As happened frequently in the U.S. Navy, it came down to alphabetical order, so Radioman Third Class Sam Winchester was bumped to the next class, which was scheduled to begin the following July.

However, this meant Safford needed to find an assignment for Winchester in the Main Navy Building. He was not yet ready for decryption work in the Research Desk—it would have been too much, too soon for the young radioman. Instead, Safford devised a plan that would serve multiple purposes.

Chief McGregor left a message for Winchester at Ma Travers's place, directing him to report for duty on the Monday before class was to start. At his desk, Safford read through the daily traffic as he waited for Winchester to arrive. When Safford heard the knock at the door he was expecting, he got up to answer it.

Safford opened the door and greeted the Sailor, "Petty Officer Winchester?"

"No, sir," the yeoman at the door answered.

"You're not Winchester?"

"No, sir. I'm Petty Officer Crocker, messenger of the watch. You've got a phone call at the quarterdeck."

"Oh, OK. Let's go. Sorry for the confusion, Crocker."

"No problem, sir," Crocker said while turning to walk back down to the quarterdeck.

"Any idea who it is, Sailor?" Safford asked as they walked together.

"No, sir, but it sounded official," Crocker replied.

Telephones had only recently been installed in the Main Navy Building, and there were still very few. Admirals rated phones in their offices, as did some captains. But not commanders. The quarterdeck had a phone, which was the main contact phone for most of the Sailors at the Main Navy Building.

As the pair approached the quarterdeck, Petty Officer Crocker picked up the telephone and spoke into the handset, "Sir, stand by for Commander Safford." He handed the handset to Safford. As Safford took it, the Sailor picked up a pen and pad and set them down on the desk for Safford to use, if needed.

"Commander Safford, here. . . . Yes. . . . What? . . . Can you repeat that?" Safford listened for several minutes, nodding occasionally.

"OK, I understand. How can I get in touch with her?" Safford picked up the pad and pen and wrote down an address and phone number.

"OK, thank you, doctor. . . . Yes. . . . Thank you."

Safford handed the phone to the Sailor and headed back to his office. Sitting down behind his desk, he replayed the telephone conversation in his head. The call was from a doctor at Northern Queen Anne's County Hospital in Chestertown, Maryland. Agnes Meyer Driscoll had been in a serious automobile accident over the weekend. She and her husband, Michael, had been with another couple and were on their way home from Maryland's eastern shore. Because Agnes was so private, Safford didn't even know that she'd gone out of town over the weekend, let alone who she was with or where they'd gone.

The doctor told Safford that Agnes was driving, Michael was in the front passenger seat, and their friends were in the back seat, when their car was hit broadside by another car at full speed in the middle of a four-way intersection. The rear half of the car on the driver's side took the brunt of the impact, and the two passengers in the back seat were killed instantly. Agnes's left femur was broken, as was her jaw in two places. Michael was the only one to emerge from the accident without major injury.

The doctors at Queen Anne's recommended surgery for Agnes's broken leg. Surgeons wanted to place a metal rod into her femur to allow it to heal. She refused the surgery for reasons she would not divulge, and Michael supported her decision. Instead, she was placed in traction and would have to remain in the hospital for at least three months. The bone was badly broken, and doctors weren't sure if Agnes would walk again. Her jaw was wired shut to allow it to heal.

Safford felt that Agnes was lucky to be alive. But her loss would be keenly felt in the Research Desk. She was a mainstay of the code-breaking operation. In her absence, they would have to depend on the people she'd trained. Safford hoped they were up to the task.

Getting back to the business at hand, Safford directed Chief Kidder to spend a Reserve weekend with Petty Officer Winchester in the rooftop classroom at the Main Navy Building. Safford wanted Kidder to set up Winchester at one of the intercept positions in the rooftop classroom to perform intercept against European diplomatic nets. These transmissions were in international Morse code and would be completely recognizable to Winchester. This solution would keep him busy until the next On-the-Roof Gang class began. It would also provide the Research Desk with additional intercept to process.

During the hours the On-the-Roof Gang class was in session, Chief McGregor could supervise Winchester to make sure he was sitting the live intercept position in the classroom. Safford had an ulterior motive in using Chief Kidder for this assignment: he wanted to continue to apply pressure on him in the hopes of luring him back into active duty.

The weekend before the twentieth class began, Kidder and Winchester climbed the ladder and stepped onto the roof of the sixth wing of the Main Navy Building. On that crisp, clear November morning, Kidder was immediately overwhelmed with fond memories. He remembered building the steel-reinforced concrete blockhouse classroom, which was a little worse for wear after almost a decade of use. He remembered all nine of the classes he'd taught, as well as each of his fifty-seven students.

The view from the roof was just as spectacular as always. "Wow," Kidder muttered aloud. He felt a fleeting moment of sadness remembering the Independence Day he'd spent on the roof with Susie. He had gotten over her, but the memory still haunted him in quiet moments.

"Yeah, this is amazing," Petty Officer Winchester agreed.

Winchester's voice jarred Kidder from his trance; he'd almost forgotten the young Sailor was with him. "Let's get you set up, Sam."

Winchester had never had a chief call him by his first name before. He supposed Kidder did it because they were wearing civilian clothes. Regardless, it made him feel like a real person again for the first time since before boot camp.

As they stepped into the classroom, more memories flooded Chief Kidder. Reciting the katakana code to the students, sending the code as students tried to keep up, choir practice . . .

Kidder had Winchester sit down at an intercept station and then sat down next to him. As Kidder fired up his receivers, Winchester followed suit. While the equipment warmed up, Kidder said, "We'll have to replace the RIP-5 for you. You'll need a regular mill."

"OK, Chief," Sam responded, quite intimidated by the confusing typewriter in front of him.

"Don't worry about that, Sam," the chief reassured him. "You'll master that thing before you leave here."

After a few moments, Harry continued, "Tune in to 15100 kilocycles. That's the Western Europe dip net. This will be easy for you—five-digit groups and it's all in straight Morse code. Usually, the code is between twenty-five and thirty words per minute. You'll do fine."

The pair tuned their receivers to the right frequency, and sure enough, Morse code rang out. With no typewriter to copy the code, Winchester simply listened. "Easy enough, Chief." Kidder nodded reassuringly.

If Safford's plan was to play on Chief Kidder's sentiment about the On-the-Roof Gang training, it had worked like a charm. Kidder left the roof that day missing the Navy and the radio intelligence operation.

⚓ ⚓ ⚓

RM3c Sam Winchester, inside the rooftop classroom in the Main Navy Building, Washington, DC, circa 1938. Winchester worked at a live intercept position during Class #20, while waiting for his class (#21) to begin.

On the first day of class, November 1, 1937, Chief McGregor arrived at work excited for class to begin. During class the following day, Petty Officer Winchester sat at one of the four intercept positions in the classroom, the RIP-5 having been replaced with a standard Underwood Model 5 typewriter. With his tobacco pipe lodged between his teeth throughout the day, Winchester typed out intercept from the European diplomatic net he'd been assigned to copy. His typewriter clacked away as the students received instruction. While this may have been a distraction, Chief McGregor thought it was a realistic representation of any intercept shack in the fleet—there was no better way for the students to prepare than in conditions close to the real thing.

After completing the rooftop training, all the students went to the Naval Research Lab for two weeks of HFDF training before transferring to their first intercept jobs. Johnson, Okins, and Phillips all transferred to Station BAKER in Guam. Briggs, Evans, Walters, and Whitlock were ordered to Station HYPO, and Ethier went to Station CAST in the Philippines.

As Chief McGregor prepared for the next class, he had a relapse of the heart palpitations he'd previously suffered in 1935. Those heart

On-the-Roof Gang Class #20, circa 1937. L-to-R (front): RM2c James Johnson, RM2c Henry Ethier, RM2c Duane Whitlock. L-to-R (rear): RM2c Charles Walters, CRM Walter McGregor (Instructor), RM3c Pearly Phillips, RM3c Ralph Briggs, RM2c Glenn Evans. Photo was possibly taken in OP-20-G spaces.

problems had cut his assignment in Station CAST short by a year and required him to spend some time in Mare Island Naval Hospital in Vallejo, California, before transferring to Washington, DC. At this point, his doctors recommended he take a less stressful job than teaching, so Commander Safford had him return to decryption duties in the Research Desk, where he could continue to work on breaking Japanese codebooks.

CHAPTER 56

AIR ACTIVITY IN CHINA

SUNDAY, DECEMBER 12, 1937
STATION HYPO, HEEIA, TERRITORY OF HAWAII

On Sunday, December 12, 1937, Radioman Second Class Markle Smith and Radioman Third Class Roy Sholes—both On-the-Roof Gang alumni—were sitting the evening "scoop" watch at Station HYPO, conducting search operations for any katakana code that wasn't on a known sked. Lately, they had been finding a lot of Japanese air activity as Japanese forces approached Nanking, China from the south and east. Since the transmissions were unencrypted, the intercept operators could actually follow what was happening, even though the less formatted traffic was more difficult to copy. Bomber and fighter aircraft regularly took off from secure Japanese airfields within China, dropped their bombs, and strafed targets in order to wear down the Chinese defenses. Intercept operators at Station HYPO—which had relatively good conditions for intercept, especially in the evening—had been copying this sort of activity for the past several weeks as the Japanese encroached deeper into China.

It was well into the evening on December 12, and Chief Keg

Goodwin should have left work hours earlier. However, Goodwin, who had recently transferred from Station CAST to become the chief radioman in charge of Station HYPO, remained at work to supervise the watch because of the increasingly belligerent Japanese military activity in China.

"Chief, I have three airborne aircraft," Smith said. The Japanese typically reported all their activities in the clear to the airfield controllers, as there was no time for encryption during this type of tactical activity.

"Nanking again, Smitty?" asked the chief.

"Yeah. Now three more airborne."

Markle Smith was the senior of the two operators on watch, and extremely proficient at intercepting the katakana code. Chief Goodwin wanted Roy Sholes, the junior operator, to get some experience by sitting "side-saddle" with Smith.

"Sholes, tune in to 330 kilocycles and start copying," the chief instructed.

With the intercept operators copying the same activity, the sound of their Underwood Code Machines echoed throughout the operations floor. *Clack, clack, clack, clack.*

"I have six aircraft all together, Chief. Six total aircraft in two sorties," Smith reported. Since the traffic was unencrypted, there was no real rhythm to the intercept, but the operators kept up. *Clack, clack, clack, clack.*

"Keep me posted, Smitty."

Several minutes passed with nothing but static in the operators' headphones. Eventually, the aircraft transmitted again, and Smith announced, "Formation one is diving . . . on attack run . . . bombs away!"

⚓ ⚓ ⚓

On the ground in Nanking, the overriding concern for the U.S. Embassy was the safety of American citizens in the city. Most had evacuated

Nanking during the prior weeks, and those that remained were safely on board the USS *Panay*, part of the U.S. Navy's Yangtze River Patrol.

The USS *Panay*, one of six gunboats built specifically for the Yangtze River Patrol fleet, was a 191-foot-long, 450-ton vessel that Kiangnan Dockyard and Engineering Works in Shanghai had built. With a compliment of fifty-nine personnel, the *Panay* was purpose-built for the river patrol duties it had performed for the past nine years: protecting American interests from Chinese bandits.

On December 12, 1937, the *Panay* was about twenty-five miles west of Nanking escorting three Standard Oil tankers with several American reporters and diplomats on board. The United States was officially neutral during this conflict between China and Japan and expected safe passage for its ships. Even so, the *Panay* flew several large American flags and continuously reported its position to the Japanese military, so as not to be mistaken for a Chinese combatant.

⚓ ⚓ ⚓

Back at Station HYPO, Smith reported, "Formation two on bombing run . . . bombs away! Formation one now strafing."

By this time, this sort of activity was routine for the intercept operators at Station HYPO, and the evening's military activity didn't appear any different to them. The bombing and strafing of Chinese targets were the same as always. Petty Officers Smith and Sholes were right on point, copying the air activity expertly and completely and reporting their intercept to their watch supervisor.

The air activity continued for about ninety minutes before each of the six aircraft returned to base. Chief Goodwin dutifully assembled the intercept logs and transcripts so they could be shipped over to the Combat Intelligence Unit at Pearl Harbor for reconstruction the following morning.

CHAPTER 57

THE PANAY INCIDENT

MONDAY, DECEMBER 13, 1937
FOURTEENTH NAVAL DISTRICT ADMINISTRATION
BUILDING, PEARL HARBOR, TERRITORY OF HAWAII

By the time Lieutenant Thomas Dyer, the Fourteenth Naval District's intelligence officer at Pearl Harbor, arrived for work on Monday morning, word had spread throughout the U.S. Navy community that the Japanese had attacked the USS *Panay* west of Nanking. The unprovoked attack was being widely reported in the press.

The Japanese attack on the USS *Panay* resulted in the loss of the vessel as well as three lives, including two Navy men: Lieutenant Edgar G. Hulsebus and Storekeeper First Class Charles L. Ensminger; and Mr. Sandro Sandri, who was a reporter for an Italian newspaper. Twelve other people, including the *Panay*'s commanding officer, Lieutenant Commander James Hughes, were seriously wounded. The casualties were transported to the USS *Augusta* in Shanghai for treatment.

Reconstruction of the activity that Petty Officers Smith and Sholes had intercepted revealed that the *Panay* had been attacked and sunk by three Yokosuka Type 96 bombers and nine Kawasaki Type

95 fighters. All of these aircraft were biplanes; the fighters were single-seaters while the bombers had room for a three-man crew: a pilot, a navigator, and a radioman/gunner. Although Smith and Sholes intercepted and transcribed communications regarding the unprovoked attack, they had no way of knowing that the *Panay* was the target, as this was not transmitted at any time during the attack.

USS Panay sinking in the Yangtze River between Nanking and Wuhu, China, after being bombed by Japanese planes on 12 December 1937.

The Japanese later apologized, claiming it was a case of mistaken identity. Despite the fact that the Japanese government paid an indemnity of over $2 million to the United States government, the message was clear: the Japanese believed China was their territory and Americans were unwanted there.

CHAPTER 58

PACIFIC HFDF NET

WEDNESDAY, JUNE 22, 1938
MAIN NAVY BUILDING, WASHINGTON, DC

To the Research Desk, the twofold message delivered by the attack on the USS *Panay* in December 1937 was just as clear. First, if hostilities between China and Japan continued, Station ABLE would no longer be safe. Second, the U.S. Navy needed to quickly expand intercept operations and HFDF activities in the Pacific.

Laurance Safford, knowing he was preparing for war with Japan, continued to press for improvements on all things related to radio intelligence.

Based on advancements in technology and the positive results at Station CAST, Commander Safford finalized plans to expand HFDF sites around the Pacific Ocean. Safford placed an order to the U.S. Navy's Bureau of Engineering for twenty Model DT HFDF systems for installation at new and existing sites. Plans for the new HFDF stations were also developed, with the sites organized into three groups: Asiatic, Mid-Pacific, and Pacific Coast.

The Asiatic group would include HFDF sites at Cavite (Station CAST), Guam (Station BAKER), and Shanghai (Station ABLE)

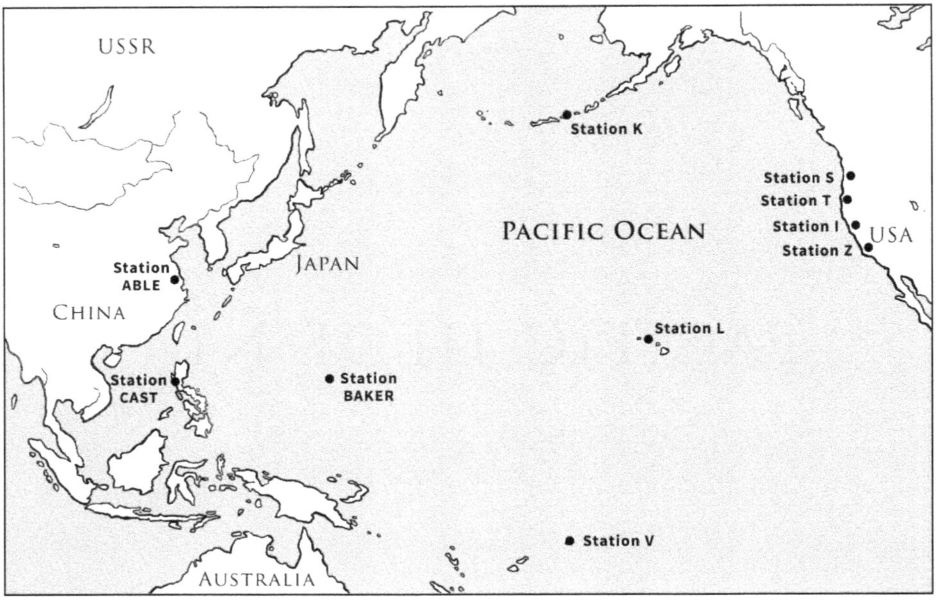

with Net Control at Cavite. Net Control consisted of gathering DF results from other sites and performing triangulation in order to pinpoint the location of a transmitter. The HFDF sites of the Asiatic Group would primarily be responsible for tracking Imperial Japanese Navy ships. Intercept operators located at the well-established intercept sites would also help man the HFDF sites.

The Mid-Pacific Group would include sites at Vaitogi, Samoa (Station V), Lualualei, Hawaii (Station L), and Dutch Harbor, Alaska (Station K). Net Control for the Mid-Pacific group would be at Lualualei. These stations were assigned the primary task of tracking Japanese merchant ships, as well as assisting the Asiatic group, when necessary, in tracking Imperial Japanese Navy ships. Four radiomen, including at least one On-the-Roof Gang graduate, would be assigned to each of these sites for HFDF work.

The Pacific Coast group would have sites at Mare Island, California (Station I), Point Arguello, California (Station Z), Point

On-the-Roof Gang operators, all chief radiomen, at Station BAKER, Guam, circa 1938. L-to-R: Martin Vandenberg, Antone Novak, Laurence Myers, Arnold Conant (Chief Yeoman), Max Gunn, Buck Dormer.

Saint George, California (Station T), and Fort Stevens, Oregon (Station S). The primary responsibility of the Pacific Coast group would be to track Japanese naval and merchant ships east of the Hawaiian Islands.

By mid-June 1938, the Asiatic and Pacific Coast groups were up and running, but the Mid-Pacific group was still just in the planning stages. Station L at Lualualei was ready, but the U.S. Navy still had no presence in Samoa or Dutch Harbor. Implementation of the plan for these HFDF sites would have to be completed in phases as sufficient numbers of trained radiomen were not yet available to operate each of the sites, and equipment still had to be procured, shipped, and installed there as well.

At the Naval Research Lab in Bellevue, engineers were making progress on reducing the size and improving the accuracy of HFDF

Model DY HFDF set.

equipment. The latest efforts concentrated on reducing the size of the electronics of the rotating Adcock system in order to fit them into a weather-proof enclosure, which the navy designated Model DY. Commander Safford ordered fifty-nine Model DY units for shipment to the fleet to supplement and/or replace the Model DT units already widely deployed.

CHAPTER 59

CLASS #21

SATURDAY, JUNE 25, 1938
MAIN NAVY BUILDING, WASHINGTON, DC

Commander Safford knew Chief Kidder was his best choice to replace Chief McGregor as the next On-the-Roof Gang instructor, so he felt it was necessary to put sufficient pressure on Kidder to return to active duty. Safford found out that Kidder had a Reserve drill weekend starting on June 25, 1938 and met him at Station M in Cheltenham. Safford asked Kidder if he would consider coming back onto active duty to teach a few classes. Although flattered by the idea, Kidder still wasn't ready to leave his life in Florida. He enjoyed working for *The Evening Independent*, which was paying him to watch baseball of all things. Life was good for him in the Sunshine State.

"I have a better idea for you, sir," Kidder offered.

Disappointed, Safford responded, "Go ahead, Chief. I'm all ears."

"Chief Wigle is doing a bang-up job at Station ABLE. The Sailors look up to him, and he is an expert at the katakana code," Kidder said. "He's been teaching some of the general service radiomen the katakana code so they can help out on the watch. And he's due for orders. I think he'd make an outstanding instructor for you."

Safford nodded along. "OK, Chief. I think you're right. I can make that happen." Switching gears, he asked, "When will we see you again?"

"I'll be back for a drill weekend next month and two weeks of active duty in September."

"Well, I hope you'll reconsider coming back to active duty. The Japanese are making a lot of noise, and I think it's only a matter of time before another *Panay* incident happens."

"I'll think about it," Kidder replied. "I think they're planning something much bigger than another *Panay*. I've been saying that all along."

Kidder wanted to come back to the Research Desk, but he kept it to himself. The truth of the matter was that he was embarrassed about what had happened to him in Hawaii. He tried to live his life with as much integrity as possible, but the accusations against him had haunted him since his forced retirement. However, this was not something he was willing to share with Safford. "I'll let you know if I change my mind."

"I hope you will, Chief. We could use you."

"Commander?" Kidder added.

"Yes, Chief."

"How's Miss Aggie? Is she getting close to coming back to work?"

"I'm sorry. I should have told you," Safford apologized. "She's making good progress. I saw her just a couple weeks ago. Her jaw is fine. After they took her out of traction, her leg needed to be in a cast for another three months. She's out of the cast now and learning to walk again. It's been a tough road for her."

"Well, I hope she comes out of this OK," Kidder said sympathetically.

"She will, Chief. Thanks for asking about her. I'll make sure she knows."

⚓ ⚓ ⚓

Main Navy Building, Washington, DC, circa 1938. Note rooftop classroom (white) on left side of sixth wing from the bottom.

Back at the Research Desk, Commander Safford was as good as his word. Within the week, Chief Daryl Wigle had transfer orders to teach at the Main Navy Building. Shortly thereafter, the twenty-first group of On-the-Roof Gang students reported for class in July 1938. In addition to Sam Winchester, seven other students were assigned to the class: Petty Officers Howard Cain, Donovan "DR" Chase, Douglas Harold, Jack Kaye, Warren Simmons, Wesley Walvoord, and Willis Wesper.

Wigle's class completed training on February 13, 1939, and all eight students were sent across town to the Naval Research Lab for HFDF training before transferring to their duty stations via the USS *Chaumont*. Harold, Winchester, and Kaye were sent to Station BAKER, while Cain, Chase, Simmons, Walvoord, and Wesper went to Station CAST.

CHAPTER 60

STATION V

SUNDAY, SEPTEMBER 10, 1938
PAGO PAGO, TUTUILA ISLAND, SAMOA

With his seabag over his shoulder, Radioman Second Class Ted Wildman, a 1937 On-the-Roof Gang graduate, stepped off the SS *Monterey* in Pago Pago, Samoa, after a weeklong journey from Pearl Harbor. The *Monterey* was a luxury ocean liner of the Matson Lines' "White Fleet." It made monthly round trips between Hawaii and Australia with stops at some of the more isolated islands in the central and western Pacific Ocean.

Pago Pago was a harbor town on Tutuila Island—the largest island of American Samoa. Wildman's top secret mission was to establish an HFDF site somewhere on the island. Chief Robert Thompson, the radioman in charge of the general service communications station on Tutuila, met Wildman at the pier. There were only about 150 Americans on the island, and all were Navy personnel. Half of them were Navy radiomen stationed at the communications station; the rest were the crew of the USS *Ontario*, a seagoing tug and the only rescue ship in the entire South Pacific.

"You Wildman?" Thompson inquired.

"Sure am, Chief."

"Welcome to Pago Pago. I think you're gonna like it here."

"I'm not even sure where we are, Chief," Wildman quipped.

"This is Tutuila. I don't know what you're doing here, Wildman, but we've got a couple of large crates waiting for you back at the site." Probing for information, Chief Thompson asked, "What can you tell me?"

Wildman was worried about this; he knew he wasn't permitted to speak too freely about his duties, even to his superiors. As far as the general Navy population knew, direction finding was still mainly used as a navigational aid in the U.S. Navy, and the fact that the On-the-Roof Gang was conducting HFDF against foreign navy communications was still being kept under wraps. Wildman knew he would have to walk the line between truth and diversion.

"Just here to set up a new DF site, Chief. I just—"

Chief Thompson interrupted, "Don't worry, Wildman. I know you can't tell me, but the look on your face was priceless!" Thompson chuckled. "Let's get you back to the base."

The two climbed into the station vehicle and headed to the base. Once there, Wildman was left alone with his crates. As he was expecting, the crates contained sufficient equipment to assemble a new Model DT HFDF suite. While not the most modern HFDF equipment, it was the one most familiar and easiest to transport and assemble for the On-the-Roof Gang operators.

Despite his specialized training, Wildman had a difficult time assembling the DT straight out of the crates. The instructions provided were vague and illegible. Eventually, he got the HFDF rig working near the fence line of the Pago Pago Navy base. The DT seemed to operate correctly, but interference from the radio station caused problems with reception. Also, a huge mountain range topped off by Mount Alava blocked any transmissions coming from the north. Wildman decided he needed a more suitable location with better hearability to the north.

Per Safford's direction before Wildman's departure for Samoa, he was to set up his Model DT HFDF suite in Pago Pago to check on suitability of the site. If needed, he should abandon Pago Pago for a better location on his own discretion. Since Pago Pago proved inadequate, Wildman, in the dead of night so as to maintain secrecy in the small Navy community, packed up his DT equipment, loaded the crates onto two donkeys, and set out into the wilderness of Tutuila Island.

CHAPTER 61

CLASS #22

FRIDAY, APRIL 28, 1939
MAIN NAVY BUILDING, WASHINGTON, DC

With the cherry blossoms in full bloom on this late April morning, Commander Laurance Safford sat at his desk in the Main Navy Building drinking a cup of coffee and reading the news from Europe in disbelief. In a speech before the Reichstag, Adolph Hitler, the dictator of Nazi Germany, announced the dissolution of the Anglo-German Naval Agreement and the German-Polish Nonaggression Pact. Under Hitler, Germany had become increasingly aggressive in annexing territories across Europe, starting with the Czechoslovakian Sudetenland, Bohemia, Moravia, and Klaipeda. With the termination of the German-Polish Nonaggression Pact, it seemed Poland was now within Hitler's sights for invasion. After both England and France guaranteed Polish independence, Safford realized a German invasion would turn into full-blown war across Europe. Since the European theater was largely the domain of the U.S. Army, more worrisome to him was that Germany had previously aligned itself with Japan as the latter waged war against China. If war broke out in Europe, was it just a matter of time before it spilled into the Pacific, the U.S. Navy's backyard?

Later in the day, with tensions ratcheting up in Europe, U.S. Army cryptologists visited Safford in the Main Navy Building. Despite years of ruthlessly competitive intelligence work, William Friedman, Safford's counterpart in the U.S. Army, was now looking for cooperation. Friedman had heard of the Navy's fledgling efforts using machines to decrypt Japanese diplomatic intercept and of the brilliance of Agnes Meyer Driscoll. Friedman thought that if the Army and Navy teamed up to create a machine to decrypt Japanese codes, they would develop a solution more quickly than if both sides worked on the same task independently.

The U.S. Army had figured out that in their encryption devices, the Japanese were using rotary selector switches similar to those used in automatic telephone exchanges. In the basement of his home, Leo Rosen—an electrical engineer in the U.S. Army—had built a model of the machine, which Friedman referred to as PURPLE. However, the Army was having difficulty making the machine work reliably, so Friedman asked the Navy to help build a new machine. Safford tasked engineers at the Washington Navy Yard to come up with an alternative solution. Within weeks, Navy engineers had reconstructed the switching mechanism, and their updated PURPLE machine put out its first decrypt. Eventually, the U.S. Navy built five of these improved PURPLE machines.

In order to protect the secrecy of PURPLE, the Army and Navy gave the intelligence output of the new decryption machine the code word *MAGIC*. MAGIC decrypts were distributed to only ten people in Washington: the President, the Secretary of State, the Secretary of War, the Secretary of the Navy, the Chief of Staff, the Chief of Naval Operations, the heads of the Army and Navy war plans divisions, and the heads of the Army and Navy intelligence divisions. If any of these recipients thought further dissemination of the decrypts was necessary, the intelligence had to be sent by attributing the information only to "highly reliable sources." No one else was to know of the existence of the PURPLE machines.

By early May 1939, the next full class of students arrived to receive training on the roof of the Main Navy Building. Chief Wigle's eight students—all second and third class radiomen—were Edward Dullard, William Eaton, Robert Ellis, Stuart Faulkner, Arthur Monroe, Hubert Price, Charles Quinn, and David Snyder. After graduation in September, Faulkner, Ellis, Snyder and Dullard were ordered to Station BAKER in Guam, and Eaton, Price, Monroe and Quinn to Station CAST.

CHAPTER 62

IJN CODE CHANGE

THURSDAY, JUNE 1, 1939
STATION CAST, CAVITE NAVAL BASE, PHILIPPINES

By mid-1939, Station CAST had become the second-largest U.S. Navy intercept site—only Station HYPO in Hawaii was larger. Of the nineteen On-the-Roof Gang alumni at Station CAST, sixteen of them worked at the intercept site on Cavite Naval Base, one performed HFDF at Sangley Point, and two others worked decryption and traffic analysis at the Combat Intelligence Unit nearby. Close coordination between the intercept and DF operations happened routinely. However, a strict "need-to-know" policy meant that very few intercept operators at Station CAST knew the details of the decryption and traffic analysis activities within the Combat Intelligence Unit.

Despite their ignorance of operations within the Combat Intelligence Unit, intercept operators at Station CAST forwarded all intercept logs and transcripts there for further processing, and the same was done with HFDF results and logs. Radiomen first class Al Pelletier and Paul Hively, who both worked in the Combat Intelligence Unit, were responsible for decrypting the four-character traffic being intercepted at Station CAST. In addition to this decryption

On-the-Roof Gang operators at Station CAST, Cavite, Philippines, circa 1939. L-to-R: RM1c Robert Williams, RM2c Willis Wesper, RM2c Howard Cain.

work, they were responsible for performing traffic analysis of the intercept and the DF results they received.

The Imperial Japanese Navy had been using the Blue Book code operationally for nearly a decade, but that changed on June 1, 1939, when they introduced two new operational codes: the "Flag Officer Code" and the "Operations Code." The latter of which was also known as JN25. At the same time, the Japanese drastically reduced using plaintext transmissions, meaning most IJN communications were encrypted from that point forward. This made breaking the new code much more important.

The changing of codes always presented problems for U.S. cryptanalysts. Each time a code was changed, significant resources had to be expended to try and break the new code. And JN-25 presented some especially difficult challenges. It included over 30,000 five-digit groups, each having a specific meaning. It was a two-part code, meaning that a random additive had been applied to the already encrypted five-digit code group. The additives were applied to the five-digit groups, and the resulting five-character group was transmitted. The additives had to be recovered daily and applied to the received five-digit number to reveal the underlying code group, and then, hopefully, the encrypted meaning of the code.

Because the JN-25 code was used much more widely than the Flag Officer Code, the Combat Intelligence Unit at Cavite concentrated its efforts on cracking it first. Plus, JN-25 was so new and effective that the U.S. Navy was rendered almost completely blind to what the Imperial Japanese Navy was up to. In fact, if it weren't for the now well-established science of traffic analysis, the U.S. Navy would have had very little insight into Japan's naval activities.

CHAPTER 63

IMPROVEMENTS AT STATION ABLE

FRIDAY, AUGUST 18, 1939

STATION ABLE, SHANGHAI, CHINA

Although the security situation in Shanghai brought on by the tensions between Japan and China was deteriorating, the Research Desk was still investing in upgrades for the site with updated intercept gear. Modern multiband receivers along with frequency preselectors and wire recorders were installed in August 1939. A new Model DY direction finding suite, which improved HFDF operations, was also put in place.

Despite the upgrades, the future of Station ABLE was still a matter of concern. Commander Safford believed the site needed to be shut down because there were too many risks involved in keeping an intercept site open as Japanese forces moved closer and closer to the International Settlement in Shanghai. If the Japanese were to ever overrun the headquarters of the Fourth Marine Regiment, all the secrecy maintained about the operations in Station ABLE would be lost. The Japanese would quickly realize what was being done in the

On-the-Roof Gang operator Raymond Parrott performing intercept operations at Station ABLE, Shanghai, China, circa 1939.

intercept room and would change their codes, processes, and procedures to become more secure. Safford believed that this security risk was too great and recommended the closure of Station ABLE to his superiors in the DNC.

However, both the CINCAF and the Director of Naval Communications disagreed with Safford's risk assessment. They believed the site was producing sufficient intelligence to warrant the obvious risk. Only Safford understood the Herculean effort it took every time the Japanese changed their codes, which they would inevitably do if they discovered what Station ABLE was up to.

Despite Commander Safford's recommendations, the Director of Naval Communications ordered that Station ABLE would remain open until there was a clear and present danger to the neutral U.S. military presence in Shanghai. Fearing this was a mistake, Safford directed LD Lankford, the new Chief Radioman in Charge of Station ABLE, to draft an emergency destruction and evacuation plan, just in case war with Japan were to come.

On-the-Roof Gang operators at Station ABLE, Shanghai, China, circa 1939. L-to-R: CRM Larry Myers, CRM Max Gunn, RM1c Robert Maxwell, RM1c Harold Layman, RM2c Merle Lynch, RM1c Alva Squires, RM2c Raymond Parrott, RM2c Ken Carmichael, RM2c James Johnson, RM2c Chester Bissell.

CHAPTER 64

STATION S MOVES TO BAINBRIDGE ISLAND

FRIDAY, SEPTEMBER 1, 1939
FORT STEVENS, ASTORIA, OREGON

By late summer 1939, having completed his tour of duty at Station HYPO, Keg Goodwin was the chief radioman in charge of Station S in Astoria, Oregon. The men at Station S were responsible for intercepting diplomatic communications between the major Japanese transmitters in Tokyo, Osaka, and Manchuria, but compared to Goodwin's last two assignments in the Philippines and Hawaii, Station S was a sleepy little intercept station sharing Fort Stevens with Naval Radio Station NUZ. The shared location benefited the intercept site since the radio station bore the cost of operating and maintaining the base.

On September 1, 1939, without warning and without consulting the Research Desk, the Thirteenth Naval District announced plans to close Naval Radio Station NUZ on Fort Stevens, forcing Commander Safford to make a tough decision. If Station S were to remain at Fort Stevens, the Research Desk would have to assume the operating and maintenance costs for the entire base. However, a move to a different

shared facility would require an initial outlay in relocation costs but would reduce recurring maintenance costs. In the end, the decision was an easy one: Safford decided to find a new home for Station S.

In order to facilitate the move, Commander Safford recalled Chief Radioman Dorman Chauncey to active duty. Chauncey had been performing his Reserve duties at Station S, but his services were once again required to help investigate a suitable new location for Station S. Chauncey's original survey work from 1932 indicated that reception of communications originating in the Far East was best in the Seattle area, so the hunt was on for space at an existing military facility in or around Puget Sound. After all options were investigated, Chauncey recommended Station S be relocated to Fort Ward on Bainbridge Island, where the Thirteenth Naval District was planning to establish a new Class A school for general service radiomen in the U.S. Navy Reserve.

Fort Ward was originally established in 1903 as a U.S. Army coastal defense post with the primary mission of protecting the Bremerton Naval Shipyard in Puget Sound. In 1935, the Thirteenth Naval District deemed the coastal defense mission unnecessary, leaving the base open for occupation. To Chauncey, Fort Ward was the ideal new location for Station S because it could fly under the radar using the new radioman school as cover.

Safford agreed with Chauncey's recommendation and allocated sufficient funds to cover the costs of the move. Two new Model DY HFDF sets were purchased and shipped to the site for installation in the new location. Chief Radioman Tru Lusk transferred from Station HYPO to help with the relocation to Bainbridge Island. Secrecy had to be maintained, so no new construction would be permitted; in other words, all intercept and HFDF operations would have to take advantage of the twenty-four buildings already present at Fort Ward, which included barracks, administration buildings, a guardhouse, a bakery, a commissary, a post exchange, ordinance facilities, and warehouses.

The first order of business was to set up the HFDF equipment that was waiting for Lusk. When operational, the DF site at Station S would serve as the Pacific Coast HFDF Net Control—the hub of DF operations on the West Coast of the United States, with Mare Island, Point Arguello, and Point Saint George as contributing outstations.

Lusk converted the old post exchange building into the new intercept operations center. He acquired fifteen new multiband receivers and three frequency meters from the Thirteenth Naval District warehouse. In addition, the Research Desk provided five new Boehme automatic wire recorders to record the automatic Morse transmissions being utilized on the Japanese diplomatic net. Lusk also managed to get three huge, rhombic antennas installed on the large parade grounds. Rhombic antennas, which the Naval Research Lab had only recently adapted for intercept, consisted of parallel wires suspended above the ground in a diamond shape and supported by telephone poles at each vertex to which the wires were attached. The three antennas gave Station S a very large frequency range in which to conduct intercept.

A mere four weeks after the decision was made to relocate Station S from Fort Stevens, the site was operational on Bainbridge Island.

CHAPTER 65

CLASS #23

MONDAY, NOVEMBER 27, 1939
MAIN NAVY BUILDING, WASHINGTON, DC

By the fall of 1939, Commander Safford's fear of a German invasion of Poland and an ensuing war in Europe had come to pass. Two days after Germany invaded Poland on September 1, Hitler ignored a British ultimatum to cease military operations there, and Great Britain and France declared war on Germany. The seemingly inevitable war in Europe had begun, and with Germany's ties to Japan, Safford wondered how long it would be before the war migrated to the Pacific.

On November 27, the Monday after Thanksgiving, a full class of radiomen arrived for training on the roof of the Main Navy Building. The twenty-third group of students were all experienced radiomen second class. They were Kenneth Barker, Arthur Groff, Raymond Hitson, Harold Joslin, Edward Otte, Rexford Parr, Russell Rogers, and Martin Smith. As Chief Kidder had predicted, Chief Wigle excelled in teaching the rooftop katakana classes, although this would be his last. Wigle was being transferred to take over as the Chief Radioman in Charge of Station M in Cheltenham, Maryland. It was time to find the next instructor, so Safford identified Chief Antone

"Tony" Novak, a graduate of the fourth On-the-Roof Gang class, as Wigle's replacement. Novak received his orders and transferred from Station BAKER in Guam to Washington, DC in May 1940.

Also in May 1940, as Chief Wigle's students completed their training, Petty Officers Barker, Joslin, Parr, and Rogers were ordered to Station BAKER and Petty Officers Groff, Hitson, Smith, and Otte to Station CAST. By this time, the upgrades and repair work Chief Kidder had completed to the rooftop classroom in 1933 had started wearing down. The concrete blockhouse was once again leaking, and the concrete was crumbling in the corners. It was obvious that further repairs to the classroom were necessary—or perhaps something more radical was in order.

CHAPTER 66

CAST MOVES TO CORREGIDOR ISLAND

THURSDAY, NOVEMBER 30, 1939
CORREGIDOR ISLAND, PHILIPPINES

The Malinta Tunnel, which was dug into the hill of the same name on Corregidor Island, had been built between 1922 and 1932. Utilizing the forced labor of a thousand convicts from the Bilibid Prison in Manila, the U.S. Army Corps of Engineers had overseen the tunnel's construction. The main tunnel, which spanned nearly 800 feet, was 24 feet wide and 18 feet high. Twenty-four smaller tunnels—each about 150 feet long and 15 feet wide—branched off of the main tunnel. This network of tunnels served as the headquarters for the U.S. Army's presence in the Philippines and also included a military hospital with a thousand beds, a warehouse for food and ammunition, and an air raid shelter.

Similar to the Malinta Tunnel but smaller in scale, the U.S. Navy's new tunnel was dug into the bedrock on Corregidor Island. The project was broken down into three subprojects: 1) the digging of the intercept tunnel (known as Tunnel AFIRM) near Monkey Point; 2) the installation of the U.S. Navy's HFDF station on the eastern

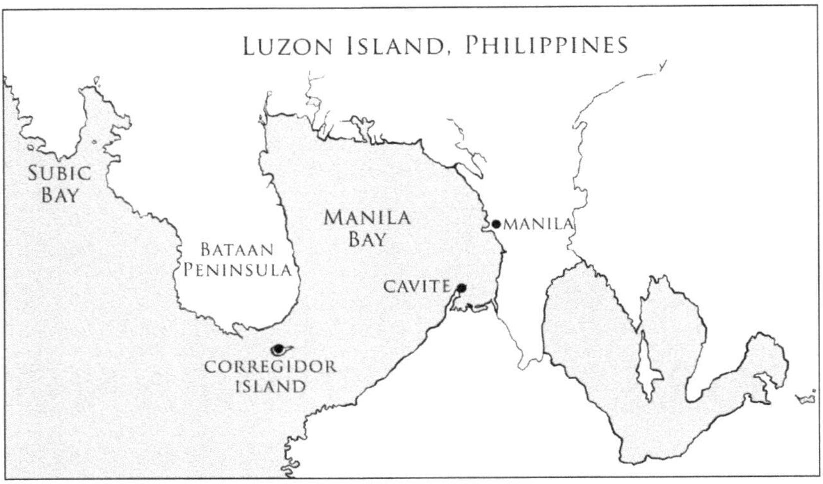

tip of the island; and 3) the construction of quarters for the Naval personnel not far from the intercept tunnel.

Mirroring the construction process for the Malinta Tunnel, Navy engineers employed inexpensive and plentiful prison labor to build Tunnel AFIRM. Using makeshift explosives, the prisoners bored into the bedrock at Monkey Point. Then the walls of the tunnel were lined and reinforced with high-quality cement that Navy engineers had imported from Japan.

By December 1939, a full three years after the project was approved, the tunnel was finally ready to be fit with the equipment needed to operationalize the new location for Station CAST. The 220-foot-long tunnel was 15 feet wide and 25 feet high and had openings at either end. The first 60 feet from the main entrance at the south side of the hill stored provisions that might be needed in emergency situations. Auxiliary diesel engines and machinery, including large air-conditioning units needed to cool the vacuum tube technology, stood farther along the passage. Air locks and 70-foot vertical conduits extended to the surface to ventilate the auxiliary diesel generator and air-conditioning systems.

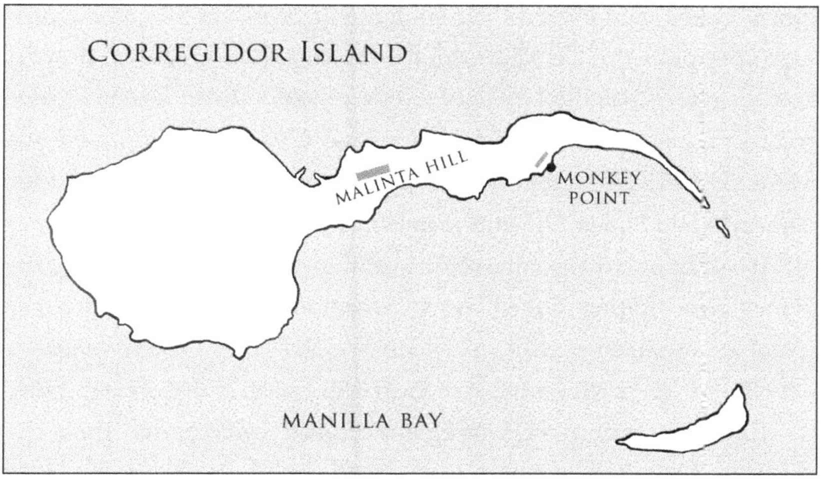

A second, equally proportioned tunnel branched off to the left near the center of the main tunnel, making its way to a third entrance on the northwest side of Monkey Point. Shooting off this tunnel to the right, a third smaller passageway housed offices and workspaces for linguists and traffic analysts. The remainder of the Navy tunnel stored electronic equipment, a photo lab, emergency supplies, auxiliary machinery, and fuel and water tanks.

Although the Navy tunnel was neither as large nor as spacious as its Army counterpart nearly a mile away, the new Station CAST was better ventilated, less humid, and quieter—all because of lessons learned from the construction of the Malinta Tunnel.

Utilizing intercept receivers from the old site at Cavite in addition to newly acquired equipment, the Research Desk designed Station CAST to be the best-equipped intercept station in the fleet. In order to maintain security, after the prisoners had finished building the tunnel, On-the-Roof Gang graduates took over the installation of the intercept equipment.

The old intercept station at Cavite ceased operations, and the On-the-Roof Gang alumni assigned to Station CAST powered down, crated, and loaded their equipment, classified files, and cipher machines onto the USS *Dapdap* for the trip to Corregidor. In total, the operators installed twenty-five receivers, three Boehme wire recorders, twenty-one RIP-5 Underwood Code Machines, and one Model DY HFDF unit at the new facility on Corregidor Island. One older Model DT HFDF suite was left operational at Sangley Point.

In addition to the intercept operation and the HFDF site, the Navy's new Station CAST on Corregidor Island also housed the Combat Intelligence Unit, to which the Research Desk provided a new PURPLE machine to aid in local decryption of diplomatic traffic.

Radio reception on Corregidor proved even better than the Research Desk had originally anticipated, which seemed to vindicate the Navy's persistence in gaining a foothold on the island. From the outset, the new Station CAST was able to perform its intercept functions better than any previous site in the Philippines.

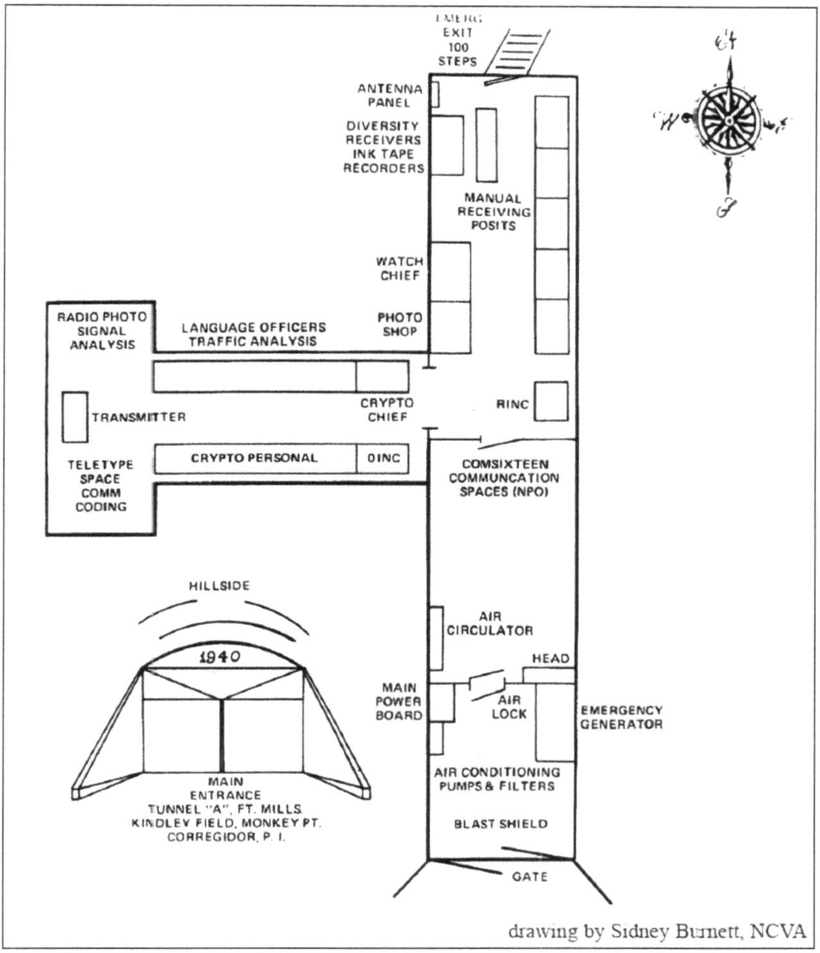

Station CAST, Corregidor Island, Philippines, circa 1940. Layout of Tunnel AFIRM.

CHAPTER 67

CLASS #24

MONDAY, MAY 20, 1940
MAIN NAVY BUILDING, WASHINGTON, DC

Chief Antone Novak arrived in Washington with ample time to prepare to teach the next On-the-Roof Gang class. After the six students checked in at Ma Travers's Guest House, they reported for duty at the Main Navy Building. Chief Novak handed out security agreements, which they each signed before class began. Gordon Carnes, Wesley Knowles, Joseph Smith, Lloyd Smith, and Harold Waldum were all radiomen second class. James Capron was the sole radioman third class.

After completing four months of radio intercept and katakana training, graduates of the twenty-fourth On-the-Roof Gang class transferred to Bellevue for two months of training in direction finding at the Naval Research Laboratory. Then all six men reported to Station HYPO for duty.

At this point, the U.S. Navy's expanding HFDF network—which the Research Desk operated and managed—consisted of sixty-five operators manning sixteen HFDF stations. The Research Desk continued to collaborate with Pan American Airways, which used katakana operators to copy the Japanese weather broadcasts in the Pacific and perform HFDF to support its air fleet with stations at Wake Island, Midway Island, and Guam, among others. Pan Am agreed that these stations would cooperate with the Navy's HFDF stations on a time-available basis.

Between the expanding intercept and HFDF sites around the Pacific and the Combat Intelligence Units in the Philippines and Hawaii, the Research Desk was finally realizing the Navy's full potential in terms of radio intelligence capabilities. Despite the work that still needed to get done, Laurance Safford felt more prepared than ever to keep track of the Imperial Japanese Navy.

CHAPTER 68

MISSING IN SAMOA

TUESDAY, JUNE 11, 1940
VILLAGE OF VAITOGI, AMERICAN SAMOA

Radioman First Class Ted Wildman had been on his own in the middle of Tutuila Island in American Samoa for several months. He had left Pago Pago to scout out potential locations for a new HFDF site on the western side of the island months earlier and had been camping in natural clearings or abandoned campsites. In Vaitogi, on the southern coast of the island, he stumbled across the old Pan Am station that had been abandoned about six months prior. Because the site was flat and had already been paved by Pan Am, it seemed ideal for HFDF. There were also small roads leading north and east from the site. The only impediment for Wildman to set up his new HFDF site was a small village of locals who had moved in. They'd set up approximately forty huts in an oblong fashion with a grassy field in the center.

When Wildman entered the village with his two donkeys in tow, the inhabitants greeted him warmly. Wildman presented the high chief with a small portable radio as a gift. In return, the high chief named Wildman an honorary chief of the village, and the villagers gave him lodging in a grass hut. Wildman then set out to assemble and install the Model DT equipment in the center of the village. Each night, after his DF work was done for the day, he entertained the villagers with music from Hawaiian radio broadcasts.

After he got the Model DT gear working, Wildman operated his one-man HFDF station and believed he was performing excellent HFDF operations. However, he was not getting any feedback on his results. Unknown to him, after he sent his regular reports to the communications station at Pago Pago, they never went any further. Chief Thompson, who was unaware of the importance of Wildman's top secret mission for the Research Desk, felt there was no reason to relay anything from him. From the perspective of the Research Desk, Wildman had simply disappeared somewhere in Samoa. Completely unaware that his reports were not being relayed to Net Control in Hawaii, Wildman continued to operate his HFDF equipment with the assumption that everything was fine.

As Wildman developed the site and as the Japanese increased their naval activities across the Pacific, the Research Desk assigned a second operator to Samoa. Radioman Second Class Glenn Evans, an On-the-Roof Gang alum, was in Hawaii awaiting orders to the Philippines. Instead, he received emergency orders to Samoa, where he was tasked with finding Wildman and assisting him in establishing the operational HFDF site.

When Evans arrived in Samoa on the SS *Monterey* in May 1940, Chief Thompson—Evans's former chief on board the USS *Pennsylvania*—met him on the pier. Knowing Thompson well, Evans quickly realized that no one on the island knew what Wildman was sent to Samoa to accomplish, and, of course, he couldn't tell anyone why he was there. With Evans's arrival and his fortuitous meeting with his old chief, operational problems started getting sorted out. Evans told Thompson about the need to forward the DF reports, and Thompson informed Evans as to where to find Wildman. Evans set out from Pago Pago in June 1940.

At Vaitogi, Petty Officer Evans was impressed with the work Wildman had accomplished. The Model DT HFDF setup, which sat on a wooden platform about eight feet off the ground, consisted of a state-of-the-art Hammarlund Super Pro receiver converted to operate on batteries. Eight-foot-long bamboo arms extended from each side to hold the dipole antennas. The entire setup, including the receiver and dipoles, could be manually rotated 360 degrees; the operator walked the complete unit around while listening for the aural "null" when the unit was pointed directly at the signal in question. When operational, Evans and Wildman took turns operating the unit when reception was best—from midday until about 2200 hours. Now that their reports were being forwarded by Chief Thompson, Wildman and Evans had Station V in Vaitogi, Samoa fully operational.

CHAPTER 69

A SCHOOLHOUSE OPTION

THURSDAY, AUGUST 1, 1940
BAINBRIDGE ISLAND, WASHINGTON STATE

Because the Research Desk was quick to act, Station S had taken over most of the better buildings on the Fort Ward on Bainbridge Island. Just as they had planned, the Thirteenth Naval District converted some of the remaining buildings on Fort Ward to house a Class A radio school for naval reservists.

The first general service radioman to arrive was Marion E. Cornelius, who was given the task of supervising the conversion of the old Army brig to the radio school. The school needed to accommodate up to forty students at a time who would come for four months of training in radio operations and the basics of communications using international Morse code. To do so, Chief Cornelius had all six cells in the brig reconfigured into one large classroom where the students would learn international Morse code, typing, naval communications operations, and elementary seamanship. Those who passed a test and graduated would receive radioman third class status and be assigned either ships in the Atlantic or Pacific Fleet.

Across the base from the general service radioman school, nine On-the-Roof Gang alumni were assigned to Station S. One of those operators was Radioman First Class Hilary "Popeye" Cyr, whom Commander Safford asked to investigate the possibility of establishing a new katakana schoolhouse at Bainbridge Island to take the place of the rooftop training.

Cyr explained to Keg Goodwin and Tru Lusk—the chief petty officers at Station S—the problems being experienced at the rooftop classroom in DC. Goodwin and Lusk then contacted Chief Cornelius, and the three chiefs developed a plan to add a Class C school—an advanced school for experienced radiomen—to the annual training calendar on Bainbridge Island. In between the general service classes, the classrooms could be used to teach more experienced radiomen how to copy the katakana telegraphic code. They drafted a recommendation, which the commanding officer at Fort Ward endorsed, and then sent it to the Research Desk for consideration.

CHAPTER 70

PAPPY REINSTATED

SATURDAY, SEPTEMBER 28, 1940

MAIN NAVY BUILDING, WASHINGTON, DC

Laurance Safford's pulse raced as he read the news that Japan had signed a Tripartite Pact with Germany and Italy the day before. Safford understood that the agreement, which created a defense alliance between the three countries, was clearly intended to deter the United States from entering the ongoing war in Europe. Although the agreement never mentioned the United States specifically, it called on the signatories to assist one another with political, economic, and military means if any one of them was attacked by a country not involved in the European War or in the Sino-Japanese Conflict. Safford realized that this wording could not have been aimed at the Soviet Union because it was already involved in both wars. Therefore, it was clearly a warning to the United States against entering either conflict. In other words, if Germany, Italy, or Japan felt the United States was participating in either war in any way, then the United States should expect retaliation.

Although Safford and the members of the Research Desk felt confident about the state of the U.S. Navy's radio intelligence operations, there was still much to do to prepare for an eventual conflict. First, Safford needed to make a decision about Station ABLE, where Japanese military activity was threatening operations. Station BAKER was also vulnerable to attack, but the threat was only theoretical at this point. Importantly, the site was responsible for over fifty percent of the intercept happening against the Imperial Japanese Navy, and there were only eight operators assigned. Station BAKER was absolutely necessary to keep tabs on Imperial Japanese Navy ships as they operated in the South Pacific. In addition, the Mid-Pacific HFDF site still needed a location in Alaska, preferably on the Aleutian Islands. Considering all these items on Safford's to-do list and the news of Japan joining forces with Germany and Italy, his confidence began to wane.

Adding to his worries, in the wake of the news of the Tripartite Pact, Safford received word that the U.S. Navy was planning to evacuate dependents of the Sailors in China, the Philippines, and Guam; this would obviously apply to the men at the intercept sites. More troubling to Safford, if the Sailors' dependents weren't safe, perhaps the men would also be in peril if war came. Even more troubling was that cryptanalysts had only made a modicum of progress toward cracking the JN-25—the Imperial Japanese Navy's Operations Code—which would need to be broken if they were to have any chance in a war with Japan. Safford began to feel the immediacy of this problem greater than ever before.

In early October 1940, Henry Tizard from the British Technical and Scientific Mission was in the United States looking to establish relationships within the American scientific and industrial communities. He also carried a secret message for the Research Desk. Tizard revealed that the Royal Navy had utilized state-of-the-art British technology to establish an HFDF site in Bermuda. He invited Safford to visit the Bermuda site as well as the Government Code and Cipher School, the British codebreaking unit at Bletchley Park north of London.

Once again, Safford found himself with too much work and too little time. He couldn't afford the time away from the office to accept the invitation from Tizard. Instead, he used it as an opportunity to put even more pressure on Harry Kidder to return to active duty. The only thing interrupting Kidder's idyllic life in Florida was his monthly Reserve duty at Station M. So in October, Safford had Kidder report to the Main Navy Building on his drill weekend, ostensibly to inspect the rooftop classroom and determine if any upgrades or repairs were necessary. Safford already knew the answer to that, but he needed a reason to get Kidder to DC.

As Safford and Kidder climbed to the roof together, the cool autumn wind howled around the classroom. To Kidder, the gusty wind reminded him of being at sea. "I always liked it up here," he remarked.

"I know you did, Chief."

"She's showing some wear again, sir," Kidder said, referring to the classroom as he would a ship.

"She certainly is," Safford agreed. "But that's not why I brought you here."

"I figured as much."

"Harry, we need you. Is there anything we can do to convince you to come back?"

"Y'know, sir, my life's pretty darn good in Florida right now."

"I assume you've heard about the Tripartite Pact, right?"

"Yeah. It's a helluva thing."

"They're coming for us, Harry. It's just a matter of time before the Japs drag us into this thing."

"I know. I've been saying that for years."

"It's real this time, Harry. How can I put this more clearly—we need you. We can bring you in as a civilian if you want. You can work in the Research Desk with Agnes and your men. How does that sound?"

Working in radio intelligence again was tempting, but the thought of living in DC after the warmth and sun of Florida did not appeal to Chief Kidder. "Could you find something for me at CAST or HYPO?" he asked.

After giving it some thought, Safford didn't see why not. The Research Desk had no civilian personnel in either Hawaii or the Philippines, but he didn't see any reason why he couldn't find a way to get Kidder out there. It just might take some time. "I tell you what, Chief," Safford began. "Come back to active duty and work in DC or Station M until I can get a civilian billet sent out to the Pacific. Then you can retire from active duty again and move out there permanently."

Kidder was convinced. Before he could change his mind, Safford recalled him to active duty and assigned him to work at Station M in Cheltenham.

⚓ ⚓ ⚓

Chief Kidder's first assignment was to travel with Lieutenant John Lietwiler to Bermuda. While this wasn't a full acceptance of Tizard's original invitation, Safford needed to be careful not to exceed United States' policy by unilaterally lending assistance to the British war effort. If word got back to the Axis Powers, it could be seen as the United States siding with the Allies and could lead to retaliation. Lietwiler would lead the delegation to Bermuda, while Kidder would be the technical expert.

Kidder and Lietwiler immediately planned their trip to Bermuda for December 1940. They would stay at the Fairmont Hamilton Princess Hotel—known to locals simply as The Princess.

Since the beginning of the war in Europe, the British government had taken over the Princess Hotel as a base of operations. The basement of the hotel became an intelligence center and way station where censors intercepted and analyzed all British mail, radio, and telegraphic traffic between Europe, the United States, and the Far East before routing the messages to their destinations.

In addition to the primary duty of censorship, the Royal Navy also had a much more secret role in Bermuda—the Government Code and Cipher School was operating an intercept station and HFDF site at the hotel. On the roof of the hotel, the school had its own version of the rotating Adcock HFDF equipment to track German U-boats as they operated in the Atlantic Ocean. After meeting with operators and touring the Bermuda site, Kidder's initial assessment was that the Royal Navy's DF equipment was far superior to that of the U.S. Navy, as it could quickly and successfully triangulate the positions of German ships operating in the Atlantic. The Government Code and Cipher School's intercept operation against the German Navy was roughly equivalent to that of the U.S. Navy's activities against the Japanese. However, the Germans used only international Morse code, so the British operators didn't need to learn any specialized telegraphic alphabets.

Sitting at an intercept position in the basement of the Princess Hotel, Kidder tuned to frequency 15100 kilocycles to show the British intercept operators what the Americans were up against. When the Japanese broadcast began, Kidder copied the katakana transmissions with a stick and paper. Kidder's British counterparts were amazed at his ability to copy the Japanese broadcasts.

"If we're ever dragged into this war, maybe we can teach you how to copy the Japs," Kidder teased.

As they departed Bermuda, both Kidder and Lietwiler believed that the British intercept site was roughly equivalent to the U.S. Navy's sites, but the British had far superior DF capabilities. With that in mind, there were certainly opportunities for the Americans and the Brits to help each other's radio intelligence operations, as long as they kept it on the down low.

CHAPTER 71

TYPHOON

SUNDAY, NOVEMBER 3, 1940
STATION BAKER, LIBUGON HILL, GUAM

On the night of November 3, 1940, Markle Smith and Al Burton, both graduates of the thirteenth On-the-Roof Gang class, were performing katakana intercept duties at Station BAKER, copying regular skeds of Imperial Japanese Navy communications. In between skeds, Burton tuned to the Japanese weather broadcast and copied it using Johnny Cooke's solution to break the code.

"Jeez, that's rough," Burton winced.

"What's up, Al?"

"Weather forecast says there's a typhoon heading this way tonight. Looks like a big one—150-mile-an-hour winds," Al answered. "The Japs are warning all their ships to avoid the Mariana Islands."

"I'll get the chief," Smith replied. "He needs to know about this. Give me your copy."

"Yeah, good idea. Here ya go, Smitty."

As Petty Officer Smith stood up and took off his headphones, Burton handed him the paper from his Underwood Code Machine then loaded another sheet into the typewriter and got right back to copying the forecast.

Smith headed directly to Chief Jimmy Pearson's office. Pearson was almost done with his tour of duty on Guam and was getting ready to transfer to Hawaii. With just another month to go, Pearson was looking forward to the faster pace of life in Hawaii after two full years on sleepy Guam.

Smith paused at the open door to the chief's office and said, "Chief Pearson, a minute of your time?"

"C'mon in, Smitty. Whatcha got?"

"Burton just copied the Japanese weather broadcast. Sounds like there's a typhoon heading this way tonight—a bad one."

"OK, Smith. You got the copy?"

"Here it is, Chief."

As Pearson read the weather report, he raised his eyebrows, surprised by the severity of the weather headed their way. According to the forecast, there wasn't much time—the typhoon would be bearing down on the Mariana Islands overnight. Pearson needed to make sure that everyone was aware of the approaching storm in order to make preparations for the forecasted high winds, torrential rains, and storm surge before any of it made landfall. He picked up the phone on his desk and dialed four numbers. After a pause, he spoke into the receiver, "Captain McMillin, please."

Petty Officer Smith lingered in the office while Chief Pearson waited for the captain to answer. Captain George Johnson McMillin was the Naval Governor of Guam, the highest-ranking Navy man on the island.

"I don't care what time it is! Wake him up!" Pearson barked.

Smitty took an almost imperceptible step back. He had never heard the chief speak in such a discourteous tone. He was glad he wasn't on the other end of the line. After a few minutes, Pearson spoke again. "Yes, sir. Sorry to wake you at this hour. I have some news for you. . . . You'll need some coffee for this."

CHAPTER 72

DEPENDENTS EVACUATED FROM STATION CAST

MONDAY, NOVEMBER 4, 1940
SANGLEY POINT, CAVITE NAVAL BASE, PHILIPPINES

Radioman Second Class Duane Whitlock, who'd graduated from On-the-Roof Gang training in early 1938 and had spent two years at Station HYPO in Hawaii, had recently arrived in the Philippines for duty at Station CAST. As a second class petty officer, he was not entitled to transportation for his wife to the Philippines, but since she was expecting their first child, he paid for her travel himself. He was the only married operator at Station CAST, and as such, when the site moved to Corregidor Island, he was allowed to remain in Cavite, where there was sufficient housing for married men. He was assigned to operate the Model DT HFDF equipment at Sangley Point, even though he had only worked as an intercept operator at Station HYPO. He and his wife, Gertrude, whom he called Gerty, believed it was money well spent to get her to the Philippines. Whitlock was looking forward to being a father and to spending his entire life together with

Gerty. After the arrival of their baby girl, whom they named Nadine, they began to establish their new life near Cavite Naval Base.

Life was good for the young Whitlock family. However, one night in early November, Duane came home after a long shift in the DF shack to find the Navy chaplain sitting in the living room with Gerty, baby Nadine in her arms. It was obvious that Gerty had been crying.

"Duane, sit down, please," Chaplain Rivers instructed.

"OK . . . What's going on?" Whitlock asked.

"Gerty has to leave, Duane."

"What do you mean?"

"The Navy is evacuating all dependents from the Philippines. Gerty and Nadine are booked on the SS *Monterey* on Wednesday."

Duane looked at Gerty and immediately understood her anguish. It was more than just having to be separated for an indefinite amount of time. The Japanese were becoming increasingly aggressive across the Pacific, and the evacuation of dependents from the Philippines could only mean war was coming. They had been married for just over a year, and now things seemed to be unraveling.

Duane looked at his wife and said, "Everything's going to be OK, Gerty, I promise."

"How can you promise that, Duane?"

He had no answer; it was nothing but wishful thinking. "Gerty, you'll go home to Hawaii. Your parents will help you there. I'll be fine here." Duane made sure not to promise this time.

There was no escaping the inevitable, so Duane and Gerty prepared for her departure. Once again, since the U.S. Navy was under no obligation to pay for the travel of his dependents, Whitlock was responsible for the cost. His pay was docked twenty-five dollars a month until he repaid the debt.

With his family gone, Whitlock was reassigned to Station CAST on Corregidor Island. Inside the tunnel, he worked as a traffic analyst in the Combat Intelligence Unit inside Tunnel AFIRM. Physically isolated on the island of Corregidor and financially isolated due to his reduced monthly paycheck, Whitlock spent his off-duty hours in the tunnel, learning to break the JN-25 code.

While performing traffic analysis one day, Whitlock broke out the call signs in the heading of a message intercepted earlier. According to the routing indicators in the heading, Whitlock deduced that a division of Japanese destroyers was planning to leave Japan, make a stop in Formosa, then head to Palau, an island just east of the southern Philippines.

Analysis in hand, Whitlock took the message to the on-watch officer, Lieutenant Jefferson Dennis, who disagreed with Whitlock's analysis and refused to put the results in the daily intelligence report for CINCAF. Dennis knew that Imperial Japanese Navy ships bound for Palau from Japan never went by way of Formosa. Instead, they first went south to Saipan or Truk—far to the east of the Philippines—before heading west to Palau. Thoroughly deflated, Whitlock returned to his desk and resumed his traffic analysis.

Two days later, a reconnaissance aircraft from Cavite reported sighting three Japanese destroyers about 200 miles east of Manila proceeding on a southeasterly course toward Palau. Whitlock's analysis had proven correct, and from that day on, Lieutenant Dennis included the results of Whitlock's traffic analysis in his daily reports.

CHAPTER 73

TYPHOON'S AFTERMATH

MONDAY, NOVEMBER 11, 1940

STATION BAKER, LIBUGON HILL, GUAM

The typhoon that swept over the area on November 3 and 4 devastated the Mariana Islands, and no more so than on Guam. The worst of the storm happened after the eye passed Guam to the south, and the island was subjected to an onslaught of devastating winds, which topped out at over 130 miles per hour. Five people died when falling trees crushed their homes; but that total most certainly would've been much worse if not for the warning On-the-Roof Gang operators had provided.

Most buildings on Guam were damaged in the storm, including every structure belonging to Station BAKER. Diesel generators provided power to only a few of the buildings on the island. In his report to CINCAF, Captain McMillin noted that reconstruction of all buildings at Station BAKER would be necessary. The DF shack was leveled, and the roofs of both the operations building and the barracks had been ripped off. The typhoon had also carried away the roof of the storehouse, and the equipment inside had sustained extensive water damage. McMillin estimated that it would cost at least $60,000 to repair or replace the buildings and equipment at Station BAKER.

Most of the receivers and Underwood Code Machines had been saved because the men had disconnected them and covered them with heavy canvas during the worst of the storm. However, the antennas and the DF equipment were all destroyed.

Asiatic Fleet commanders immediately authorized the renovation of all Station BAKER buildings and the replacement of all antennas and equipment necessary to get the station back up and running. The Research Desk dispatched a new Model DY HFDF set to Guam for installation.

Without any intercept to perform, On-the-Roof Gang graduates stationed in Guam pitched in with the restoration efforts. While their primary concern was to get intercept operations up and running again, they couldn't do anything about that until power was fully restored and new antennas were installed on the island.

Engineers from Cavite Naval Base arrived on the island exactly one week after the typhoon struck. They carried with them sufficient equipment to get Station BAKER back on its feet, but their priorities were to restore full power to the island, renovate Captain McMillin's quarters and offices, and then—and only then—could they begin restoring the intercept station.

When McMillin heard this, he immediately reprioritized the engineers' orders: power first, but then he wanted the intercept operations up and running before any work was done on his own quarters. He understood the importance of having the intercept site tracking the Japanese Navy.

CHAPTER 74

CLASS #25

MONDAY, NOVEMBER 18, 1940
MAIN NAVY BUILDING, WASHINGTON, DC

At the Research Desk, Commander Safford received the report from Keg Goodwin and Tru Lusk at Station S and decided to accept their recommendation for a new school at Bainbridge Island to replace the katakana training that had been conducted on the roof of the Main Navy Building since 1928. In DC, Chief Novak prepared to teach the twenty-fifth On-the-Roof Gang class, which would be the last one held in the nation's capital. With the decision made to transfer katakana intercept and radio intelligence training to Station S as soon as possible, classes at the Main Navy Building would no longer be necessary.

However, although the twenty-fifth class would be held at the Main Navy Building, it would not be taught in the rooftop classroom for two reasons. First, the structure was no longer habitable. The leaks had become completely unmanageable and the walls were crumbling. Second, the Research Desk wanted to push through at least a dozen students for the final class, and the rooftop classroom could only accommodate eight. Instead of the roof, the class would be held in the Research Desk workspaces during evening hours, after the regular staff had gone home. The twelve students chosen for the last radio intelligence class in the Main Navy Building were Maynard Albertson, Elmer Disharoon, Reece Finley, Stanley Gramblin, James Howard, Roy Lehman, Howard McConnell, Hugh McGall, Earl Rank, Raymond Rundle, Arthur Swain, and Merrill Whiting.

After the students completed their training in February 1941, eleven of the twelve new operators were sent to Station HYPO in Hawaii. The twelfth man, Petty Officer Swain, was sent to Station M in Cheltenham, Maryland.

The U.S. Navy's official radio intelligence training would move to Bainbridge Island as soon as the training facilities were ready. With that, the list of perhaps the most exclusive club of U.S. Navy radio intelligence operators ever assembled—the On-the-Roof Gang—was complete.

⚓ ⚓ ⚓

When Chief Kidder and Lieutenant Lietwiler returned from their expedition to Bermuda in January 1941, the results were beyond anything Commander Safford could have hoped for. Desperate to slow the destruction German U-boats were wreaking in the Atlantic, the Royal Navy needed the help of the U.S. Navy, particularly with radio intelligence, so the British were prepared to open up their deepest secrets to gain such cooperation.

At the Research Desk, Commander Safford learned that the Royal Navy had shared technical details of their radio intelligence efforts with Chief Kidder, including the fact that the Brits were operating an extremely effective HFDF site from the Princess Hotel in Bermuda using a variation of the rotating Adcock DF set. In exchange, Kidder agreed to start sending bearings from US-based HFDF sites in the Atlantic to the Royal Navy's Net Control in Bermuda. Both countries would fully share results in order to improve locational data of German submarines. This had to be a tightly held secret because if any of the Axis Powers suspected anything about this cooperation, it could pull the United States into the war. As important as the agreement on direction finding activities was, Kidder and Lietwiler also secured an agreement with the Royal Navy to cooperate on codebreaking. This agreement, which was the first of its kind, meant that resources could be used more efficiently on both sides of the Atlantic and the results would be shared as a matter of routine procedure. It was a win-win for both sides: the British would receive assistance for their U-boat problem, and the Americans would obtain help in breaking foreign diplomatic codes, including those from Japan.

Thrilled with the results of the Bermuda expedition, Safford began planning the initial engagement on codebreaking with the British at Bletchley Park. But meanwhile, Safford was having a devil of a time dealing with the U.S. Navy bureaucracy in trying to get Chief Kidder a civilian position somewhere in the Pacific. It seemed like a civilian position in the Philippines was simply too difficult, so Safford concentrated his efforts to placing a civilian billet in Hawaii. Even this was difficult to get past the navy bureaucrats, but Safford wasn't going to give up. In the meantime, Chief Kidder worked at Station M and waited.

CHAPTER 75

STATION K

MONDAY, DECEMBER 2, 1940
DUTCH HARBOR, AMAKNAK ISLAND, TERRITORY OF ALASKA

Radiomen first class Clarence "Al" Detterich and Robert "Buck" Dormer, both 1937 On-the-Roof Gang graduates, were transferred from Guam to establish a new DF site at Dutch Harbor, Alaska. They boarded the USS *Henderson* in Guam and made stops at Midway Island and Pearl Harbor before arriving in San Francisco. From there, they boarded a train to Seattle and then to the Bremerton Navy Yard in Washington State.

After several frustrating weeks awaiting transportation in Bremerton, Detterich and Dormer finally boarded a U.S. Fisheries ship bound for Dutch Harbor. They made the trip up the breathtaking inland passage and across the Gulf of Alaska, arriving on a bitterly cold morning.

Dutch Harbor was a port town located on Amaknak Island within the Aleutian Islands archipelago. Sheltered within Unalaska Bay, Dutch Harbor protected ships from the harsh conditions of the Bering Sea.

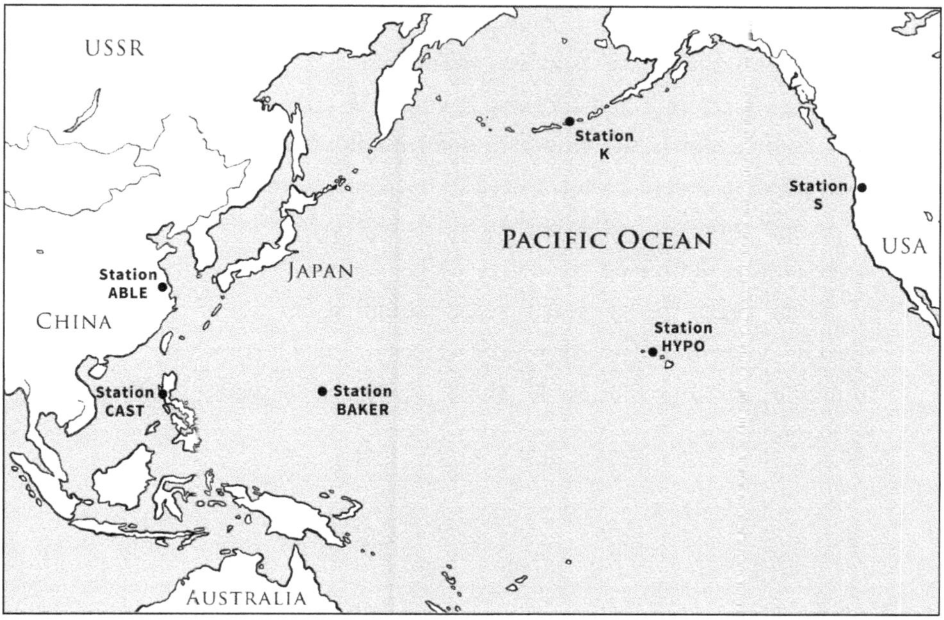

As with all of the Aleutian Islands, Amaknak was rocky and mountainous. No trees grew naturally on the island, although some low-lying brush occasionally interrupted the fields of grass that painted the hills of Amaknak green.

The U.S. Navy base and the Army's Fort Mears provided the majority of the population of Dutch Harbor, and a small town developed to support their needs. Detterich and Dormer were formally assigned to the Naval Radio Station at Dutch Harbor, call sign NPR, at which twelve radiomen and one machinist worked. They were all berthed in a small Quonset hut at the nearby Naval Aerological Expedition, whose mission was to observe and report Siberian weather to the U.S. Weather Bureau.

Detterich and Dormer installed an older Model DT HFDF suite in a tall cylindrical building, halfway between the Aerological Expedition area and the main radio station. They called it "the silo" and installed a second receiver below the DF equipment where they could copy Imperial Japanese Navy communications.

Once Detterich and Dormer got the DF equipment operational, they trained newly arriving radiomen on how to operate the gear. Their mission was to perform HFDF on Japanese merchant and navy ships, but they also utilized their skills to copy some katakana messages as time permitted.

Over time, the general service radiomen became proficient at the DF operation. This allowed Detterich and Dormer to perform intercept, making Station K, the U.S. Navy's newest HFDF site, fully operational.

CHAPTER 76

CODEBREAKING IN DC

TUESDAY, DECEMBER 31, 1940
MAIN NAVY BUILDING, WASHINGTON, DC

With the help of the Combat Intelligence Units in Pearl Harbor and Corregidor Island, by the end of 1940, the Research Desk was making some headway toward cracking each of the five encryption systems that the Imperial Japanese Navy was using: the Administrative Code, the Merchant Ship Code, the Material Code, the Intelligence Code, and the Operations Code.

The Administrative Code system was a relatively simple transposition code whose keys changed every ten days. The Combat Intelligence Unit at Pearl Harbor was responsible for recovering the keys to this system. Decryption of this code system revealed intelligible text from nearly all intercepted messages after key recovery, which the Combat Intelligence Unit was able to complete in about a day or so.

Decrypted intercept from the Merchant Ship Code system produced texts that were almost 100 percent readable. The cipher changed quarterly, and the keys had been predicted for several quarters into the future. The Merchant Ship Code had the widest distribution of all the systems since both merchant and fishing vessels on the Imperial Japanese Navy's communications nets used it. Even so, the Merchant Ship Code was never used for highly sensitive messages and rarely produced intelligence of significant value.

The Materiel Code system, also known as the "HE" system to U.S. Navy cryptologists, changed ciphers at random intervals of every ten to thirty days. At the end of 1940, Lieutenant Junior Grade Prescott Currier was leading a team at the Research Desk to decipher this system. The code was used when transmitting technical details of a ship's construction, including speed, tonnage, height and beam length, weaponry, and more. Unlike some of the other codes, decrypted messages from the Materiel Code produced intelligence about communication capabilities rather than intentions.

The Intelligence Code system was also known as the "I Code." The Research Desk was responsible for the recovery of the I Code, but this system was not used extensively, and specific code recoveries were few. For that reason, plus the fact that the Research Desk didn't have the time or resources to expend on this system, the team had been neglecting the I Code in favor of the other, more important code systems.

The Operations Code system, or JN-25, was the most important system for the U.S. Navy to break because it was believed that all operational navy communications used the code. However, the decryption unit at the Research Desk was making slow progress toward breaking the JN-25. The JN-25 used an additive key cipher, and although the method of key recovery was well defined, the process was a laborious one, requiring an hour to several days to recover the key, which changed daily. Only a few code groups had been recovered, so it was unknown when JN-25 messages could be read. The decryption unit at Corregidor was tasked with helping the Research Desk crack the JN-25 code.

In addition, the Japanese were using the weather transposition code—the simplest of all the codes in use. Keys for this code were available at all intercept sites, so they all had the ability to copy and decrypt messages using this code.

Lieutenant Commander Alwin Kramer, a Japanese language officer, was in charge of the decryption unit at the Research Desk. The team consisted of Radioman First Class and On-the-Roof Gang graduate Al Pelletier and three civilians: Fred Woodrough, Dorothy Edgers, and Phil Cate. Kramer spent most of his time on Japanese diplomatic ciphers and used Woodrough and Edgers as his principal assistants.

Pelletier and Cate worked on recovering JN-25 code groups, first focusing on place names, ship names, dates, numbers, naval organization, and movement reports. While they occasionally came across information in the traffic that might have been worthwhile to operational commanders in the Pacific and Asiatic Fleets, the decryption team never reported such information. Operational reporting from decrypted messages only happened at Corregidor and Pearl Harbor. The Research Desk focused solely on recovering code groups.

In addition to the radiomen and naval officers trained as cryptanalysts and Japanese linguists, the Research Desk employed ten yeomen to process traffic using an IBM keypunch and punch cards. The yeomen were given the same high clearance level as everyone else that worked in the Research Desk, and Commander Safford made efforts to keep them within the radio intelligence community from one assignment to the next.

The members of the decryption unit also used their PURPLE machine to create automatic decrypts of Japanese diplomatic traffic. The PURPLE machine was made up of two typewriters connected by four rotors and a switchboard. A PURPLE operator would type in the encrypted message using one of the machine's typewriters, and the second typewriter would automatically type out the decrypted text, which then had to be translated. The decrypted and translated messages were marked with the code word *MAGIC*, and the

Research Desk was processing from fifty to seventy-five MAGIC messages per day. Working with its counterparts in the U.S. Army, the Research Desk selected about twenty-five of these messages per day for distribution to the ten people with clearance to read the MAGIC correspondence. These messages were considered so secret that only a select few couriers were given clearance to deliver them to the intended recipients and then bring them straight back to the Research Desk for record-keeping.

CHAPTER 77

INTELLIGENCE COOPERATION

SATURDAY, FEBRUARY 15, 1941
MAIN NAVY BUILDING, WASHINGTON, DC

By mid-February 1941, intercept at Station HYPO and the follow-up analysis from the Combat Intelligence Unit at Pearl Harbor indicated that Japan was sending a large naval force to French Indochina, stoking the fears of an attack on Singapore. However, despite the deployment of the Japanese naval force, the attack never materialized. During the deployment, traffic analysis conducted by the Combat Intelligence Unit at Pearl Harbor indicated no communications from the Japanese aircraft carriers. The resulting assumption was that the carriers had remained in Japanese waters to protect their homeland—the assumption turned out to be correct.

Following a series of high-level diplomatic exchanges between the United States and Great Britain in late-1940 and early-1941, the two countries formally agreed to share intelligence, including codebreaking procedures and results. Despite the competitive nature of intelligence activities in the U.S. Army and Navy, the War Department directed the formation of a commission comprised jointly of Army and Navy personnel.

After some hurried coordination, the U.S. Army and Navy decided on a group of four individuals to represent America's codebreaking activities. The Army's delegation included Captain Abraham Sinkov and Lieutenant Leo Rosen. The Navy selected Lieutenant Junior Grade Prescott Currier and Ensign Robert Weeks for the assignment. The American delegation's purpose was to exchange information and learn how the British radio intelligence efforts were conducted. The Americans were to deliver to the British two PURPLE machines capable of decrypting the high-level Japanese diplomatic cipher. Currier also took a U.S. Navy RIP-5 Underwood Code Machine to give to the British. Additionally, the team brought along approximately 2,000 JN-25 code groups—everything the U.S. Navy had compiled on the Imperial Japanese Navy's Operations Code, to date.

On January 17, 1941, the four Americans boarded the HMS *King George V* in Annapolis, Maryland. Publicly, the visit was an educational event for U.S. Navy midshipmen to get a closer look at the newly commissioned British battleship. Only the CO of the *King George V* knew about the American delegation's intelligence mission.

⚓ ⚓ ⚓

On a crisp late-February morning, Chief Radioman Sandy McGregor arrived at the Main Navy Building for work in the decryption section of the Research Desk. Unusually, McGregor was late, arriving after 0830, even though he normally arrived for duty as early as 0700.

He sat down at his desk between those of Chief Billehus and Petty Officer Al Pelletier. Sweat dripped from his forehead after the two flights of stairs. He took deep, uneven breaths, attracting the attention of Pelletier, who had been a rooftop student of McGregor's in 1936.

"Good morning, Chief," Pelletier said as he immediately sensed something was wrong. "Chief, are you OK?" he asked.

McGregor could do nothing but nod—he was too out of breath

to answer verbally. Pelletier noticed how pale McGregor looked, and stood to check on him.

"Gee, chief, you don't look so hot."

Chief Billehus joined Pelletier in approaching McGregor to make sure their shipmate was all right. Just then, McGregor suddenly hunched over, hitting his head on the desk and falling hard onto the asbestos tile floor. As he fell, he grasped at his desktop, papers full on intercept logs landed all around him. By the time Pelletier and Billehus reached McGregor, he was prostrate on the floor.

They rolled him on his back and saw that McGregor was in serious trouble. He was only taking short, gasping breaths and his face was as white as the paper surrounding him. They yelled for help, but they knew there wasn't going to be much anyone could do.

Chief Sandy McGregor was still alive as the ambulance drivers placed him on a stretcher and carried him out of the room. Everyone hoped they could get him to a hospital in time to save him.

⚓ ⚓ ⚓

The American delegation arrived at Bletchley Park two weeks later. Alastair Denniston, the Director of the Government Code and Cipher School at Bletchley, was there to greet them. The Americans were initially shown some, but not all, of Bletchley Park. They were also taught the game of rounders, which seemed like baseball played with a broomstick. However, there were also reminders that Great Britain was a country at war.

On March 7, Denniston took the Americans to Café de Paris, a London nightclub on Leicester Square, a favorite with Londoners because it was underground and, therefore, seemed safe during the nightly German bombing raids known as the Blitz. The raids had taken their toll on the city's streets and ravaged buildings across town. The number of casualties could've been much worse, but Londoners had become very familiar with hiding out in makeshift bomb shelters in the subway system during the attacks.

When the men arrived at Café de Paris, the club was very crowded, noisy, and filled with men in uniform dancing to the music of bandleader Ken "Snakehips" Johnson. The Americans marveled at the resilience of the British people. Their country was at war, yet they managed to forge a normal life in between German aerial attacks. The team enjoyed the camaraderie in the nightclub and returned to their lodging at Bletchley Park around midnight.

The very next night, a German bomb tore through the nightclub's ventilation system and exploded on the dance floor, killing thirty-four people including "Snakehips" and most of his band.

The American visitors were shaken by the news, but their British counterparts seemed to take it in stride. Their focus remained on the business at hand and with the PURPLE and RIP-5 machines. When the Americans shared their Japanese Operations Code recoveries, they learned that the Brits at Bletchley Park had made some progress on the JN-25 as well, so the two sides shared what they knew. Between the two groups, they had recovered roughly 20 percent of the JN-25 codebook. This wasn't sufficient to read full messages but combining forces to decipher the JN-25 code could only be helpful.

Cooperation on intelligence matters between the Americans and the British was off to a good start. Still, it took weeks of deliberation for Prime Minister Winston Churchill to eventually decide that Britain would fully reciprocate. On their last day at Bletchley Park, the Americans were finally let in on Britain's greatest intelligence secret: a machine called the Bombe that mathematician Alan Turing had designed to automatically decipher messages created by the Enigma, the German's encryption device. This revelation came as a bit of a surprise to the Americans, who understood it to mean that the British were ready to cooperate at the closest levels.

CHAPTER 78

CODEBREAKING IN HAWAII

TUESDAY, MARCH 11, 1941
FOURTEENTH NAVAL DISTRICT ADMINISTRATION
BUILDING, PEARL HARBOR, TERRITORY OF HAWAII

In March 1941, Lieutenant Commander Joseph Rochefort, having completed Japanese language training in Japan and an assignment as the Eleventh Naval District Intelligence Officer in San Diego, was assigned to lead Pearl Harbor's newly established Combat Intelligence Unit. At the same time, Lieutenant Commander Edwin Layton, Rochefort's friend and fellow Japanese language student, became the Pacific Fleet's intelligence officer. Rochefort and Layton had known each other as language students in Tokyo, and they were looking forward to working with each other in Hawaii.

After just a couple months in Hawaii, Rochefort gave up correcting people when they called his unit Station HYPO. Station HYPO was the intercept site at Heeia; Rochefort's unit, the Combat Intelligence Unit, was located across the island in the basement of the Administration Building of the Fourteenth Naval District at Pearl Harbor. As such, Rochefort referred to his workplace as "the dungeon."

The Combat Intelligence Unit at Pearl Harbor was established to process, decrypt, and translate intercept from Station HYPO more quickly. Originally, transcripts of intercept had to be forwarded—by courier and air mail—to Washington, DC, for processing. So, by the time it was decrypted, most intercept was badly outdated. Together with the Combat Intelligence Unit in the Philippines, intercept from On-the-Roof Gang operators could be processed much more quickly into viable and tactical intelligence for commanders in the Pacific and Asiatic Fleets.

Joseph Rochefort in Hawaii, circa 1940.

From the outset, the Research Desk assigned the Combat Intelligence Unit at Pearl Harbor the primary task of breaking the Imperial Japanese Navy Admin Code, since both the Combat Intelligence Unit in the Philippines and the Research Desk were working on the Operations Code, or JN-25.

Rochefort's Combat Intelligence Unit team included cryptanalysts Lieutenant Joseph Finnegan, Lieutenant Thomas Dyer, Lieutenant Junior Grade Wesley "Ham" Wright, and Lieutenant Jack Holtwick, as well as Lieutenant Junior Grade Forrest Biard, who was a Japanese linguist, and U.S. Marine Corps Major Alva B. Lasswell. Additionally, chief radiomen George "Red" Hopkins and Jimmy Pearson, early On-the-Roof Gang graduates, were assigned to the dungeon to provide intercept expertise, traffic analysis, and assistance where needed.

In the meantime, Station HYPO was outgrowing its spaces across island. The intercept location provided excellent results but could not accommodate the U.S. Navy's expanding needs, as more and more

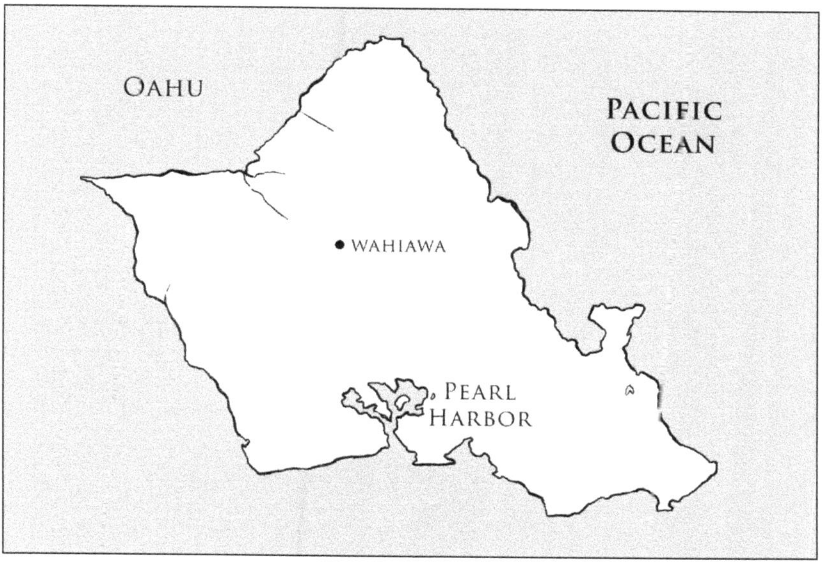

On-the-Roof Gang graduates were being sent to Hawaii. There were only eight intercept positions, and Station HYPO needed more. Martin Vanderburg, the Chief Radioman in Charge of Station HYPO, requested assistance from the Research Desk in finding new location for the intercept operation with more space.

Safford assigned Rochefort at the Combat Intelligence Unit the task of finding a new location for Station HYPO. Rochefort learned that the Fourteenth Naval District planned to move the large radio station at Wailupe to a new site a short distance northeast of the town of Wahiawa near Schofield Barracks, a large U.S. Army post in the west-central part of the island. Rochefort sought and received permission from the Research Desk to piggyback on the plans and move Station HYPO to Wahiawa as well. Rochefort worked with the district communications officer to develop plans for a joint station, which would house both the general service radio station and Station HYPO. They planned to move into this new facility in late 1941.

CHAPTER 79

PLANS FOR PAPPY

SATURDAY, APRIL 5, 1941
MAIN NAVY BUILDING, WASHINGTON, DC

The loss of Chief Radioman Walter "Sandy" McGregor was felt keenly in the Research Desk. He had been one of the leaders of the fledgling organization. He had suffered with a chronic heart condition throughout his career, which kept him from being assigned outside of Washington, DC for the final six years of his life, during which time he taught five classes of the On-the-Roof Gang training and became an expert codebreaker. He would be missed.

In early-April 1941, after their stay at Bletchley Park, American codebreakers Sinkov, Rosen, Currier, and Weeks sailed back to the United States on board the HMS *Revenge*. With them, they brought a complete British version of a Marconi-Adcock HFDF set. Although they did not bring back a Bombe machine, they carried with them a "paper" copy—a full schematic and list of algorithms pertaining to the Enigma machine that would allow the Americans to build their own Bombe.

In exchange, the British were hoping for some operational assistance from the Research Desk. The British wanted nothing more than to establish a DF site in Greenland, which would give them a 360-degree view of the Atlantic Ocean with their DF network. However, because Greenland wanted to remain neutral during the war, the British did not have permission to do so. In order to protect Greenland's neutrality, the British asked the United States to establish a DF site there and share the results.

Since the U.S. Navy already had HFDF sites all along the East Coast of the United States, it was a relatively simple process for Safford to add another site to the network. He easily got the approval to establish a DF site in Greenland, and he knew just the right person to get it done. *He's not going to like this*, Safford thought.

CHAPTER 80

OPERATIONS IN SAMOA

MONDAY, JUNE 2, 1941
VAITOGI VILLAGE, AMERICAN SAMOA

In the year since Glenn Evans had arrived in Samoa, he and Ted Wildman had been providing excellent DF results to Net Control at Station L in Lualualei, Hawaii. By the summer of 1941, Evans had been promoted to first class, so the U.S. Navy paid for travel for his dependents. As such, Glenn immediately sent for his wife, Jane, who was still living in Hawaii. He had met her in Honolulu, where she was a nurse at Queens Hospital. After she arrived in Samoa, she was the only medical professional in Vaitogi, and began to provide basic medical care for both Americans and the local population.

In June 1941, Radioman First Class Paul Hively arrived in Samoa. Known as Pete to his friends and family, Hively had spent the previous five months at Mare Island learning how to operate and maintain HFDF equipment. Hively was there to relieve Ted Wildman, who was on his way to the Naval Research Laboratory in Bellevue to teach advanced radio technician training.

The Navy also sent five new radio operators to Station V as HFDF operators. Freshly out of Class A school, they were all very junior and barely knew international Morse code, let alone the katakana code.

On Tutuila Island, Hively and Evans settled into a wonderful existence living in what seemed to be paradise—the climate was neither too hot nor too cold. Living in grass huts was idyllic, and the locals were welcoming and friendly. Most importantly, the HFDF results from their South Pacific vantage point provided unique intelligence on the location of Japanese Navy vessels.

The results were so good, in fact, that the Research Desk sent engineers to Samoa to rehabilitate the old Pan Am buildings to expand the HFDF operation. They also installed a new Model DY HFDF set with sixteen-foot arms and twelve-foot dipole antennas. The upgraded model was easier to use and provided more accurate lines of bearing.

Over time, Evans and Hively sensed that Japanese communications were becoming increasingly intense, as more frequent and longer messages crowded each of the skeds. The approximately 150 Americans on the island—Navy men who manned the small base and maintained the USS *Ontario*, the only rescue ship in the South Pacific—began to feel uneasy because they realized they were on a tiny island that barely rated any defense from the U.S. Navy. If a war with Japan were to break out, they would be on their own.

CHAPTER 81

KEEPING TRACK OF THE CARRIERS

TUESDAY, JULY 29, 1941
FOURTEENTH NAVAL DISTRICT ADMINISTRATION BUILDING, PEARL HARBOR, TERRITORY OF HAWAII

From his office in the dungeon, Lieutenant Commander Rochefort read the reports of 140,000 Japanese troops invading southern French Indochina. This did not come as a complete surprise given that the Japanese had been aggressive toward French Indochina since September of the previous year. Plus, radio intercept, direction finding, and traffic analysis all revealed the large naval force steaming south from Japanese waters toward the Gulf of Tonkin.

Once again, traffic analysis picked up no messages to or from the Japanese aircraft carriers, and the assumption was that they remained in Japanese waters. Later reports confirmed this traffic analysis: the Japanese carriers never left port.

This was the second time a Japanese naval force had moved out of Japanese waters without aircraft carriers, and each time, American traffic analysis had noticed they were absent from communications. If

Entrance into the 14th Naval District Administration Building. The Combat Intelligence Unit was located in the basement, or "the dungeon."

Rochefort had learned anything from these Japanese movements, it was that traffic analysis could detect the composition of an Imperial Japanese Navy task force. Along with decryption and codebreaking, Rochefort viewed this development as an arrow in his radio intelligence quiver if or when war ignited with Japan.

CHAPTER 82

STATION ABLE CLOSES

MONDAY, SEPTEMBER 1, 1941
STATION ABLE, SHANGHAI, CHINA

With the recent escalation of Japanese aggression toward China, the safety of the men and operations at Station ABLE was becoming untenable. To Commander Safford at the Research Desk, the facility in Shanghai offered Station ABLE little in the way of physical security. Given the growing Japanese presence in the city, the risk to the U.S. Navy's radio intelligence program was no longer acceptable.

By the summer of 1941, On-the-Roof Gang graduate LD Lankford was the chief radioman in charge of Station ABLE. In early September, he called an "All Hands" meeting after the midwatch, which meant that everyone was required to attend regardless of where they were in their shift schedule. At the meeting, Lankford addressed his six men: Arthur Groff, Jack Kaye, Warren Simmons, Martin Smith, Rod Whitten, and Sam Winchester. All were all radiomen first class and On-the-Roof Gang alumni.

As the men gathered around the intercept room, Lankford motioned to Whitten and Groff, who were on duty, to take off their headsets. They stood along with the rest of the operators assembled there.

"Men, you may have heard some of this before, but the situation around the International Settlement is bad and getting worse. We can see the Japanese bombing Chinese targets right across the Whangpoo."

"We know, Chief. We don't leave the International Settlement while we're on liberty," Simmons said.

"That's good, Simmons. But things are changing for us."

The men murmured to each other in anticipation of the news. Lankford was reluctant to say what he had to say, but he knew he had to do it. "Station ABLE is closing," Lankford said abruptly. "You're all going to Station CAST. The Research Desk says we're to pack everything up."

The men were shocked by the news. Even though the Japanese were intensifying their attacks on Chinese forces, they never felt unsafe in the compound of the Fourth Marine Regiment.

"Chief, are you sure?" Petty Officer Kaye asked.

"Yes, and that's not all. We have two weeks, so it's time to get cracking." Lankford went on to explain that effective immediately, there would be no more intercept from Shanghai.

Lankford shared the plan with his men: Station CAST would immediately take responsibility for Station ABLE's intercept duties while the men at Station ABLE shut down and moved out of the Fourth Marine Regiment's Headquarters in Shanghai. All records and equipment would be transferred to the Philippines—nothing was to be destroyed. But they needed to make it look as if they were never there, so antennas would be disconnected and dismantled, and the equipment would be powered down and crated along with safes full of intercept logs and other records for shipment to Station CAST.

Lankford's men met the two-week deadline and departed as planned. Everything—equipment, files, and personnel sailed from Shanghai on board the USS *Isabel* en route to Corregidor Island, except for Chief Lankford himself. Since the Navy didn't want to cause any confusion about who was in charge at Station CAST, Lankford was headed to Station HYPO to take over as chief radioman in charge there.

CHAPTER 83

STATION AB

FRIDAY, SEPTEMBER 12, 1941
GAMATRON ISLAND, GREENLAND

From the moment the British asked the United States to open an HFDF site on Greenland, Commander Safford knew he would ask Chief Kidder to lead the effort. Safford knew Kidder had his heart set on a transfer to the warmer climate of the Pacific, but nearly a year after putting in his request, Kidder was still working at Station M in Cheltenham, Maryland.

The U.S. Army already had a small presence at Bluie—America's official code name for Greenland—so it offered the Research Desk a location referred to as Bluie West 3. Bluie West 3 was located on Simiutak Island, off the southwestern coast of Greenland. The Americans had difficulty pronouncing Simiutak, so they called the island Gamatron instead. Gamatron was an uninhabited island that was occasionally used by the local Inuit people as a burial ground. As such, some of the locals considered it sacred or haunted.

In order to create a cover story for the new HFDF site, the U.S. Navy announced it would open a new radio station on Gamatron Island, and Chief Harry Kidder was nominally attached to the

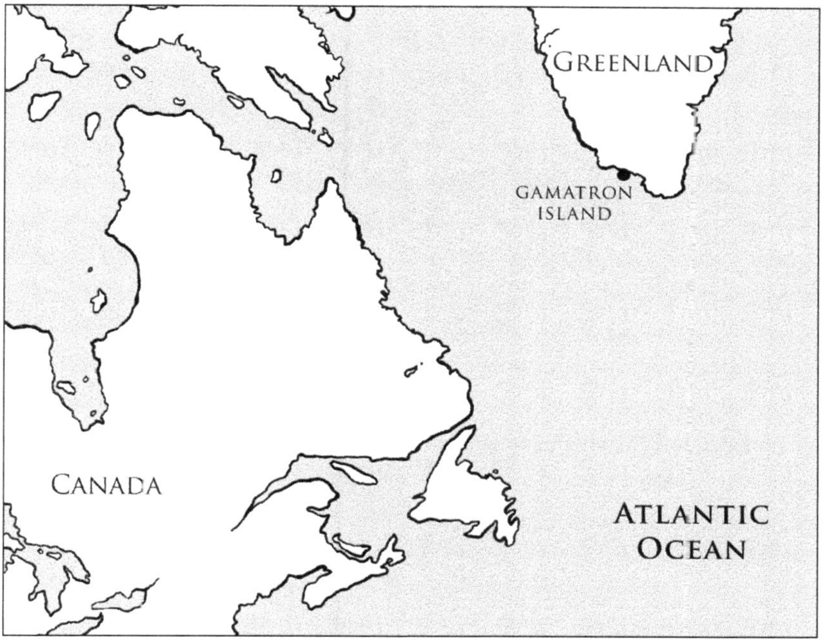

fourteen-man team sent there to get it up and running. In reality, Kidder was on his way there to independently establish the HFDF site, which the Research Desk designated Station AB. Kidder carried with him a complete Model DT HFDF set, which he would set up and begin to operate after his arrival. In September, the team boarded the U.S. Coast Guard cutter USCGC *Tampa* in Boston for the trip to Greenland.

Gamatron Island was a rocky outcropping, approximately a mile long and a half mile wide. Deep fjords surrounded the island on three sides. Davis Strait, leading from the Labrador Sea to Baffin Bay, bordered the other. Other than members of the U.S. Navy, the only inhabitants were a few white fox and nests of ptarmigan. Drinking water for the men stationed on Gamatron Island came from a lake-sized puddle of melted glacier ice that was filled with little red crustaceans about the size of raisins.

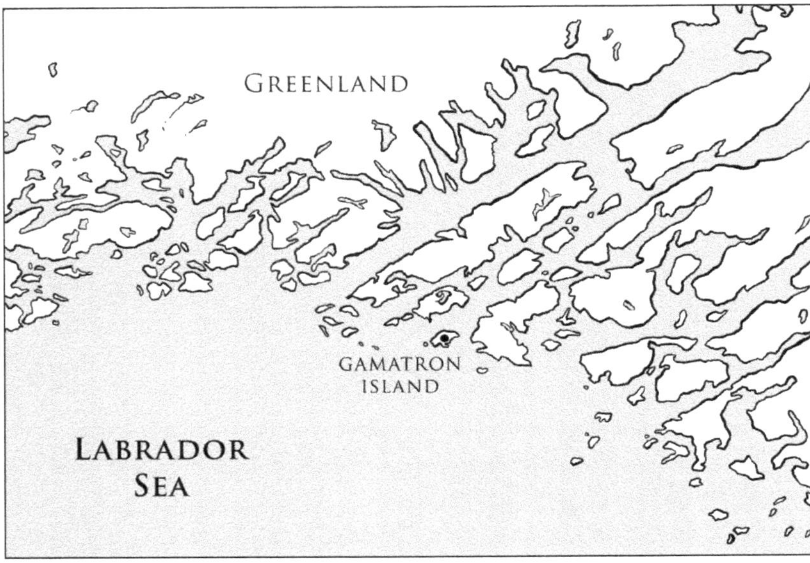

The naval facility on Gamatron Island had four main buildings: a mess hall, a recreation hall, the commanding officer's quarters, and the radio station. The only other buildings were a boathouse and a few Quonsets for the crew's quarters.

The crew's Quonsets were large enough to hold eight men and their belongings. For heat and to warm up water for washing and bathing, each Quonset had a cast-iron wood stove in the center. Lines were strung between the bunks to hang clothes to dry.

As a chief petty officer, Kidder rated a smaller private Quonset. Kidder was not happy about being in Greenland, but he knew he had a mission. He set up the HFDF gear south of all the Quonsets in order to have a clear line of sight to the ocean. However, he recognized immediately that the weather might pose a problem in operating the gear. Wind gusts on the island frequently reached up to 100 miles per hour and would last for days at a time. Walking between the DF shack and his Quonset was often difficult due to the high winds and sleet. Having to climb a ladder outside, the

Quonset huts at the Navy camp on Gamatron Island.

equipment would be hazardous in the cold, windy, icy Greenland winters. In his first report back to the Research Desk, Kidder requested for a more modern Model DY setup that could be installed inside a proper shelter. In addition to the DF equipment, Kidder set up a modern multiband receiver with the hope of hearing some katakana transmissions.

Chief Kidder had Station AB operational long before the worst of the winter set in. His mission in Greenland was a far cry from working as a civilian in Hawaii as Safford had promised. Kidder missed the warmth of the Pacific Ocean and wondered how long he would be required to stay in the frozen tundra of Greenland.

CHAPTER 84

STATION CAST ABSORBS STATION ABLE

MONDAY, OCTOBER 20, 1941
CORREGIDOR ISLAND, PHILIPPINES

Shortly after the closure of Station ABLE in September, the men and equipment arrived at Corregidor Island from Shanghai. If Tunnel AFIRM was hot and crowded before the new arrivals, it became even worse when the men and equipment from Station ABLE moved in.

In addition to copying the diplomatic nets they inherited from Station ABLE, the men of Station CAST also picked up intercept from the Berlin-Tokyo circuits, which had previously been conducted at Station BAKER. Since Station CAST had a PURPLE machine, it only made sense for them to perform intercept that needed PURPLE decryption.

Despite the increasing workload and the number of personnel crammed into the tunnel, operations at Station CAST were superb. Conditions from Corregidor Island made for intercept that was a

On-the-Roof Gang operators at Station CAST, Corregidor Island, Philippines, circa 1941. L-to-R (front): Wilson Mason, Warren Simmons, Victor Long, Martin Smith, Jack Kaye, Duane Whitlock, Charlie Johns. L-to-R (row two): Donovan Chase, unknown (ducking), Tack Walvoord. L-to-R (row three): Douglas Harold, unknown, unknown, unknown, Joseph Smith. L-to-R (row four): unknown, unknown, Harold Jones.

marked improvement over what was retrieved from any of the previous sites in the Philippines. Coverage of ABLE's and BAKER's nets were performed easily at CAST. And Station CAST had sufficient intercept equipment—receivers, antennas, DF sets, and Underwood Code Machines—to expand its operations.

The additional personnel and equipment from Station ABLE produced a greater volume of intercept traffic and analysis at Corregidor, so the problem of getting the information to Washington grew. The U.S. Navy's solution was a new encryption device called the Electronic Cipher Machine (ECM) Mark II. Intercept sites around the world received the encryption devices, including Station CAST.

Instead of using couriers to send messages and files to Washington, DC, the information could be sent encrypted via radio. Operation of the ECM Mark II was the responsibility of yeomen, who had been given security clearance to work in radio intelligence.

Throughout the fall of 1941, analysis and operational reporting from Station CAST was beginning to show a disturbing pattern of Japanese military preparedness. Radioman First Class Duane Whitlock, who was now working full time as a traffic analyst in the Combat Intelligence Unit, prepared an updated report for the Chief of Naval Operations on the state of the Japanese Navy. The report revealed the Japanese Navy had assumed a wartime disposition and was recruiting and inducting its merchant ships in alarming numbers. Whitlock's analysis accounted for no less than 200 such ships in ports bordering the Formosa Strait just north of the Philippines.

The Combat Intelligence Unit also produced reports that detailed the composition of two powerful Japanese naval task forces converging on the Philippines: one from the north preparing to join the transports in the Formosa Strait area, and one from the Mandate Islands to the east, closing in upon Palau and the southern Philippines. These developments made it clear that if the Japanese were to attack, the Philippine Islands would most likely be their target.

Because the JN-25—the Japanese Naval Operations Code—still hadn't been cracked, any intelligence gleaned from intercept operations came from messages encrypted in other codes or through traffic analysis. Advancements toward breaking the JN-25 code moved forward only as Japanese errors allowed. The problem with trying to make any headway toward breaking the code was that five-digit additives had to be recovered before meanings could be assigned to the underlying five-digit code groups. But paradoxically, the five-digit code groups had to be recovered before breaking the additives. Many months and reams of intercept had to be performed in order to recognize sufficient mistakes by the Japanese code clerks before any foothold into the complex operations code could be obtained.

Even so, with the Combat Intelligence Unit in the Philippines, along with cryptanalysis in Washington, DC, such a foothold was beginning to appear. However, it was by no means a very sturdy one, as breaks in the JN-25 code moved ahead at a snail's pace. Days or weeks would pass with only two or three additives discovered out of the many thousands that the Japanese were using.

CHAPTER 85

DEPENDENTS EVACUATED ACROSS PACIFIC

FRIDAY, OCTOBER 17, 1941
USS *HENDERSON*, APRA HARBOR, GUAM

By October 1941, evidence was building that the Japanese intended to drag the United States into a military conflict in the Pacific. In addition to the analysis and reporting happening at the intercept sites in the Philippines and Hawaii, things were taking an ominous turn diplomatically. Anticipating the possibility of a major attack at one of the intercept or DF sites in the Pacific, the Research Desk began planning to evacuate the Sailors' dependents from those sites.

For the Sailors on Guam, news of the world came from the *Guam Eagle*, a small local newspaper that On-the-Roof Gang operators produced from news broadcasts out of Hawaii. The radiomen simply typed out news broadcasts they copied and then mimeographed the newsletter for distribution to the U.S. Navy community on Guam.

However, bowing to pressure from its readers, the *Guam Eagle* focused mainly on sports scores instead of foreign relations or diplomatic activities. The first solid indication the Sailors on Guam had of the ongoing world events occurred when Captain McMillin, the naval governor of Guam, ordered all dependents back to the United States on the next eastbound transport ship in October 1941. More than a hundred dependents of U.S. Navy personnel boarded the USS *Henderson* bound for Hawaii, which was assumed to be within the safe protectorate of the U.S. Pacific Fleet. Among them was Marie Joslin, the wife of Radioman First Class Harold "Hal" Joslin, a 1940 On-the-Roof Gang graduate assigned to Station BAKER.

En route from Guam to Hawaii, the USS *Henderson* stopped at Wake Island to pick up more Navy dependents. Pan American Airways requested assistance from the U.S. Navy in doing the same. One of those Pan Am dependents was Isyl Cooke, the wife of On-the-Roof Gang alum Johnny Cooke, who had been working for the airline for several years.

From Wake Island, the *Henderson* headed southeast to American Samoa to pick up more dependents. At the time, Radioman First Class Glenn Evans was due to rotate from Samoa to Station S on Bainbridge Island, so he boarded the ship with his wife, Jane.

Two weeks later, the USS *Henderson* arrived at Pearl Harbor and off-loaded more than 200 wives and children of U.S. Navy servicemen. Confident that the Japanese would never attack so far east, U.S. Pacific Fleet commanders felt that the military families would be safe in Hawaii. The women and children were given the option of continuing on to the mainland or remaining in Hawaii until the situation in the Pacific settled down. In the meantime, the *Henderson* would remain at Pearl Harbor for two weeks of maintenance.

While the *Henderson* remained docked at Pearl Harbor, several ships of the U.S. Pacific Fleet quietly slipped out to sea. Their missions were secret and preparatory to presumed Japanese Navy strikes in the western Pacific. The USS *Lexington*, one of three aircraft carriers assigned to the Pacific Fleet, left Pearl Harbor to ferry seventeen

Vindicator dive bombers to Midway Island. Along with five destroyers and the heavy cruisers USS *Chicago*, USS *Portland*, and USS *Astoria*, the *Lexington* formed Task Force 12. After delivering the aircraft to Midway, Task Force 12 was scheduled to perform training and scouting in the western Pacific Ocean.

The USS *Saratoga* left Pearl Harbor for a short period of repairs in Bremerton, Washington, before it was scheduled to head to San Diego to pick up its air group, which consisted of bombers, fighters, and torpedo bombers.

The USS *Enterprise*, three heavy cruisers, and nine destroyers, all of which made up the U.S. Navy's Task Force 8, left Pearl Harbor. The mission of Task Force 8 was to deliver twelve Grumman F4F-3 Wildcats to Wake Island to help shore up the defenses there. Task Force 8 was due back to Pearl Harbor on December 7.

To the crew of the USS *Henderson* watching from the dock in Pearl Harbor, the ships that departed the port seemed like an endless parade of the U.S. Navy's power and might. After the procession of Navy ships out of port Pearl Harbor, there were no U.S. Navy aircraft carriers remaining at Pearl Harbor.

CHAPTER 86

STATION S OPERATIONS

WEDNESDAY, NOVEMBER 19, 1941
STATION S, BAINBRIDGE ISLAND, WASHINGTON

The night before Thanksgiving, Radioman First Class Elmer Dickey was sitting an uneventful midwatch. Throughout the night he copied several encrypted messages in the katakana telegraphic code that he'd learned during his training as an On-the-Roof Gang student.

At 0515 hours, toward the end of his shift, Dickey heard a Japanese radio operator call all stations for an important message on frequency 9160 kilocycles. It was not out of the ordinary for Japanese radio operators to call their next message important, so Dickey didn't pay particular attention to this one, which began with the code indicator "BUTWJ," a known indicator for a global audience on the diplomatic circuits. As he was taught to do in his On-the-Roof Gang training, Dickey sat tall in front of his Underwood Code Machine and placed his fingers on the home row keys to wait for the transmission to begin. The katakana code began to ring out in his headphones, and Dickey instinctively hit the corresponding keys on his RIP-5: *clack, clack, clack, clack, pause. Clack, clack, clack, clack, pause. Clack, clack, clack, clack, pause.* At the end of the message, he noted that it was an eighty-one group message sent at roughly twenty-five words per minute.

When the message was complete, Dickey followed procedure: He typed up the text of the encrypted message text along with its heading onto paper tape and then contacted the person standing watch at the Research Desk in DC. When the connection was made, he fed the tape into the ECM Mark II machine for automatic transmission. He imagined the operator in Washington, DC, catching the tape as it spewed out of the machine on his end.

When his watch ended at 0700, Petty Officer Dickey briefed his relief, Glenn Evans who'd recently arrived from Samoa, on all the messages he'd copied over the midwatch. There were twelve encrypted messages, each of which he'd forwarded to the Research Desk watch Officer in Washington, DC. All in all, it was nothing extraordinary.

Evans assumed the watch, waiting for the next Japanese sked. Larry Myers, who was also an On-the-Roof Gang graduate and the chief radioman in charge of Station S, joined Evans on watch. It wasn't unusual for Myers to join one of his men and take the second intercept position. He'd noticed an uptick in the volume of traffic being processed at Bainbridge Island, so he regularly pitched in. Most of the intercept they were processing came from the diplomatic nets. In comparison, the Japanese Navy nets they were responsible for intercepting were relatively quiet.

As Myers sat at the intercept position and placed the headphones over his ears, he and Evans gave each other a quick nod hello. Evans was waiting for the next sked and didn't want to start a conversation. Right on cue, he heard the Japanese radio operator tuning up to send the next message. Evans sat up, placed his fingers on the home row, and began to copy.

As Chief Myers watched, Petty Officer Evans copied a forty-eight group message on 9160 kilocycles, which carried the same "BUTWJ" indicator that Dickey had copied overnight. *Clack, clack, clack, clack, pause. Clack, clack, clack, clack, pause.* Evans processed this intercept and sent it along to the Research Desk watch center. Chief Myers was proud of his men for doing everything by the book.

None of the messages intercepted at Station S caused any concern for the operators, nor the chief. To them, it was just another day intercepting the Japanese katakana code.

CHAPTER 87

WINDS INSTRUCTIONS

TUESDAY, NOVEMBER 25, 1941

MAIN NAVY BUILDING, WASHINGTON, DC

At the Research Desk, the on-watch cryptanalyst recognized the indicator "BUTWJ" and other aspects of the messages intercepted by Station S on 19 November — the diplomatic messages were addressed to all Japanese embassies and consulates worldwide. These messages needed to be decrypted by the PURPLE machine.

The daily PURPLE key usually took cryptanalysts at the Research Desk a few days to break, and the daily key for November 19 was finally available. The PURPLE operator worked through his stack of diplomatic intercept from that day, finally decrypting the two "BUTWJ" messages intercepted at Station S and sending them to the Japanese linguists for translation in folders marked "MAGIC." The PURPLE-to-MAGIC process was a well-rehearsed dance of technology, intellect, and intrigue.

The translations of the "BUTWJ" messages from November 19 revealed a set of instructions for all receiving stations. Japan would secretly communicate its intentions regarding diplomatic relations with three named countries by coding it into a broadcasted weather phrase. These plaintext weather phrases would be broadcast on several frequencies in the event that code machines were no longer available for use. The three possible phrases were each unique and signified the state of relations with one of the three countries:

- *HIGASHI NO KAZE AME* (East Wind Rain) meant that Japan's relations with the United States were in danger.
- *KITA NO KAZE KUMORI* (North Wind Cloudy) meant Japan's relations with the Soviet Union were at risk.
- *NISHI NO KAZE HARE* (West Wind Clear) meant that Japan's relations with Great Britain were threatened.

The translated instructions stated that each phrase would be repeated as a special weather bulletin, twice in the middle and twice at the end of the daily Japanese language shortwave voice news broadcast and during plaintext news broadcasts in the katakana code. When the message was heard, each diplomatic facility was to destroy all code machines, codes, and important papers.

The instructions also indicated that specific radio stations would broadcast these weather messages at certain times and frequencies:

Station	**Frequency (kc)**	**Schedule**	**Reception Area**
JVJ	12275	1800	Pacific Coast
JUO	9430	1830	Western Hemisphere
JVJ	12275	1830	Western Hemisphere
JVJ	12275	1900	Pacific Coast
JHL	5160	2000	East Coast
JHL	5160	2100	East Coast
JHP	11980	2230	Europe

After the translations were verified, Commander Safford sent instructions to all intercept and DF stations to be on the lookout for any of these phrases—in voice or in katakana code—during news and weather broadcasts. Looking for these so-called Winds Execute messages was advisory tasking only. In other words, it was not to interfere with the copying of any of the stations' normal skeds.

CHAPTER 88

STATION CAST LISTENS FOR WINDS MESSAGE

FRIDAY, NOVEMBER 28, 1941
STATION CAST, CORREGIDOR ISLAND, PHILIPPINES

By late 1941, two dozen On-the-Roof Gang alumni were assigned to Station CAST, which had four intercept positions manned around the clock. Like at Station HYPO, general service radiomen were assigned to assist the site with additional traffic analysis and DF operations. Cleared yeomen, including Petty Officer Ken Grisham, who had recently arrived in the Philippines via the USS *Chaumont*, operated the ECM Mark II secure communication system and the PURPLE decryption machine.

After teaching the last official rooftop class in DC, Tony Novak had been transferred to the intercept site at Station CAST as the chief radioman in charge. It was there that he received Commander Safford's message to search for the Winds Execute messages. Having four intercept positions gave Novak the flexibility to devote one of his men to looking for the weather message at all times.

Novak wrote his orders in the daily instructions for the intercept watch: each shift, one man would dedicate his time to searching for the Winds Execute message. But secretly, Novak doubted the wisdom of these instructions. *Even if we copy it, what would it help?* he thought. It was a common belief among the officers and men of the Asiatic Fleet that war with Japan was imminent and that the Japanese were likely to attack without warning. But the Winds Execute message wouldn't reveal when or where such an attack would take place. Plus, current estimates from Washington, DC held that the Japanese would first attack U.S. bases in the Philippines, so Novak wanted to find clear evidence of this in the intercept. Still, he assumed Safford knew what he was doing when he wrote the order, so he dutifully assigned his men to look for the coded weather message.

Radioman Third Class Martin Smith, a more recent On-the-Roof Gang graduate, was assigned to search for the Winds Execute message when he heard on Japanese news broadcast station JVJ that all listeners should tune in at 0700 the following morning for some important news.

Recognizing the potential importance of the message, Chief Novak ordered all intercept positions at Station CAST to tune to all the specified frequencies to listen for the important news the next morning. Following Novak's orders, operators Duke Carnes, Charlie Quinn, Eddie Otte, and Cappy Capron ignored their normal Japanese naval skeds and tuned to the different frequencies specified in the instructions. But 0700 hours came and went, and no Winds Execute message or notice was heard on JVJ or any other station.

⚓ ⚓ ⚓

By this time, Admiral Thomas C. Hart, the Commander in Chief of the Asiatic Fleet, was preparing for war. And like Chief Novak, he believed the Japanese were planning a surprise attack on Cavite

Naval Base in the Philippines, the home of the Asiatic Fleet. In late November, Hart ordered many of the Asiatic Fleet ships, including the USS *Houston*, the flagship of the Asiatic Fleet, out of Cavite in case of attack.

On December 1, 1941, the USS *Houston* got underway from Cavite Naval Base with a full complement of more than a thousand Sailors aboard. The *Houston*'s first stop was scheduled for the next day at the port town of Iliolo, on the southern shore of Panay Island, where it would be safe from any potential Japanese attack.

CHAPTER 89

ANOTHER IJN CODE CHANGE

MONDAY, DECEMBER 1, 1941

MAIN NAVY BUILDING, WASHINGTON, DC

A young yeoman working as messenger of the watch stood in the lobby of the Main Navy Building keeping an eye on the doors as Sailors and officers arrived for work. He was anxiously awaiting the arrival of Commander Laurance Safford, who had several messages waiting for him.

Safford walked through the main entrance, his eyes adjusting from the bright sunshine outside, and stepped into the lobby.

"Commander, I'm glad you're here," the yeoman called out. "They need you upstairs right away. I was told to tell you it's urgent."

"Thank you, Sailor. I'll head straight up."

His mission accomplished, the messenger of the watch strode back to the desk at the quarterdeck and sat down. Safford picked up his pace, taking two steps at a time as he headed up to the Research Desk.

Agnes was already at her desk when Safford walked in. "It's not good," she said.

"What's wrong?"

"Looks like all the IJN codes have changed again. Nothing is breaking. We're hearing the same from HYPO and CAST. They can't decrypt anything, either."

This was one of Safford's biggest fears. Just as diplomatic negotiations with Japan were breaking down, the United States needed radio intelligence more than ever to help detect a potential Japanese strike. Safford knew the next question he had to ask, but he hesitated, not wanting the worst news of all. When he finally gained the nerve, he asked Agnes, "How about PURPLE?"

"We still have PURPLE, Commander," Agnes said.

Momentarily relieved by the thought of the PURPLE decrypts, Safford snapped back into reality when Agnes reminded him of the potentially devastating loss of the Japanese naval codes. "But we've never gotten anything tactical out of PURPLE," she said. "We need the naval codes to know what's going on with the IJN."

Agnes was right, of course, but there was nothing Safford could do about that. He wanted to check the MAGIC folder to see if there was anything revealing in the traffic.

Reading the traffic, he learned that Japanese embassies in DC, London, Manila, Singapore, and Hong Kong had been ordered to destroy their code machines immediately. The Japanese embassy in Washington had also been directed to burn all codes except one.

"Oh, this is not good, Agnes," Safford groaned.

Nodding, she got back to work. It was time to try to figure out the new code. But she knew it was going to be a long few weeks before they were going to achieve any sort of success with cracking the new code.

Safford realized that war with Japan was near, but the White House wanted more than intuition and estimates. President Roosevelt was waiting for unequivocal evidence that Japan was going to declare war on the United States. And so far, Safford didn't have it. Instead, he did what he could. He drafted a message to the Pacific and Asiatic

Fleet commanders, informing them of the Japanese diplomatic activities. He assumed they would understand the implications.

In addition to trying the break the new Imperial Japanese Navy's codes, the Research Desk was responsible for the dissemination and usage of U.S. Navy codes and ciphers. Safford knew exactly what needed to be done to protect those codes and ciphers from capture at outlying stations in the event of war. He drafted messages to the U.S. Navy attachés in Tokyo, Bangkok, Shanghai, and Peiping, directing them to destroy all cryptographic aids. They were to confirm their compliance by sending the word *boomerang* in plaintext and then report the final destruction of the last cryptographic system and other confidential papers by sending the word *jabberwock* in plaintext.

In the hours that followed, messages stating *boomerang* and *jabberwock* came trickling in until there was complete accountability of all U.S. cryptographic material around the fleet. With that accomplished, Safford turned back to the pressing issue: the U.S. Navy's intercept and codebreaking enterprise was in trouble because of the change in the Imperial Japanese Navy's Operations Code. Despite the fact that they had only cracked a small percentage of the previous Operations Code, JN-25, they were making progress and could even decrypt partial messages. Now that the Imperial Japanese Navy had abandoned the JN-25 code, the U.S. Navy was blind to its presumed enemy's intentions outside of DF and traffic analysis—which would not be enough to thwart a surprise attack.

Suddenly, Safford remembered the Winds Execute message and immediately ordered all U.S. Navy intercept stations to redouble their efforts in searching for it. While it wouldn't provide the timing or location of a potential Japanese attack, it could provide confirmation that an attack was imminent.

It wasn't much, but at that point, it was all they had.

CHAPTER 90

STATION HYPO LISTENS FOR WINDS MESSAGE

TUESDAY, DECEMBER 2, 1941

STATION HYPO, HEEIA, TERRITORY OF HAWAII

Over the past eighteen months, Station HYPO had grown into the largest U.S. Navy intercept site in the world, with eight intercept positions and thirty On-the-Roof Gang graduates working as operators. Together with other operators trained in Hawaii to copy the katakana telegraphic code, Station HYPO filled each of the eight positions around the clock.

Although the plan was to relocate Station HYPO from Heeia to Wahiawa, contract problems and material shortages plagued the move that would eventually double the number of intercept positions at Station HYPO. Initially, the move-in date was scheduled for September 1941, but as the end of the year approached, that date got pushed back until at least March 1942.

The changing of the Imperial Japanese Navy's codes created a sense of urgency at all U.S. Navy intercept sites, as would any change of codes. The first step in breaking any new code was to intercept as much traffic as possible and look for patterns in the code or mistakes that the Japanese operators had made. However, orders from the Research Desk prioritized finding the Winds Execute message over copying traffic using the new codes. As a result, LD Lankford, the chief radioman in charge at Station HYPO, directed six of his eight intercept operators on each shift to search for the Winds Execute message on the specified nets.

Ensuring there would be sufficient experience on watch at any given time, Lankford broke protocol by assigning at least one On-the-Roof Gang-trained chief petty officer or senior first class petty officer to each of the four watch sections. His chief petty officers were normally given only day shifts. However, Lankford didn't want Station HYPO to miss anything that might have indicated when or where the Japanese would attack, and assigning chiefs to the watch gave him some level of comfort.

Overnight, the intercept watch consisted of Chief Radioman Homer "Charlie" Kisner, supervising eight On-the-Roof Gang operators, charged with finding the Winds Execute message. The traffic volume was low, and they were able to find only a few transmissions from Japanese shore commands. The transmissions were mostly encrypted into groups of four katakana characters—these messages would have to be decrypted by Commander Rochefort's team at Pearl Harbor. Intercept operators dutifully logged all of these encrypted messages onto intercept logs, which would be couriered to Pearl in the morning. None of the operators heard what they believed to be anything close to the Winds message.

The following morning, On-the-Roof Gang graduate Radioman First Class Elliott Okins was sitting next to several other operators looking for any information on the Winds Execute message. Okins was the senior operator in the watch section, responsible for making sure everyone on intercept duty knew what they were responsible for.

As Okins did his work, Chief Lankford approached and said, "Okie, I'm heading over to Pearl today to check in with Rochefort in the dungeon. I have to try to figure out why we're spending so much time on this 'Winds' thing."

"All right, Chief. I've got this. You go ahead," Okins replied confidently.

Five graduates of the last rooftop class—Reece Finley, Stan Gramblin, Roy Lehman, Ray Rundle, and Merrill Whiting—were on duty with Okins, who turned to the men and said, "Everyone clear on what we're looking for? 'HIGASHI NO KAZE AME.'" He repeated it clearly so that everyone understood, "We need to find 'HIGASHI NO KAZE AME.'" The men nodded in understanding and got to work.

CHAPTER 91

STATION BAKER LISTENS FOR WINDS MESSAGE

TUESDAY, DECEMBER 2, 1941

STATION BAKER, LIBUGON HILL, GUAM

By December 1941, Don Barnum, who had graduated from On-the-Roof Gang training in 1933, was the chief radioman in charge of Station BAKER in Guam. It was a much smaller intercept site than CAST or HYPO and had only six other On-the-Roof Gang operators assigned. Working a four-section watch, Barnum had assigned one rooftop-trained operator to each section. During the day, when intercept traffic was heaviest, he supplemented the watch with an additional operator.

As the inevitability of war loomed over the men at Station BAKER, they worried more and more about what would happen to them if or when the Japanese attacked Guam. Would the Navy send reinforcements to help defend Guam? Or would they be left to defend themselves with a few dozen Marines armed with not much more than rifles? Either way, Don Barnum seemed to worry most about it, and leaned heavily on his senior operator, Radioman First Class

Markle Smith, from On-the-Roof Gang Class #13. Smith was up to the task, leading the rest of the operators with confidence.

During the afternoon shift on December 2, 1941, Radioman Second Class Hal Joslin and Markle Smith were on intercept duty. Don McCune, a general service radioman who operated the Model DT HFDF equipment at Station BAKER five days a week, was also there.

Rob Ellis, Eddie Dullard, Stuart Faulkner, and Rex Parr—the other On-the-Roof Gang operators assigned to Station BAKER—were all in the barracks just uphill from the intercept site. Some were sleeping after an overnight watch, while the others simply relaxed in the tropical warmth of Guam.

Petty Officers Smith and Joslin sat at their positions listening for anything that sounded like the Winds Execute message. They had abandoned the sked normally on their intercept plan; on this particular day, it was the Winds Execute message or bust.

Smith looked at Joslin and said, "You know what this means, right, Hal?"

"No, what?" Joslin replied. At Station BAKER, the operators never really knew what they were copying because they weren't trained in decryption. They simply copied their code groups and sent them off for decryption.

"Code change. If we're abandoning our normal intercept, it must mean they can't break the code, so they want us to find something that'll be useful to them."

Joslin nodded in understanding.

"Be careful, though," Smith warned. "The messages we're looking for will sound like normal weather reports. We're looking for weather reports that are repeated twice at the beginning and twice at the end of a transmission. If you don't hear that, it ain't what we're looking for."

"Got it, Markle."

With that, Smith and Joslin got back to work listening for the Winds Execute message.

CHAPTER 92

STATION S LISTENS FOR WINDS MESSAGE

WEDNESDAY, DECEMBER 3, 1941
STATION S, BAINBRIDGE ISLAND, WASHINGTON

With just two intercept positions, Station S at Bainbridge Island was similar to Station BAKER in size and capabilities. The Research Desk had given Larry Myers, the chief radioman in charge, instructions to maintain one of the positions on the Tokyo-to-Washington diplomatic circuit while the other searched for the Winds Execute message. Myers passed along the instructions to his operators, and they complied.

On December 3, 1941, Petty Officers Hilary "Popeye" Cyr and Fred Thomson were on watch duty. For the previous forty-eight hours, operators at Station S had been unsuccessfully listening for the Winds Execute messages.

"Popeye, what do you think? Are we chasing ghosts?" Thomson asked.

"I couldn't tell you, Fred. At least we still have the dip net to copy."

"I suppose that's still breaking, if they want us to copy it."

"I suppose," said Cyr.

Just then, Thomson began to copy as he heard a Japanese operator tuning in on the diplomatic net he was guarding. Popeye turned to his receivers and continued stepping through the broadcast stations that might contain the weather messages they were looking for.

Thomson's right. We are chasing ghosts, he thought.

CHAPTER 93

STATION M LISTENS FOR WINDS MESSAGE

THURSDAY, DECEMBER 4, 1941
STATION M, NAVAL COMMUNICATIONS STATION,
CHELTENHAM, MARYLAND

At Station M in Cheltenham, Maryland, Daryl "DW" Wigle—the chief radioman in charge of intercept operations—had briefed all of his operators on the need to search for the Winds Execute message. Station M only had two intercept positions, and Wigle dedicated both of them to finding the elusive message. Chief Wigle was lucky enough to have five On-the-Roof Gang trained intercept operators at Station M, all radiomen first class. They were Ralph "Red" Briggs, Robert "Buck" Dormer, Arthur Swain, Clarence, "John" Taylor, and Howard Troup.

Two days after the Research Desk intensified the search for the Winds Execute message, Red Briggs sat the day watch, anxious to copy any Japanese broadcast he could find. He was on high alert for any weather reports that might contain the encoded message as Chief Wigle had described.

Early on in his watch, Briggs thought he'd copied the sought-after message and yelled, "Chief!" He tore off his headphones and threw them on the desk to concentrate on reading the message he'd just copied.

Chief Wigle rushed over to see what Briggs wanted. But as Briggs read back the message he had just copied, he was disappointed to realize that it wasn't right. Although it was quite similar, the message he'd intercepted was not the Winds Execute message they were seeking.

Toward the end of his watch, having been similarly disappointed several times, Briggs copied the Japanese Overseas News Broadcast from Station JHP in Tokyo on 11980 kilocycles. Again, Briggs excitedly threw off his headphones to concentrate on reading his own copy. He breathed heavily reading through his intercept. This time he was sure he had it. He'd copied the Winds Execute message!

He called Chief Wigle over. Indeed, his intercept log showed that he'd copied "HIGASHI NO KAZE AME," but it appeared only once, even though the directions said it would be repeated twice at the beginning and twice at the end of the broadcast. Still, he was sure this was it.

Wigle was suspicious of the intercept. As Briggs himself had recognized, the phrase should have been repeated twice at the beginning and end of the transmission, but it wasn't. In addition, the phrase was misspelled in Briggs's own intercept log. What he read was "HIGASHI NO HAZE AME." It was a minor misspelling, but together with the lack of repetition, Chief Wigle didn't believe this was the actual Winds Execute message— especially after several false alarms from Briggs earlier in the shift.

"I don't know, Briggs," Wigle said reluctantly.

"This is it, Chief! I know it is."

"It's not what we were expecting. The phrase should have been repeated twice at the beginning and end. You copied it only once, not four times. And you've got a spelling mistake."

"I know, Chief, but you know the Japanese. They're a mess on their skeds. They always make mistakes like this."

Briggs was right about that, but Wigle wasn't convinced. Still, understanding the importance of the message, Wigle prepared the message for transmission via ECM Mark II to the Research Desk. When he sent it, he made sure to include his own assessment that this was not the actual Winds Execute message.

CHAPTER 94

WINDS MESSAGE CONFUSION

FRIDAY, DECEMBER 5, 1941
MAIN NAVY BUILDING, WASHINGTON, DC

By Friday morning, Laurance Safford had been awake for almost forty-eight hours, and his day was just beginning. There was too much going on for him to take any real breaks. Instead of going home for a full night's rest, he took occasional catnaps at his desk. He was feeling punchy from the lack of sleep, but adrenaline and coffee kept him afloat.

Several times over the past few days, Safford had received reports about the Winds Execute message. Despite the fact that he had provided explicit details to all the intercept sites, no one else seemed to be able to identify false messages and mistakes, and it frustrated him. The lack of sleep didn't help his frustration.

The Research Desk had also alerted radio operators at the Federal Communications Commission (FCC) to be on the lookout for the Winds Execute message. Unfortunately, they were the culprits of several of the false alarms.

One of the more significant erroneous intercepts occurred when an operator at the FCC monitoring station in Portland, Oregon, overheard a weather broadcast from Tokyo station JVW3 that appeared, at first, to fit the Winds Execute format. The operator heard "KITA NO KAZE KUMORI," which indicated a break in relations with the Soviet Union. Less than an hour after the Portland operator copied the weather phrase, the FCC watch officer in Washington, DC, reported the intercept to Lieutenant Francis Brotherhood, the watch officer on duty at the Research Desk.

Brotherhood thought the message seemed to be missing something from what he had been led to expect, but he brought the intercept to Commander Safford anyway. Safford read the intercept and recognized that the "KITA NO KAZE KUMORI" phrase occurred only once in the broadcast, instead of the required two times in the beginning and at the end of the news program. Also, the same broadcast carried other weather phrases not in the instructions, indicating the broadcast was an actual weather forecast instead of a coded message. Most telling, the call sign JVW3 was not on the list of stations that would broadcast the warning. It was obvious to Safford that, yet again, this was not the Winds Execute message.

Unfortunately, word of the intercept, though not verified, spread around the Main Navy Building, and Safford was called to the office of Rear Admiral Leigh Noyes, the current Director of Naval Communications. Safford had to explain the problem with the FCC intercept.

This cycle of mistaken Winds Execute intercept, Safford's recognition that the message was invalid, and then explaining to Admiral Noyes what had happened occurred several times throughout the day. One of those false alarms came from Red Briggs's intercept at Station M.

Because of his exhaustion, one false alarm ran into the next for Safford, who, by the end of the day, had essentially been awake for more than sixty hours. He was tired, confused, and needed sleep.

On the evening of Friday December 5, Laurance Safford finally went home to catch up on his sleep. As he faded in and out of sleeping in the taxi on the way to his apartment in Washington, DC, he thought about all the false Winds Execute messages from that day and wondered if any of them had actually been the tip-off he was waiting for. He struggled to keep them all straight in his mind, but it was no use; his brain was no longer firing on all cylinders. He needed to get home for some much-needed sleep. His plan was to be up and ready for work early on Saturday morning.

CHAPTER 95

STATION S INTERCEPTS 14-PART MESSAGE

SATURDAY, DECEMBER 6, 1941
STATION S, BAINBRIDGE ISLAND, WASHINGTON

During the middle of his day watch, Petty Officer Dickey, who was guarding the Tokyo-to-Washington diplomatic net, began to copy a message that was off sked. The header of the message indicated it was a fourteen-part message addressed only to the Japanese ambassador to the United States.

As he was instructed while in On-the-Roof Gang training, Dickey sat up straight, put his fingers on the home row of his Underwood Code Machine, and prepared to copy. "Chief, over here!" he called out.

Chief Tru Lusk, who'd recently been recalled to active duty after several months in the U.S. Navy Reserve, was sitting at the station next to Dickey. He looked over at the output of Dickey's intercept and recognized the message header's meaning. This was an important message, so Lusk tuned his own receiver up to the same frequency and began to copy. *Two intercept operators are better than one*, he thought.

As expected, the body of the message was encrypted. Parts one through ten came in clear and strong; however, as Dickey and Lusk copied part eleven, the signal began to fade in and out. Even so, between the two of them, they still caught it all. But after part thirteen, it faded away completely, so they didn't hear the final part of the message at all. Hearing only static in their headphones, both operators took their fingers off their typewriters.

Chief Myers, who was standing over the two intercept operators, had witnessed what had happened. "OK, guys, give me what you got," he instructed. "Then check all the diplomatic nets for a retransmittal."

When the two operators got back to work, Dickey remained on frequency, while Chief Lusk began to spin up to other frequencies.

Chief Myers quickly scanned the two operators' intercept logs to see which was more complete. He wanted to send the better of the two intercept logs to Washington, DC, for decryption. After reading them, he recognized that they were identical: Dickey and Lusk had copied exactly the same thing—character for character—despite the fact that the messages were several hundred groups in length.

That's a testament to their exceptional training, Myers thought as he transmitted the message to the Research Desk.

CHAPTER 96

WHERE ARE THE CARRIERS?

SATURDAY, DECEMBER 6, 1941
14TH NAVAL DISTRICT'S ADMINISTRATION BUILDING, PEARL HARBOR, TERRITORY OF HAWAII

In the basement of the Fourteenth Naval District's Administration Building at Pearl Harbor, Joseph Rochefort's team continued to scour Station HYPO's intercept logs for the Winds Execute message, but it simply didn't seem to exist. And Rochefort knew that at some point, he would have to dedicate his cryptanalysts back to trying to break the new Imperial Japanese Navy codes. This Winds Execute issue was just getting in their way.

As Chief Radioman and traffic analyst Jimmy Pearson sat at his desk in the dungeon combing through the Imperial Japanese Naval intercept from Station HYPO, he discovered a worrying fact. He hurried to Rochefort's office and knocked on the open door.

"Come in," Rochefort said. With his feet propped up on his desk, Rochefort was smoking a pipe and wearing his robe over his uniform. Sailors working in the dungeon had gotten used to seeing Rochefort in this state. After normal business hours, he frequently dressed like this to stay warm and comfortable in the cold, damp basement.

"Sir, HYPO is still producing intercept from the IJN nets, but there's a problem."

"Go ahead, Jimmy. Tell me," he said. Rochefort was not comfortable with strict Navy protocol, so he called everyone who worked in the dungeon by their first names.

"We don't have much traffic from HYPO to go through, but we've lost the aircraft carriers."

Rochefort took his feet off his desk, leaned forward, and looked directly at Pearson. "Lost? Explain."

"We know all the call signs for the carriers. We know all the call signs for most of the IJN. We should still be seeing them in traffic, but we're not."

Rochefort took a deep toke on his pipe. He had seen this before, most recently when the Japanese had sailed into the Gulf of Tonkin in July. In those cases, the carriers could not be found in communications, because, as it turned out, they were all in port.

"Go on," Rochefort said.

"There doesn't seem to be enough traffic, either. We've never seen comms levels this low," Pearson said.

"Could it be that HYPO is simply preoccupied with the Winds Execute messages, and they're just intercepting less?" Rochefort asked.

"It could be, sir. But it seems more like the Japanese are just not communicating—as if they're all in port."

"OK, Jimmy. Keep looking for the carriers. They're most likely in port, but check with HYPO to see what they think about the dip in communications. They've got some sharp operators up there."

"Aye, aye, sir," Pearson responded. Dejected, he got back to the traffic to see if he could locate the carriers in the communications.

Rochefort worried that the Japanese aircraft carriers could not be located. He was never comfortable with not knowing where enemy forces were. Regardless, there was nothing he or the traffic analysts could do.

⚓ ⚓ ⚓

In Wahiawa, Station HYPO had more than enough intercept positions to search for the Winds Execute message while continuing to copy the most important Imperial Japanese Navy skeds. As was their usual practice, all intercept logs were forwarded to the dungeon for processing.

The intercept operators at Station HYPO were also confused about the lack of communication from the Japanese. On the day watch, Petty Officers Jim Capron and Ray Rundle waited for Imperial Japanese Navy skeds that never came. The silence was eerie to them, so they took the opportunity to update their logbooks with recent call sign changes. The busywork was good in the sense that it distracted them from the obvious lack of katakana code to copy.

Elliott Okins, the on-watch supervisor of Capron and Rundle, was so concerned with the lack of communication from the Imperial Japanese Navy that he reported his apprehensions to Chief Lankford, who then relayed them to Rochefort's team working in the dungeon.

⚓ ⚓ ⚓

Rochefort decided to remain on duty in the dungeon overnight. It wasn't as if there was a lot of work he needed to do, since there were a scarce few messages to decrypt or analyze. He simply felt better if he was at work and ready, just in case something happened.

As dusk settled over the Hawaiian Islands on the evening of December 6, 1941, Joseph Rochefort felt a great unease about the situation. He listed his concerns to himself: *Code change. No Winds Execute message. No aircraft carriers. No locational data on the Japanese fleet. Comms nets drying up. No news of a diplomatic solution with the Japanese.*

And there was nothing he could do about any of it.

CHAPTER 97

THE FINAL PART

SUNDAY, DECEMBER 7, 1941
MAIN NAVY BUILDING, WASHINGTON, DC

Having returned to work the day before—after his first full night's sleep in a week—Laurance Safford arrived at the Research Desk early on the morning of December 7, 1941. Even though it was a Sunday, Safford sat at his desk anxiously awaiting the decryption of the final part of the fourteen-part message intercepted from the Japanese. The day before, Station S had initially intercepted only thirteen of the fourteen parts. Luckily, the day's diplomatic keys had already been broken, so the PURPLE machine was able to turn out a clean decryption. Instead of waiting for the final part of the message, there was consensus among the Army and Navy radio intelligence organizations to deliver the first thirteen parts to the MAGIC recipients immediately. President Roosevelt's naval aide delivered the results to the White House in a folder marked:

MAGIC
EYES ONLY

The first thirteen parts of the message contained the Japanese perspective of their diplomatic negotiations with the United States over the preceding twelve months, but the message was not a declaration of war against the United States. The final part of the message was key to understanding if the Japanese were planning to declare war on the United States.

In the early morning hours of Sunday, December 7, Station S finally intercepted the last part of the message and forwarded it to Washington, DC. Safford tapped his fingers on his desk as he waited for the PURPLE machine's decryption. He anticipated that the fourteenth and final part of the message would be instructions for the Japanese ambassador to declare a state of war against the United States.

The wait for the PURPLE decryption seemed like it was taking an eternity to Safford on this cold but dry December day. As Safford sat alone in his office, he was keenly aware of his every sense. The morning sun streamed through the venetian blinds in his office, creating parallel lines of warm light across his face and arms. With his eyes shut, he breathed deliberately, listening for footsteps outside his door, but this early on a Sunday, there were few people in the passageways.

Safford understood the White House decision regarding the first thirteen parts of the message—without a direct declaration of war, the United States would not preemptively attack Japan. Everything hinged on what was said in that final part of the message, which was, ever so slowly, being decrypted next door to Safford's office.

Finally, footsteps, and then a knock on the door. Before the second knock, Safford hollered, "Enter!"

The on-watch cryptanalyst handed Safford another MAGIC folder. Safford was so singularly focused on the folder that he had no idea who was delivering it to him. He stood and opened the folder at his desk. Putting on his coat in preparation for his drive to the White House, he read part fourteen carefully. The closing two paragraphs read:

Thus, the earnest hope of the Japanese Government to adjust Japanese-American relations and to preserve and promote the peace of the Pacific through cooperation with the American Government has finally been lost.

The Japanese Government regrets to have to notify hereby the American Government that in view of the attitude of the American Government it cannot but consider that it is impossible to reach an agreement through further negotiations.

There was no explicit declaration of war.

MAGIC folder in hand, Safford dashed out of his office.

CHAPTER 98

KIDDER IN GREENLAND

SUNDAY, DECEMBER 7, 1941
STATION AB, GAMATRON ISLAND, GREENLAND

Harry Kidder lay in his cot; he had no desire to get out of bed on this frigid Sunday morning in Greenland. He had been there for three months, and it was getting old. From inside his Quonset, he could hear the wind howling outside. He sat up and took a deep breath, realizing he had to dress and get outside to operate his HFDF gear despite the bitter cold.

He splashed water on his face, dressed, and put on his wool cap, parka, and mittens. He stood at the threshold of his Quonset—humid, still, acrid air behind him; biting, cold air in front of him. This was the last place he wanted to be. He couldn't help but think back to his days in Alaska as a young Army private and wonder how he'd gotten himself into this situation again.

He had certainly come full circle. As he stood there, he reflected on his life and career, recalling the excitement of forging the new radio intelligence discipline in the U.S. Navy and thinking about his parents, Susie, and the men he'd trained and where they all were. He thought of Miss Aggie and of Laurance Safford, the two smartest people he'd ever met. And he wondered if any of it mattered. He was alone and cold on a rock in the northern Atlantic Ocean and he knew the Japanese were preparing for war in the Pacific.

Sleet hit him on the side of the face on that early Sunday morning in December as he stepped out into the abyss.

CHAPTER 99

DAY OF INFAMY

SUNDAY, DECEMBER 7, 1941
CENTRAL PACIFIC OCEAN, 250 MILES
NORTH-NORTHEAST OF OAHU

In the predawn haze, six Imperial Japanese Navy aircraft carriers of the Combined Fleet turned into the wind. For the past eleven days, the *Akagi*, *Hiryu*, *Kaga*, *Shokaku*, *Soryu*, and *Zuikaku* had been steaming eastward from Hitokappu Bay on Iturup Island in the southern Kuril Islands under the command of Vice Admiral Chuichi Nagumo, who was on board the aircraft carrier *Akagi*. The strike force of thirty-two ships departed Hitokappu Bay and had reached its destination undetected by maintaining a strict radio silence throughout the entire eastward journey. After Admiral Nagumo received radio orders to "climb Mount Niitaka," the carriers assembled into strike formation on the morning of December 7, 1941.

At 0600 hours, as the sun rose over the broad blue Pacific Ocean, the first wave of 183 dive bombers, torpedo bombers, high-level bombers, and fighters took off from the Japanese aircraft carriers and headed for Pearl Harbor—where the heart of the U.S. Pacific Fleet was docked. From the seat of his Nakajima B5N2 torpedo bomber—tail number AI-301—Commander Mitsuo Fuchida directed the air attack. Nagumo and Fuchida hoped to catch the entire U.S. Navy fleet—especially the aircraft carriers—in port, by surprise.

Flying through thick cloud cover, Commander Fuchida thought for a moment that he'd flown past Oahu. But a sudden parting of the clouds revealed the island's north shore several miles ahead. At 0740, Fuchida arrived with the first attack wave on Oahu's north shore near Kahuku Point. This first group then banked and flew along the northwestern coast of Oahu. The high-level bombers continued southwest along the coastline, while the torpedo bombers and dive bombers banked and passed directly over Wheeler Army Airfield toward Pearl Harbor.

As the dive bombers and torpedo bombers approached Pearl Harbor, they rejoined the high-level bombers and got into attack formation. To Fuchida's disappointment, the American aircraft carriers were absent. Instead, the torpedo planes would have to concentrate on the vessels lined up along Battleship Row. After observing no American defensive activity at Pearl Harbor, Fuchida slid back the canopy of his plane and fired a single dark blue flare known as a "black dragon." It was the signal to attack.

The formation banked and made a direct course toward Battleship Row. At 0753, Fuchida ordered Norinobu Mizuki, his telegraph operator, to tune his Model 96 continuous wave transmitter to frequency 330 kilocycles and send the prearranged code indicating they had achieved the goal of complete surprise back to Admiral Nagumo and the Combined Fleet:

· · — · · · · · · · — · · · · · · · — · · · · ·

トラ トラ トラ

TORA TORA TORA!

EPILOGUE

SUNDAY, DECEMBER 7, 1941
MAIN NAVY BUILDING, WASHINGTON, DC

The U.S. Navy and the Research Desk had suffered the worst intelligence failure in history, and there was little cause for optimism. Still, there were blessings that neither the members of the Research Desk nor the graduates of the On-the-Roof Gang recognized at the time.

First, the U.S. Navy's aircraft carriers were all safe. It was only due to a combination of dumb luck and poor planning, but none of the aircraft carriers were in port at Pearl Harbor on the morning of December 7, 1941.

Second, the American industrial machine had already shifted to wartime mode after Congress passed the Lend-Lease Act in March 1941. This industrial machine would be critical for the Allied war effort.

Lastly, by the time Japan attacked Pearl Harbor and dragged the United States into World War II, the U.S. Navy's ability to intercept, process, and react to enemy communications was greater than ever before. A score of U.S. Navy officers had been trained in the Japanese language and/or cryptanalysis and were working to crack the Imperial Japanese Navy codes. Additional U.S. Navy radiomen stationed around the Pacific were being trained for DF operations.

Dozens of cleared yeomen worked in the Research Desk and at the Combat Intelligence Units in Hawaii and the Philippines, helping with decryption and processing.

The U.S. Navy had intercept stations at Guam (Station BAKER), the Philippines (Station CAST), Hawaii (Station HYPO), Washington State (Station S), and Maryland (Station M), along with numerous DF stations around the Pacific and Atlantic Oceans. The Research Desk had upgraded most intercept stations with the latest in radio technology.

Perhaps most importantly, 176 Sailors and Marines had received specialized training to intercept the Imperial Japanese Navy's katakana code on the roof of the Main Navy Building in Washington, DC. Of those, more than a hundred were still on active duty or could be recalled from the Reserves to perform radio intercept, DF, traffic analysis, and cryptanalysis for the U.S. Navy. The On-the-Roof Gang was poised to make a huge difference in the war against Japan.

APPENDIX A

ACRONYMS AND ABBREVIATIONS

Acronym/Abbreviation	Meaning
BUENG	Bureau of Naval Engineering
BUPERS	Bureau of Naval Personnel
CINCAF	Commander in Chief Asiatic Fleet
CINCLANTFLT	Commander in Chief Atlantic Fleet
CINCPAC	Commander in Chief Pacific
CINCPACFLT	Commander in Chief Pacific Fleet
CIU	Combat Intelligence Unit
CNO	Chief of Naval Operations
CO	Commanding Officer
COMINT	Communications Intelligence
COMSTA	Communications Station
CPL	Corporal
CRM	Chief Radioman
CW	Continuous Wave
CY	Chief Yeoman
DCO	District Communication Officer
DF	Direction Finding

DNC	Department of Naval Communications
ECM	Electronic Cipher Machine
FCC	Federal Communications Commission
GPM	Groups per Minute
HF	High Frequency
HFDF	High Frequency Direction Finding
KC	Kilocycles
LANTFLT	Atlantic Fleet
LF	Low Frequency
MC	Megacycles
MF	Medium Frequency
NCVA	Naval Cryptologic Veterans Association
ONI	Office of Naval Intelligence
PACFLT	Pacific Fleet
PCS	Permanent Change of Station
PFC	Private First Class
PI	Philippine Islands
RI	Radio Intelligence
RIP	Radio Intelligence Publication
RM1c	Radioman First Class
RM2c	Radioman Second Class
RM3c	Radioman Third Class
RMS	Radio Materiel School
SGT	Sergeant
VLF	Very Low Frequency
XO	Executive Officer

APPENDIX B

ON-THE-ROOF GANG CLASS ROSTERS

Class #0 (self-taught)

Harry Kidder, CRM, USN
Malcolm W. Lyon, CRM, USN
Orville Coonce, RM1c, USN
Dorman Chauncey, CRM, USN
Stephen Lesko, SGT, USMC

Class #1 1 Oct 1928–21 Jan 1929

Instructor: Harry Kidder

Guy O. Billehus, RM1c, USN
Burton E. Cloyd, RM1c, USN
Joseph Goldstein, CRM, USN
Keith E. Goodwin, RM1c, USN
R. W. Hoffman, RM1c, USN
Truett C. Lusk, RM1c, USN
Martin A. Vandenberg, RM1c, USN

Class #2 15 May 1929–10 Sep 1929

Instructor: Harry Kidder

Donovan S. Broughton, RM1c, USN
Earnest E. Dailey, RM2c, USN
Charles E. Daniels, RM1c, USN
Oliver W. Grew, RM1c, USN
Maximillian C. Gunn, CRM, USN
Clarence E. Reynolds, RM1c, USN
Murrel D. Wood, RM1c, USN

Class #3 Nov 1929–Feb 1930

Instructor: Harry Kidder

Charles A. Cameron, PFC, USMC
Ludolph G. Guillet, RM1c, USN
George W. Hopkins, RM1c, USN
Laurence F. Myers, RM1c, USN
Daryl W. Wigle, RM1c, USN

Class #4 5 May 1930–20 Aug 1930

Instructor: Dorman Chauncey

John B. Cooke, RM3c, USN
Albert H. Geiken, RM3c, USN
Edward R. Keesey, RM3c, USN
Leroy A. Lankford, RM1c, USN
Antone Novak, RM2c, USN
James W. Pearson, RM3c, USN

Class #5 Dec 1930–Apr 1931

Instructor: Dorman Chauncey

Phillip M. Miller, PVT, USMC
Maurice M. Overstreet, PVT, USMC
Walter B. Robertson, PFC, USMC
Charles J. Smith, PVT, USMC
Hubert N. Thomas, SGT, USMC
William A. Wilder, CPL, USMC

Class #6 10 Aug 1931–20 Dec 1931

Instructor: Dorman Chauncey

Joel H. Easter, CPL, USMC
Carl H. Gustaveson, CPL, USMC
John Hibbard, CPL, USMC
Clifton Shumaker, RM1c, USN

Class #7 1 Feb 1932–28 Apr 1932

Instructor: Malcolm Lyon

Jesse B. Byrd, CRM, USN
Fred L. Freeman, RM1c, USN
Walter J. McGregor, CRM, USN

Class #8 1 May 1932–2 Jul 1932

Instructor: Malcolm Lyon

Sidney A. Burnett, RM2c, USN
R. P. Clifford, RM2c, USN
Carl L. Congdon, RM2c, USN
Prescott H. Currier, RM3c, USN
Victor L. Long, RM2c, USN
Joseph L. McConnel, RM3c, USN
John H. Roop, RM3c, USN
Richard Willis, RM2c, USN

Class #9 1 Oct 1932–4 Feb 1933

Instructor: Harry Kidder

Richard A. Hardisty, SGT, USMC
William A. Knefley, RM2c, USN
Virgil W. Morgan, PFC, USMC

Class #10 20 Mar 1933–1 Jun 1933

Instructor: Harry Kidder

Donald W. Barnum, RM3c, USN
John H. Gelineau, RM3c, USN
Benjamin Groundwater, RM2c, USN
Thomas G. Hoover, RM3c, USN
Orville L. Jones, RM2c, USN
Homer L. Kisner, RM2c, USN
E. H. Marks, RM3c, USN
Walter C. Rathsack, RM2c, USN

Class #11 5 Jul 1933–1 Dec 1933

Instructor: Harry Kidder

William J. Edens, RM1c, USN
Clarence F. Gentilcore, PFC, USMC
Ralph S. Horne, RM3c, USN
William K. Muse, RM2c, USN
Alvin Rainey, PFC, USMC
Donald D. Ritchie, RM3c, USN
Charles S. Southerland, PFC, USMC

Class #12 Dec 1933 –Apr 1934

Instructor: Harry Kidder

Harry L. Butler, PVT, USMC
Harold V. Jones, PVT, USMC
Joseph A. Petrosky, PVT, USMC
Norman F. Robertson, PVT, USMC

Class #13 Apr 1934–Sep 1934

Instructor: Kidder/Billehus

Albert G. Burton, RM2c, USN
Hilary E. Cyr, RM2c, USN
Garwin S. Diehl, RM2c, USN
Frank E. Estes, RM3c, USN
Eugene S. Givler, RM3c, USN
Charles J. Johns, RM3c, USN
Wilson L. Mason, RM3c, USN
Markle T. Smith, RM3c, USN

Class #14 Sep 1934–Mar 1935

Instructor: Kidder/Billehus

Ivan S. Benjamin, RM3c, USN
Carl A. Jensen, RM3c, USN
Norman V. Lewis, RM2c, USN
Leo J. Potvin, RM2c, USN
Meddie J. Royer, RM2c, USN
Edward W. Schroeder, RM3c, USN
Howard H. Troup, RM3c, USN
James D. Willmarth, RM3c, USN

Class #15 Mar 1935–Jul 1935

Instructor: J. Bryan Byrd

Cecil T. Carraway, PFC, USMC
Curtis W. Crowe, PVT, USMC
Lombard R. Hingle, PFC, USMC
Jesse L. Randle, SGT, USMC
Carl G. Suber, PFC, USMC
James W. Winborn, PFC, USMC

Class #16 Jul 1935–Nov 1935

Instructor: Byrd/McGregor

Isaac C. Bemis, RM3c, USN
Elmer Dickey, RM3c, USN
Alfred D. DuRoss, RM2c, USN
Robert G. Maxwell, RM3c, USN
Kenneth B. Selch, RM3c, USN
Rodney L. Whitten, RM3c, USN
Clifford O. Wilder, RM3c, USN

Class #17 Jan 1936–May 1936

Instructor: Walter McGregor

Kenneth E. Carmichael, RM3c, USN
Paul V. Hively, RM2c, USN
Harold E. Layman, RM2c, USN
Robert H. Ledford, RM3c, USN
Merle E. Lynch, RM3c, USN
Clarence P. Taylor, RM3c, USN
Robert R. Williams, RM3c, USN

Class #18 Jul 1936–Nov 1936

Instructor: Walter McGregor

Chester H. Bissell, RM3c, USN
Walter H. Johnson, RM3c, USN
Rex H. Jule, RM2c, USN
Samuel O. McCurdy, RM2c, USN
Albert J. Pelletier, RM2c, USN
Roy C. Sholes, RM3c, USN
Fred R. Thomson, RM3c, USN
Frank J. Weiland, RM3c, USN

Class #19 Jan 1937–Jul 1937

Instructor: Walter McGregor

Clarence A. Detterich, RM2c, USN
Robert L. Dormer, RM2c, USN
Harvey J. Howard, RM2c, USN
Edward N. Kelly, RM2c, USN
Raymond E. Parrott, RM2c, USN
Alva E. Squires, RM2c, USN
Theodore J. Wildman, RM2c, USN
William C. Young, RM2c, USN

Class #20 Nov 1937–Mar 1938

Instructor: Walter McGregor

Ralph T. Briggs, RM3c, USN
Henry E. Ethier, RM2c, USN
Glenn E, Evans, RM2c, USN
James H. Johnson, RM2c, USN
Elliott E. Okins, RM3c, USN
Pearly L. Phillips, RM3c, USN
Charles A. Walters, RM2c, USN
Duane L. Whitlock, RM2c, USN

Class #21 Jul 1938–Feb 1939

Instructor: Daryl Wigle

Howard A. Cain, RM2c, USN
Donovan R. Chase, RM2c, USN
Douglas W. Harold, RM2c, USN
Jack G. Kaye, RM2c, USN
Warren A. Simmons, RM2c, USN
Wesley H. Walvoord, RM2c, USN
Willis H. Wesper, RM3c, USN
Samuel H. Winchester, RM3c, USN

Class #22 Apr 1939–Aug 1939

Instructor: Daryl Wigle

Edward J. Dullard, RM3c, USN
William W. Eaton, RM3c, USN
Robert R. Ellis, RM2c, USN
Stuart T. Faulkner, RM2c, USN
Arthur L. Monroe, Jr., RM2c, USN
Hubert A. Price, RM3c, USN
Charles G., Quinn, RM3c, USN
David W. Snyder, RM2c, USN

Class #23 Oct 1939–May 1940

Instructor: Daryl Wigle

Kenneth H. Barker, RM2c, USN
Arthur D. Groff, RM2c, USN
Raymond L. Hitson, RM2c, USN
Harold E. Joslin, RM2c, USN
Edward Otte, RM2c, USN
Rexford G. Parr, RM2c, USN
Russell W. Rogers, RM2c, USN
Martin H. Smith, RM3c, USN

Class #24 May 1940–Nov 1940

Instructor: Antone Novak

James B. Capron Jr., RM3c, USN
Gordon O. Carnes, RM2c, USN
Wesley S. Knowles, RM2c, USN
Joseph E. Smith, RM2c, USN
Lloyd T. Smith, RM2c, USN
Harold P. Waldum, RM3c, USN

Class #25 Nov 1940–Feb 1941

Instructor: Antone Novak

Maynard G. Albertson, RM2c, USN
Elmer W. Disharoon, RM2c, USN
Reece Finley, RM3c, USN
Stanley E. Gramblin, RM2c, USN
James C. Howard, RM2c, USN
Roy E. Lehman, RM2c, USN
Howard E. McConnell, RM2c, USN
Hugh W. McGall, RM2c, USN
Earl L. Rank, RM1c, USN
Raymond A. Rundle, RM3c, USN
Arthur D. Swain, RM3c, USN
Merrill F. Whiting, RM2c, USN

Lightning Source UK Ltd.
Milton Keynes UK
UKHW012208170820
368394UK00002B/66/J

9 781735 152707